CROMA VENTURE

SPIRAL WARS; BOOK FIVE

JOEL SHEPHERD

1

E rik awoke. The wall display by his bedside said the time was 06:15. He'd gone to sleep at ten, and it just felt like eight hours. One thing to be said for four months of relative safety in one spot, without people chasing them and trying to shoot their collective asses off, was that *Phoenix's* overworked, overstressed crew were finally getting some decent sleep.

He reached for his AR glasses, the first thing every Fleet captain did upon waking, and put them on. *Lien Wang* was still there, close now out of jump. ETA until lunar orbit was barely three hours, with a shuttle arriving at Defiance close after that. He lay on his back, blinked on the ID icons and read the details for the tenth time.

Lien Wang was a radium-class scout, made for long-range reconnaissance. Civvies often thought that would make for a small ship, but *Lien Wang* was nearly half the size of *Phoenix* — the bulk of it engines, powered by similar technology. It was slim and low-mass for its size, and could power in and out of star systems a long way from their gravitational center, sometimes undetected. In the war such ships had been invaluable, gathering intelligence on tavalai movements.

The scout's Captain was Angelo Sampey, a hundred and twenty

year old veteran known to anyone who was anyone in Fleet. And he'd come, yesterday's encrypted message had said, through tavalai space bearing the IDs of the Inspection Force, to talk directly to *Phoenix*. Beyond that, there had been no further information.

Erik could guess. Humans had won the war, but not just any human ship was allowed through tavalai space. Inspection Force were empowered by the peace treaty to travel through tavalai space and see that the disarmament provisions were being observed. With any other race than the tavalai it would have been inadequate, but the officious, law-abiding tavalai had thus far observed all provisions, and treated all Inspection Force vessels with polite formality.

Recon vessels like *Lien Wang* were rarely used for Inspection Force duties. Inspection Force ships tended to be larger with a significant shuttle component to allow for large bureaucratic visitations to the surface of various planets. They also needed berthing for all the inspectors and accountants who would check tavalai records, and the ambassadors who would attend to the various documents of treaty upkeep and reaffirmation. Tavalai didn't take inspection vessels seriously unless they came loaded with bureaucrats, and Fleet was of the opinion that if tavalai equated such things with agreeable civilisation then it was a small price to pay for strengthening their cooperation.

But *Lien Wang* was stripped of all excess weight, and carried just one shuttle. Which meant that whatever temporary ID she carried for safe transit through tavalai space, she was no part of the regular Inspection Force. She'd come directly from human space. And as much as Fleet HQ would have great interest in seeing Defiance for themselves, no tavalai authority would have granted the IF identification for that purpose alone. *Lien Wang* was here to see *Phoenix*, sent direct from whoever was now in charge of human affairs back home. Erik was certain of it.

So, then. He climbed from bed and sat on the edge of the mattress, trying to muster the purpose to begin his morning exercises while putting the glasses on review, to catch up with the night-shift's reports. Lieutenant Rooke's second-shift were keeping the *Phoenix* refit going non-stop, and progress was spectacular. Then there were preparations for great meetings, as the high denominations of the parren House Harmony always did everything grandly, this time to discuss the vexing issues of the drysine data-core that *Phoenix* had unleashed upon the Spiral. But today Erik could muster no enthusiasm for any of these things.

He took his slate off the bedside table and removed his glasses to look at it properly. Words unadorned, descriptions, thoughts. All utterly inadequate. He wanted to delete the lot and start again, but he knew from experience that a new version would be no better. He stared at the dry, stale words, and was disgusted with his own inadequacy.

The adjoining door to Trace's quarters opened and she entered, in sweat shirt and stretch pants, her brown skin bright with the sheen of exercise, sipping a dark green smoothie. "Morning," she said. "Do you have those tennis balls in storage?"

"Bottom shelf," said Erik, pointing. Trace went and crouched by the little kitchenette, retrieving the items.

"I need them for the kids to practice with," she explained. Erik nodded. Trace glanced, and guessed what he was looking at. "Hey," she said gently. "I've read them all. They're fine."

"They're not. I could give them to Lisbeth and she'd do far better, even if she didn't know them as well."

Trace went across and sat on the bed beside him. "Erik, it's not your job to summarise a life, or to give meaning to everything we lost. The families will do that for themselves, in time. No one's looking at you to tell them all what it's for."

"Yours are better than mine too," Erik said bleakly. "I'm not good at this, Trace."

"That's bullshit," Trace said calmly. "But even if it were true, so what? You'd be a carrier captain, not a poet."

Erik stared at the slate. Sixty spacer lives. Fifty-two marines. Trace wrote the condolence letters to the marines' families, Erik to the spacers'. They'd done it four months ago, directly after the Battle of Defiance, but in all those months they'd not yet found a courier they trusted to take it all the way back to human space unmolested. Only now, with *Lien Wang*'s arrival, did he have to finally send the things. And only now, at the prospect of all those families receiving these letters in person, did the feeling truly hit him — that he'd let every one of these men and women down.

Erik took a deep breath. "Captain Sampey's down at 09:40 at the tower. I want you there."

"I'll be there," Trace confirmed. "Just us?"

"Just us."

"Shouldn't Lisbeth be there too? Fleet need a briefing on parren affairs, Lisbeth's the best placed to give them one."

"Lisbeth's got her own appointment right after us," Erik explained, climbing off the bed and heading to the kitchen for some coffee. "Gesul insisted. He'll get his own as well, condition of *Lien Wang*'s entry."

"That's fair," said Trace, also getting up. "It's their city. With any luck, Rehnar won't try to kill us all while Sampey's here."

"Or even after Sampey leaves," said Erik, without optimism.

* * *

THE PRESSURISED HABITAT was called Aronach Dar, which sounded fancy but was actually just a parren numerical grid reference to describe its location on the city surface. Aronach Dar was a great dome, a kilometre across and containing a giant spinning wheel like any orbital space station. That wheel spun to create one full human gravity for all occupants... but the rim was angled at fifteen degrees to account for the Defiance moon's gravity as well. The dome enclosed the entire wheel for protection, and there were thankfully no windows anywhere, or the blur of this giant merry-go-round would make motion sickness in even the most hardy spacer.

Erik walked to the cafeteria, still something of a novel experience for a spacer, as no Fleet warships had the room for one. Crew leapt to their feet to the cry of 'Captain on deck!', then sat once more at Erik's 'at ease'. He sat with Lieutenant Commander Justine 'Giggles' Dufresne and Commander Dylan 'Bucky' Draper, a pair of youngsters who'd been no more than lieutenant reserve pilots before their lives had been turned upside down, and now found themselves second and third-in-command on one of humanity's most powerful warships.

Draper was thirty-three, Trace's age, and had a round, freckled face, sandy-brown hair and prominent front teeth — thus 'Bucky'. His background was middle-class suburban, from Columbia on the world of Esparza. One parent was a teacher, the other ran a small business, and he'd grown up so utterly unremarkable, in his own words, that he was completely astonished to look around and see how far he'd come. But he'd excelled at sports and academics, and several good teachers had encouraged him to follow his fanciful dream of Fleet Academy, where he'd risen even further. He was really far too young for his current position, but then again, the higher he'd risen so far, and the larger the challenges thrown his way, the better he'd done. Erik just hoped that the trend continued, now that the suburban boy from nowhere-in-particular found himself second-in-command of the *UFS Phoenix* at an age where most of his school friends' lives revolved around party weekends to break the monotony of middle-class jobs.

Justine Dufresne was more typical of a senior Fleet officer — the daughter of a wealthy spacer family, she'd grown up on a station and counted many proud Fleet veterans and martyrs in her close family. Like many from that background she had a bad case of 'spacer humour', which was to say that she had none, or little enough that it was rarely observed. Naturally the crew called her 'Giggles'. The sims showed that she was if anything a slightly superior natural pilot to Draper... but Erik had distrusted the sim's high weighting to what he called 'obstacle courses'. When he threw more complex situations at them, requiring judgement calls on unknowable factors like politics and alien psychology, Draper always did better. Given what *Phoenix* had been through lately, Erik was certain that Draper's total skillset better qualified him for the rank of commander than Dufresne's. Dufresne, it was widely suspected, was displeased with that assessment, but had thus far been civil about it.

She was also an old guard Fleet loyalist, and was only on *Phoenix* because she'd been stuck aboard when the shit had hit the fan at Homeworld. If she'd been planetside at the time, Erik knew there was no chance she'd have joined *Phoenix* in going renegade against the rightful authority of Fleet, no matter what the crimes Fleet HQ committed against her. In the intervening months her attitude had softened considerably, having seen firsthand what they were up against and exactly how crooked her beloved Fleet leadership had become. But still Erik sometimes wondered, if and when they came face-to-face with Fleet authority once more, just which way she'd go.

Lieutenant Wei Shilu joined them at the table, and there was no standing attention for him as the only three spacers requiring it were already here, and Major Thakur was elsewhere. "Wei, how's the arm?" Erik asked him.

"It's getting there," said Shilu, flexing his left. He wore a glove on the synthetic hand, pressure to help get sensation into reluctant fingertips. To Erik the arm looked as mobile and natural as any regular arm... though apparently it did not yet feel that way to *Phoenix*'s first-shift Coms Officer. "It's been waking me up at nights, though. That's its latest trick, after the pins-and-needles."

"Waking you up how?" asked Draper past a mouthful of light soup.

"Well it's odd. You know how when you're trying to get to sleep, and you keep getting little itches? And you scratch them, and they go away... and I never thought about it before, but why don't you get those itches while you're sleeping? And the answer is obviously because they'd wake you up. So it's not that you don't get the itches, it's that your brain decides not to notice them... or that's what the Doc says, anyhow. But I'm getting itches on the arm now, and they *do* wake me up. The brain's supposed to numb them while I'm asleep, but for some reason it's not happening with the arm."

"I'd have thought," said Erik, "that the only thing worse than an itchy synthetic arm would be a synthetic arm that wasn't *able* to get itchy."

"I guess," said Shilu, looking unconvinced. "My balance isn't the same, either."

"Oh go on, you'll be dancing Swan Lake again in no time," Draper insisted. "It's your arm, not your leg."

"Shows what you know about dancing," Shilu sniffed. Wei Shilu had been a professional ballet dancer for a while, putting all academic pursuits on hold to follow his passion. That had lasted until a sard attack on New Congo, killing thousands, whereupon he'd been no longer able to enjoy his dancing, he said, for the feeling that it was all so frivolous when all these other men and women were out in space giving their lives to keep him safe. "Proper balance is an all-body thing, it takes arms *and* legs."

Lieutenant Hausler joined them in the growing chatter of new arrivals, the squeal of chair legs, the clatter of utensils. Happy sounds, Erik thought, remembering family breakfasts, his parents, sisters and household staff talking over food, coffee and emerging schedules. "Groundcrew says PH-1 is prepped for departure anytime, Captain," said Hausler, sitting his lanky frame on Erik's left with a tray. "Now if my damn co-pilot can just drag her ass out of Medbay, we'll be good to go."

"What's wrong with Cory?" asked Erik.

"Dunno," said Hausler, eating without concern. "Lady issues, I think."

"Well I'm sure she appreciates you sharing that with everyone," Dufresne said primly.

Hausler shrugged. "You bet. We'll have a full load, Charlie Platoon's coming too. Manifest says the Major's not coming?"

"She's already gone with Jersey, playing with her babies," Erik explained. "Borrowed my tennis balls this morning."

"Well there go your tennis balls," said Draper. "Someone had those in personal storage? Who?"

"Yep," said Erik, still eating. They'd belonged to Ensign Remy Hale, Engineering's XO, who'd died with all the others in the defence of Defiance. Officers at the table saw Erik not elaborating, and a brief silence followed, filled only with eating. If there were spare personal items lying unclaimed of late, there was usually just one reason why. Draper looked faintly mortified, realising his mistake. He did that kind of thing more than he should. The Commander of *Phoenix*, and still just a naive kid in some things.

Tif arrived at the table with Skah, to everyone's relief. "Hello Skah!" said the table in rough unison, and the little kuhsi boy looked delighted despite them saying it to him nearly every morning. He scrambled on his bench at Hausler's side opposite his Mummy, and Hausler ruffled the boy's wide, floppy ears.

"Herro!" he told them. "Hausrer, you want sone of ny breakfast?" Skah's tray was mostly meat, sliced and cooked in several different styles. Kuhsi digestion handled little else.

"I think we'd better save your breakfast for you, kid," Hausler told him. "We don't want to run out of meat or you'll have nothing to eat."

"If rittuw boy keep eating so nuch," his mother observed, "we run out of neat anyway." Skah scowled at her, and chomped on a slice with sharp teeth. Those teeth weren't so little any longer, and the big incisors looked as though they could put a hole in someone. Or two holes. Luckily for the crew, Skah's temper was never more than boisterous. "He cun frying with ne this norning. Rewtenant Crozier say it's okay. You renenber to say thank you to Rewtenant Crozier, Skah."

"I wiw!" Skah said indignantly. "But Rewtenant Crozier nad at ne."

Shilu frowned at Hausler. "Mad," Hausler translated. "Why is JC mad at you, Skah?"

"Because I run into her, nake her spiw her drink." Skah's smile was embarrassed — not easy to see with a kuhsi's naturally pursed lips, but obvious to anyone friendly with Skah. "And other narines aw raugh." About the table, officers repressed grins.

"Skah!" Tif said crossly, evidently hearing this for the first time. And followed it with a rebuke in Gharkhan — likely that she'd told him a thousand times not to run in the hallways, Erik thought.

"Yeah," said Hausler around a mouthful, "I think if Lieutenant Crozier was angry at you, Skah, she wouldn't have let you come flying with her and your mother this morning. It takes a lot more than a spilled drink to upset JC."

"Don't encourage hin," his mother objected. Always unflappable, Hausler just smiled.

"Which sector this morning, Tif?" Draper asked her.

"KT-486," said Tif. "Stiw no one there, even now. Rooks rike factories, naybe. We rook for technowogy before parren get everything, so naybe good prace to rook."

"Is it reawy coow, Nahny?" Skah asked, excitement reemerging as fast as it had gone.

Tif smiled at him reluctantly. "Very coow." Her mouth tried to pronounce the L, but the tongue just didn't want to go there, between the sharp front teeth.

"Do yourself an injury," Hausler observed.

Tif flexed her finger claws at him in mock warning. And noticed Skah trying to eat a large meat slice with his fingers. "Skah! Put..." and she began again in Gharkhan as Skah put the meat down, and his mother leaned across the table, extending one finger-length claw and slicing the meat into smaller strips with that scary-sharp blade.

"I'm glad my mother never had those," Shilu observed.

"Me too," said Erik with feeling.

* * *

THE ELEVATOR CAR opened onto the inner hub of the rotating wheel, typically enormous like all the architecture on Defiance. A ten-meter-high inner circumference, rotating only slowly here in the middle, with an inner wall broken in parts by large, reinforced windows. On the far side of the wall were shuttle berths in the vacuum, lit with great floodlights. Opposite those berths, on the pressurised side of the wall, platforms adjoined from lower-level assembly points, filling the otherwise open space.

Erik led Hausler and several Operations techs down stairs to the berth level and found Charlie Platoon in the final stages of suiting up, clustered in squads and sections, buddy-checking their armour and systems. They'd been up an hour before the spacers to get breakfast then prep their armour. Lieutenant Jalawi saw Erik coming and bounced over, armour whining and thudding with a familiar noise not loud in itself, but nearly deafening when multiplied by forty other suits.

"Yo Captain!" Jalawi shouted above the noise, stopping with his visor up and saluting. Erik returned it — for formal purposes, Assembly on a warship was to be considered 'outdoors', allowing the giving and receiving of salutes, and so Assembly qualified here as well. Normally Jalawi was shorter than Erik, but now Erik had to tilt his head back. Jalawi was always reliable — full of business-like good cheer, his wide, brown face filling the helmet. The man was a bull, but a friendly one. "Loading's in five, we'll be ready in two!"

"Our co-pilot's in Medbay, so we might be a little longer than that!" Erik replied.

Jalawi shot Hausler a look of concern. "What's wrong with Cory?"

Hausler put his hands up. "If it's morning sickness, wasn't me."

"We're going to leave Third and Heavy with *Phoenix*," Jalawi told Erik, continuing his mock-accusing stare at Hausler. "I'll take the tower with First and Second. Got a poker game to finish with that thief Lassa."

"That's Lieutenant Lassa to you, Skeeta," Erik told him. A spacer lieutenant being one rank higher than a marine lieutenant — an O-3 against an O-2.

"Yeah well she cheats, I'm sure of it." Erik didn't think for a moment that Dreyfus Jalawi and Angela Lassa were actually passing tower duty by playing cards. Jalawi was just a world-class stirrer.

Sergeant Hoon bounced over in the light-G, and also saluted. "Captain."

"Sergeant," said Erik. Hoon was smallish, but tall within his armour. His face was weathered, Asian eyes narrow, and though it wasn't apparent to look at him, two of his limbs were synthetic. The most combat-experienced person in Phoenix Company, second on all of *Phoenix* only to Chief Petty Officer Goldman, he was now Charlie

Platoon's XO following the death of Jalawi's previous XO, Staff Sergeant Spitzer, four months ago.

Charlie Platoon had less holes in it than one might have thought considering the casualties in that desperate battle for Defiance. That was because Echo Platoon now ceased to exist — its commander, Lieutenant Chester Zhi, having been killed and the platoon suffering casualties second only to Bravo, Trace had had no choice but to simply disband Echo and fold its survivors into the remaining four platoons. That had still left a platoon's worth of wounded, but in the four months since, most of them had now returned, or were about to, save for three who could not be rehabilitated to marine-level performance by any level of medical technology and were now retraining as spacers for the rest of the journey.

The survivors of Echo hated it, and non-Echo marines were wise not to bring it up in their presence. Trace had reported on a few fights that broke out directly after, defused only by her loud insistence that Lieutenant Zhi wouldn't have liked it — a rebuke that brought a few of them to tears. Echo Platoon, Phoenix Company, dated back to the commissioning of *Phoenix* herself, and like all of *Phoenix*'s platoons had a combat history rarely matched elsewhere in Fleet. To lose it was a blow to everyone's morale, not just that of Echo's survivors. Even today, Trace reported that tension remained, despite the best efforts of the Company's surviving officers.

For a moment Erik thought Hoon might speak to him, but instead he turned to his Platoon Commander. "LT, main channel's a bit fuzzy, only seventy-eight percent resolution. I thought we could boost vitals onto the second-tier to clear the network, we need to preserve bandwidth and I don't trust the local relays."

"Sure, let's do that," said Jalawi, excusing himself. "What's your settings?"

Erik made his way with Hausler to the berth, reflecting that he'd barely spoken five words to Hoon since he'd come aboard at Joma Station... half-a-year ago now. Hoon didn't talk much, Trace said. But she liked him, and said he was just as good as the legends told, so that was good enough for Erik.

He was buckling himself into PH-1's observer chair behind Hausler when Ensign Cory Yun edged past him in the narrow space. "Captain."

"Ensign," said Erik, and abandoned his buckles to get up and take her shoulder. Yun looked at him in surprise — a small, pretty face beneath her big flight helmet. She looked more worn and tired than she should have, considering everyone's sleeping improvements. "How you doing, Ensign?"

"I'm okay sir. Just coming down with something, I think. Doc says it's nothing serious, gave me some meds."

Erik didn't believe it. Cory Yun was usually a more cheerful, talkative version of her pilot's drawling cool. Since the fight four months ago she'd been much the same, but patchy, like someone with a bad case of mood swings. Hausler had refused to see it, but Lieutenant Jersey had been concerned, and told Erik. Today, Erik thought, was one of Yun's off-days, and he doubted she'd been in Medbay for a cold.

"Cory," he said with what he hoped was the right amount of gentle firmness. "If you need a day off sometime, we can do that. The roster's not that full, and we're not getting shot at."

Yun's surprised laughter was all defensive denial. "I'm *fine* Captain! Seriously, it's just a cold!" She turned and clambered over the shoulder of Hausler's chair with a practised squeeze against the canopy. Erik sat and resumed buckling, concern growing.

The irony was that none of the shuttle crews had actually been shot at in the Battle of Defiance. There had been nothing they could do against the forces they faced, and getting killed needlessly would have deprived Phoenix Company of much-needed mobility. So they'd hidden, avoided contact, and watched the battle unfolding around them. And, Erik thought grimly as the pilots took the shuttle through pre-flight, they'd had to sit helplessly and listen on coms as their marine friends had died, and call desperately for *Phoenix*, who had clearly been hit and was not responding at all. Ensign Yun and the other shuttle crews had all thought they were about to be left alone — pilots without a mother ship, unable to help as their family died around them. And that, perhaps, was more traumatising for Cory Yun than the prospect of having been killed herself.

They were a broken crew, Erik knew, gazing now out the canopy at the great steel dome overhead, lit from below with the glow of floodlights. The strongest among them held the family together, but the cracks were showing. Morale had been so strong for those first frantic, exciting, terrifying six months. Today everyone insisted they were just as keen, but it was coming to feel like a facade, like the lies people told themselves to avoid facing unpleasant realities. Like the look on Ensign Yun's face when she'd refused Erik's offer of a day off. Harder work and even the risk of combat might have kept them focused, but *Phoenix* was crippled, stripped and under repair, and there'd been little for the non-technicians to do but settle down and wait, in the grip of this strange new alien routine.

We'd better start making some progress soon, Erik thought grimly, as PH-1's engines roared and the grapples released, propelling them up toward the dome exit above. Or we're going to start imploding under the stresses we're pretending don't exist.

2

Aronech Dar was only four kilometres from the the great shipyard berths where *Phoenix* was undergoing her rebuild, and seven kilometres from the great Tower District from where human and parren command centres overlooked this entire portion of the city. Theoretically it might have been possible to use Defiance's own transit systems for such short distances, but even were it possible, it would have taken a lot of man-hours and been a security headache. This was not a human city, and with every day Defiance became a little less unoccupied.

Erik gazed out now at the vast steel horizon in the short minute he'd have before arrival. Every trip it seemed that there were a few more lights somewhere, gleaming in industrial clusters, lighting domes and valleys, hard-shelled surfaces and a maze-work of exposed beams. Here and there across the surface, parren shuttles roamed, a blink of multi-coloured running lights. On one nearby industrial section he saw what looked like construction equipment, newly erected, and a number of small, suited figures dwarfed by the architecture, no doubt repairing some life-support system in this the organic-friendly part of Defiance.

Overhead, if he'd bothered to look, he'd have seen the occasional thruster flare of an incoming or outgoing shuttle, heading to or from orbit. Beyond that, ships were impossible to see with the naked eye, in the blackness of space without any nearby source of sunlight. But they were up there, accumulating dozens of them, some military but lately many that were not. Those were Erik's greatest concern, for they bore parren dignitaries and leaders from various factions and houses across parren space. Military parren were predictable in that they did what they were told. But parren house rivalries were always alarming, and on the matter of this newly discovered treasure-trove of hacksaw technology in particular.

After a minute, Hausler swung them tail-first and made a short burn, cutting the small vertical thrust that kept them up and letting the lunar gravity bring them in. Beneath them were great circular holes in the steel, like the perfect burrows of some strange subterranean animal. About those burrows were enormous gantries and mobile arms, most lying idle, but one ablaze with white light. Hausler brought them neatly to a low hover above a neighbouring platform, then cut thrust entirely at several metres to let gravity bounce them gently down.

"Thanks for the lift," Erik told the pilots, unbuckling and hitting the cockpit door release.

"Our pleasure Captain," said Hausler. "I hope you have a pleasant and productive day."

"I always do, Trey. You fly safe, you hear?"

"I'll be as safe as a tavalai's money, Captain."

Erik beat the first marines to the dorsal hatch, confirmed the connection himself with Spacer Alexander on the far end, got good pressure to override the shuttle airlock and popped both doors together. A short heave got him up, then through the overhead opening into the adjoining access arm.

"Thanks Levy," he told Alexander. "Heavy and Third Squad are coming up behind."

"Yes Captain," said the tired-looking spacer. "Nothing here to report, we're the same as yesterday."

Erik nodded and bounced in the low-G, knowing that Jalawi

would have already told the Alpha Platoon marines currently guarding *Phoenix* that their replacements were here... but the Alphas wouldn't leave their posts until personally relieved. It wasn't strictly necessary or effective to guard the ship, nor their control center in the Tower District. There were easily enough parren forces here that if some factional warlord decided to wipe out the humans, they could do it easily. But *Phoenix* was important, if currently controversial, and besides, Erik had the best possible mole deep inside the most powerful local administration, and he was confident of her ability to keep them informed of possible dangerous developments.

The docking arm ended in a wide assembly area, a thick steel floor for heavy use, and centred by a double-doored, pressurised elevator. Erik figured that the marines would be a minute at least assembling here, and the elevator was fast, so he got in alone and hit the main observation level. Doors hissed and his ears popped, and he put his feet firmly into the floor straps to avoid hitting the ceiling as the car accelerated downward.

For a moment the curved glass-panel windows showed nothing, then the car broke into the gantry structure as it fled down the side of the vast hangar. And there, beyond the flashing blur of passing beams, was *Phoenix*. She stood on her tail within the great hole where Fleet regulations said no human starship should ever be. Support arms held her on all sides, blazing light on her matte-black flanks. Seeing her like this, in proportion to things on the ground, gave Erik the clearest sense he'd ever had of how big she was — four hundred metres long, and taking an elevator down her flank was like descending an enormous skyscraper in a big city. The workers on the ground far below looked like ants, and even now the Engineering second-shift crawled upon their latest points of interest, and cut new attachments into the old hull with showers of orange sparks.

Erik's eye picked out the new additions as he descended — the coms dishes, the scanning modules, the rail-gun turrets. New, armoured ammunition feeds, snaking along the hull-cage that contained the habitation cylinder. The cylinder had a new paint job too — just as spookily-black as the last one, but even less reflective.

Despite all the floodlights, *Phoenix* sat dark and impassive, seeming to drink in the glare like a black hole. A shape this big and regular couldn't be particularly radar-stealthy, but Lieutenant Rooke insisted that the new material would decrease radar reflectivity by another sixty percent. And then there were the stealth counter-measures, which some in Engineering were calling a 'cloaking field'... Rooke discouraged that, saying it was nothing of the sort, only to then explain how it kind-of was, using a strange set of field generators to bamboozle incoming radar. 'A field of what?' Erik had asked, but hadn't received a reply he could understand.

But the changes to the forward third of the ship were nothing compared to what had been done to the rear half. *Phoenix*'s familiar old lines were gone completely, replaced by something that looked almost evil in its alien monstrosity. It was no bigger, and Rooke insisted was actually seven percent lighter — no small saving on a warship that needed mobility to survive. The powerplant that it contained was a brutal thing, even by the physics-bending technological standards of the old *Phoenix*. The jump engines first, directly behind Midships and ahead of the primary powercore, radiating the jump lines that forked and looped forward, past Midships to the hull cage about the crew cylinder. *That*, Rooke said, they'd have to test to precisely discover the performance of. Big, was all he'd say when Erik asked him for predictions. Very big.

The main powerplant was an atom-smasher, like all modern starship drives, pulling power out of quantum states using understandings of those mechanics that humanity probably wouldn't have reached by now if they hadn't been handed all these things ahead of their time by the chah'nas and alo. But this particular powerplant did it differently to anything the crew had seen or even heard of before. The power it created was cheap, but it was not easy, and now Rooke's Engineering heads were huddled to try and figure how they were going to maintain the thing once in operation, given that their understanding of the technology was limited and their current maintenance tools and procedures obsolete. More concerning for Erik was the distinct probability that this engine, if fired at full power, would kill everyone on *Phoenix* by sheer G-force alone. Exactly how he was going to use it in combat, if it came to that, he had absolutely no idea. Given how things had gone for *Phoenix* over the past ten months, he was pretty sure it was going to come to that eventually.

The car reached hangar control, decelerated fast, then was enclosed by the pressurised compartment. Double-doors hissed and unlocked, then opened, and Erik yawned as he walked in, equalising against the small mismatch. Immediately the car resealed and shot upwards once more to bring the marines down. The control room was wide, with posts for many people, all presently unoccupied, display lights flashing as they monitored various of *Phoenix*'s new systems. A wide strip of windows overlooked the repair bay, and before it stood Lieutenant Rooke himself, sipping on coffee and gazing at his beloved warship.

Erik joined him, and it took Rooke another two seconds to glance and do a double-take. "Oh, Captain! I'm sorry, I didn't... I mean, I was just..."

"Thinking, I know." Erik gazed out at the familiar, yet now alarmingly alien ship that had for many months been his only home. "If you'd rather think, you can report to me later. Thinking's important."

"No, that's okay sir." Rooke was nearly thirty, but looked more like twenty-five... if that number meant anything today with ageing treatments as they were. African-black, middle-height and slender, he was no athletic specimen to look at, and rumour was he would have flunked Fleet's spacer standards by some record margin if it weren't for the augments every recruit received just managing to push him over the line. More rumour said that he'd *still* managed to flunk those standards, but Fleet had given him an exception for being such a genius with tech. As Captain, Erik had seen Rooke's files and knew that Rooke had actually passed those physicals, though borderline. The files had also shown the Academy's assessment of his intellect, by whatever latest measurement the psychs now thought best to measure that nebulous concept. The number had been eye-wateringly high, and Erik had never been more pleased of the fact than now.

"I like to get here early during shift change," Rooke explained, indicating the empty control room. "It's the best time to review everything and gather my thoughts. I sometimes worry I don't get enough time to just... think, you know?"

"I know exactly what you mean," Erik agreed, with feeling. "How's it looking?"

"Same as before, Captain. Good progress. Better than good, actually." He sounded both excited and worried at the same time. "She's going to be a beast, Captain. I mean, she was already a beast. But if I'm right about the numbers, I think she'll be doing things even those deepynines can't match."

"Big engines won't help us if the crew pass out above 12G," Erik reminded him. "Machines don't G-LOC."

"Oh, it's so much more than that, Captain." Rooke shook his head faintly, coffee mug at his lips. "I'm not even sure they'll be able to see us. The engines are one thing, the computers... oh yeah, that's another thing. Ensign Kadi got the computer's flight sim working. So you can sit the chair if you like."

Erik blinked. "Today?" Rooke nodded, with the barely restrained smile of a kid with a secret he was dying to share. "Is it good?"

"I think you should just sit the chair, Captain. It's not any of our speciality anyway, only you can tell how it flies."

Erik's smile grew at the younger man's manner. "You think it's cool though, right?"

"Well it *looks* fucking awesome." Rooke grinned. "But looks aren't everything, I guess."

"So I'm told. What would you say to some extra manpower?"

It was Rooke's turn to blink at him. "From where?" Because obviously, they weren't inviting parren to come and look at their deadly new creation. The parren were too busy trying to build their own, with apparently mixed success, if Lisbeth's tales were true.

"The Major's almost done with her babies," said Erik. "She thinks. The first couple, anyway, might take another five days to be sure. Their technical skills are instinctive, she says. You program them with the capabilities you want, they'll learn it in days."

"Wow." Rooke gazed at the gantries around the ship, and the second-shift workers toiling away. Engineering was the one group of *Phoenix* crew who hadn't all moved to parren daytime hours. They had just enough people to maintain a round-the-clock effort on *Phoenix*, and so that was what they did. To help, Rooke had been recruiting technically able crew from non-Engineering specialities, even if it meant higher ranks taking instruction from Engineering spacers and petty officers. If they'd only kept a single-shift, completion would still be months away. "We'd have to guard them too. Around-the-clock. Do we really want to leave them alone with *Phoenix* for that long?"

"We'll see," said Erik. "Everything's a judgement call at the moment, there's no handbook on any of this. We're the first humans to ever do anything like this."

"Don't think we'll be the last, either," said Rooke. He sounded more excited at the prospect than Erik thought was wise. And he wondered now, again, what Captain Sampey of *Lien Wang* would think.

* * *

Tif flew at a steady three kilometres off the surface, maintaining just a gentle vertical thrust to keep them level. There was quite a bit of traffic over Defiance these days, utterly unlike when they'd first arrived, and traffic control now gave shuttles a correct altitude for each direction they might fly. With all intersecting trajectories operating at different altitudes, and all co-altitude flights heading the same way, statistically unlikely collisions became nearly impossible.

Tif looked across the horizon now, and her visor overlaid the blips of moving shuttles and a few larger runners and smaller skips. All were parren, most from House Harmony, though not necessarily friendly to each other, in the way of parren. Nearly as bad as kuhsi, Tif thought sourly to herself. An entire sector down south glowed with red navigation barriers, invisible walls erected by traffic control to shield all unauthorised entry. The number of those forbidden sectors was also growing. Tif gathered that the big hacksaw-brain underground in Sector KS-320 was not off-limits to humans yet, but not for want of parren trying. Hannachiam was Styx's friend, and Styx was technically a member of *Phoenix's* crew. That *couldn't* be making the parren happy. It meant that Hannachiam would listen to humans first and parren second... and Hannachiam basically controlled everything on Defiance.

A bright light flared off to the left — Tif looked, and saw a thruster tail maybe ten Ks distant, kicking in full power on its way to orbit. "Look Skah," she said. "Off to the left, a big shuttle heading to orbit."

She rolled the shuttle thirty degrees left to let the boy see — he was in the rear observer chair, which only put his eyes level with the cockpit rim, limiting his field of view. Rolling the shuttle took the thrust off-vertical, pushing them left, so she cut it, tilted the nose up instead and gave them a light tap from the mains to avoid losing altitude.

Skah made an impressed noise from the back, and she smiled. "Is that a big one, Mummy?" he asked.

"That's a big parren cargo shuttle," she agreed. "It's three times bigger than us, so it has bigger engines. But it still can't accelerate as fast because it's much heavier."

"Do you like that one, Skah?" asked Dave Lee from the front seat, in English.

"Very good," Skah agreed in the same. "Big ship."

Coms crackled. *"Hello PH-4,"* came Lieutenant Angela Lassa's voice — usually second-shift Coms but working from the Control Tower now. Most of the bridge crew spent their day with *Phoenix*, working on their speciality systems with Engineering and learning how all the amazing new tech was going to work. But Coms was more use in the tower, so Lassa and Shilu took turns there. *"We are reading a lot of parren activity near Sector KX-18. We'd appreciate it if you could swing by and take a look at what's going on."*

"Hello Tower," said Lee before Tif could reply. "We've been

receiving a flight alert to stay clear of that sector. They really don't want us over there."

"*Don't penetrate their flightspace,*" Lassa replied. "*Just go past it. See what you can see.*"

"Tower, PH-4 copies," said Tif. Lee flashed the course change onto her screen, and Tif checked to see if there was any traffic around to be upset by that correction. "Rewtenant Crozier, did you hear that?"

"*Hello Tif, I did hear that,*" Crozier confirmed from her command post in the back. "*Bravo Platoon has no objection to this course change.*" That was irony, Tif was pretty sure. Bravo Platoon had no say in the matter, like all marines on spacer vessels. Crozier had Bravo First Squad plus Bravo Heavy Squad back there, as *Phoenix* shuttles had been flying 'exploration' missions every day since arrival. They'd found some interesting things, including the dead chassis of drysine drones that the Major was now taking charge of rehabilitating in the base of Control Tower. They'd recovered other technology too, and often just gone looking at interesting things, expanding their knowledge of the city. Tif was happy to fly the missions as it kept her busy, and suspected that was the *main* reason the Captain insisted they be flown. There wasn't too much about Defiance they couldn't learn directly from Hannachiam. But the Captain wanted them to stay occupied, and Tif was fine with it. Flying over Defiance was never boring.

"Hold course for a moment, Lieutenant," said Lee. "We'll relay our course to parren control first, just to be polite. Give it ten seconds first."

Tif waited, then swung the shuttle's tail out and wide, and gave them a mild 2-G push. Thrust grumbled rather than roared, and she gained altitude with the new heading until she was at the required two-point-one kilometres.

"That wasn't hard," Skah complained from the back, in Gharkhan.

"We're trying not to upset the parren," Tif explained. "This is a parren city, we have to be polite. Look ahead, Skah. That's Tega Nen Sector. That's where the big arches are."

"I can't see," Skah complained. Tif swung them sideways once more, and tilted so he could. Looking left, in their direction of travel, Skah got a good look at the enormous two-kilometre-long arches, looming high above the city surface. They looked like the ribs of some great tube whose skin had been torn away, leaving only the skeleton. Light flickered across them, as their new parren owners explored and worked. "What for?" Skah wondered.

"We don't know," Tif admitted. "They look nice, though."

"Someone in Engineering told me that Hannachiam said they were something to create a magnetic field," Lee volunteered in English, evidently listening to their alien discussion on translator. "No idea what for. Hacksaws got up to all kinds of weird stuff." He laid in the second part of their new course and transmitted that to parren central. Tif saw that it took them within two kilometres of the forbidden zone. Normally they'd get no closer than three... but Control Tower had asked them specifically.

Tif waited, then cut vertical thrust to drop them on the new, required altitude, swinging to give them another shove through a ninety-degree course change. They flew lower, leaving the amazing high arches, and now passed over what looked like another old terrestrial shipyard — big vertical holes in the steel ground, surrounded by machinery arms and plants. This one was still abandoned, like most facilities on Defiance. What the place must have looked like in the height of the Drysine Empire, with all of this stuff alive with activity and crawling with drones, Tif could barely imagine.

"Here ahead," said Lee after a few more minutes. "On the right, the square blocks. That's Komaren Es."

Tif looked, and saw yet another unique surface feature — kilometres of regular, square shapes, as though someone had half-buried a bunch of six-sided dice. The gaps between them glowed with illumination, creating a three-dimensional gridwork of light and dark. Atop one of the near squares, scan showed her a large combat shuttle had landed. About it, a series of com signatures that were parren and encrypted.

"Parren marines on the ground," said Lee. "There are more shuttles down in the gaps between those cubes, I can read their com signatures."

"*Those marines look like top-cover,*" came Lieutenant Crozier from down back. "*They don't usually do that unless they've found something important.*"

"Kind of dumb to give that away, though," Lee remarked. And then, with sudden alarm, "We have a ground missile lock on us. It's coming from those grounded marines."

"*Phoenix* Controw, prease advise," Tif requested calmly. Missile locks were Lee's expertise, but she knew enough to know that these were the marine-suit missiles. With recent upgrades to PH-4's countermeasures it was nearly impossible that any of them could hit... and probably not from that big combat shuttle, either. This looked like a warning rather than a serious threat.

"*Hello PH-4,*" said Lassa from the tower, "*recommend you stay silent, do NOT retaliate in any way, do not change course. Just fly by, it looks like a warning more than a threat.*"

"PH-4 copies," Tif replied. "Dumb parren cood just say 'go away'."

"*They're parren,*" Crozier said drily. "*They never make a small threat when a big one will do.*"

Abruptly, some of the lights between the cubes went out. "Whoa," said Lee. "I'm reading a big energy spike, a whole bunch of coms in that district just went to static. It's like something's jamming them."

"I can't see missiw wock," Tif complained. "Is that our systen or their's?"

"I'm getting green on all systems," Lee replied, just as puzzled. "It must be them. It's like something cut them all off, or jammed their systems completely."

"*PH-4, this is Tower Control,*" came Lassa's voice once more. "*We're getting some alarmed-sounding encryption from parren ships in orbit and a few of the control bases on the surface. Whatever just happened down there, they're upset about it. I think you guys had better come home and sit this one out, we don't want things getting ugly.*"

"PH-4 copies, Controw," Tif replied, already calculating her course for home before Lee could feed it to her. It was almost as though something hadn't liked the parren aiming missiles at PH-4. But what?

* * *

ERIK MET Trace opposite loading berth one in the command tower, and waited. The *Lien Wang*'s shuttle came down precisely on schedule, a dim flare of thrust through the airlock viewports. Not bright, as the Defiance moon's gravity was barely a sixth of humanity's preference. About them was open storage space, where crates of gear unloaded from *Phoenix* but so far not needed were kept, directly by the landing pads.

"*Rehnar's people are lodging an official protest,*" Lassa told him from tower control high above. "*They're demanding PH-4's pilot be punished for an illegal flightpath. I'm sorry Captain, I shouldn't have pushed Tif into it.*"

"I'm not sure you did the wrong thing, Lieutenant," said Erik. "Clearly Rehnar's people have found something important out at Komaran Es and they don't want to share. Contact Lisbeth and request that she try to find out what it is through channels."

"*Aye Captain.*"

"Large energy signatures out that way," Trace remarked as the call ended. "Engineering's best analysis is advanced manufacturing. Whatever it is, Rehnar seems to have gotten it up and running again."

"Yeah," said Erik, watching the activity from the shuttle berth ahead. "Lots of secrets still on Defiance. For all the exploration, even the parren haven't seen more than ten percent yet."

Spacer Lang indicated when the shuttle acquired an access tube match, then a pressure seal. Soon there were figures entering the airlock, and airlock scan showed no weapons. Given recent relations between Fleet and *Phoenix*, that was probably wise on the visitors' part. The inner door opened, and a pair of men emerged. They wore spacer jumpsuits, pressure-tight linings beneath, airmasks in full webbing on their torsos and other equipment besides. Erik was pleased neither he nor Trace had bothered to don the full uniform, no matter how tempting to make a display before the visiting officers. *Phoenix* crew were a working crew, and evidently so were *Lien Wang's*.

The leading man wore a captain's eagle wings on his shoulder, while the second, taller man was a Commander. They bounced, an easier motion than walking in light-G, and Erik recognised Captain Angelo Sampey from pictures — average height, dark, flat features with more curly black hair than Fleet regs typically allowed.

"Captain Debogande," he said with an easy smile, and extended a hand. Erik took it, a little relieved that Sampey was not choosing to question his rank here. He'd taken the rank himself by necessity, and Fleet HQ could challenge its validity if they chose.

"Captain Sampey," Erik replied. "You'll know Major Thakur, of course."

"Major," said Sampey, and shook her hand as well. "This is Commander Adams, Fleet Intelligence." Ah, thought Erik, shaking his hand as well. Of course Fleet would send a spook. He didn't know Adams, but was sure he'd be someone quite senior.

"This place is just incredible," said Adams, with genuine awe. He was a tall man, pale with thin, greying hair. "I've never seen anything like it."

"We have," Erik said grimly. "It's eye-opening just how much like this there still is, for an era that I was assured had been completely destroyed. Who sent you?"

"Fleet Admiral Reiko," said Sampey. That was the new second-in-command of all United Forces, Erik knew. Replacing Fleet Admiral Anjo, who'd been eliminated by the Guardian Council after making the critical mistake of deciding to eliminate *Phoenix's* old commander, Captain Pantillo, and putting half of Fleet's senior captains perilously offside in the process. "We heard that the *UFS Phoenix's* rampage across the galaxy had finally come to a halt." The disarming smile couldn't quite disguise the edge to Sampey's voice. "So we pulled a few strings and figured out a way to reach you before you set off again. The repairs are progressing?"

"They are," said Erik. And left it at that, whatever the awkward silence. "And what is your intention in being here?"

"To learn, Captain," said Sampey. "That's all, I promise. No threats, no instructions, no demands. We just want to learn what's been going on, and the reasons behind all the... alarming things going on in tavalai space right now. And parren space too, by the looks of it."

Erik nodded. "Well then. We have a briefing prepared. If you'd like to come this way?"

* * *

ERIK TOOK the Captain and Commander through it, in the room by the bridge they'd been using for a meeting room. It had a wide view over the steel canyon in which this cluster of tall towers was located, and the many domes and features beyond. Much of it was aglow, the long-dormant city of Defiance coming back to life as might a desert plain after heavy rains.

Erik was surprised how long the briefing took. He handled most of it, seated at the circular table and resorting to holographics when there were things Sampey and Adams really needed to see for themselves. There were quite a few of those, and the open-mouthed astonishment on the faces of the two very experienced officers gave him more satisfaction than it probably should.

By mutual agreement between himself and Trace, he concealed very little. Styx, he discussed openly, and their success with a reconstructed drysine drone. Aristan and the power struggles within House Harmony were all unavoidable. And the drysine data-core, most of all, captured their undivided attention. Trace told those portions of the story that she was best placed to, and spacers on bridge duty brought them parren tea and light snacks.

When they were finished, with a final description of the Battle of Defiance that had left *Phoenix* shattered in space, and a hundred and twelve of her crew dead, nearly two-and-a-half hours had passed. Sampey and Adams did not bother to disguise their incredulity.

Adams put both hands on his head, stretched out his long legs, lips pursed in a silent whistle. Sampey gazed past them all at a blank wall, momentarily oblivious to the spectacular view.

"I really don't know what to say," he said finally. "I've seen a lot of things in my time, but this..." He didn't finish, and gazed at the wall a moment longer.

"The data-core," said Adams. "What progress have you made with it? Your AI queen was certain there would be technology here that could read it?"

"No, wait wait wait," said Sampey, holding up a hand to keep his colleague in check. "We have a lot of other things to discuss here first. Especially regarding *Phoenix*'s status in light of all this."

"There's nothing more important than the data-core," Adams corrected, pulling himself fully upright, leaning elbows on the table. "The data-core changes everything. It changes the whole Spiral. The parren are demanding access, yes?" Looking at Erik beneath arched brows.

"Yes," said Erik. "Defiance is theirs. We're valued guests so long as we don't screw them around."

"And the fact that you've unilaterally decided to unleash upon the Spiral the greatest arms race since the Machine Age doesn't concern either of you one bit?" Adams said it without malice, but Erik was reminded of an older instructor at the Academy, asking a deadpan rhetorical question to let a couple of youngsters know they'd screwed up. But neither Erik nor Trace had been youngsters for a long time.

"Which part of the briefing did you not understand, Commander?" Trace asked calmly. "We could go back over it and talk more slowly if you'd like?"

"You..." Adams grimaced, breaking off his sentence with a hard gesture from both hands, gathering the enormity of his thoughts. "The Spiral is filled with competing factions. The Triumvirate War wasn't just two sides, it was lots of sides, we just happened to all be formed into two sides for convenience. That happens because everyone's seeking an advantage... but now there's this data-core, containing a whole bunch of technology so advanced it could swing the balance of power one way or the other. And now you're going to, what, let it go? Across the Spiral? Let everyone get their hands on it? This will start more wars than any single thing since..." Again the waving hands, seeking an answer to his own rhetorical question.

"The alo are aligned with the deepynines, Commander," Erik said calmly. "The deepynines already know all this stuff, or most of it. It's already out there. We're just trying to catch up."

"Your major concern can't seriously be the fate of other species," Trace added, in a tone that was almost scorn. "Fleet is concerned with the fate of humanity. That's it. The alo/deepynine alliance will be eyeing us next, we need this technology if we're to have even the slightest chance of survival, and you'd deny it to us on the basis that someone *else* might get hurt?"

"What's your evidence the alo/deepynines are after us next?" Adams retorted with animation. "Okay, I'll buy that there *is* an alliance, I don't think that's arguable with the evidence you've acquired. But we have a multi-level, multi-signature *relationship* with the alo, the depth and sophistication of which you wouldn't know about because most of it is classified. Your very ship is based on their technology..."

"Which was spying on us," Erik interrupted. "And working against us, with covert codes that even Styx couldn't completely unravel. Did you miss that bit too?"

"It was spying to find lost drysine colonies, sure! That makes sense, the deepynines are terrified of drysines. But what evidence that they're truly going to break our alliance, attack and invade us?"

"The fact that they're making alliance with the sard, who will always be our enemies, god willing," said Erik. "Because I'd hate to belong to any species that actually made friends with the sard."

"Deepynine behaviour has not changed at all," said Trace. "Look at what they just did to Mylor Station — forty thousand dead civilians for no strategic purpose other than to send a warning. If the drysines hadn't won the drysine-deepynine war, I'm not sure there'd *be* any organics left in this part of the Spiral. If they'd then expanded as far as Earth, there wouldn't be any humans either. Previous AI races were murderous, but deepynines were almost uniformly genocidal."

"Which would work for me as an explanation," Adams persisted, "if they hadn't just teamed up with the alo!" And made a shrugging gesture at them both, challenging them to explain themselves. "Who are most certainly organic, and... Major, you saw them fighting on the Tartarus, as you call it? You said alo and deepynines seem to share a bond that looks like 'love'. Your words."

"I know," said Trace. "We can't explain it either. Deepynines seem to hate other organics just as much as they ever did, but alo are an exception."

"You said in the final part of your report that that might have a connection to the reeh?" Captain Sampey reinterjected himself.

"The data-core places an early record of the alo out in reeh space," Trace confirmed. "We've been following contacts through House Harmony to see if we can gain access to the croma. The Croma Wall, of course, stands between this entire portion of the Spiral, and all reeh space." She glanced at Erik. Erik gestured for her to continue. Having spent more time in close proximity to drones, Styx and deepynine enemies, she was probably better placed for this kind of analysis anyway. "Alo are biomechanoid, in part. What little we know of the reeh says they certainly are. Our working theory is that reeh space might have been where alo and deepynines met, after the drysine-deepynine war. Maybe a deepynine queen fled in that direction. We'd like to find out, because if deepynines start using reeh technology against us... well from what we've heard, we've no defence against that either."

"You can't go off to see the reeh," Sampey said flatly.

"We don't want to meet the reeh," said Erik, "we want to meet the croma."

"Who are right next door and aren't known to be that friendly, and we'd like to not piss them off either. Look, guys. I must differ from my friend Commander Adams here — I find the idea of an alo/deepynine alliance, exhibiting the kinds of behaviours you've identified, right on humanity's doorstep, to be pretty fucking terrifying. Our back is turned to them and we're vulnerable. I understand, and believe it or not, Fleet HQ will understand."

Trace glanced at Erik, warily, as though concerned that he might be falling for it. Erik barely acknowledged, and just met Sampey's gaze with a flat, disbelieving stare.

Sampey saw that unity and sighed. "Whatever you believe about Fleet HQ, I can assure you that what you've shown me here will blow their socks off. That's not to say they'll be happy. What you've achieved is incredible, but the methods you've taken to achieve it have been dangerous at best, and may yet hurt us very badly.

"But, I mean, gravity bombs." He looked amazed. "And if your Lieutenant Rooke is correct about the upgrades to *Phoenix*'s performance, then the benefits to Fleet could be..."

"Except that everyone else will have those upgrades too," Commander Adams said with exasperation. "So we haven't really gained anything at all, just made everything more dangerous."

"The deepynines don't have gravity bombs," Erik replied. "They were as surprised as we were."

"Sure, but now they know they're possible, they'll work on them until they invent them..."

"In decades or centuries," said Erik. "Drysines were far more advanced on gravity tech. Drysines had more inquisitive minds, it doesn't come as naturally for deepynines."

"We're going to still be living with the alo and deepynines in decades and centuries, Captain," Adams said crossly.

"That's what we used to say about the krim," said Trace. A silence followed.

"Captain," Sampey tried again. "My point is that *Phoenix* has done enough. If you come home now, I promise you'll be well treated. Your record at this point is inarguable — the worst thing your enemies say about you is that you're only in it to somehow advance or aggrandise yourself. But what you've done... what you've *all* done... out here, is so completely selfless and brave that those arguments will collapse like sand in water when people hear about it.

"But the reeh are a whole different game. I'm no expert, probably

Commander Adams could tell you more. But the reeh are just flat out scary. That empire could overwhelm the croma if they really wanted, the only reason they don't is that they've pissed off all their neighbours simultaneously and are constantly fighting everyone. The croma are just one neighbour. We're not doing anything to get the reeh looking in our direction suddenly. Fleet can't allow it. If you come home now, bygones will be forgotten, I'm sure of it. But if you tear off again to go and destabilise some *other* dangerous alien race that humanity previously had no problem with... then I'm afraid you're truly on your own."

"Bygones," Trace said flatly, looking from Commander to Captain and back again. Suspiciously. "The last ultimatum Fleet gave us came via my old friend Colonel Khola in barabo space. We broke that ultimatum to go with *Makimakala* and fight the deepynines and sard at Tartarus. We haven't heard a thing about our status back home since then. Exactly what bygones are we talking about now?"

3

Lisbeth thought the chair was about the most ridiculous thing she'd seen in four months on Defiance. It had no great artistry to it — just a simple, straight-backed plastic thing, made by people with no real knowledge of chairs, and presented for the human guest to sit on before the leader of all House Harmony. Lisbeth wore her spacer's jumpsuit beneath, with no choice but for that informality considering the airless expanse to be traversed by any visitor to this Incefahd tower. A red sash about her waist was the sole offering to parren style, and some neat pins in her hair to keep the brown curls orderly after a half-hour in an EVA helmet on the way here.

The walls of this upper-level in the tower had been stripped, joins still visible where workers had not yet filed them away to nothing. What remained were structural supports only, though Lisbeth remained unsure that aesthetically fastidious parren would not bring the ceiling crashing down if it could create a more perfectly formal space. But the last she'd glanced at her AR glasses, the pressure indicator had suggested all in good order, and neither she nor this esteemed company were about to be blasted to vacuum. Red carpets and red wall decorations completed the effect — a royal place, she supposed, and the walls were lined with many bureaucrats, big-hatted officials, grand-robed dignitaries and colourfully-attired guards.

God forfend that parren would put the razzle-dazzle aside for even a steel and airless place like Defiance, where sensible folk would all be surely attired as she was — with pressure-suit linings and emergency mask and hood near at hand in case of rapid decompression. Semaya stood at her side in a parren-equivalent jumpsuit with green ties. Behind them all, Timoshene and his small group of Domesh warriors, black robes now replaced by black jumpsuits, hoods and dark interactive glasses similar to what *Phoenix's* crew would wear. The robes were merely a style, and Timoshene had been unbothered to replace them with attire that achieved the same fully-covered result.

"This new human warship," said Rehnar, kneeling in the usual parren preference. Here he knelt upon a poga — a raised platform — so that the human would not loom above him, difficult though that would be from this ten meter distance. "This *Lien Wang*. Is this not the name of the human captain who sacrificed his life to commit total genocide against the krim?"

"*Her* life, Rehnar-sa," Lisbeth corrected. Half-a-year of full emersion in the Porgesh tongue, and she was finally confident to ditch the translators entirely. Semaya assured her that she would catch any small mistake before it got out of hand, and that the degree to which parren would be impressed by a human's fluency would outweigh any possible mistake. "Lien Wang was a woman. One of the greatest human heroes. This visiting ship is named in her memory."

"Genocide," Rehnar repeated, big, dark blue eyes lidded. 'Korosar', the Porgesh word was. In Porgesh, Lisbeth grasped that the horror of the concept was as much a matter of aesthetics as morality. Parren were dismayed by the brutal and blunt. Genocide, to parren, meant the work of barbarians, unfit for the fine appreciations of life. The moral matter of annihilating billions of lives bothered them less.

"The krim started it," Lisbeth said coolly. A small murmur of looks and gestures circled through the robed figures who flanked the walls. That was unusual, among disciplined, ever patient House Harmony parren.

"No doubt the crew of the *Lien Wang* will be most eager to learn of the data-core, and to take its knowledge back to her human rulers," said Rehnar.

"I am not privy to those discussions," said Lisbeth. "It seems likely."

"I forbid it," said Rehnar. "The data-core is the property of House Harmony. Its contents will not be shared with foreigners."

"This has been discussed," said Lisbeth, too wise by now in parren brinkmanship to suffer more than a mild acceleration of her heart.

"Unsatisfactorily," Rehnar said darkly.

"*Phoenix* possesses the data-core," said Lisbeth. "*Phoenix* crew suffered and died to win it and keep it. *Phoenix* acknowledges House Harmony's rightful claim to the contents of the drysine data-core, but *Phoenix* holds a claim on the behalf of all humanity."

"Unacceptable. This is parren space. House Harmony space. By parren law, *Phoenix* was in the service of this house in all its actions to acquire the data-core, and thus has no grounds to decide who sees the data-core's contents."

"*Phoenix* served in parren space under agreement with Gesul of the Domesh," said Lisbeth. "The Domesh made no such restriction, and *Phoenix* made clear from the beginning that she reserved the right to pursue the interests of humans above all other considerations."

"Domesh Denomination does not rule House Harmony," said Rehnar. "Incefahd Denomination does. The Domesh have no authority to make such agreements where they contradict my will."

"Retroactively," Lisbeth said firmly, her eyes not leaving Rehnar's. 'Tego dolara', the Porgesh phrase was. It meant much the same thing as in English. "As in human law, Rehnar-sa, no parren can arrive on the scene of an ongoing circumstance and retroactively impose his will upon legally sanctioned actions that have already occurred. *Phoenix* acquired the data-core at great cost, in the belief that she could share that information with all humans. Not even the ruler of a great parren house can alter that understanding retroactively, particularly not when *Phoenix* has paid such a price for the acquisition in blood."

Rehnar's slim nostrils flared. Lisbeth knew she took quite a risk, dressing him down in his own court like this. But lately she'd had less and less choice.

"I warn you, *Phoenix*," said Rehnar. "And your sponsor, Gesul of the Domesh. Gesul swore allegiance to Tobenrah of the Incefahd, and remains bound by that oath of fealty today, to foreswear all competition between the denominations for the greater good of all parren. Tobenrah fought within that bond to win this world and this city, and he died gloriously for the honour of House Harmony and the Incefahd. *Phoenix* also swore an oath to Tobenrah and the Incefahd, to assist him in conflict against Aristan's people on Chirese, in exchange for Tobenrah's commitment to side with humans against the alo/deepynines. Tobenrah is now dead, I have gained his place atop the Incefahd, and thus your oath to him remains in force with me."

"*Phoenix* follows your instruction faithfully, Rehnar-sa," Lisbeth gave the traditional phrasing. "But *Phoenix* fulfilled its commitment to Tobenrah until his brave and glorious death in the battle of Defiance, and so considers its part in that bargain complete. It was *Phoenix*'s Major Thakur who defeated Aristan in an honourable catharan, witnessed now by most of parren space, that sent the Domesh forces at Chirese into disarray, and thus prevented Aristan's ascension to supplant Tobenrah as the head of House Harmony. That Tobenrah remained leader of this glorious house, and was not supplanted by Aristan, is entirely the doing of the *UFS Phoenix*, Rehnar-sa."

And thus, she could have added, your own position here today is also. But stating it so boldly would have been dangerously impertinent.

Rehnar's eyes flashed with anger. "Humans and Domesh are not the only ones to have died here. Best that you do not forget."

"No, Rehnar," said Lisbeth, with a faint bow of her head from that awkward sitting position upon the ridiculous chair. "But humans on Defiance are not helpless, no matter how outnumbered. Best that no one forgets."

* * *

"HE'S GOING to attack Gesul, isn't he?" Lisbeth said in a low murmur as she and her entourage changed back into their pressure suits. The basement beneath the Incefahd tower was filled with lockers and storage, surrounded by many airlock doors and the endless hissing cycle of visitors coming and going. Incefahd guards stood wary, watching their guests while other parren operated the airlocks. "Gesul is a threat to the House Harmony leadership now, whatever Gesul says about not wanting it."

"It is not up to Gesul," Semaya agreed. She looked incongruously slim within the bulk of her pressure suit, her neck narrow above the helmet rim. She'd nearly died in the Battle of Defiance, riding on Gesul's ship the *Stassis* when it had been crippled and left spinning and powerless. Surviving vessels had rescued the *Stassis*'s remaining crew, and Semaya with them. Lisbeth thought the experience had changed her, but with parren — and House Harmony parren in particular — it was hard to tell. "The Jusica are conducting a count of followers through all parren space. Should Gesul be found to have more, the Domesh will be the ruling denomination of House Harmony."

"The Incefahd changed the course of rivers to prevent the Domesh ascending with Aristan in power," said Lisbeth. "They claimed that was all about Aristan, but I doubt they'll be happier with Gesul."

"Rehnar's greatest displeasure is that he feels Gesul has inherited all of Tobenrah's good work," said Semaya. "Tobenrah fought and died against the deepynines, and brought great glory to the Incefahd denomination. And yet it is Gesul and the Domesh who benefit, although the Domesh should have been discredited by Aristan's failure and selfishness at Chirese. All the newly phased parren are flooding to the Domesh, because it is Gesul who survived the battle with glory and not Tobenrah. Such are the fortunes of war."

So newly-phased parren were supposed to choose denominations based on which interpretation of Harmony-phase psychology most appealed to them personally, Lisbeth thought. But instead, as with humans, they ended up siding with the most charismatic leader and not taking much note of what his teachings or policies were. Gesul was the beneficiary of that now, which supposed good sense on the part of his followers, because Lisbeth knew Gesul well enough to like and admire him greatly. But previously Aristan had been the recipient of that parren cult of personality, and the power that his megalomania had nearly managed to acquire was frightening to contemplate.

Parren populism could be alarming. The surges and tides of parren popular opinion, driven by a psychological phase-change embedded and irreversible in their biology, could favour good people or bad, and drive all parren en masse either toward the heights of sanity and prosperity, or straight over a cliff. Parren artists had been writing plays about it for millennia, these cyclical highs and lows, this simultaneous enlightenment and insanity. Lisbeth had once thought those plays somewhat melodramatic, but now that she'd seen it at a closer range than even most parren playwrights got to experience, she thought that if anything they'd been underplaying the random fragility of it all.

Something small, winged and insect-like buzzed before her face, and Lisbeth unzipped the pouch on the front of her pressure suit. The little machine landed and climbed inside, theoretically unable to escape once contained, but Lisbeth doubted that and others of Styx's claims about the bugs' harmlessness. Perhaps some of the watching parren guards noticed — it did not matter, all parren knew of *Phoenix*'s association with drysine technology, and all of *these* parren knew about the bugs. Hiding them would not fool anyone, and parren respected displays of power and authority. But too much power and authority, in the wrong company, could get you recognised as a threat and killed. It was the endless tightrope walk of life amid parren authorities, and it seemed to Lisbeth that lately the rope was growing thinner, and the crosswinds stronger.

Timoshene joined them at the designated airlock — he and his assigned guards now in the advanced and sleek armour of parren marines, with a visor display that would create wrap-around panoramics inside his helmet, and advanced targeting for the rifle and other weapons. Lisbeth was pleased for the protection, but it did not make her feel as secure as her time amongst *Phoenix*'s marines had. Parren armour was good, but *Phoenix* marines considered them toys, and speculated as to how many hits that rifle would need to even penetrate human armour.

Outside the airlock, *Defiance*'s grey steel mechanical innards surrounded, some of it the straight forward structural right angles that Lisbeth's engineer-trained brain made simple sense of, and some of it organic and baffling like the entrails of an alien creature. Incefahd-installed floodlights lit this portion of passage — a winding tube that snaked away like an animal's burrow. It had been a mass transit system once, beneath the towers that soared overhead, but all trace of train or carriage was now long gone. Instead there sat a familiar parren design of ground car, with fat wheels on independent suspension about a central chassis. Some larger cars were pressurised, but this one was not, used for short trips beneath the towers.

Lisbeth climbed the ladder easily and pulled herself in, Semaya and the guards distributing themselves evenly about the remaining seats, and several propped on the rear with rifles ready. "No, let me drive," Lisbeth admonished Timoshene as he attempted once more to take the driver's seat. "How are you supposed to protect me from attack if you're busy driving? There's only two possible directions, forward and back, and besides, I'm a qualified shuttle co-pilot and you're not."

She could not see Timoshene's expression through the reflective glare of floodlight on visor, but he relented to take the middle of the seat row behind. Lisbeth settled in, pleased to have something more to do than be hauled from one location to another like a bag of vegetables. In parren company, that wasn't always easy.

After making sure all were prepared, Lisbeth powered up the engine and sent them forward. She hadn't mentioned to Timoshene that 'shuttle co-pilot' didn't actually involve much flying, and was mostly about operating systems that the pilot was too busy to manage personally. But this big electric rig was about as simple as vehicles got — a hand throttle, a steering wheel that was mostly redundant in a giant tube, and a few indicators showing speed, power levels and powerplant health.

Through the open superstructure as they left she saw more vehicles rolling in, similarly loaded with passengers and armoured guards. *"Rousha Denomination,"* said Semaya on coms, whose job it was to know such things. *"A lot of them. Here to discuss the data-core, no doubt."*

Semaya was now the head of Lisbeth's personal staff, by Lisbeth's own appointment. 'Chief of Staff', she'd explained the human term to the parren woman — the person who managed the affairs of the office and all the people in it. Semaya was far too cool and graceful to show any great emotion at the appointment, but Lisbeth could tell she'd been pleased. Back at the office, whose personnel were split between the gravitational habitat and the Domesh Tower alongside the one occupied by *Phoenix*, she had also (as nearly as she could translate their parren names and functions) a Chief of Communications, a Chief of Assessment (whose job it was to advise her on the political state-of-play between denominations), a Chief Scientist (who Semaya had warned was actually a plant from a big Incefahd research institution, there to learn as much as possible about Styx and *Phoenix* both), and a full seven Denominational Liaisons who were tasked with keeping in personal contact with people from each denominational head office, who often knew things unannounced in the official releases. Happily, all of them answered to Semaya, who in turn answered to Lisbeth. Plus of course there was Timoshene and his twelve-strong security team, tasked with protecting them all from attack, and Lisbeth in particular.

"I'm more concerned about Alired myself," said Lisbeth, as the big tires bumped on the lower skeleton ribs of the tunnel. "And the extent to which Alired is coordinating all this House Harmony activity against Gesul."

It was the commonest speculation, and one did not need to be an expert in parren politics to see it happening. If the Jusica's count of followers put Gesul ahead of Rehnar, then Gesul and the Domesh Denomination would assume control of House Harmony. The leaders of the other Harmony denominations, Rehnar's Incefahd Denomination most prominently, preferred that it did not happen.

House Fortitude, the greatest of the five parren houses, and currently the outright rulers of all parren space, also preferred that it did not happen. Harmony ruled by Incefahd was manageable, but Harmony ruled by Domesh was a destabilising concern that Fortitude had long sought to prevent — first with Aristan leading the Domesh, and now with Gesul. And so House Fortitude had sent an ambassador to Defiance, to organise and instruct on the wishes of House Fortitude and the Supreme Leader of all the parren. That ambassador's name was Alired. Lisbeth had met her on several occasions, and liked her less on each.

The trip back to the Domesh Tower took barely ten minutes, a slow crawl through the framework tunnel that was nonetheless faster than the alternatives. Along the way they passed many engineers and technicians, examining various ancient systems, some still functioning, some long since decayed. The anti-aging technologies on Defiance had not saved everything, and while some sections of the enormous alien city appeared almost pristine, others were a mouldering shell.

At the tower's basement access Lisbeth drove them out through the gap Domesh engineers had cut in the tube, then parked the car in its long-term bay. Its passengers dismounted as a tech came with a big cord from its generator to recharge it, and Lisbeth noticed some *Phoenix* marines nearby, talking with parren marines. She would have stopped to chat, but such informalities were unknown to parren on official business, so she settled for a wave. The marines waved back — a group of four, Second Section, Third Squad, Bravo Platoon, her Augmented Reality visor informed her, or Bravo 2-3 in marine-speak.

She didn't know those guys, and hadn't been on *Phoenix* long enough to get to know more than a handful very well. But those she did know continued to regard her like family, however little she saw them these days.

On the other side of the airlock, before the lockers of suit-transition, Hiro Uno was waiting for her. With him was a human man Lisbeth didn't recognise — middle height and strongly built, he had the look of a military man save that he wore a plain spacer jumpsuit and his hair was several grades too long for even the relaxed grooming standards of a Fleet carrier crew one year away from external inspection. So he wasn't *Phoenix*, then. It didn't leave many options.

Timoshene stepped before them immediately, helmet off and staring down at both men with menace. "Timoshene, don't be silly," Lisbeth told him. "You know Hiro, he's worked for my family for many years."

"This other is not *Phoenix*," Timoshene said bluntly. "There is no passcode access. How did you enter?" This directed at Hiro. Hiro heard on his earpiece translator, but looked at Lisbeth, both amused and wary.

"*Phoenix* has the tower next door," Lisbeth retorted, feeling very much like a pre-school teacher scolding an unruly five-year-old. "Humans come and go from the Domesh Tower all the time, I'm quite happy to meet anyone Hiro has brought to see me."

"This human is from the other ship," Timoshene said stubbornly. "He could be an assassin."

"If he's a friend of Hiro's, he probably *is* an assassin," said Lisbeth. It was a thought she would have kept to herself among humans, but among parren it was more likely to increase respect than diminish it. "But Timoshene, you must understand the consequences for a human of assassinating the daughter of Alice Debogande, and the brother of Erik Debogande. It would be catastrophic for all involved. Besides which, I trust Hiro implicitly, both his loyalty and his judgement."

Parren didn't really do family. They had families, and loved them, but those bonds were always weaker than the bonds of house and the great change of the flux that sent parren scattering to all corners. It was a constant source of misunderstanding between herself and her parren comrades, as they could not quite grasp what Family Debogande *was* — not a denomination of like-minded ideologues, not a house describing a psychological state of mind, but rather a bloodline of kin that also operated as a great unit of power in human space. Whatever else they were, parren were meritocrats, and their leaders did not ascend to the top purely by accidents of birth or marriage. They'd never really done kings and queens at any point in their social evolution, and regarded all those who ascended in that way as suspect, the same way a *Phoenix* spacer might judge an officer who'd climbed the ranks on rumours of favouritism from high-placed friends. And sometimes Lisbeth was left with the uncomfortable feeling that they were probably right.

"His name is Daica," said Hiro, and Lisbeth was astonished at the momentary disorientation that sudden switch to English caused her brain. "He is a representative of the human government. There are private matters to be discussed, Lisbeth. Regarding your family, and its affairs back home, while you have been gone."

"No," said Timoshene, a blunt obstacle in Hiro's way. "No private affairs. Lisbeth is an advisor to the ruler of the Domesh Denomination."

"A role she will struggle to fulfil if she cannot hear sensitive information from the human government for herself," Hiro said calmly, after the translator pause that Lisbeth no longer needed. "If she is not privy to sensitive human information, what possible use is she to Gesul?"

LISBETH SETTLED in her personal quarters, and waited for the aides to settle food and drink on the small tables before each of her guests. The aides were the lowest rung in her office — four of them, all wide-eyed kids from various worlds in parren space, who fetched the

drinks and did the odd tasks that every office required. Lisbeth was
uncomfortable with how brusquely they were treated by others in
her office, but happily it was never a permanent position, and all
high-ranking parren had begun their duties in such posts, Gesul
included. They departed, as Hiro watched with a private, impressed
smile. His companion, now Lisbeth's guest, looked out the curved,
massively reinforced windows at the airless view of alien cityscape
beyond, with all the awe that it deserved. Lisbeth put her AR glasses
over her eyes and blinked through a series of security protocols,
assuring her that the installed technology in this room was doing
its job.

"We are secure," she informed the new man. "There's anti-
bugging technology in this room that parren technology cannot
penetrate."

Daica, Hiro had said the man's name was. "Who installed that
technology?" he asked, still gazing out the window. "Given that this is
a parren facility?"

"I did," said Hiro. "It's drysine and it's ridiculous, like all things
drysine. What the local parren don't realise is that it can probably
isolate and recover every data-feed taking place in this tower,
communications or otherwise."

"And they let you install it?" Daica wondered. "Surely they'd
suspect, given how you've been messing around with drysine coms
tech lately?"

Hiro shrugged. "Parren be strange."

"Superior capabilities are a mark of status among parren,"
Lisbeth explained, sipping the steaming tea the aides had left.
"Parren compete upwards, not down, and superior abilities are
encouraged, not repressed."

"They're elitists," Hiro translated, dipping a small instrument in
his own tea. It gave him a reading on his glasses. Only then did he sip.
Daica watched, then did the same.

"Spies," Lisbeth said distastefully. And to Daica, "What branch
are you?"

"Federal Intelligence," said Daica. His face registered cautious surprise at how good the tea was. Lisbeth wondered if he'd been out of human space before in his life. "The same branch as Hiro." Meaning quite a bit more than just 'Federal Intelligence', Lisbeth knew. Most of Federal Intelligence sat in offices and processed data. A small, elite few went out and gathered that data. An even smaller, even more elite group possessed specialised and often lethal skills for the gathering. Hiro was a former member of this group, and Lisbeth suspected that Daica was too.

"Old friend?" she asked. Daica glanced at Hiro. Hiro just smiled. Lisbeth sighed, knowing she'd never get a detailed answer. Hiro had 'retired', but in truth no one ever really retired from *that* organisation. And Alice Debogande had surely known that, in hiring Hiro, the advantages and connections from his presence went both ways. Surely it had benefited Hiro's former bosses to have a theoretically 'ex' agent within the Debogande household, as it had also benefited Alice to have a conduit to the highest spymasters in human space right in her office. Hiro's branch of Intelligence was *not* Fleet, it was civilian, and those two sides didn't always get along.

"You've got parren servants now," said Hiro. "To go with the personal bodyguards."

"They're staff," Lisbeth corrected, wary of her former family security making fun of her. He and Jokono had always worked for Alice, not for Alice's children, and had not been shy of reminding them. "I have an office. Call it a human liaison office, in Gesul's administration."

And she was surprised that Hiro did not make fun, but smiled proudly. "Amazing," he said.

"Amazing," Daica added with feeling. "There's been hardly any non-parren who've achieved it, let alone humans. Maybe back in the Parren Empire aliens in high administration would have been a thing, but not for thousands of years. And your Porgesh... you learned all that in six months?"

"It's been high immersion," said Lisbeth with great understatement. "And I've been taking the memory enhancers, they help."

"So," said Daica, nodding. Like Hiro, Lisbeth thought he seemed quite casual and laid back. It had surprised her at first, meeting Hiro as a younger girl. Hiro had been a significantly powerful person, a top spy, yet he was flippant and good humoured. Only after a while had she come to realise how the flippancy worked as a cover for evasiveness, and created an air of general vagueness that allowed him to avoid answering most questions directly. And the thing with casual, laid back people was that you could never really tell what they were thinking, or what mattered to them. People liked Hiro, and were at ease with him, talking eagerly and hoping to impress him... all good things for a spy. And the fact that he was so damn handsome didn't hurt his chances at getting information from female contacts, either. Human ones, anyway.

"I came out on *Lien Wang*," said Daica. "As you've gathered. I'd heard a few things about your situation when I left, but nothing like this." He gestured around. "You've made yourself quite an asset to all human kind, Lisbeth. We've not had this degree of influence in parren society ever."

It made Lisbeth immediately uncomfortable. "No, look." She held up her hand. "You've misunderstood my position. There's no such thing as 'parren society'. It's not a singular thing, all the houses compete and all the denominations compete within the houses. I have some influence in House Harmony, but no more than that. And if humanity attempts to use me to further human causes, I lose all my status and thus my usefulness to anyone. Parren serve only one master. Divided loyalties are almost entirely unknown to them."

"Really?" Daica's eyebrows raised. "Isn't there a long tradition of servants turning on masters?"

"No." Lisbeth shook her head firmly. "The servant was *always* serving one master. He was only pretending to serve the other. That's the difference."

"Infiltration," Hiro explained to his colleague. "Parren don't follow casually — they're committed. Right down to the lowest rungs of society. It's not ideological, it's psychological on the genetic level."

"Nearly," Lisbeth corrected with a faint smile. "The denominations are ideological, there's some conscious choice involved. The houses are structurally psychological, there's no choice in those. But yet, even denominational loyalties are absolute — parren choose their denominations, but then commit to them absolutely. Absolutism is a universal parren characteristic."

"But you *clearly* serve two masters," Daica pointed out. "I mean, you're a Debogande, and Erik's the captain of *Phoenix*. They're not dumb, surely they can't ask you to choose?"

Not a stupid man at all, Lisbeth thought. Not surprising, given his background. "I'm alien, so it's tolerated," she said uncomfortably. "And I was snatched against my will by Gesul's predecessor, so Gesul's people feel some responsibility for the situation. So long as Gesul and *Phoenix* remain allies, it won't be a problem."

"And if that relationship changes?"

Lisbeth did not particularly want to discuss those contingencies with a man she'd only just met. Not long ago, she would have tolerated the endless smalltalk and probing. But this was her office, and this man was here to see *her*, not the other way around. "Daica," she said, with the faint irony of knowing that it was unlikely to be his real name. "Why are you here?"

"Well first," said Daica, shifting gears in the manner of a man at ease in any situation, "there's the matter of your family."

Lisbeth frowned. "What matter?"

Daica held up both hands. "I want to make clear that this is not something my bosses cooked up to threaten you or your family. I think Hiro can vouch for me on this — the challenge does not come from our side of government, it comes from Fleet."

Lisbeth felt her alarm growing, from that small, manageable twinge that she'd become accustomed to ignoring, to something more like the dry-mouthed, heart-thumping fear that she would never get used to, nor learn to enjoy. "Threaten my family? What threat?"

"Fleet Intelligence are building a case against your mother," said Daica. Almost apologetically, like a defence lawyer telling his client something unpleasant but unavoidable. "Money transfers to alien financial entities. That sort of thing."

Lisbeth stared. "The barabo?" It was nearly funny. And then it wasn't. "I mean, off the record..."

Daica smiled. "Lisbeth, I'm a spook. There is no record." At which Hiro gave her a faint nod of agreement. Until very recently, Hiro had been in the direct employ of Alice Debogande. By some measures he still was... among other things.

"Okay..." Lisbeth took a deep breath. "So Mother made financial transfers to a barabo trading company to support *Phoenix* in barabo space. After that... well, I wasn't there, but I'd guess the tavalai have been picking up the tab in tavalai space... or the Dobruta did anyway... and now it's House Harmony in parren space."

Daica nodded. "Financial dealings with alien entities is illegal. We all know it goes on and there's very little that can actually be proven, particularly when you're dealing with the barabo, because the barabo never actually write anything down. But whatever recent conciliations toward *Phoenix* by Fleet, *Phoenix* is still technically a renegade vessel. And so this isn't just a matter being handled by financial regulators and the like — this is Fleet Intelligence, the big guys who can prove anything if they set their minds to it..."

"Because *Phoenix* is a renegade vessel," Lisbeth murmured in shock as the implication of it rolled over her. "A Fleet-level security issue."

"Probably the biggest Fleet-level security issue there is right now," Daica added helpfully.

"They're looking for leverage, Lisbeth," Hiro explained. "Making financial transactions to unreliable alien entities in support of a renegade vessel is a pretty serious deal. They're angling for a treason charge."

"Yes thank you, I got that Hiro," Lisbeth said impatiently. Spending half-a-year at this level of parren intrigue and treachery made some things quite transparent to her. "Mother's got the best lawyers in human space, what are their odds?"

"On a fair and level playing ground?" said Hiro, with meaning. "Pretty good. What do you think are the odds of *that*?"

Lisbeth said nothing, thinking and gnawing her lip. "Treason," she said finally. "They can't drop that on Alice Debogande without serious repercussions. I mean, the penalty is death." She forced herself to say it, with difficulty.

"Fleet hasn't liked Debogande Inc for a long time," said Hiro. "Long before this whole mess. They do business with the Debogandes because they have to... and that's exactly what they don't like. They don't like *having* to do anything. They don't like being cramped for options. In strategic terms, they call it flexibility."

"They'd break the companies up?" Lisbeth surmised. It was a horrible, nightmarish thing to contemplate, but she'd gotten accustomed to contemplating those on this journey too. "They don't need to for procurement, there's plenty of other good ship-builders out there, Fleet buy from us because we're better than most of them..."

"It's just a threat at this point," Daica interrupted, hands again raised, calmingly. "It gives them options, and pressure against your mother. They got into trouble pulling the nuclear trigger too early before, with Captain Pantillo. They're not going to rush into it this time... but they will if they don't get what they want."

"And what do they want?"

"Leverage against *Phoenix*. Control over all the forces that *Phoenix* has unleashed."

"*Phoenix* hasn't unleashed anything," Lisbeth retorted. "*Phoenix* has uncovered things *before* they're unleashed, for which Fleet should be eternally grateful."

"Fleet doesn't like anything they can't control," Daica said patiently. "I've heard talk in senior places that right now, humanity's foreign policy is being run by *Phoenix*. I mean, turmoil with the tavalai, now with the parren, a suddenly resurgent deepynine force allied to the alo and making alliances with the sard. You might be right, Fleet might stand to benefit a lot from all of this. All of humanity might. But right now Fleet aren't even being consulted, and they'd like their hands back on the controls."

Lisbeth shook her head firmly. "Well screw that, they're not going to get anything from Erik. Erik loves Mother as much as I do, but he's convinced he's on a mission to save humanity from future annihilation. He thinks the alo and deepynines could be just a few years away from pulling the trigger and there's not much we could do about it, and that the entire Triumvirate War was just very long battlespace preparation by the alo to weaken the tavalai in advance. He won't stop now, no matter what they threaten. And if Mother was here, she'd tell him not to."

Daica nodded in cautious agreement. "You'll notice I didn't approach Erik."

Lisbeth's eyes widened. "Me?" Suspicion followed. "Wait a moment... *you're* acting as an agent for Fleet Intel? Getting me to do what they want?"

"No, my bosses want to *protect* your mother. Fleet's grown into a mini-tyranny, Lisbeth — you know this as well as anyone, after what happened to Captain Pantillo and your brother. There have been many others, just less well publicised. It was inevitable, Fleet does an amazing job of keeping us safe and they take that mission very seriously. So seriously that they don't like to be crowded by any rival authorities, including Captain Pantillo, the Worlders, Debogandes, etc. My side of government wants to stop Fleet's mini-tyranny from becoming a mega-tyranny, and your mother is one of the most important countervailing voices doing that.

"We'll be helping the people constructing the case in your mother's defence. But she's going to need all the help she can get, Lisbeth. Anything you can give us, any proof that you're providing invaluable intelligence for the human cause, would be gold for that defence."

"Daica," Lisbeth said carefully, to be very sure he understood. "I'm granted a very special leeway by Gesul in light of my unique circumstances. I can be both in *Phoenix's* service, and in Gesul's, for as long as *Phoenix* remains a friend and ally of Gesul. Humanity as a whole? Particularly represented by Fleet? They're neither friend nor ally to any parren, Gesul or otherwise."

"I understand that," said Daica, solemnly.

"You're asking me to betray their trust. You're asking me to be a double agent."

"Nothing so drastic. Just provide Fleet with intelligence on internal parren workings."

"Parren see that as betrayal. They're not big on moral shades of grey."

"Fleet's already getting briefings from Lisbeth and Erik," Hiro attempted.

Daica shook his head. "No, a briefing is something parren leaders would approve of. Fleet will need the stuff they wouldn't."

Lisbeth exhaled hard, and gazed out the window at the vast alien view. "I can't. There's too much else at stake."

"Well that's your choice to make, of course," said Daica. "But I have to tell you, Lisbeth — my bosses are telling me that there are a lot of people in Fleet who see this is a grand opportunity to remove the Alice Debogande thorn from their side once and for all. And if Fleet wants it, Fleet will get it."

* * *

"SKAH, *I really think you should do the puzzle.*"

"I don't want to do the puzzle." Skah sat in bed, AR glasses on, looking at the data files that Mummy had brought him. The files were from Chogoth, and they'd come all the way out here on the human ship, *Lien Wang*. All human ships, and most alien ships, carried the latest news that had reached them, so *Lien Wang* would have been carrying all kinds of news, not just from Chogoth. But Mummy was interested in news from Chogoth, and she'd sat with him at bedtime and instead of a story had watched some of the vision with him, and the news reports, and explained to him what it all meant.

It hadn't been fun in the same way that a story was fun, but it had been compelling all the same. Sometimes Skah forgot what it was like to be surrounded by kuhsi. He knew he wasn't a human — he wasn't stupid. But sometimes he thought it would just be so much easier if he stayed with humans forever, and never had to worry about kuhsi ever again. Sometimes he thought Mummy felt the same way... but then she brought him news from Chogoth, and told him he shouldn't forget where he came from. That was confusing, because for a long time now she'd been telling him that he was from *Phoenix*, and this ship and its human crew were their clan now.

"The puzzle will help you with your maths," Styx insisted on his glasses earbuds. He often talked to her like this, in bed, when no one else was around. Often the *Phoenix* coms people would know who was talking to who, but Skah didn't think even Lieutenant Shilu knew that Styx was talking to him so often. He was pretty sure they wouldn't like it. Sometimes he was so overcome by the desire to share with his friends the things he and Styx would talk about, but then he remembered that he'd promised her not to. And it was even more fun, really, to have a real secret of his very own. And worse yet, if he told them, and Styx got into trouble, she might not be allowed to talk to him any more.

"Mummy says my Daddy was Lord Khargesh," he said. They spoke Gharkhan, and that was good too, to have someone other than Mummy to speak Gharkhan to. He was getting very good at English, but English had so many difficult sounds that his mouth just couldn't make. "Lord Khargesh was the Lord of Koth. That's a big nation on Chogoth."

He watched his visuals on the glasses. There was a big city, somewhere in Koth. The streets were wide and there weren't many tall buildings. Lots of kuhsi were out in the streets, and there were a lot of trucks and air vehicles. There was shouting and screeching, and banners being waved, and then there was white smoke and scary-looking security men with big sticks and sonic blasters. Some kuhsi fell, others ran away, and a few more charged with claws bared, and there was fighting. Kuhsi could be frightening, Skah thought... and tried flexing his own claws. Trimmed a long time ago, they barely moved. It would be years yet until they regrew properly within their finger sheaths.

"Would you like to be the Lord of Koth?" Styx asked.

That was funny, and Skah smiled... but the images on his glasses weren't funny at all, and the smile faded. "I'm the twenty-third in line, Mummy says," he replied. "And besides, they've put a different man in charge now. They killed my Daddy. My Daddy was the real Lord of Koth." He knew it should have made him sad, but then he'd never known his Daddy. And Lord Khargesh had had many children — hundreds, with many different women. That was normal for big kuhsi lords. "Mummy says some people want to put one of Lord Khargesh's heirs back in charge of Koth. She says they don't like the new Lord. And then she says some other kuhsi say there shouldn't be lords at all, that everyone should vote for a new lord." He didn't really know what that meant, but Mummy said it was important, so he believed her. "What do you think, Styx?"

"I don't know very much about organic systems of government," said Styx.

"Don't be silly," Skah laughed. "You know much more than me."

"How do you know that?"

"Because you're the smartest person in the history of the galaxy." Styx usually corrected him when he said something wrong. That she didn't do it now told him that she wasn't going to disagree with him.

"I think that Chogoth is going through some very large changes," said Styx. *"The kuhsi were not very advanced when humans discovered them. Some humans said they should be left alone, and that bad things would happen to kuhsi society if they introduced too much new technology too quickly. But the humans had a lot of enemies, and they needed some new friends, so they introduced high technology to a society that wasn't really ready for it. I think what happened to your father is a result of those troubles. Some people don't like change."*

"Are those the bad people?"

"Not always. Not all change is good."

"The deepynines wanted to kill all the drysines," Skah said slowly, thinking hard. "That's change too, right?"

"Yes exactly, Skah."

"And the krim wanted to kill all the humans. That's change too."

"And the humans, quite understandably, thought that change was very bad, just as the drysines thought the change the deepynines wanted was very bad. I'm pleased that you understand, Skah. When we first met, I don't think you would have."

"Mummy says I'm growing up, and I need to think about these things. How do you know if change is good or bad?"

"Objectively, it's very hard."

"What does 'objectively' mean?"

"It means that you take yourself out of the equation. Something might be bad for you, but good for everyone else. Objectively means that's a good thing, if you can accept that the bad thing happening to you and your people is necessary."

Skah frowned. On his glasses now were journalists, talking in a studio with big holographic displays and a live audience. It was funny to see kuhsi like that — talking in fancy clothes like civilised people. Kuhsi seemed so savage, sometimes. Like animals. "I don't think I could let something bad happen to Mummy or *Phoenix*," he said. "I wouldn't care if it was good for someone else."

"You know," said Styx, *"I think you might be right. I'm not sure there is any such thing as 'objectively'. Ultimately there's just survival, and there is no greater or more moral motivation than the survival of yourself and your people. Now, I really think you should do the puzzle. I designed it myself."*

"You made a puzzle for me?" Skah frowned. "Why?"

"Because I find you very interesting, Skah. Will you do the puzzle?"

"I suppose." He flipped the news images from his glasses, replaced by a series of complex three-dimensional shapes. "What do I do?"

4

Trace sat in the technical bay amidst several dozen creepily advanced fabricators, and tried to bounce the tennis ball off Peanut's main eye. One of Peanut's four small manipulator arms always intercepted it, grabbing with multiple-articulated claws and tossing it quickly back. His head was roughly spherical, protected within an articulated hood-shield, and darted with rapid, birdlike intensity to follow the ball.

Trace was unarmoured, but behind her Staff Sergeant Kono was fully suited, big Koshaim rifle in hand and surveying all the bay's activity. He wasn't pleased that Trace was unarmoured, but it was Kono's job as Command Squad leader to be protective. Command Squad's primary function was to make sure the Major didn't get herself killed. But Trace was insistent that Peanut, Bucket and Wowser should get to know what humans actually looked like under those thick metal shells, to get them accustomed to the idea that cooperation between machines and organics was normal. In his full armour, Kono looked nearly as much the machine that the drones did.

Peanut's vibroblades were inactive, and a drysine drone's primary weapons systems were modular and thus could be removed when not on combat operations, or replaced by tools for non-combat tasks as required. His body was the size of a large man, in two primary segments — a torso to which all legs attached, and a rear abdomen containing powerplant and weapons attachments. The arrangement provoked obvious comparisons to spiders, but at this range it didn't really work. The abdomen was multi-segmented and flexible, for one thing, with interlocking armour plates that allowed a degree of bending, with the intricacy of some three-dimensional artwork. The legs were also not exclusively side-mounted like a spider, but could rotate around the torso to create any convenient three-dimensional configuration. Drone legs were not really meant for walking, despite first appearances — AIs had never found planets very interesting, and thus their drones were not optimised for gravity but rather for various degrees of micro-gravity, where the legs would pull them floating through structures while holding equipment and manipulating things at need.

Peanut had ten limbs — the four small ones to grasp small objects before his face, like Trace's tennis ball, being by far the most dexterous. Trace was sure Peanut could do perfect origami with those arms if shown how, and probably at three times the speed of the fastest human. The remaining six legs were big — the rear two were often used in conjunction with rear weapons attachments, but were primarily for propulsion, haulage and large-scale manipulation.

At close inspection it was obvious that the drones could hardly be described as 'machines' in the simple way humans understood such things. The shell and armour surfaces were varied in texture, embedded with multi-phase sensors on the molecular level, giving a surface sensitivity comparable to human skin. Petty Officer Chenkov had shown Trace the intricacies of sensor networks embedded into Peanut's small hands on the forearms, and it had been like looking at organic brain structure, a maze of microscopic connections. Humans typically understood 'machine' to mean less complicated than 'organic', but with hacksaws Trace was not certain it was true. They'd been self-evolving for tens of thousands of years, dividing into different branches of civilisation as one group would pursue some technological advancement the others lacked, and chased it to an extreme. The constant fracturing had led to wars, but also to competition, which had resulted in synthetic life so complex and nuanced even a human could see the semantical issues that arose from insisting that it was not actually 'alive'.

Trace flicked her hand again, but did not let go of the ball. Peanut's little arms flashed to where he thought the ball would be, froze as he realised his mistake, and Trace flicked the ball before he could recover, hitting him on the big, main eye. He did a fast double-take, lurching back half-a-step as though discombobulated.

"Wake up Peanut," Trace told him. "Look at where the ball actually is, not just where you think it is."

Peanut's eye flicked to her face, then to the ball, as though sizing that up. Trace was certain he was reading her expression for clues... or trying to. Drones, in her limited experience, didn't seem very good at that. But then, she'd never seen one grow old enough to learn properly. Peanut's word comprehension was pretty good now, but she suspected all three drones were supplementing language comprehension with facial and body language cues. And just because he understood what she was saying didn't mean he'd automatically follow her commands. Loyalty, with hacksaw drones, seemed a nebulous and potentially treacherous concept. Particularly with Styx around.

On cue with her thoughts the big bay doors opened, and like a scene from a horror movie, there stood Styx, a looming steel dinosaur with flared head-shield atop a long neck, and a segmented body several times more complicated than the drones' and twice as large. She entered the bay near where Private Jess Rolonde was showing Bucket the toy cube that Trace had once shown to their previous drone companion, whom they'd known only as 'Kid'. Bucket flicked the rotating parts of the cube around to make colours and patterns align, then showed it to Jess. Bucket seemed to like Jess in particular.

And Jess, having once struggled to be within ten metres of Kid was now among the most active participants in the new drones' training.

"Hi Styx," said Rolonde, barely even looking.

"Hello Private Rolonde," said Styx. Once, Styx had communicated by hacking nearby speakers or earphones. Now, to go with her new body, she had a very accurate synthesiser — a voice of her own. "How is Bucket?"

"Much smarter than Peanut," Rolonde replied. "He's had this mastered in an hour. Peanut's had it for days and still hasn't gotten it."

"Some degree of natural variance in capability is to be expected," said Styx, stalking through the bay, sweeping past various humming fabricator shells with that creepy-smooth, flowing gait of hers. "What the final end product will be, only time will tell."

Bucket had gotten his name because they'd utilised many old parts to complete his chassis — 'a bucket of bolts', Petty Officer Chenkov had called him. Peanut was Peanut because that sometimes seemed to describe the size of his brain. And Wowser had once seen Corporal Rael unzip his jumpsuit and remove a newly soiled shirt, only to stumble back five steps in staring shock. Rolonde had found it funny, and named the drone for a prude who disliked the sight of naked skin. Trace had found it more concerning, for it described a synthetic brain that equated 'organic' with 'different', and possibly even 'alarming'.

"We're just doing morning warmups, Styx," said Trace. "Would you like to administer the technical uploads yourself?"

"Yes," said Styx, pausing by the large computer module in the bay's center, a stack of alien systems that now served as a command mainframe for the drones while they recharged or reloaded.

Chenkov looked up from his mainframe displays, observing the drones' systems and vitals. "Can't you do that from, like, anywhere in the tower?"

"Yes," Styx said patiently. "But this bay has inadequate visual coverage for remote surveillance, and sometimes it is better to observe things in person."

"Better yet," Chenkov pressed, "why can't you just simulate antici-
pated results in a psycho-structure and tell us what's about to
happen?"

"Because there is a randomness built into the mathematics of the
universe that makes pre-judging results folly," said Styx. "And..."

"But surely if you've got the brain-power of yourself and
Hannachiam," Chenkov interrupted with youthful enthusiasm, "and,
like, way back in Drysine Empire time when you had *thousands* of
brains that powerful, all linked together in network psycho-struc-
tures... I mean, wouldn't that be enough to iron out most of the kinks
in those numbers? And let you, well, maybe not predict the future,
but be able to anticipate the results of an experiment before you've
conducted it?"

Trace had to smother a smile, still tossing the ball with Peanut.
Chenkov was too absorbed in his idea to notice the faint sideways
glance from that single, malevolent red eye when he'd interrupted.
Trace wondered if there'd once been a day when organic beings more
senior than Chenkov had died for less.

"A false premise does not become less false because you apply
more intellect to it," Styx replied, her synthetic voice showing no
more inflection than usual. "The universe is not perfectly simulat-
able. My people tried, with vastly more processing power than you
describe, and still failed. Intellect affords no greater likelihood of
accurate prediction in the real world if the premise preceding such
calculations is wrong. The only way to ascertain the correct premise
is to observe and record. Any other form of knowledge accumulation
is not physically possible. The omnipotence of great minds, so often
described in human literature, is not science, but magic."

"Oh," said Chenkov. Like an enthusiastic puppy who'd gone
bounding to his master hoping to play, and had instead received a
whack on the nose.

"Don't worry Chenk," said Private Leo Terez. "She still loves you."

"What books are you talking about when you say 'human literature', Styx?" asked Irfan Arime, watching from a nearby seat in his

marine jumpsuit. Arime had been badly hurt in the battle of Defiance, and was not back to full health, let alone operational capability. But he was well enough to leave Medbay and come down with his Command Squad buddies to hang out with the new pets. Command Squad, like a lot of Phoenix Company units, remained one marine short of its full eight, there being insufficient available manpower to replace the loss of Private Kumar four months ago.

"Sherlock Holmes makes a good example," said Styx.

Arime grinned, propped against a ceiling beam with his leg out, jumpsuit unbuttoned in the heat from the many fabricators, and to let his bandages breathe. "No shit? Detective stories?"

"Those books provide an instructive insight into human misconceptions of omnipotent intelligence. The author constructs a false, fictional scenario wherein he allows the primary character to appear omnipotent in his unfailing ability to select the correct answer from limited datasets. Such limited datasets exist only in fiction — the real universe is nearly limitless. It is the greatest folly, before such limitless possibility, to presume the certain accuracy of such a limited tool as intellect — organic or synthetic. Sherlock Holmes is not a detective, he is a magician."

"Great," said Kono. "Styx's book reviews. Could be a column in the *New Worlder*."

"I don't think she gets out of those books what we do," said Trace.

"*You* read those books, Major?" Arime asked her.

"No."

"The last book the Major read was the marine field manual," Corporal Rael joked.

"Right," said Rolonde. "Thirty-four times."

Trace just smiled, tossing the ball rapidly. And glanced at Styx, to see the unblinking red eye watching her. Wondering, perhaps, that the most elite human marine she'd met was happy to tolerate this teasing. Trace greatly doubted that Styx either approved or disapproved. She just learned, as always. Day by day she learned more about the organics, and grew wiser... and perhaps other things as well.

"How much use do you think Engineering will get out of these guys once the uploads are complete, Styx?" she asked.

"Assuming the uploads are successful," said Styx, "there should be no functional limit. They will continue to build on the base of knowledge the uploads will entail, simply by learning. And from what I have observed, Lieutenant Rooke should make an adequate instructor."

"He'll be thrilled," Kono said drily. "Finally people he can talk to on his own emotional level." A few of the marines chuckled.

"That's pretty harsh, aimed at the guy who's done more than anyone to save and rebuild *Phoenix*," Trace said sharply. A silence fell.

"Yeah," Kono agreed, subdued. "That was dumb. I shouldn't have said that."

He knew better than to apologise to *her,* at least. Kono was one of Phoenix Company's elite non-coms, and he could be grim and sarcastic at times. Trace thought there was entirely too much of it going around at the moment. She didn't drop the hammer on her people often, finding that well-led, quality people rarely needed it, and that the hammer was far more effective when used sparingly. But lately she'd been dropping it more than she wanted.

Again, she caught Styx looking at her. This, too, Styx learned.

Halfway up the elevator on her way back up the tower, Trace stepped off, having been informed she had a visitor. Down several corridors she came to the mid-level cargo storage, where walls were replaced by open space for stacked crates from *Phoenix* and elsewhere. Several marines worked here in full armour, loading the newest arrivals, food from their parren suppliers, parts for their basement fabricators, miscellaneous gear that was nothing the marine commander would know about. Warrant Officer Kriplani was here, updating his storage manifest and directing the marines.

Ahead, Third Squad Delta Platoon were on airlock guard duty, fully armoured and watching over their guests. Those guests were parren, in the spacer jumpsuits of their kind, these ones an off-white with more utilitarian pockets and functionality than Trace was accustomed to with ornamentive parren. There were ten in the hallway in total, warriors all by Trace's judgement. Their weapon holsters were all empty, their builds wiry and strong. Unusually for parren, they did not stand to close attention while waiting, but stood at comfortable ease, a few even leaning against a wall, but watchful and always professional. Also unusually for parren, four of the ten were women.

Unusually for *House Harmony* parren, Trace corrected herself. She glided to a halt in her low-gravity bounce, and one of those parren women stepped forward. She was slim and small, but she had a hard edge to her stare, a directness that the ever-decorous House Harmony would never allow. On her hairless head she wore a scarlet skullcap, a far more practical decoration than Harmony parren wore, yet also more outlandish in its alarming colour.

"Major," said Staff Sergeant Jakobson, visor-up in his armour, "this is Alired, House Fortitude's ambassador to Defiance."

Trace was about to extend her hand, but Alired knelt down on one knee instead. Trace blinked, astonished, as all of Alired's guards did the same. So House Fortitude was not without ceremony and display, then — it seemed a constant among all the parren houses. But where House Harmony parren placed great store in symmetry, these parren were not precisely in line, and each of their kneeling stances was slightly different. It felt... spontaneous, she supposed. If that were possible, with a people who did everything all at once.

Alired spoke, rising to her feet, and Trace's earpiece provided the translation. *"Major Thakur. You have won great honour with the parren people. Allow me to grant you a gift, from the leadership of House Fortitude to you and all the crew of the warship Phoenix."* She rose, and produced from her pocket a slim band of wooden beads. Alired placed it into Trace's palm. *"It is worn on the wrist. It was one of the few surviving artefacts from the Fortitude warship Cobana. Our forensics tells us it was the possession of a common crewman. Please accept, on behalf of his house, and his family."*

Cobana had been assigned to the defence of Cason System, the system containing the world of Pashan and its moon Cephilae. House Harmony ships, then in unwelcome alliance with *Phoenix*, had destroyed *Cobana* when she had been a helpless inconvenience, unable to fight back. *Phoenix* had then destroyed the ships that had done it, and Trace herself had later killed their commander and then-Domesh leader Aristan in single combat. That combat had been recorded, and vision had since spread throughout parren space. Few parren alive today, Lisbeth had assured Trace, would not have seen it. Lisbeth was the most successful and high-ranking human to ever ascend the ranks of parren power, but it was Trace who was by far the most famous.

Trace considered the bracelet for a moment. Alired and her security watched, narrow-eyed and not entirely worshipful. This was a test, as all these games and gestures parren liked to play were tests. House Fortitude loved *Phoenix* because *Phoenix* had killed the hated Aristan, whom all the non-Harmony houses had despised, and because *Phoenix* embodied the kind of muscular power and will-to-action that Fortitude psychology embodied. And House Fortitude loathed *Phoenix*, because *Phoenix* had brought great glory to House Harmony beneath Aristan's successor Rehnar, in whose possession now rested this great alien city of Defiance, access to the drysine data-core which held the sum total of all drysine civilisational knowledge, and a glorious military victory against the alien alo/deepynine invaders. These things had in turn produced an enormously large number of new phasings, which had sent the Jusica institution running throughout parren space to conduct a new count of denominational numbers. Word was that many of those new phasings had gone to House Harmony, and the lion's share of *those* were choosing Gesul of the Domesh Denomination as their personal leader.

Phoenix, in the eyes of Fortitude, had delivered them what they'd always least wanted — House Harmony ascendant, and led by a Domesh. But Fortitude could not attack or threaten *Phoenix* directly, because Fortitude could not help but respect such power, forcefully wielded in the name of strengthening parren defences against hostile aliens. Fortitude were just angry that it wasn't them who were bene-fitting.

Trace considered the bracelet for a long moment. Then she slid it onto her wrist, and made a fist. The parren seemed satisfied with the gesture. *"You are invited,"* said Alired. *"At Fortitude headquarters, we invite you to a ***."* The translator gave her static on that word. *"A formal training. A lecture, you might call it. The warriors of House Forti-tude would be honoured to hear of your techniques."*

She was being invited to train Fortitude warriors, Trace realised. No doubt it was a great honour, particularly when delivered by a high-ranking ambassador like Alired. "I am not the greatest fighter in unarmed combat on *Phoenix*," Trace replied. "My victory over Aristan was found in tactics, not in technique. And human techniques in armed combat are classified. I fear I would make a poor instructor."

"Never," said Alired, with a faintly devilish smile. Definitely not like House Harmony, Trace thought. *"You belong with us, Phoenix. House Fortitude are warriors too."*

"Harmony fought well for Defiance," Trace said calmly. "And they were victorious."

"Fortitude warriors would have done better."

"Easy to say," said Trace. "You weren't here."

Alired's eyes flashed. *"But true nonetheless. Our power is undisputed in parren space."*

"I am Kulina," said Trace. House Fortitude, she'd been warned, would lose all respect if you rolled over before them. There was no such thing as polite agreement between Fortitude's senior leaders. "Kulina are small. We do not boast of size. *Phoenix* is small, compared to the human Fleet. Our smallness is what makes us great. We are elite. There is no greatness in size, only in quality."

Alired's growing smile suggested that she liked this answer. *"So you will accept this invitation?"*

"It would be my honour," said Trace. "But I am very busy. All that I am, I give to my ship. Finding time for outsiders can be difficult, please understand. I will look to find a time."

"A warrior's answer," said Alired. *"Duty first and always. Know that*

you will always be welcome in House Fortitude, Major Thakur. The spirits of the Cobana crew will welcome you."

Trace held up her wrist. "I am pleased to have avenged them." That was true enough. *Cobana* had not been so much killed in combat as murdered.

Alired made a sweeping gesture, not quite a bow, then swung with theatricality to bounce, in low-G stride, toward the airlock. Her warriors followed in similar style. Trace watched them go, as behind her, Staff Sergeant Kono came to examine her new bracelet.

"Nice," he said. "Tricky buggers, aren't they?"

"I asked Gesul about House Fortitude," said Trace, as *Phoenix* crew operated the airlock for the parren to enter on their way back to their shuttle. "He said that on the world he grew up on, there was a species of reptile that seems a lot like a snake. When one snake encountered another snake of the same species on the edge of their territory, they'd rise up on their coils to see who could stand higher than the other. If the smaller one was wise, he'd run away. If he didn't run away, the larger one would usually strike first and kill him."

"And he thought Fortitude were like those snakes?" Kono asked.

"'Walk tall when they confront you,' he said. 'Hold your chin up, and look them in the eye. Let them stand taller, or prouder, and they will devour you.'"

* * *

THAT 'EVENING', 1800 Defiance time, Erik sat with Trace and those senior crew not currently on duty back in the Aronech Dar habitat, where they could all have the relief of full gravity while eating the day's final meal. It was parren food again, which most of the crew were acquiring a taste for, to the displeasure of those who hadn't.

"I spoke with Lisbeth today," Erik told them. The 'room' was just back of the kitchen, an open space between ovens and storage units where *Phoenix*'s two chefs, plus some rotating help from regular crew, loaded trays and meals, and now sent the clattering piles of dishes back through the washer they'd brought down from *Phoenix*. The officers' table was two smaller tables shoved together, and held all bridge crew ranked Lieutenant or higher, plus Trace and Dale representing the marines, and Hausler for Operations. Engineering remained unrepresented as Lieutenant Rooke, of course, had sent back a harried reply upon notification of this meeting, requesting that someone send him a summary. Erik doubted he'd find time to read that either. "The situation with Rehnar is bad. Speculation is that Gesul might win the count, making him the official ruler of House Harmony. Everyone doubts Rehnar will let that happen, so he'll probably move against Gesul soon. He's got support from the other denominations, but how much support is unknown."

"How much is being orchestrated by House Fortitude?" Kaspowitz asked around a mouthful of tuku — a flightless, domesticated bird, they'd been told. The crew called it parren chicken.

"It's a sensitive thing," Erik admitted. "None of the Harmony denominations want to admit they're doing Fortitude's bidding. But if Gesul wins, we have the Domesh winning control of House Harmony, and *all* the other houses will hate it nearly as much as they did when Aristan was head of the Domesh."

"So if Gesul wins, we'll have helped to start a parren civil war," Lieutenant Commander Dufresne said bluntly. "That's charming."

"Anyhow, you can read about it," said Erik, toying with his food. "Lisbeth's given us a full writeup, she can explain it far better than I can. The real thing I wanted to talk about here is the Major and I meeting with Captain Sampey and Commander Adams of *Lien Wang*."

An attentive silence on all sides, beneath the hum and crash of kitchen machines. Somber stares. A few faintly hopeful. Erik suspected that at this time, most of them just wanted to go home. Whether that was possible or not, he suspected, was largely up to him. Again.

"News from home is that the Worlder disturbance is getting worse," he told them. "It's not a full scale civil war by any means, but it turns out that the Worlders actually have some warships, and are using them from hidden bases somewhere out in deep space, away from populated systems, to launch raids against undefended Fleet shipping. Freighters mostly, there's been some casualties, speculation is the Worlders are after supplies as much as anything — weapons especially. Fleet's caught and destroyed a couple, but there's no decrease in attacks, so more speculation says they might have more ships than thought, or even a shipbuilding capability."

"It's almost like they remember what we did against the krim for five hundred years," Kaspowitz said sarcastically.

"It's almost like Captain Pantillo was right all along," Shilu added sombrely. There were nods and murmurs of agreement around the tables.

"Sampey says Fleet have offered to let us come home with clean records," said Erik. More anxious silence, at that. "If we agree to pledge total loyalty, etc, etc... and if we come home immediately, share everything we've acquired with the data-core with no questions asked, and basically reincorporate ourselves into the chain-of-command."

"Which they broke," Dale said loudly. Some of these soft, spacer pussies might have wanted to go home, but Dale was letting everyone know he thought otherwise. Erik repressed a smile. He'd found Dale's tough guy routine aggravating in the past. Now he was coming to realise that it wasn't a routine, it was just Dale. And some larger appreciation of why Trace found him so invaluable to the operation of her company.

"And we'd have to abandon any thought of going out to croma space and try and track down the origins of the alo," Erik continued. "Obviously."

"Where are we standing with that anyway, Captain?" Draper asked. "I was up to date until you met with that parren scholar, Juresh. Then I lost track."

"Because we haven't heard back from her yet," said Erik. "She's got contacts in one particular croma household, it takes time for messages to travel back and forth. And the croma don't trust outsiders much, they'll only accept outside contacts if it's through a trusted intermediary. So we can't move until we get Juresh to approve it for us, basically."

"Captain," said Stefan Geish, the only Second Lieutenant present. He was as old as Kaspowitz, a much-decorated veteran of his post, yet had shown no interest in promotion, and had a conspicuous lack of that sparky, charismatic drive that Fleet always preferred to see in their full Lieutenants. But for experience alone, Erik valued his inputs more than he did from his Commander and LC — on these matters at least. "God forbid I should try to speak for everyone, but it strikes me that the data-core is the most important thing on anyone's table right now. The parren are all queuing up to get a look at it, likely if they start blowing each other up it'll be access to the data-core that does it — Gesul's got access now and that makes him far too powerful for the others to tolerate.

"I think we've gotta go home, sir. We have to bring them the data-core — yeah they'll probably fuck it up, Fleet fucks a lot of things up lately, pardon my Porgesh. But they're all we've got, and we've gotta take the chance to drum into their thick heads just what they're facing out here. And the data-core not only does that, it gives them the technology they'll need to fight it."

There were glances, and a few, faint nods. It was the value of Stefan Geish — he could be brusque and sometimes rude, but he said what the majority were thinking but lacked the conviction to say out loud.

Erik nodded to himself, then looked at Trace. "Major?"

"I'll follow your lead, Captain," she said calmly.

* * *

THE CALM DIDN'T last when they were back in his quarters.

"Okay, here are the things we lose if we go back home," Trace said, in a tone that suggested he was going to hear her list whether he wanted to or not. Erik sat on his bed, activated the wall-screen with a feed from the *Phoenix* control tower of all their current deployments, and pulled off his boots. Trace joined him on the bedside.

"First," she said, "if we hand over the data-core, we lose all our leverage. We have our reputation with the Captains, plenty of whom have been sticking their necks out for us it seems, but that still leaves plenty of senior officers in Fleet who'd rather see us dead than rehabilitated. We're trouble. Fleet doesn't like trouble. To them, we're a virus that spreads disorder and dissent. The Fleet immune system will react accordingly, whatever nice things they say to us now.

"Second, the reason no one gets to meet the croma is the same that almost no one gets to meet the senior parren — lack of leverage. We've got plenty right now. We go home, we lose all that with croma and parren alike. Not to mention, we leave Lisbeth hanging out to dry, all alone in parren space without all the political capital our presence gives to Gesul."

"We do that if we go see the croma, too," Erik reasoned, gazing at the wall screen. The icons showed Rooke still in place, working on the ship. Lieutenant Lassa was in charge of the night shift at Phoenix Tower, protected by two squads of Delta Platoon, the other two watching over *Phoenix* in her repair bay.

"Not to the same extent," Trace persisted. "Away from human space, we're still independent. We're still in the game. Back home, we surrender autonomy to Fleet, we're not a player anymore.

"Third, we don't know anything about alo or deepynine motivations. We don't know how they met, why they get along, what their long-term goals are. We don't even know what the extent of their technological advantage is. If it's based on what the reeh have, we could be in real trouble because I'm not sure anyone in the Spiral has any counter to that. So what if they've got some kind of secret weapon, or hidden motivation up their sleeve that we could conceivably figure out by chasing our leads out to croma space? And we give that up just to go home?"

Her eyes bore into him, with her usual controlled intensity.

"I know," Erik said simply. Looking at the screen instead of at her was probably cowardly, but he knew how hard it was to match Trace's intensity on most things.

"So why do you want to go home? Lay it out straight."

"I think we've done enough," Erik said simply. "We just got hammered, Trace. We're lucky anyone survived at all."

"Who cares?" said Trace. Erik did look at her. She was utterly serious. "You know I love my people. All of our people. But we didn't embark on this so that we could *live*, Erik. This isn't just some ass-kicking Kulina thing — that wasn't the oath that *any* of us swore."

"Sure, we're all prepared to sacrifice," said Erik. "And we have. But we've been lucky too, Trace. We took some huge risks in what we've done so far. And Sampey's right — we did destabilise tavalai space, we did destabilise parren space, we might even have accelerated any aggressive timetable the alo and deepynines have against us. And I'll defend all of those actions to my last breath, because I think they all turned out for the best, for humanity as a whole. But odds are we're going to stop being lucky sometime. And the consequences for everyone when that happens, when we finally screw something up and make things *worse* for everyone..."

"So don't screw up," Trace said bluntly. "I believe in you."

"This isn't about belief. It's about statistics — take enough chances, one of them will blow up in your face."

"No, it only becomes about statistics when you run out of self belief."

Erik sighed. "I'm warning you Trace, don't push me too hard to stay out here. There's already one very big reason not to go home that's clouding my judgement, and it's not Lisbeth."

Trace frowned at him. Quite predictably, she didn't get it. "What?" she asked finally.

"You," said Erik. "If we go home, Fleet may leave the rest of us alone, but the Kulina are another matter. You might survive if you went into hiding, but you'd never do that. Probably they'll find a way to kill you."

Trace gazed at him. Erik looked away, swallowing hard against the lump in his throat. "You don't think that's the reason I'm arguing for..."

"Don't be stupid," Erik interrupted with a faint smile. "Geez, you'd think you thought I didn't know you at all."

Trace thought about it. "Sure," she said. "They'd probably get me. You can't let that sway your thinking though." And she looked away with a roll of her eyes, and shook her head, then laughed. "Damn you're clever. You've got me arguing against myself."

"It's the Debogande people-influencing gene," Erik explained. "We're born with it. Look what Lisbeth did with the parren."

"Look," said Trace, "you may have good reasons for going home. Certainly it's what most of the crew want, even the marines. But I won't let you make that decision because you've suddenly acquired a few bruises and it hurts. This isn't a school excursion. If you're not prepared to die on this job, you shouldn't have joined."

"It's a balance," Erik said quietly. "The potential good we might do, the potential bad we might do, and the dead certainty that more of our crew will die either way."

"It's an extraordinary threat," Trace disagreed. "It requires extraordinary efforts to beat it. I don't think it's why we're here. I think it's why we're *alive*." Erik smiled at her, repressing the emotion that he knew she didn't like, and clasped her hand. Trace clasped it back, then gave him a light whack on the cheek with her other hand. "And don't let me *ever* catch you making command decisions based on my welfare. I'm not your wife."

Erik grinned. "You'd make a great Debogande."

Trace snorted. "I don't think your mother would approve."

"You kidding? She'd *love* you. Finally a woman in the family who gets out of bed before she does."

Trace laughed. She had a nice laugh, all the more pleasant for being so rare. Erik wished she'd do it more often. "Get some sleep," she advised, and left with a kiss on his forehead. Erik watched her go, and wished she hadn't done that. It made the prospect of sleep less likely.

* * *

TWO HOURS INTO HIS SLEEP, an uplink call woke him. "This is the Captain," he said, reaching groggily for his AR glasses in case the call were emergency enough to require immediate situational awareness.

"Hello Captain, it's Jokono." Ensign Jokono, that should have been, but the life-long policeman sometimes forgot military protocols.

"Go ahead Joker."

"A parren shuttle carrying the scholar you were talking to regarding contacting the croma took off from Sector KV-140 twenty-one minutes ago. It crashed nineteen minutes ago, directly into the side of the Tower District geofeature cliff. All aboard were killed, including your scholar."

Erik should have felt more shocked, but he'd seen so many shocking things of late that his nervous system couldn't muster the energy. "Is it possible that you could investigate? I don't know who has authority over this, or what your relations are like with them."

"Yes Captain, I'm on the ground at the crash site now. I thought I'd delay informing you until I had more concrete information, given you were sleeping. Best to only wake you once. It will be hours before I have anything else to report, it can wait until your morning."

For the thousandth time, Erik felt relief to be working with a crew of such professionals. "Good work Joker. I'll speak with you then, and in the meantime try not to step on any toes."

"Yes Captain, I'll do my best."

Probably murder, Erik thought as he lay looking at his situational display. It was too convenient that that particular scholar, who was key to *Phoenix*'s onward journey to see the croma, just happened to be in a shuttle crash. Surely there were a lot of parren who didn't want *Phoenix* making that particular contact... though what their reasons might be, he couldn't guess. Parren always had reasons.

A year ago, such developments would have kept him awake much of the night fretting on possible answers. This year, he was asleep barely a minute past the end of Jokono's call.

* * *

IN WHAT FELT like only a few minutes later, Erik got another call. "Captain," he said loudly enough to drive the exasperation from his voice. He hoped. The glasses told him it had in fact been thirty-three minutes.

"Hello Captain," said Lieutenant Lassa, on night-duty at the tower. *"A new contact just arrived at jump point. It's Makimakala. Captain Pram says he'd like to meet with you at the earliest. Thought you'd like to know."*

Erik actually smiled. He'd been expecting this particular visitor for some time now, and was surprised it had taken so long. Which was probably not smart — tavalai left to their own devices were usually punctual, but tavalai bureaucracy could make a man late for his own funeral. *Makimakala* had to deal with more bureaucracy than most.

"Very good, Lieutenant," he said. "Tell Captain Pram it will be nice to see our old friends again."

"Yes Captain."

This time when the call ended, he was asleep again in twenty seconds.

* * *

LIEUTENANT TYSON DALE hadn't been too upset to get pulled from his bunk. Four months of waiting around might have been nice for everyone else, but for him they'd been hell. For all his love of the United Forces Marine Corps, Dale was quite unsentimental about his service. He'd joined to fight, not to drill, not to get promoted, not to climb the greasy pole through the back offices of Fleet bureaucracy. To come all the way to this amazing city, only to pass each day with dull routine, had tested his patience.

He stood with First Squad, widely spread upon a ledge halfway up a Defiance cliff. This cliff was part of what was known as the Tower District geofeature, and made one wall of a canyon in which the enormous spires of the Tower District were located, like so many chopsticks bundled together in random patterns. The canyon was nearly two kilometres wide, and Dale had heard various explanations for the technical details of Defiance's sub-surface design that resulted in such oddly natural-looking features. None of it directly affected his job, and so he mostly didn't care. But it sure looked amazing to be here, in person, gazing out at the perfect detail that only an vacuum could provide.

A vacuum with no sunlight. Defiance's moon was many lightyears from any sun, having been thrown into deep space by a catastrophic science experiment many millennia ago, carried out by some earlier incarnation of the AI Machine Age. The steel canyon was now alive with artificial light, much of it restored when Hannachiam had brought the power back on, and more coming up each day as parren engineering teams multiplied. The Tower District looked spectacular, multi-coloured striations of light dividing various levels in the sixty-or-so clustered towers. Half of them were occupied now, so many parren importances had moved to Defiance in recent months — nearly all of them House Harmony, an even split of scientists, bureaucrats and soldiers. Shuttles and surface runners buzzed the scene with running lights flashing, and every few minutes a bright trail of flame would light on the horizon, then climb vertically to reach a ship's passing orbit. There were hundreds of those now, and in just four months the population of Defiance had grown from zero to three hundred thousand and climbing. And yet, despite these localised patches of growth, most of Defiance remained unexplored.

"Wish Tricky could have seen this," Private Reddy said sombrely on First Section coms, gazing at the view.

"Yeah," said Sergeant Forrest. First Section was currently only three marines, Private Cillian 'Tricky' Tong's place having not yet been filled, despite Echo Platoon's dispersal amongst the others. He'd been Reddy's best friend, and none of them were taking it well. Another reason why Dale preferred active duty. On active duty you had less time to think about anything else.

To their left along the ledge was a curious sight. The remains of a parren shuttle, embedded in the canyon wall. Scorch marks and burning were always limited in a vacuum, but still there was very little left, courtesy of the velocity of impact. And here along the ledge, away from the cluster of parren in EVA suits with floodlights and forensic gear, came Ensign Jokono in his plain spacer suit, bouncing with a careful eye to the precipitous drop on his left.

Close coms opened. "Hey Joker," said Dale. "Find anything?"

"The parren insist otherwise," said Jokono. He'd done some EVA work in his time on various stations, but most of that had been in senior roles, and the head of station security on a five-million population station didn't go wandering outside often. *"There is much work to do, but they say their flight control's latest data showed no evasive manoeuvres, just a straight-line plunge into this wall at over eight hundred kilometres an hour. Until they can get cockpit audio they won't know much, but at those speeds there might not be much to find."*

"Maybe it was low cloud," muttered Private Reddy.

"Looks like someone murdered our contact, Joker," said Dale. "Gonna be hard to get to the croma now."

"It's certainly a possibility," Jokono admitted, coming to a halt beside Dale. *"But if so, I'd like to know in whose interest it was to stop us from going. Most parren have little do with the croma, and plenty would like us to leave parren space. It seems odd."*

"Do croma have spies or assassins among parren?" Forrest wondered.

"An interesting idea, Sergeant. I admit I have no idea, expertise on the croma seems thin even among the parren, who are closer and more scholarly than anyone else. But again, it seems difficult to conceive that parren could serve foreign masters. Among any other species you would have the possibility of mercenaries or paid assassins, but it's almost unheard of among parren. Parren kill as an act of selfless service. They derive all social status from that service, money is insignificant by comparison."

"Well," said Dale, "sounds like you got yourself a puzzle. Tell us what you need to do next and we'll keep you safe while you do it."

"Thank you Lieutenant, there's actually not much more I can achieve here — I'm not a crash investigator but the parren who is has assured me he'll keep me up to date. He's one of Gesul's, I've no reason to doubt him. What I'd like is to visit the Domesh Tower and ask if I can access that shuttle's crew manifest — such requests work better with parren in person, I've found. If it was an assassination, it could have been the suicide version, perhaps a saboteur aboard who brought the shuttle down."

"Domesh Tower, got it." Dale changed channels. "Hello PH-3, this is Alpha Commander, do you copy?"

"Hello Alpha Commander, this is PH-3," came Lieutenant Jersey's reply. *"We are on standby awaiting your next move."*

"Hello Jersey, Jokono wants to go to the Domesh Tower to do some research."

"We can do that. Hello Phoenix Command, this is Air Jersey, we are on route to retrieve Alpha and Jokono, followed by a short hop to the Domesh Tower. ETA on pickup is two minutes, Alpha please standby for immediate departure."

5

Erik and Trace had just sat down with Captain Sampey and Commander Adams for their second briefing when Erik received an emergency call on his uplink. He held up a hand to forestall whatever Sampey had been saying, and indicated his ear. "This is the Captain, go ahead."

"*Captain, it's Shilu,*" came the voice. "*We have blanket jamming outside the tower. All of Defiance communications are down.*"

Erik hurriedly indicated to Trace to join the command channel. "Everywhere? What about landlines?"

"*We're trying that now, there's immediate interference but I can't see how they can keep the landlines shut down when Hannachiam has so much control. But she might not know what's going on immediately, and... well, who knows what she'll think to do about it if we can't contact her to ask for help.*"

"What *is* going on, Lieutenant Shilu?"

"*Sir... by your leave I've put Styx onto it, but it looks like battlespace preparation. It could be aimed at us, but with our assets that could be catastrophic for whoever attempted it. Given that these are parren, my best guess is it's a local powerplay, but there's no telling who at this point.*"

While Shilu was speaking, Trace was giving orders to put all

Phoenix crew on red alert. Sampey and Adams watched with patient alarm.

Erik was about to reply to Shilu when the lights went black, then flickered back to life at half-power. "Shilu? Shilu, can you hear me?"

"*Hello Captain,*" Styx's calm, feminine voice interjected. "*I believe this tower complex is specifically under attack. I have detected and disrupted multiple network assaults and attempts to establish a barrier matrix about us, but external forces appear to have gained physical control of regional power and communications nodes. No amount of network activity can regain those nodes for us, though a ground assault may achieve the same.*"

Both Sampey and Adams' eyes went wider still when they realised who was talking. Neither had made that particular acquaintance yet.

"They'll have air support, other fire support plus established defences around those nodes," Trace replied to Erik's unasked question, listening on the same channel. "We've barely got enough marines in the tower for local defence, taking those nodes back will take more forces than we've got available. We could move a platoon from elsewhere, but..."

"We can't leave *Phoenix* defenceless," Erik completed her sentence. "Nor Hannachiam, nor our habitat." They were spread too thin between the various sites that required defending, a strategic inevitability that neither Erik nor Trace had seen any way around. They'd known it could come to this if there was trouble, and now here it was, staring them in the face. "Plus we won't have anything close to air superiority, and moving a platoon under those circumstances is just begging to lose it."

Defiance had various ground transportation systems, but restoring them to full function had been low on the list of priorities for the parren engineers now working on such things. Besides which, this whole assault would be well planned, and Erik doubted it was safe to move reinforcements by any form of transport right now.

Erik shook his head clear of too many racing thoughts, and stared at Trace in disbelief as it occurred to him. "They've *seen* Styx. They complain endlessly how Hanna's our friend. There's no way they risk it against us, we could completely trash them."

Trace nodded fast as she realised the sense of what he was saying. "It's Gesul. They're after Gesul. Do we..."

An echoing thud through the walls and floor cut her off, followed by several more. "Was that...?" Erik asked, and received a fast, distracted nod from Trace as she monitored a dozen things on her AR glasses, then issued some terse instructions. Erik recalled his own glasses with annoyance, pulled them from a pocket and got a full spread of visuals as he settled them on — command channels mostly not responding, only local tower systems and coms being restored, likely by Styx finding ways to bypass the jamming and severed wires faster than anyone else could manage.

"Captain, what's going on?" Adams ventured. Sampey looked annoyed at his Intelligence colleague for interrupting the commanders with superfluous questions.

"Looks like the other parren factions are after Gesul of the Domesh Denomination," Erik told him distractedly. "He occupies the entire tower right next to us, so that puts us in the firing line too. You could get out on your shuttle now but I don't recommend it — the airspace will be locked down, they'll be shooting down anyone trying to leave and might not distinguish between our tower and Gesul's..."

"*Major!*" one of the marines was calling. "*The interlink levels with Gesul's tower have been closed! There's some kind of override, we can't get through to them!*"

"Don't try to break through yet," Trace replied. "We don't know what's going on, we don't want to declare we're taking sides without meaning to, we could make ourselves a target right along with Gesul."

"*Major,*" came another. "*The acoustics through the walls tells me there's shooting in the lower tower next door. They're definitely after Gesul.*"

"We will remain on full defensive, everybody knows the plan. Don't assume they're not after us, don't assume the assault will only come from the ground-up, and don't assume the guys next door won't attack us as soon as they've finished with Gesul."

The plan for tower defence had been well in place since the early days of their occupation. The lower floors were rigged with a variety of boobytraps and ammunition stores dispersed along the line of possible fall-back to provide retreating marines with a ready supply of reloads. Right now Charlie Platoon were the marines on station in the tower, meaning Lieutenant Jalawi had command under Trace.

"We have two squads of marines deployed at our shuttle pad for local defence," Sampey volunteered. "They are at your command if you need them."

"Thank you," Trace said distractedly, following five things at once. "Please contact them with instructions to integrate to local tacnet, deployment instructions will follow from there." She finished her preliminary review and glanced at Erik. "You should get topside, I'll get a suit..."

A new signal appeared on Erik's glasses, a big, flashing icon, urgent in its power. Erik guessed what it was, and opened it. *"Captain Debogande and the crew of Phoenix,"* said the translator-voice. *"This is Rehnar of the Incefahd. Gesul's time as leader of the House Domesh denomination is coming to an end. I pledge to continue a cooperative relationship with the warship Phoenix following Gesul's removal. This action is not aimed at any human on Defiance. Declare your neutrality and you shall all remain safe. Assist Gesul, or interfere in any fashion, and you shall also be eliminated. This will be your single warning."*

The transmission ended. Erik exhaled sharply, hardly surprised. Trace shook her head with a grimace. "This is yours," she said. "I'm marine commander on the ground, but this is political and strategic, it's beyond my skillset. Tell me what to do."

Erik nodded. "Styx, can you hear me?"

"Yes Captain, I am attempting to reroute communications to the control bridge, the jamming is intense."

"I want full coms restored to all of our units elsewhere on Defiance as a matter of priority. Major, you get your suit on and join me at the bridge until we have full coms in the tower — Jalawi can handle tower defence and I'll need your input if we get coms back across the rest of Defiance. Captain Sampey, if you're willing, you and Commander Adams can join us on the bridge."

"Yes Captain," said Sampey. "We are yours to command as well."

Erik nodded his thanks. "And Styx?" As they got up and made for the door. "Tell me what we need to do to get back in contact with Gesul. I want to talk to him."

* * *

LISBETH SAT in front of her wall coms unit, finger hovering over the record icon, and could think of nothing to say.

It was crazy. She'd been through so much since she'd left home. She'd seen and done incredible things. Now there was a human ship in orbit, duty-bound to return a report from *Phoenix* on everything that had happened to her in the past crazy year. Erik had made no guarantees about how positive that report would be, but he'd told her to prepare a message to send home to the family, just in case that became viable. But all of the things she really needed to talk about were serious business, and that was no way to begin a conversation with family she hadn't seen in a year. She tried to think of some fun, frivolous things to open her message with, and could think of nothing. Perhaps she was finally becoming a serious grownup, she thought wryly, with nothing on her mind but work. Like Mother.

Oh yes, there it was, the main reason for her hesitation. Mother liked plans. Whenever there'd been discussions about Lisbeth's life, Mother had always insisted to know the future. Where is this all going, Lisbeth? Have you taken all the variables into account? Where do you see yourself along this path in five years time? Ten years? For a young woman looking forward to the next party or boyfriend or holiday, it had become quite exasperating, and she'd learned better than to float any old idea of what she might like to do or Mother would demand a multi-year chart and spreadsheet to figure out the implications.

'So where is this parren business taking you, Lisbeth?' she could imagine Mother asking her now. 'Have you considered whether this is something you really want to be involved in?' Well, no. She hadn't really considered that, it had been violently thrust upon her. But it was special, and it was spectacular, and it was important, and for once in her life, while she was here, she didn't feel like the insignificant little sister of all these great and grand Debogande children. She felt like she was doing something that mattered... and more than that, she'd seen what the alo were up to with the deepynines, and it stripped her of any wistful dreams of a safe and happy homecoming. Yes she could go home, but she could never be safe again, not with that threat brooding out in the dark. No one was safe, not Mother, not Diedre, not the great captains and admirals of Fleet itself.

Tell Mother that she now fancied *she* might play some great role in stopping that threat? In saving the human race from a second great extinction? Put like that, she didn't quite believe it herself... except that humanity would need all the help it could get from as many alien races as could be persuaded to help. The parren were powerful, or would be if they could ever put aside their petty differences to concentrate their forces. Plenty of neighbouring species would really prefer them not to, but if the deepynines and alo attacked, even parren domination would seem preferable.

Lisbeth took a deep breath, and touched 'record'. "Hello all!" she said cheerily, imagining the whole family seated to watch the recording. "It's me! I'm in the parren habitat of an abandoned drysine city... *long* story, believe me! Anyhow, I'm safe and well, I have a lot of friends here and I'm in no immediate danger..."

The door hummed open without announcement and Timoshene strode in, tall in black armour, skull-fitting hood and mask... he never just barged in unless something bad was happening. Spoke too soon, Lisbeth thought sourly.

He did a fast search of her room, without speaking. "That bad, is it?" Lisbeth enquired in Porgesh.

"Keresh," Timoshene said shortly, and Lisbeth's eyes widened. 'Coup', was perhaps the closest translation. An assassination attempt, but more than an assassination — a move by one faction against another. "Lai to," he added, and left, closing the door behind. 'Stay here,' that was.

Months ago, Lisbeth might have sat still, been scared, and waited for someone else to direct her. Now she got up, in as much exasperation as fear, and went to her locker. Within was a heavy jacket, a gift from Major Thakur, lined with thin body armour sufficient to stop most small firearms. With that gift had come another — a snubnosed Dush-73 electro-mag, small enough to tuck in a pocket, only five-millimetre but with a magfire's high muzzle velocity it would put holes through anyone not armoured. This was Hiro's gift — one of his spares and certainly not a marine weapon. She pocketed the Dush and three spare clips in a magnetic bundle, then donned her Augmented Reality glasses and blinked the personal protection icon.

The bugs flashed in four locations — two in the bathroom where she'd installed a sunlight-simulating lamp on the counter so they could recharge, and another two in the room with her. One assassin bug had been enough to grant her both fear and respect in parren society. Four made her something of a weapon, despite Erik's understandable concerns that the bugs could not be trusted because the only one who could program them was Styx. Of all the *Phoenix* crew, Hiro was the most well-versed in their use, and he'd in turn checked with Hannachiam (he insisted) and had received an all-clear on the bugs' software. How on earth he'd managed that when Hanna had no idea nor interest in what day it was, Lisbeth did not know. Gesul had once asked Hanna if Defiance was safe, and she'd responded with images of wildflowers. But then Lisbeth figured that if Styx decided to kill her, she'd have to kill everyone else around her too, because she was too important to both *Phoenix* and Gesul for that assassination to go unanswered. It didn't stop anyone sane from believing it was possible.

Her coms weren't working, not on the glasses, nor on her wall unit. In fact the glasses were barely working at all — just a few local relays to otherwise autistic processors in her room and elsewhere. Anything reliant upon the broader Defiance network was dead. Going out of her room would be pointless — her security preferred her to remain where she was, and doing otherwise achieved nothing. All of her staff would be now confined to the office, just up the corridor on this habitat level save for Risa and Dolumev, who were doing a shift at the Domesh Tower. There wasn't even a window in the parren habitat, the entire wheel was enclosed in a massive dome for radiation and other protection. She initiated a scan of network functions within range, and sat crosslegged on her bed while waiting for it to run... and was not particularly surprised when her audio abruptly crackled.

"Hello Lisbeth, this is Styx."

"Hello Styx, I take it we're being jammed?"

"Yes Lisbeth. Most communications pathways are blocked but I have established some more. I dare not route additional traffic through it, even this simple audio link is being rerouted every few seconds to prevent Rehnar's people from detecting and blocking it."

"Well it sounds like they've gone to a lot of trouble if even you're finding it hard to talk. It's bad, then?"

"Rehnar is assaulting the Domesh Tower. The Phoenix control tower is not under attack, we have been assured by Rehnar that Gesul is the only target. Domesh facilities are under close military observation, including yours, but it appears unlikely that there will be any attack other than the one upon the tower. Your brother is concerned that that could change if others join Gesul's side."

Timoshene returned while Styx was talking and Lisbeth ignored whatever he said, holding up a hand to indicate she was uplinked. Timoshene frowned, and waited. "Which of the other factions is with Rehnar?" she asked. Timoshene said something in Porgesh... difficult to process when she was speaking to Styx in English. 'Do you have an external link?' she thought he said, and nodded impatiently.

"It is unclear," said Styx. *"There has been no announcement. There is only fighting in the tower, it is moving from the base up toward the top. Gesul's forces appear to be making a strategic withdrawal."*

"Styx, the other denominations are supposed to announce," Lisbeth said firmly. Other parren were gathering in the doorway beyond Timoshene, perhaps realising what was going on. Maybe she had the only external link in the entire habitat. She blocked them from her vision, turning side-on to look at the wall. "When a keresh happens the other denominational leaders are supposed to announce what side they're on. If that hasn't happened, it means they're staying neutral. It's just Rehnar, which means Gesul's outnumbered but not by much. The other denominational leaders probably favour Rehnar, but they are restrained by their fear of you and Hanna, and by a parren sense of etiquette in such conflicts. Rehnar must prove himself alone and without help — if he cannot defeat Gesul in a limited contest, he does not deserve to be head of House Harmony."

"Rehnar is the head of the Incefahd, which rules all House Harmony," Styx returned. *"His forces here outnumber Gesul's three-to-one, more if one counts non-military personnel. Furthermore, the communications blackout indicates parren participation and forethought beyond just the Domesh, whatever those other leaders say."*

Why was Styx taking the trouble to talk to *her*, Lisbeth wondered? True, Styx could conduct twenty conversations at once with no difficulty, but if relayed communications were so problematic, this still represented some kind of effort, particularly given the risk if detected. Certainly Styx overstated her confusion with the politics and psychology of organics, but Lisbeth did not think it was *entirely* a lie. And Styx had not spent the time in close proximity to Gesul, and other high parren powers on Defiance, that Lisbeth had. Styx was looking for advice, for herself and for Erik. Situational awareness on a matter she was less well equipped to deal with than Lisbeth was.

"Styx, the laws of the keresh dictate that the target is allowed to defend himself to an equal degree of violence as represented by the threat," she said. "That means Rehnar has put himself in play." Dear god, she couldn't quite believe what she was suggesting. "The fastest way to kill the snake is to cut off its head. Of all your capabilities, that one could be the most useful now."

"That is your brother's decision, Lisbeth. I would never take such an action unilaterally."

"Then tell Erik... look, can you get a link direct to him? Or to the Major?"

"They are quite busy. I will relay this communication in full."

"Gesul's defeat is not in the best interest of *Phoenix*, Styx. I've had this discussion with Erik many times and we are in agreement. Rehnar does not like us, he does not like our mission, and he particularly does not like you."

"That being so, for Phoenix to remove the head of House Harmony, under any circumstances, would be an extraordinary interference in the affairs of parren by outsiders. I am not always confident in my analysis of organic politics, but on this I am quite sure."

Semaya was gesturing most demonstrably for a parren, in a way that suggested huge importance. Lisbeth nodded for her to go ahead, straining her brain to change languages. "Lisbeth, our records show that new House Harmony ship at the jump-point was two jumps ago at Lumarei System!"

Lisbeth winced. "Hang on a moment Styx, parren here are talking to me..." and in Porgesh, to Semaya, "Lumarei System? What are you saying?"

"It was monitoring the count! The Jusica were conducting a count, to see if Rehnar remains head of House Harmony by number of supporters!"

Lisbeth's eyes widened. "He lost!" Semaya made a firm gesture of hand against fist — an affirmative, the parren equivalent of a serious nod. "Styx! Tell Erik that Gesul's parren think that the Jusica were counting the numbers of followers to see if Gesul had overtaken Rehnar — that ship that just arrived was watching the count, and now it's come rushing here to tell Rehnar something, and Rehnar attacks! He's lost, only the count hasn't arrived yet! That makes Gesul the true leader of House Harmony, Rehnar is trying to remove him before it can be enforced!"

"This is conjecture."

"Look, ask Gesul yourself! He's only next door..."

"The connecting doors are down, there are external overrides, we do not control them."

"Then hack them yourself, surely you can do that?"

"No Lisbeth, this is a mechanical system and network connections have been severed. Rehnar's people appear aware of my abilities and are well prepared. If we blast through the doors we will be violating Rehnar's instruction and involving ourselves directly on Gesul's side."

"Laser-com between the two towers, then! Hell, you could use morse-code..." Which parren did not know, of course.

"I believe it is being tried. Again, laser-com can be spotted, and would be a violation of Rehnar's instruction." Erik had to make a choice, Lisbeth thought desperately. Probably he was the only one who could.

"Styx," she tried again, "if Rehnar dies quickly, this entire question will end. Could it be an accident?"

"Nothing would rouse parren suspicions against us more at this moment. I judge most parren would prefer outright murder, by their rules."

"Then maybe that's what you should do!"

"ACOUSTICS INDICATE the fighting has moved to the tower's mid-level," said Trace, standing before the control room's huge, curved window before the view. She didn't need access to one of the room's posts for command — with internal tower coms operational once more, external jamming was largely negated in the immediate vicinity, and her armour suit contained all the gear required. "Sounds like it's becoming more intense, they'll be running out of space to fall back into."

The tower bridge consisted of Erik, the second-shift bridge crew of De Marchi, Lassa and Zelele, plus Erik's first-shift Scan Two, Second Lieutenant Jiri. The rest of *Phoenix's* bridge crew were all at the ship, supervising the reconstruction. Trace finished some instructions to Jalawi, whose marines were covering all approaches from Gesul's neighbouring tower, and stomped back to Erik.

"I don't like you being here," she said in a low voice off-coms as the other posts all announced what they could see and hear, attempting to accumulate a picture of the unfolding attack. "This place isn't armoured for an assault, Rehnar knows exactly where it is and that glass won't stop a missile."

"He could blow this whole tower and there's nothing we could do about it," Erik retorted. On near-coms he heard a blast from the acoustics, the only way they were going to hear the fighting on this airless moon. "Lisbeth thinks we should kill Rehnar — what do you think?"

"We don't know where he is," Trace said pointedly, leaning close, her visor raised. "The only person who could know is Hanna, but we can't contact her. If we try and fail, we're fucked."

"Captain," called Jiri, "three new marks airborne at 281, they're coming this way." Erik glanced at the display — that was from one of the big Incefahd military bases. Incefahd airborne shuttles now totalled fifteen, with more no doubt on standby. Between them they had everyone covered — *Phoenix* at her repair facility, this tower complex, the rotary surface habitats, everything. And then there were the ships in orbit, where Incefahd's advantage was larger still.

"They can't escalate," Erik muttered. "That's against keresh rules, it won't turn into ship combat no matter what happens down here. And we've got gravity bombs even if it did."

"Hanna's got gravity bombs," Trace corrected him. Those weapon bays were now crawling with parren techs, but no one had wanted to disable them in case the deepynines came back. Neither had they been able to figure out how to transfer firing control to someone other than Hanna, a fact that remained central to Rehnar's issues with how Defiance was being run at present.

"I think he's got us good," Trace added. "We can't risk the fight escalating, Rehnar could kill our crew in the habitat if he wants, or *Phoenix* itself, and neither we nor Gesul can ask for help because of the jamming. If we did move a platoon for reinforcements it would get shot down, and the other parren all assume Rehnar's ascendence because he's the head of House Harmony. They might challenge if they could talk to Gesul, but they can't."

"If it turns out Gesul really *has* won the count," Erik muttered, "Rehnar's going to have hell to pay when word gets out."

"Which won't help Gesul if he's dead. Makes you wonder if Alired put Rehnar up to it."

"From what we know of House Fortitude's leadership, I think we can count on it. We need Hanna. Styx, are you there?"

"Yes Captain."

"Explain to me again why all your communications wizardry can't let you get in contact with Hanna?"

"Captain, communications run on operable hardware. In a civilian environment such as Kantovan System there were unguarded hardware nodes everywhere and I could function without restraint. Here on Defiance the Incefahd technicians appear to have shut down most of the nodes within range of our tower in anticipation of this event, and the heavy jamming is nothing I am equipped to..."

There was a silence, filled only by the terse commands and questions from about the bridge. "Styx?" Erik pressed in alarm.

"Captain, disregard my last. Hannachiam is in contact, I am directing her to your controls."

Erik took a seat for the first time, eagerly. "Hanna? Hanna, are you on coms?" Silly thing to ask, how could she be? Hanna didn't speak.

Erik's main display was overridden, a simple image appearing in its center. It was Gesul, in his EVA suit, standing at Erik's side and talking. They'd done that many times — gone to speak with Hanna in person, together. Gesul found her fascinating, and had been to see her as often as possible over the past six months, with or without company. And Hanna, as nearly as anyone could tell, had appeared to enjoy his company and his endless, curious questions. The image rotated now, compiled by multiple cameras and blended together — no doubt it would work better as a hologram, Hanna's preferred means of communication.

"Yes Hanna," said Erik, heart thumping as he guessed her question. He could only hope he was right — he'd been wrong plenty of times before. "Gesul is in danger. He will be dead shortly if we don't help him."

The image faded, and Erik's screens returned to normal. A tower-display, tacnet showing the positions of Charlie Platoon spread between the tower's various interconnections with the Domesh tower next door. Then a sudden eruption of new coms activity. External. His eyes widened.

"Captain," said Styx. "The jamming has stopped. It appears Hannachiam has disabled it. All coms nodes are open, I can disable nearly every system arrayed against us if you choose. Against Gesul as well."

Because parren technology had gone significantly backward since the days of the drysine/parren alliance, while Styx was the original article, many thousands of years superior to anything under Rehnar's command. Rehnar's people, given four months to examine Hannachiam and her network systems, must have thought they'd found a way to shut her down, for long enough, at least. But unsurprisingly, they'd missed something.

"If we do this," Trace told him, "it will change everything. We'll be playing kingmaker for House Harmony, probably against the wishes of House Fortitude itself. Humans choosing the leaders of all parren. It's unprecedented."

"We've *already* chosen the leaders of House Harmony," Erik said grimly, staring at the screen where Hanna's single, simple image had appeared. "We put Gesul in power, or you did." Trace gazed back, sombrely. "And I led the attack where Tobenrah died. Parren value strength, they tell us this all the time. Then Rehnar tries this right under our nose, when *we* hold all the cards, and he asks us to be polite little weaklings and undermine the respect in which we're held? If we let him do it, we ignore every lesson parren have been teaching us since we arrived here."

He stared at Trace. She nodded once, in agreement. That was all he needed.

"Major Thakur, new orders," he said. "Ground operations. Save Gesul's leadership, eliminate Rehnar's threat. How you do it is up to you, though I believe we now have the tools to avoid escalation."

"Yes Captain," she said shortly, and snapped down the visor on her armoured suit. It lit with full displays, hiding her face. "Styx, prepare to disable all airborne weapons platforms on my command.

Leave flight control systems intact, we don't want fatalities unless they start shooting."

"Yes Major."

"Lieutenant Lassa, prepare to signal the other denominations that *Phoenix* declares for Gesul and the Domesh. Assure them that our capabilities are now overwhelming and Rehnar's defeat is assured. We would prefer him alive, and we assure all non-involved parties that their lives are in no danger once he is gone."

"Yes Major, on it."

"Lieutenant Jalawi, give me your best strength estimation of Rehnar's forces in the tower."

"Could be nearly a hundred, Major," came Jalawi's grim assessment. *"They've been staying inside, haven't been risking the outside, probably scared they'll get picked off from next door."*

"Lieutenant, I want you to punch in below them and trap them between Charlie Platoon and Gesul's forces at the top of the tower. Lieutenant Hausler will get airborne in PH-1 and apply covering fire as necessary, probably Gesul's airborne forces will join as well."

"Yeah, they'll be fish in a barrel pretty quick," said Jalawi. *"And I reckon they'll abandon the tower pretty quick too, probably head for neighbouring towers, maybe even ours."*

"If they run, let them go. The objective is to secure Gesul's safety, we don't have enough forces to stretch our perimeter chasing retreating Incefahd. How you do it is up to you, Lieutenant, just make sure we don't get breached or flanked when you go in."

"Can't guarantee that completely, gonna need to take enough with me that I can't leave much guard behind. I suggest everyone in the tower grabs a rifle."

* * *

IRFAN ARIME IGNORED the pain in his side to cover the curved angle past the hydroponics bay. He was on Medbay level by the landing pads, where Doc Suelo kept a rapid response center open. It took ten minutes less time to evac a casualty to the tower than to the habitat, plus the low-G was better for blood loss and stabilisation. Fifteen minutes ago Arime had been in the Medbay himself, getting yet another check to his ongoing series of operations and procedures from the fragmentation wound he'd received four months ago. Several internal organs were synthetic now — no big deal with *Phoenix's* bio-fabrication tech, but getting them all to work at optimum, in conjunction with everything else, had been a challenge for doctor and patient alike.

Now he was in one of the tower's spare armour suits, struggling against both the poor calibration to his personal preferences and the pain in his side. Tacnet was a mess, internal tower coms were still being disrupted by something, and 3D vertical displays were difficult to read even in a perfect mental state. But Charlie Platoon's rush into the neighbouring tower had left the human tower's many levels exposed, and now some of those connecting passages had been blown back the other way as Lieutenant Jalawi had predicted. Thus his own mad rush for the spare suit, conveniently at the same level as Medbay — equal to the docking pads so shuttles could deposit patients with minimum transit time — and now to his standing here alone, in no real condition to fight, single-handedly covering the Medbay approach.

"Irfy it's Jess," came Rolonde's voice in his ear. *"I see your position, I'll be there shortly."* Or not entirely alone. Other than Charlie Platoon, there was Command Squad. For several years now Jess Rolonde had always had his back, and he her's.

"Copy Jess. Medbay's locked up, Doc and a corpsman got themselves guns. Won't be pretty." Medbay was central to the tower, beside the elevators and thankfully away from any windows. Those windows were tougher than most steel but that hadn't stopped many breaches in the neighbouring tower, leading to sectional decompressions. Just like in a warship, anyone without full suits had to lock themselves someplace airtight and hope.

There was a lot of shouting and shooting on coms. Without even looking at tacnet, Arime could tell that Charlie Platoon were skinning them. The coms chatter just had that tone. In bad fights, voices got elevated, sometimes screechy. Now they were loud but controlled, commands clear, responses calm. But to judge from the scatter of red dots on the tactical picture, a lot of Charlie's success was simply that the Incefahd parren realised their impossible position, squeezed between two forces, and were displacing fast. A lot had gone out the windows, using jumpjets to fly clear in the low-G, decompressing large regions of tower. And more had come into the human tower, blasted the hardware nodes that supported local security systems with unnerving precision, and were now up to who-knew-what. With large sections of local security down, no one could see them... but there weren't that many sensitive targets in the tower. The control bridge was the obvious one, but very well guarded, with the rest of Command Squad and a section of Charlie Third Squad remaining behind. The eight marines from *Lien Wang* had been on this level where their shuttle had landed, but then redeployed to counter infiltrations on the higher levels where they'd been in some shooting. That left Medbay level, which also included the main dock and warehousing, and then the lower, secret high-tech bays.

"Jess, what about the drones?"

"No idea, I think the Major's got it covered. I'm in the elevator now, thirty seconds."

Arime's handball relayed him a view of two corridor approaches behind him on the far side of Medbay — he'd stuck the spherical remotes to walls and corners and had the whole thing covered, visually at least. But it was still a lot for one person.

Enhanced audio heard something from the hydroponics bay ahead. He couldn't see most of it from the corridor, just leafy fronds from rows of multi-level planted beds, waving in a faint breeze from nearby airvents. There again, the audio gave him a visual spike, software confirming what ears alone could not. Arime turned up the sensitivity and was nearly deafened by a small control-rattle from one of his armoured legs as a myomer actuator hypertensed. He turned down the armour settings to 'stealth mode', which all marines knew was something of a joke, but at least standing still it allowed acoustic settings to go higher without interference. But now, past the dull hum of his suit's powerplant, he heard nothing.

"Jess," he murmured. "I think something's in the hydroponics bay. Careful opening that door, my coverage doesn't go past five metres to your right."

A rear sensor blanked, one handball offline. Then the other, and ahead something popped, then a crack of metal bouncing off the curved wall, the angle heading straight for him. Arime knew he couldn't dodge, braced against the wall, flipped fire control to grenades and pulled the trigger repeatedly even as the blast knocked him back and sideways, blinding all senses. The suit snapped itself from stealth mode without having to be told and he flipped back to rifle and put several shots through the corridor wall ahead to deter any advance.

"Jess, I lost coverage on your position!" he yelled. "Coordinated assault, in front and behind, don't leave the elevator!" If they'd seen her coming down, he thought desperately, they'd probably timed it to ambush her. The thought sent him backward, pumping several more grenades for cover as fire hit the wall to his right, shots tearing through hydroponics on the way, sending plants and tubes scattering.

He scrambled back around the bend to the Medbay door, the elevator on the opposing wall of the intersection just beyond... a grenade airburst just before him, rattling armour with shrapnel as Arime ducked to an armour-supported squat and returned fire, but right-handed he didn't have the angle around the right-curving corridor...

More explosions and heavy fire, tacnet showing him Rolonde's position in the elevator car, difficult to read what level she was on from the top-down view, but evidently it was this one because there was holy hell exploding ahead. Then from behind came an awful screech and howl that most human marines had never heard in combat, but Arime knew only too well. He flattened against the wall and looked back, as opposite the hydroponics bay flailed a tangle of spidery limbs, and the shriek of huge vibroblade forelegs sent bits of corridor cladding and parren armoured limbs flying in all directions.

And then he could see them on tacnet — two innocuous blue dots, like any friendly units, dancing in the corridor amid several red dots that flickered and died. A brief thunder of rapid cannon and a last red dot vanished, then armoured feet clattered on the floor and walls, twin hacksaw drones moving with astonishing dexterity in his direction.

"Yo Peanut!" yelled Arime, indicating with his left hand to the far wall. "Covering fire, right here buddy! Bucket, get close, right behind me!"

Peanut screeched to a halt where Arime indicated, claws gripping for brakes in the low-G against the left-side wall, angled twin rotary cannon over his shoulders and fired. Corridor walls ahead disintegrated, and Arime switched his rifle to left-handed carry for a better angle, pressing forward along the wall as rapid fire tore past his left shoulder and return fire came back from somewhere within the carnage ahead.

Arime pinpointed it and fired, blew a parren armour suit nearly in half, then Bucket came charging past as Peanut's fire stopped, Arime following. More shooting as the drone fronted an intersection corridor, then Arime got an angle on the hard-left corridor, saw one parren bounding away and put a round through his back. And then there was silence, save for bits of shredded corridor wall collapsing, and electrical fires breaking out from severed wiring.

"Jess!" Arime edged toward the elevator doorway, not taking his eyes off the adjoining corridors. "Jess, you okay?"

"Hey, is that Bucket?" She stepped out alongside him, armour scratched from shrapnel, the elevator doorframe chewed as though by some giant, hungry animal. "Where the hell did they get guns?"

"Styx," Arime suggested, gasping air. "Wild guess."

"Fuck me," said Rolonde, looking at the devastation, and the multiple parren bodies on the ground. "These guys really aren't armoured for this shit."

"*We're* barely armoured for this shit," Arime agreed.

"You okay?" Rolonde asked him with concern.

"Yeah sure, why not?" He knew he couldn't really answer the

question for a few minutes yet. When the adrenaline went up like this, it drowned out all other sensation, pain included. "Where's Peanut?"

The second drone hadn't followed him in. Arime looked back the way he'd come and saw Peanut on the floor, writhing in distress, several legs missing. Arime swore and went back that way. Kneeling, he found himself face-to-face with those hacksaw rotary cannons — only small calibre to maximise ammunition capacity, but with muzzle velocity to turn armour to swiss cheese.

The shot had hit Peanut along the left torso, where a shoulder might be on a human. One of his forward manipulator arms was gone, and the main vibroblade leg too, with intricate armour stripped in a furrow down his side. Fluid was leaking, a slow ooze from many thousands of synthetic capillaries that looked disconcertingly like blood. The drone's head darted and squirmed, now looking up at him with what might be hope of reassurance.

"Hey Peanut," said Arime, disconcerted further at how distressed he felt to see it. "You're gonna be fine, buddy. We'll take you back downstairs and get you fixed, you'll be just like new. You did real good, saved my ass for sure."

"Careful Irfy," said Rolonde, still guarding the intersection, now far enough for coms only. *"Bucket's coming back."*

Arime looked around and saw Bucket springing lightly up the corridor... and thought it might be an idea to get out of the way. Neither drone had been properly trained for combat that humans knew of, but here they were, fully armed and capable. Styx's doing, no doubt, and while Arime was grateful for it, neither did he want to stand directly in front of it with weapons primed.

Bucket stopped before his wounded comrade and considered him. A spike appeared on local coms, something alien and high-density, utterly untranslatable. Peanut stopped writhing, picked himself up awkwardly on remaining legs, then shuffled to retrieve his detached limbs. Arime wondered what Bucket had said. If 'said' was the correct term. When drones talked, their speech was data. Data also programmed and reprogrammed. What humans would take as suggestions, drones could take as commands, depending on who'd issued it. Humans talked, but drones remote-controlled. But Bucket was no higher rank than Peanut. Who was truly in charge? Or was it an equal-ranked hive mind of some sort?

They'd been around these strange, frightening aliens for so long now, but still they knew so little. Only Styx could talk properly, and she was so good at disguising what she really thought that you couldn't trust a damn thing she said.

"*Irfy, it's the Major,*" Arime's earpiece informed him. "*Sitrep?*"

"We got charged, Major. Me and Jess are good, Peanut and Bucket came to help, didn't even know they were here, I guess Styx sent them. Peanut's hurt... damaged, whatever... think he'll be okay."

"*Good work, all of you. Charlie Two-Three are on their way to relieve you. Once you hand off, go down and check on Styx, take Peanut and Bucket with you. I've had only cryptic comments from her, I think there was some trouble down there but it's not showing up on tacnet. And guys, be careful.*"

"Major, shouldn't Irfy stay here?" Rolonde suggested.

"I'm fine," Arime retorted.

"*Sorry, but I want you two with the drones. You know them better. And Styx.*"

They took another elevator down, as the one Rolonde had ridden in was a wreck. And it was surreal, Arime and Rolonde squeezed in with two hacksaw drones, two humans in amidst the tangle of legs that splayed about the car for balance as the downward acceleration began. Attempting to contact Styx brought no reply, which was very disconcerting given how she'd been the one to get the tower's systems back online. So she'd been functional until just recently, and now fell silent? If she'd been attacked and required help, she would have reported it — Styx was neither proud nor suicidal, just ruthlessly practical. Maybe that was why the Major kind of liked her, Arime thought. It wasn't a thought to share on coms.

As the car decelerated, they heard from the Major again. "*Guys, I've just learned that a section of Lien Wang's marines have diverted to the basement to give you cover, they've come down the third elevator. They did*" *not do so on my orders. I do not judge them hostile but be very careful of them around the kids."*

"We copy, Major," said Arime.

"Great," Rolonde muttered. "They diverted to come and get a look at Styx themselves."

"If you came all the way out here, and heard our story, wouldn't you?" Arime replied.

The car halted on the basement level, opening onto an expanse of engineering levels, wide floors and machinery, infrastructure for this and the adjoining towers, mostly the life support that the original drysine owners of Defiance had permitted the organic inhabitants to maintain on their own. Directly ahead, tacnet showed blue dots, and Rolonde took the lead, holding up a hand for caution.

"Hello *Lien Wang* marines," she said. "We are Privates Rolonde and Arime of Phoenix Company Command Squad, who's there?"

"Hello Command Squad," came the reply, audible only on coms at a further distance. *"This is Master Sergeant Arianne of the UFS Holbein, currently assigned to Lien Wang. We have parren casualties on the ground, we're watching the corners and waiting for you guys."*

"*Lien Wang*," said Rolonde, "be advised that we have alien friendlies with us. Do not be alarmed and for god's sake do not point your weapons at them."

She indicated to move forward, taking point as Bucket followed, then the limping Peanut, with Arime walking mostly backward, swivelling his Koshaim side to side while watching the rear. Ahead he heard an exclamation on coms.

"Holy shit," said someone else.

"This is Bucket, that's Peanut," said Rolonde. "Peanut's hurt, we're getting him home for repairs. In the engineering space are Wowser and Styx, also friendly. Be polite."

Arime arrived at the meeting spot between huge air pipes and processors, and glanced around to see four unfamiliar marines in full armour, all paying far less attention to their perimeter than they should. They were staring at Bucket and Peanut. Arime had to remind himself that there had once been a time when hacksaws of

any kind had been little more than a rumour, a ghost story told by
Fleet veterans to frighten the greenhorns. Everyone knew that the
Machine Age had been a real thing, but they knew it the way that a
Homeworld resident might know that the last ice age had been a real
thing — so long ago and far distant from everyday reality that it may
as well have never happened. Until it came around a corner and
stared you in the face, vibroblades, many legs, rotary cannon and all,
powerplants humming like a distant swarm of wasps.

On the ground between the *Lien Wang* marines were several
parren of the same armour and insignia as the Incefahd parren
they'd seen upstairs. Their armour had been chewed by multiple
high velocity rounds, and there was matching damage on the
surrounding pipes and processors. Evidently it hadn't been enough to
endanger the tower's lifesupport or there'd have been warnings.

"*Looks like rapid fire, high velocity,*" said Sergeant Arianne, eyeing
the parren's damaged armour, then looking at the twin cannon on
Bucket and Peanut.

"That'll be Wowser, I think," said Rolonde. "Entrance is there...
hang on a moment." She switched channels. "Styx? It's Jess and Irfy,
we're outside with four *Lien Wang* marines, what's the situation
here?"

"*Hello Jess,*" came Styx's cool voice on coms. "*We had a small
encounter, a few ill-advised parren made a probe into the basement. All
have been dealt with, I did not see the point in troubling the Major with it.*"

Arime frowned. Tacnet would usually contribute data into the
broader network automatically. If the Major did not know that there
had been a firefight down here, it meant that Styx, locally at least, had
turned it off. What was going on?

"I copy that Styx," said Rolonde. "We're coming in now." She
walked forward, rifle at cross-arms and muzzle down, standard carry
position for the huge Koshaims so they didn't catch on clutter. It was
not an entirely relaxed carry position, however, and the *Lien Wang*
marines seemed to get the idea, all falling in behind with Arime,
letting Rolonde and the drones go first. Largely, Arime thought, they
just wanted to look at the drones for longer. If they thought a couple

of standard drysine combat drones were impressive, they were going to love what came next.

Peanut kept trying to turn sideways as he limped, to look at these strange new marines. He looked to Arime like an anxious dog in new company, wondering if the newcomers were friendly. "Don't worry Peanut," he told the drone. "They're friends. All humans are friends." Which was, he thought, perhaps the biggest lie he could ever tell a hacksaw drone.

"Hello Wowser," said Rolonde to the third drone, who stood in the middle of the floor with a good vantage, twin cannon scanning elsewhere. Wowser did not even acknowledge their presence. Peanut was the least accomplished, technically speaking, but at least Peanut responded to people in ways a human might think he understood. Wowser was all alien drone, all the time, and it sometimes gave Arime the creeps.

Peanut stumbled and crashed into a fabricator as he lost balance, clearly disoriented. "Here buddy, hold my arm," Arime told him, offering his right for the remaining manipulator arms to grab. "I'll lead you." And he flipped coms to talk to the bridge once more. "This is Private Arime, we need a tech down here asap, I don't know if a drone's damage gets worse the longer he's not treated but Peanut's in some trouble."

"He will be fine," said a cool, familiar voice from across the bay. An audible voice, not a coms transmission. "His systems will not suffer irreversible damage if repairs commence shortly, self-maintenance has already begun. He will sleep now."

Peanut immediately curled into a corner between fabricators and powered down. That had been a command, Arime realised, not a suggestion. Just in case anyone was stupid enough to forget who the drones really answered to.

"Styx?" Rolonde asked, advancing past Wowser and the *Lien Wang* marines toward where Styx was, behind the big armour-plate assembler. "What are you doing back there?"

"An experiment," said Styx. "One I did not think humans would approve of." Arime heard Rolonde's small gasp, and bounced quickly over. Behind the big-framed, multi-armed assembler, Styx loomed over her prey like a mantis upon a new kill. As Arime came closer, he saw that the object of her attention was a parren armour suit. This parren armour suit was missing all four limbs. Styx's vibroblades, twin weapons half-as-large again as the drones', hummed with recent activity, and the stubs of the parren's arms and legs glowed hot on IR vision.

"Holy mother of god," said Sergeant Arianne when he saw her. All four *Lien Wang* marines stood frozen where they'd moved behind for a view. Arime turned, and was close enough to see their eyes through the armoured visors. Several registered outright shock of the kind that could quickly turn to unreasonable fear.

"Don't move," Arime told them. "Don't be threatening. Whatever she looks like, she's a member of the crew and she's got more right to be here than you do. And she will defend herself." With all four marines focused on Styx, none had seen Wowser climbing to a high vantage on a fabricator behind, twin cannon angled in what was suspiciously close to a covering position. And here to the side was Bucket, less aggressive, but between him and Wowser they now had the *Lien Wang* marines in a fatal crossfire if they chose. Styx did not leave things to chance and human judgement. Styx always took precautions.

Beneath her claws, the parren suit was still moving. Struggling, trying to protest. "Styx?" Rolonde said coldly. "Is that parren still alive?"

"The suit has kept him that way, yes. The gels retard blood loss, as with your marine armour. Drugs and implants fight the shock. But this one's lack of response to my questions has been simple stubbornness. Drysines did always find that a most AI-like quality, among parren. House Harmony have it most, though House Fortitude are close. If this one were House Creative, he would have answered my questions by now."

"Styx," said Arime, feeling cold. *Now* he felt the pain in his side, and his head felt light. "We don't do that kind of thing here."

"I know," said Styx. "And thus it falls to me. I will not allow our operations to be compromised by parren disputes. All measures must be taken to identify the extent of the threat."

"And yet you've found nothing," said Rolonde. "Let him go, he might still survive."

"And cannot be allowed to. He will not report what he has seen here." One big vibroblade hummed, then smashed through the parren's helmet. Arime closed his eyes, recalling the fate of his good friend and *Phoenix* legend Master Sergeant 'Stitch' Willis. Cut in half, by blades like that, wielded at Styx's command. Styx turned to them, nonchalant as she switched to a more important matter. "I did not think the attacking parren force in the lower levels significant enough to trouble our defences by asking for reinforcement. They were outmatched."

"And you wanted a toy," Rolonde muttered.

"I understand human sentiment on the matter," said Styx. "But my commitment to *Phoenix*'s security is absolute. For hundreds of years did I serve, command and fight alongside the parren. I fear that *Phoenix*'s methods must evolve, in what humans would describe as a more ruthless direction, if we are all to survive what lies ahead."

6

Erik's network vision displayed the grand procession direct onto his helmet visor. He didn't even know exactly where the place he was looking at was on Defiance, only that it was very large and very wide, with suspiciously few structural supports to keep the roof up, and was filled with thousands of parren all standing in rows with not an EVA suit in sight.

"Stands to reason the parren would put all their restoration work into finding a pressurised room large enough for their fucking ceremonies," Erik said to Trace. "I mean, god forbid they stick a crown on someone's head before any less than five thousand."

"I don't think that would pass any safety inspection in human space," Trace agreed, seeing the same vision. In the airless hangar above Hannachiam's 'residence', coms were the only way they'd hear each other. Surrounding them were inflatable, pressurised habitats as would be used on any airless world — an odd sight here, colonising a vast steel expanse of floor that had until recently held the relics of an ancient battlefield. Machines did not need air, and so nearly all of Defiance was like this — unpressurised steel floors, nothing airtight unless specifically made for organic 'guests' who'd only materialised in the last part of the last millennia of the Machine Age. Those pres-

surised habitats were rare, just the few recently revived places like Aronach Dar, granny flats put out by the drysines to accommodate visiting relatives. Or maybe dog kennels, Erik sometimes thought.

Suited parren civilians now made their way between habitats, working on generators and other support equipment that would not fit inside the crowded workspaces. Most of these parren were House Harmony, and Erik could see a number of them not working hard, no doubt pausing to look at their own visor displays and the great ceremony unfolding there.

"Do you know if Lisbeth is there?" Trace asked.

"To the right of the altar," said Erik. "Third across, red robe."

"Oh yeah," said Trace as she peered. *"Fancy that. The first human in all history to achieve any kind of rank with the parren."*

"Yeah," said Erik, unable to not feel the pride. "Of course it will upset all the folks back home who complain that Debogandes get too much status as things stand."

"They want things to be fair," said Trace. *"There's no such thing as fair. Attempts to impose fairness upon an unfair universe usually end in disaster."*

"Major," said Sergeant Kono. *"Descending now."*

Erik and Trace turned and looked, and from the big hole in the upper level floor that remained the primary access to Hannachiam's level, some big, squat armour suits were descending on low thrust. Between them dropped a non-armoured EVA suit, yet just as wide at the shoulders and chest. Too wide for humans, and far too wide for parren. They landed, and began low-G bounding toward the humans — unmistakably tavalai and gazing about at the research camp spread across this level.

Captain Pramodenium made an exasperated gesture at all the parren activity, and Erik actually grinned, and bounced the last few metres to his old friend with enthusiasm. Pram grasped gloves with gloves, wide-set tavalai eyes rolling to look about with mischief. *"What have you gone and done now, crazy human?"* he said on coms in his perfect, gravelly English. *"I leave you for only a short time, and now look at this nonsense."*

"I'm sorry that we violated your protocols," Erik said solemnly. "If we filled in the correct forms, do you think your leadership would forgive us?" Pram actually laughed, a chortling grunt that sounded more animal than sentient. "Djojana Naki," Erik continued to the karasai at Pram's side. "I see you've kept the old man in one piece since we last met."

"No simple task," Naki growled via the translator. His Captain had learned English because tavalai spacer academies taught officers to study their enemies, but karasai were taught simply to shoot them. Erik was very glad that Naki had not been given reason to shoot at *him*, because Trace rated him highly. She added her own greeting now, more subdued and professional, but genuine enough.

Pram stepped aside with Erik and pointed toward an arch-like structure that emerged from within a series of cordons and measuring equipment. *"Is that her over there?"* he asked. There was no mistaking the eagerness in his voice.

"What happened to those lectures that we should never give an artificial sentience a gender?" Erik said with amusement.

Pram gave him a sideways look through the visor. *"I hear that your personal monstrosity has acquired a body now?"*

"And an alarming habit of dropping in on conversations you could have sworn were private," Erik warned him.

Pram grunted. *"My warnings about that one stand. But* this*! I have only heard stories of this, very vague, lost in history. She was pure speculation, little more than a fantasy tale among scholars who once heard a story from someone who heard a story. No proof, and no direct record. And now you've found her!"*

"There were a number like her," Erik replied. "Not many, but several. She knew their locations, but we know that nothing survived there. She was very sad to learn that she is the last."

"Sad." Pram stared at him, big eyes both wide and skeptical behind his visor. *"You're sure?"*

Erik smiled. "Hannachiam is the product of drysine interactions with organics. Drysines took those parts of organic sentience they found most interesting and created an entirely new form of sentience to explore them more thoroughly. Hanna's like a midway point between organic and machine. She's more emotional than we are. In some ways, she's pure emotion. And she's a friend of mine. Come, let me introduce you, she's always pleased to meet interesting new people."

* * *

ERIK AND TRACE led Pram and Naki out from the elevator to Hannachiam's control level. The space about them was large but not vast, the walls a tangle of cords and connections, organic like the vines of some impenetrable jungle. From amidst the tangle, projector arms made rows, now glowing with a regular, pulsating holographic light. Erik walked to where a circle of smaller holographic panels surrounded a platform and saw the projectors focusing to create a new shape, glowing in that channel of light.

It was a horse, he saw, and it galloped and whinnied, running circles through the air about the exposed platform. Erik laughed. "Hello Hanna," he said. "Yes, that's very much like the horses I used to ride at GreenOaks." As the further big panels made the shapes of tall trees and a vista of forested mountains as background for the galloping steed. "I told Hanna about horses on my family's ranch on Homeworld," Erik explained to the others. "She seems intrigued. I've told her about all sorts of stuff on Homeworld, but she's much more interested in animals and people than buildings and cities."

Pram, Erik saw, was gazing about within his helmet visor, eyes wide at the surrounding displays. *"All of this is her?"* he asked. *"How does she know what a horse is? Does she have access to Phoenix databases?"*

"I'd imagine so," said Erik, looking at the near control panels and finding them mostly blank. That was odd. "She can't really answer questions like that — she has no actual speech function and the chronological ordering of events isn't how she perceives things. So she can't, you know, tell you how she's done something, or explain cause-and-effect very well... Hanna?" As the near panels remained unresponsive, despite him inserting fat, gloved fingers into the sheet of light. "Why aren't your controls working?"

The projectors flashed, and multiple beams intersected to create a figure standing to Erik's left. A figure in a parren EVA suit, equipped with tools and fiddling with something.

"*Someone was down here,*" Trace observed. "*Looks like security vision.*"

"Hanna," Erik said with frustration. "Has someone been messing with your controls?"

The holography faded, was then replaced by scenes of a parren ceremony, thousands upon thousands standing in orderly rows, now chanting and moving in unison. Flags waving in the sun, and the glint of ceremonial steel weapons. So not the current, ongoing ceremonies to install Gesul as head of House Harmony.

"*I don't recognise those,*" Pram admitted. "*Who does she mean?*"

"I'm not sure," said Erik, touching more panels, looking for a response. "Hanna's not always clear. She doesn't always distinguish between individuals and groups." The parren scenes now gave way to stage plays, that great parren passion, and actors gesticulating dramatically. "Anyhow, it looks like the hand controls are down. Hanna? I've brought some friends to visit you. This is Captain Pramodenium and Major Naki, they're from the tavalai warship in orbit overhead. They are Dobruta... you know what the Dobruta are, don't you Hanna?"

The holography faded, replaced with rippling displays of multiple images about the circle. Underwater scenes, of tavalai swimming in little more than loin cloths. Some held spears, and others hand tools that they used to scrape shellfish off the sides of underwater rocks. None wore breathing apparatus. The visuals looked impossibly old, like scenes of tavalai pre-history.

Pram and Naki stared. "*What is this?*" Pram whispered. "*Where is this from?*"

"Well she does invent some imagery," Erik cautioned the tavalai. "She can generate visuals in realtime, it's not real, it's just like a movie — her processing power is pretty obscene. And the machines aren't

old enough to have taken visual footage in tavalai pre-history —
tavalai were civilised before hacksaws existed."

"There were worlds where tavalai reverted to old ways of living," the
translator replied for Naki. *"After the machines destroyed most modern
industry. This footage could have been taken by tavalai at the time, and
found later by drysines. Most today is lost."*

"I'd be wary of that," Trace echoed Erik's caution. *"Hannachiam
talks and thinks in dreams. Her thought patterns are abstract, it's all
emotion and imagination. Likely you're seeing what she's imagining."*

Images followed rapid-fire, chasing each other around the circle
— tavalai warship interiors, tavalai spacers in zero-G, tavalai councils
convening in great institutions, tavalai crowds on worlds gathered to
hear some debate. Scenes of tavalai civilisation, most of it recent to
Erik's eyes. In Hannachiam's time tavalai had not been nearly as
powerful as this.

"Well Hannachiam," said Pram, *"you seem to have a healthy respect
for the tavalai. This is a pleasant surprise. Many of your kind in your time
did not."*

Images of devastation, a city of some kind. Debris strewn across a
street, and tavalai bodies. Amidst them, a small tavalai child, sitting
helplessly among the dead, and now staring up at the viewpoint
camera in vacant horror. Now a shift, and a tavalai child was lifted
from a crib by steel manipulator arms. Robotic arms, it became clear,
as the viewpoint pulled back enough to show the owner of the arms
was a multi-legged drone. About the drone were hundreds of similar
cribs, and tavalai adults, all taking notes in what looked like a repro-
duction lab of some kind, appearing quite calm and unthreatened.

Erik looked at Pram again. He just stared, speechless. Erik fancied
that his large, semi-amphibious eyes might be a little moister than
usual. Tavalai did that too, Erik had discovered, at moments of great
emotion. Pram was Dobruta, and had devoted his life to the elimination of hacksaw technology, in the hopes of preventing its horrors
from ever visiting his people again. Now he was learning that with
Hannachiam at least, it hadn't been at all that simple.

"She does have that effect on people," Erik said quietly.

"So I hear that we have our history all wrong," said Pram. *"That the hacksaws, after tens of thousands of years treating organic beings like vermin, finally evolved into the drysines. And drysines, it appears, made peace with the parren, and invited Drakhil of the Tahrae to join them. And some tavalai joined too, and others. Fighting* for *the machines, not against them, as our history has always taught."*

An image shifted — a tavalai sitting crosslegged in an old wooden hut, weaving baskets from water reeds, thick, webbed fingers surprisingly nimble. Opposite her, multiple drone manipulator arms wove a similar basket, pausing to consider the woman's work, then to copy. Pram gave Erik a disbelieving look. Imagining drysine drones sitting in pre-historical tavalai huts was too much even for him.

"She's imagining," Erik said patiently. "It's how she talks. I think she means coordination. I don't think any of the drysines expect us to believe they coordinated with organics out of love, not even Hanna. But organics think in different ways, and drysines came to see that as a strength. Studying those strengths led them to create Hanna."

An eruption of images followed — diagrams, drawing, parren and tavalai artists with paintbrushes and pencils, engineers with holographic schematics... and now, abruptly out-of-place, a human orchestra playing some grand old classical tune. His fault, Erik knew, as he'd been introducing her to Tchaikovsky's symphonies at Lieutenant Shilu's suggestion, and Hanna would actually listen to them in real-time instead of just processing them for content in milliseconds as Styx would. It suggested a positive relationship between emotion and time, given that Hanna was all emotion, and Styx was not. Now more images — parren commanders seated about what looked like tactical displays, arranging battle plans.

"Creativity," Pram murmured, gazing about. *"She's talking about creativity. Organics and machines do it differently. Hannachiam, are you suggesting that organic creativity helped the drysines to beat the deepynines in the great war?"*

The displays faded to peaceful blue skies above golden grass, rippling in a gentle wind. "Serenity usually means 'yes'," Erik translated. "She finds your assertion harmonious."

"Hanna," said Trace. *"Did* you *help to plan the great war?"*

Again the female tavalai, weaving baskets in her hut. Beside her now sat a tavalai child, handing her mother new strands of reed as she needed them. Erik smiled. "She helped," he translated that as well. "I've asked her before. I think she was more inspiration and process. And I think that war terrifies her."

The image changed to Pram himself. It was hard to see where the viewpoint cameras were situated that could create such an image. As the viewpoint circled, Erik decided that it was a graphical composite, influenced by many perspectives, but primarily a creation of Hanna's imagination. Now the side-screens displayed an aerial image of a large building compound, surrounded by a jungle of trees. Large shuttles parked on an elevated pad, their small size demonstrating the building's immensity. More screens showed an interior, a formal setting, many distinguished tavalai seated about the walls of a wide circular chamber. Erik saw many Fleet uniforms, and the obvious ribbons that tavalai wore instead of medals.

"That is on the world of Lamaran," Pram translated for Erik and Trace. *"The Dobruta head quarters."*

"Where does she access such images?" Naki wondered. *"She was deactivated long before the Dobruta existed."*

"There are tens of thousands of parren on Defiance now," Erik explained. "They bring their databases with them. Hanna's quite caught up on current events."

"No one thought to restrict her information flows?" Pram wondered. *"Not that I think it would have been wise or necessary... but parren are conservative. An old mind might interpret new information in destabilising ways. Keeping new databases from intersecting with Defiance mainframe systems would not have been impossible, given some forethought."*

"Styx shares with her," Trace explained. *"Styx has that autonomy, as Phoenix crew. We couldn't stop her if we wanted to."*

"Ah," said Pram, grimly. Erik was sure the wise old tavalai captain was beginning to grasp why so many parren found *Phoenix's* presence on Defiance unsettling. With Styx around, Hannachiam could not be controlled or commanded. Not that Hanna had shown any great need

to be controlled or commanded, as she was entirely accommodating of most reasonable activities on Defiance. But parren being parren, they did not like loose ends, to say nothing of loose cannons. Particularly not cannons as powerful as alien super-sentiences who controlled the entire city, and now practised functional autonomy according to her own friends and conscience. And now she had chosen Gesul over Rehnar as head of House Harmony. Parren who did not prefer that change would not forget. "*Well, Hannachiam, the Dobruta's information of recent events in parren space tells us much alarming data about the recent deepynine attack. The slaughter of so many innocent parren lives on Mylor Station has caused us particular alarm.*"

Rain on the screens. The shore of some distant alien beach at dusk, waves crashing upon the sand as the wind blew and rain fell. A small shack far away, a light in the windows as smoke rose from the chimney.

"Sadness," Erik translated for the tavalai. "I'm not sure how she associates rain with melancholy, considering she's never actually been on a planet. But I don't think physical locations make much difference to an imagination this powerful. Maybe she's watched a lot of movies."

"*Amazing,*" Pram murmured, gazing at the scene. "*It makes tavalai very sad too, Hannachiam. And very alarmed that it could happen again. I understand that you have been assisting parren and human researchers to understand the weapons that were used to kill those civilians?*"

"Limited progress," Erik admitted. "We're using some analytic equipment we built from scratch using data-core schematics. It's incredible, but if drysine tech was lacking in one field, it was the biological sciences. Machines never had much use for it."

"*Well,*" Pram said grimly. "*If you have nothing to share with me, I have something to share with you.*"

* * *

TIF SAT LOCKED into the simulation chair, strapped so tight she could barely move, inflation bladders compressing her limbs every time she 'manoeuvred'. Inflation bladders were rarely used on starships to combat G-compression, because starship G-forces always came from aft, where the engines were located, and did not drive blood from the head — the main problem that inflation bladders were created to combat. In the simulator the compression was used to simulate the forces of G itself — poorly, Tif thought, but it was certainly distracting and constricting, and sometimes made it hard to breathe, just like the real thing.

Worse, the chair spun within a gimbal of three concentric rings, and played havoc upon the natural orientation of a pilot's inner ear. That did not bother Tif much — all pilots beyond a certain level of experience learned to disregard what their own bodies were telling them, and trust the instruments. By far the worst bit was the 3D holographical display that now presented a real-time evolving tactical scenario before her eyes of staggering complexity. Solving the problem it presented was like trying to play Styx at chess while being spun about in blindfolded freefall while people threw rocks at her.

"*Watch your off-side orientation,*" came LC Dufresne's blunt instruction over coms. "*Thirteen degrees infraction is too steep.*"

That described the optimum orientation between a perfect firing alignment that allowed all guns a sight of their firing arc, and the pitch at which the warship had to maintain in order to continue this degree of course alteration. Tif set her jaw and reoriented, but now her course wasn't shifting rapidly enough, and the incoming ordnance that Scan highlighted on her graphic would intercept her in less than thirty seconds instead of her preferred thirty-five.

Engineering showed the jumplines fully charged, but the possibilities on this gravity slope about a G2 star threw her jump-pulse projections off-optimal. She dumped V in a massive pulse of jump engines, used the slower V to rapidly spin and reorient the ship to a better firing alignment, then pulsed up once more to gain V ahead of the changing intercept-point with that incoming ordnance.

"*Your course reset is offline by point-five degrees,*" Dufresne told her coldly. "*Intercept angle on targets three and four are now sub-optimal, readjust.*"

Tif battled the frantic sensation that her brain was about to explode with data-overload... a horrible feeling, the mental equivalent of drowning. Armscomp blared at her that fire-volume at the primary targets was insufficient at current attitudes, so she gave a barrel roll with a tail-swing to let it get the next full volley off, then hammered thrust up to the full-performance 10.5Gs to set up the next jump pulse when the incoming ordnance arrived, pre-setting attitude with a swing back to her previous trajectory...

Suddenly Scan was telling her the second target, which had been trailing her to this point, had abruptly pulsed and was slashing at her rear quarter at high-V with ordnance incoming. She pulsed up early... but the jumplines hadn't quite reached full charge, and was held up on a two-second delay, during which time one of those big, obvious incoming rounds that she'd had on her Scan the entire time slammed into her and presumably killed everyone on the ship.

The displays went blank, and the gimbal came back to neutral. Tif flicked her wrists to clear the arm restraints and pulled off her helmet, biting back the guttural growl of frustration she knew alarmed some humans. She was sweaty and tired, heart hammering, eyes sore and limbs aching. It always astonished her that even here, sitting in a simulator without any actual G-stresses upon the body, a simulator pilot could burn hundreds of calories and feel like she'd hunted a rogue raslan barehanded.

Commander Draper came to help her with the restraints, sometimes difficult for sim-dazed pilots with their heads still spinning in circles. "Fleet training command regrets to inform you that you are dead," he told her cheerfully, as was Draper's way. That was tradition, she'd been informed — for senior pilots to tell juniors exactly how dead they were, in case they hadn't yet grasped what those simulator results would mean in real life. And it was a senior pilot's way of putting a junior in her place, telling her just how far she had to go.

She tasted blood in her mouth, and put a finger inside her lip. It came out red, to her annoyance. "Seriously Tif," said Draper. "You should consider a mouthguard."

"And you aw understand what I say with nouthguard?" Tif said drily. "You don't understand now."

"How dare you say that about my mother," said Draper, crouching to undo her legs. "I think the kuhsi god is not the god of ergonomic design. If I'd been born with that mouth and teeth, I'd demand my money back."

Tif repressed a snort. "Ask gods cone back as hunan. No teeth, chew food rike awd rady. No thanks." Draper laughed, finishing the straps and giving her a friendly whack on the arm. Tif liked Draper. Unlike her, he was a hell of a warship pilot. And unlike Dufresne, people liked him.

"How I do?" she asked her instructors. They were in *Phoenix* itself, as the simulator functions were all integrated up at the bridge, and too difficult to run successfully off-ship. Engineering Bay 14, grey steel and greyer storage compartments, extra wiring still exposed where Engineering had run cords to the new setup. It was all temporary, the simulator gimbals mounted on the rear G-wall, with *Phoenix* in the bay, sitting on her brand new tail.

"You died," said Dufresne, reviewing the screens arrayed before her chair, replaying that last sequence of manoeuvres. Tif was having difficulty hearing, then recalled that her ears were still bound and reached to undo the bandana that held them there, flat beneath the helmet.

"I die good?" she asked Dufresne. "Or I die bad?" Blood recirculated into her ears, hot and painful. But now she could hear properly.

"Dying is usually bad, Second Lieutenant," Dufresne told her. "Please try to recall that if you're ever flying this ship in combat." Unlike Draper, Dufresne meant it without humour. If a kuhsi senior had addressed her like that, Tif would have been upset, but Draper caught her eye and winked. "You progressed nearly halfway through the assigned simulation. A full report will have to await our full assessment, but you appear to have fallen short on multiple objective counts, and achieved satisfactory results on a few."

"The first time I tried that scenario," Draper told her, "I died about a minute short of where you survived to. So you did better than me for a beginner."

"She took a lot of shortcuts to survive that long," Dufresne said with disapproval. "Thus bypassing multiple assigned objectives."

"I survive ronger," Tif told her. "Other objective stupid. First thing is survive, yes? Crazy scena... scena-rio." She had to bite out the awkward word. "No one rive aw through. Inpossibu."

"The Captain survived the entire scenario in Academy training," Dufresne said coolly. "And Captain Pantillo before him. With high ratings for secondary objectives as well."

Tif felt her heart fall through the floor. She'd been sure it was impossible. There were just too many enemies in all the wrong places, and the sheer volume of information to be processed was too much. Draper put a hand on her shoulder, and gave a hard look at Dufresne.

"What the Lieutenant Commander fails to mention," he said, "is that among the very good pilots who have *never* successfully completed this scenario, her name is right up there."

"Yours too," said Dufresne, unruffled as she continued to scroll through the data.

"Exactly," said Draper. "There's no shame in failing here, Tif, the entire scenario is designed to push you to your limit just to see where that limit is. We only run it on advanced pilots, and you're now certainly one of those. Only a few total freaks like Captains Pantillo and Debogande have ever passed."

It made Tif consider the plausibility of crew-wide rumours that Dufresne was actually a better pilot than Draper, but had been knocked back for the Commander's rank because no one wanted her in charge. "How about AI ship?" she wondered. "Drysine ship..." she waved a hand at Dufresne's screens. "Too nuch data for ne, head exprode. AI fry no probren, yes?"

"I have no idea," said Dufresne.

"Actually no," said Draper. "The Captain was saying he discussed it with Styx, and Styx is surprised with the capabilities of human pilots. She says AIs don't have a problem with data-overload like we do, but human pilots acquire an instinct after a while that allows them to take short-cuts without *having* to process all that data. So being able to run all the data doesn't guarantee an AI will necessarily make better decisions — some AIs get sidetracked by irrelevant data that a human or kuhsi would ignore, there's apparently dangers to being *too* smart. The more important thing is to know which data matters and when, and that's something organic brains are naturally better at than AIs — we have a better biological sorting mechanism. AIs think themselves to death and drown in complexity."

"The computer gives you a rank of forty-two percent," Dufresne said primly as she finished her calculations. "As you can see, Second Lieutenant, it's quite a bit different from flying a shuttle."

Tif couldn't argue with that. "Deep space with junp engine," she said tiredly. "Lots options, deep view..." she demonstrated with her hand, indicating the ridiculous depth a pilot had to process, well beyond the visible light horizon, toward things the ship's scanners insisted hadn't actually happened yet. "Don't need new skill. Need new brain."

She hauled herself dejectedly to her feet, as Draper went and peered at the Lieutenant Commander's screens. "The computer also says," he added, "that the Fleet Academy mean-average for a pilot of your experience would expect you to be scoring at twenty-seven percent. And your forty-two percent would place you in the... top one percent of all trainees." He smiled broadly at her. "But I already expected that."

The news did not cheer Tif as much as it was supposed to. "Books say trans... trans-i-shun hard. Good score eary not say pirot nake trans-i-shun. Need change brain, brain sonetine say no."

"Well there's no arguing with that," Draper admitted. "But if I had to choose between being a twenty-seven-percent pilot on the wrong side of the transition, or a forty-two-percenter, I'd choose where you are now. Now, let me show you the next assigned reading and lectures — the LC and I will try to grade your papers faster this time."

7

On Captain Pram's insistence, Erik and Trace were ushered into PH-1's cockpit upon return to the shuttle. When disembarking without an external airlock, the shuttle's entire rear hold would be decompressed first, leaving the forward hold just rear of the cockpit sealed with an extra pair of pressure doors to protect cockpit integrity. Erik, Trace and Pram used it now as an airlock to access the cockpit, and stood in bulky pressure suits beside the observer chairs with barely enough room, Erik stooping slightly beneath the overhead.

"Guys, noise cancellation, please," Erik told Hausler and Yun, who by regulation had to remain in the cockpit while the shuttle was grounded. Both activated helmet headsets so they could hear nothing else, and gave thumbs up to indicate they'd done it. The cockpit was pressure-guaranteed, as pilots couldn't fly in full EVA suits, and would have to seal up with a safety hood, and plug their flight suits into emergency air if the cockpit were holed. More important right now, the cockpit was the most secure place for a top-secret conversation.

"We can turn off all coms," Erik told Pram, "but there's no guarantee Styx can't surreptitiously turn them back on...

To his surprise, Pram waved away the concern. "She will hear of this eventually, there's no preventing it. I'm more concerned in the near-term about the parren." He considered them for a moment, big, amphibious eyes rimmed with the wrinkles of ageing skin, just as with humans. That made him somewhere over two hundred human years old, Erik guessed. The mouth, twice the width of a human's, pursed with displeasure, thick lips pressed thin with tension. "I understand the *Lien Wang* is here to try and persuade you to go home?"

"They told you that?" Erik asked warily. As much as he liked and trusted Pram, he could never forget that Pram served an alien government with which humanity had recently been at war. What-ever else he was, Pram was a dutiful servant of the collective tavalim, and would screw all of humanity in an instant if it ensured his own race's survival. And Erik, of course, would do the same in return.

"It seems the logical thing," said Pram, inner eyelids blinking rapidly in the dry human air. "What happened to your plans to head to croma space and search for the origins of the alo?"

It would be too much, Erik supposed, to hope that Pram hadn't heard about *Phoenix*'s plans. And if he knew, that meant all the major tavalai institutions and leadership knew. "Well you probably heard that the parren scholar we were speaking to about establishing contacts with the croma just crashed into the side of a steel cliff," Erik replied. "So that's proving harder than expected."

"The Dobruta have croma contacts," said Pram. "We can get you there."

"How?" Trace interjected with suspicion. "Croma are nearly as far away from tavalai space as human. You have no significant relations with them, croma have few enough relations with their neighbours, let alone those even further away."

"The Dobruta have an unusual role in tavalai affairs," said Pram. "Making friends with strange aliens is our job." The big eyes swiv-elled with an inward intensity that might have constituted a pointed look.

"Why give us contacts?" Erik persisted on Trace's line of questioning. "What's in it for you?"

"A lot," said Pram. "Nearly all of which I am not at liberty to discuss with you."

"Well I'm sorry," said Erik. "But the last time we took assistance from one tavalai department, we nearly brought down the tavalai State Department."

"And gained Drakhil's diary, and from that, the drysine data-core," Pram retorted. "I think humanity gained significantly from the venture."

"And we went into it with our eyes open," said Erik. "You're right, we knew exactly what we were getting into. Without similar knowledge on this occasion, I can't accept your offer of contacts or introductions. Because we both know very well, Pramodenium, that tavalai institutions are not authorised to make these offers unless they have some significant larger agenda in play. I need to know what that is."

Pram looked out the canopy for a moment at the steel hangar bay walls, and the flatbed parren vehicles rolling by, crowded with EVA-suited engineers and scientists. Then he looked back. "I will deny that I told you this, if asked. I will lose my job if it is discovered. Possibly my life. There is still a death penalty for tavalai military personnel, for which the Dobruta marginally qualify. I could get that penalty for telling you this."

"I appreciate your risk," said Erik. "But the entire crew of *Phoenix* has had that penalty hanging over our heads for some time now, either inflicted by our enemies out here, or by our own Fleet back home."

Pram appeared to consider that, and accept it. "Our scientists received samples from Mylor Station, after the attack. They've been analysing them."

"How did you receive samples?" Trace interrupted.

"Do you want to hear my information or not?" Pram replied. Erik gave Trace a faint shake of the head when she looked his way. "Analysis of those samples indicated what I imagine parren scientists have found — bio-synthetic nano-technology designed to rapidly interfere with biological life processes so as to cause rapid death. We've not seen that precise technology, but it's not surprising that someone else may have it. It's frighteningly advanced, but in a galaxy of V-strikes from jump-capable starships it's hardly a worse existential threat than we already face from many sources.

"The worse news is that..." and Pram coughed, interrupting himself to wipe at his lips, an anxious mannerism. Erik saw that his hand was faintly shaking. An unpleasant chill started somewhere in his stomach, and worked its way up his spine. "Well, it gets quite complicated," Pram resumed, the tremor having moved to his voice. "Obscenely complicated, in fact. The technology is on a level that makes it difficult for our scientists to even follow. Fortunately there is a small unit of such scientists who have been tracking these developments for centuries, largely emanating from the direction of the reeh.

"The samples concern not the parren who died at Mylor Station, but those who survived. Their DNA has been mutated. Only to a very small degree — too small for previous technology, advanced as it was, to even detect. But those mutations effectively make a kill-mechanism, which when activated will kill that person very quickly."

"Then we have to tell the parren authorities immediately," said Trace. "They have to round up and treat those parren survivors immediately..."

Pram held up a hand. "Other tavalai vessels have already done that, from the moment we made the discovery. But you see, it gets worse, because there are synthetic nano-particles that can wrap themselves with organic tissue to make synthetic-organic hybrid particles, thus rendering them invulnerable to the host's immune system, and almost untraceable to modern medicine, drugs or counter-treatments. Their function is manifold, but the end design is to edit DNA, cause the mutation to spread, then to spread to neighbouring organisms much the same way as a cold or any other infectious disease would spread..."

"Oh no," Erik breathed. Now he was scared. It was a different kind of fear to anything he'd known before. Previous threats, humanity had discovered ways of combatting. This did not sound like one of those.

Pram nodded. "The DNA-editing spreads, like any infection, but the host remains unaware that it is even taking place. Our scientists think it can be activated at a signal — we don't think a radio signal or anything quite so simple, but close, and perhaps even worse. If an entire population were infected in such a way, over a period of years, decades or even centuries..."

"Then they can start a war by popping in from jump and wiping out entire planetary populations with a signal," Trace surmised. She sounded completely flat, devoid of emotion. Erik suspected it was too much for her to even process.

"Tavalai authorities have ordered a tavalim-wide survey to check for those DNA modifications," said Pram. "Already we've found infected portions of the population... not large so far, but we also suspect there are far more forms of infection that we don't yet know about. If the alo/deepynines have weaponised this technology, they may be evolving it to the point where they can kill every other species in the Spiral, once they've acquired proximity, with the touch of a button. And if they've done it to our population, on the opposing side of the Triumvirate War, then one can guarantee they've done it to yours."

* * *

THERE WAS silence in the Aronach Dar briefing room, save for the woosh of the giant dishwasher, and the hum and buzz of automated appliances from the kitchen. Erik had never seen his senior crew look so frightened in any situation where no one was shooting at them.

"What if Pram's lying?" Commander Adams of *Lien Wang* said finally, with a note of desperate optimism. "The tavalai are in political chaos right now, State Department is in crisis, there's renewed concern that humanity might resume the war while they're weak, beat them down further. Come up with a common enemy, distract the humans, get them looking the wrong way."

"If that was their strategy," said Erik, "they wouldn't send Pram running here to see *Phoenix*, they'd send others to see you guys back at Homeworld or Heuron. They'd need to convince Fleet Command, not *Phoenix*. We're irrelevant to that plan, save in making it look consistent."

"We don't know that they haven't," Adams objected.

"And secondly," Erik continued, "even if that were true, so what?" He didn't want to be saying this. Just days ago he'd been arguing with Trace about why they should all go home. But now, everything changed. "Even if there's only a chance he's right, it's our duty to do everything we can to investigate. And right now we're in a position that no one else in Fleet is. We've a huge headstart, we've alien contacts they're in no position to gain or access, and we've learned how to operate out here, with alien allies, in a way that I don't think most Fleet officers, with their regulations and protocols, could manage. This is our play. I don't think we have a choice."

There was no argument from those surrounding. Many faces were pale, no doubt thinking of families and friends back home. Entire civilisations. Worlds. Systems. All full of humans who might already be infected with a DNA mutation no one even knew to look for, and could kill them with a simple trigger, rendering entire systems uninhabited of human life.

"Pram was trembling," Trace added. "We both saw it." Glancing at Erik. "He's a brave man, but he was terrified for his people."

"And he said he'd give us the medical evidence from tavalai doctors and scientists," Erik added. "He can't show everything, because the way the technology affects tavalai DNA is about the most highly classified secret the tavalai have. But he says he can give us enough to let our doctors and scientists know what to look for. Doc Suelo's going to look over it, but he's a military fixer not a cutting-edge theoretical scientist, as he told me quite strongly when I talked to him just earlier. So this stuff needs to go back home on *Lien Wang* with all urgency."

He looked at Captain Sampey and Commander Adams. Both

looked shaken and quiet. "Of course," said Sampey. "We'll make immediate preparations."

"Just wait long enough until we can get you a tavalai escort," said Erik. "You might run into another Fleet inspection ship on the way back or you might not — either way, a tavalai escort would clear the way of any bureaucracy, give you the fastest path back home."

Sampey nodded gratefully. "Appreciated, Captain."

"I don't think there's any choice at all," said Romki. He was seated along the table on Erik's right, with Lisbeth. This was no longer a purely military matter. They needed all the best minds on this, irrespective of their place, or lack of one, in the military hierarchy. Romki looked remarkably calm, in the manner of a man accustomed to extremely complex answers who had just discovered one that was incredibly simple. "We must treat this as the highest level of emergency. Military or civilian, we must all agree now that our own lives, hopes and dreams become irrelevant. If we die doing this, so be it. If the worst case scenario were to occur and we did nothing, we'd all be dead anyway and most of humanity with us. We must be prepared to willingly sacrifice everything to defend against this threat."

Trace gave Romki an approving nod. "Does anyone disagree with the Professor?" she asked the table. Varying degrees of 'no' came back, from the fearful to the hard and determined. From Lieutenant Dale, a loud 'Hell no'.

"So if we're going," said Kaspowitz, with the skepticism of an older man who'd seen the difficulties of simply moving from point A to point B under normal circumstances, "how are we going? Our best parren contact with the croma is dead, and croma don't just accept any visitors."

"Captain Pram says the Dobruta have croma contacts," said Erik.

"How?" Kaspowitz persisted. Everyone at this table knew from experience to be skeptical of tavalai 'assistance'.

"Apparently they go back a few thousand years. The Dobruta invited croma to discuss joint patrols against possible Machine Age survivors. The croma weren't very interested, the Machine Age never advanced much beyond their territory. They said they'd taken care of it. But the Dobruta have persisted, it's pretty much the Dobruta mission in life — putting the containment of Machine Age technologies ahead of even State Department policy."

"They missed a bit," Dale said grimly. A few smiles around the table. Alo space had always been off-limits to Dobruta. There'd been speculation that tavalai insistence on the opening of alo space to such inspections had helped convince alo that tavalai power in the Spiral needed to be taken down several large notches.

"And who are their contacts, exactly?" asked Kaspowitz. "Croma aren't monolithic, there's lots of groups."

"The only monolithic species in the Spiral is humanity," Romki said mildly. "You want to talk to us, you talk to Fleet Command." Everyone looked at him blankly. "Do go on."

"I won't even attempt the proper pronunciation," said Erik, checking his slate notes. "But the faction is Croma'Dokran. The current rulers of all croma space are Croma'Rai. Croma'Dokran aren't very friendly with them, Pram says, but he's fairly vague on the croma too. Nobody knows very much, not even their parren neighbours."

"And Pram's contact is leadership in Croma'Dokran?" Shilu asked.

"That's right."

"Captain Pram wouldn't happen to have any translation notes?" Shilu asked hopefully. "Work on basic law and customs? I've looked but it's pretty thin, and mostly repeats itself — you know, they're big, they're slow, their architectural style is fortified and they've made a fetish of strength and impenetrability. I've read that a dozen times using different big words each time, and still learned nothing."

The Coms Officer looked hopefully at Romki and Lisbeth. "I'm sorry Lieutenant," said Romki. "The croma are so far outside my area of expertise I'd only be guessing. I'm happy to cooperate with you on making best guesses on whatever we encounter, but until then I won't be much help."

"Same here, Wei," Lisbeth said apologetically. "It was all I could do just to get Gesul's people to find Jarush for Erik to talk to. And now that she's dead, I don't think many others will be stepping forward."

"Figures," Shilu sighed.

"I think you're about to have another issue," Lisbeth continued. She wore a plain jumpsuit, evidently not having had time for anything more elaborate, whatever her now standard ceremonial requirements. Her brown hair frizzed as nature intended, without its more recent restrictions. Erik thought she looked much better this way, but wasn't game to say so. "If the tavalai are telling the parren about this, it will get back to House Fortitude and their ruler Sordashan as soon as the fastest ships can get there."

"And what happens then?" Erik asked.

"It's hard to be sure... but my guess is that House Fortitude will invoke their status as the ruling house and take full jurisdiction over all missions from parren space to further investigate this matter. *Phoenix* is in parren space on the invitation of House Harmony, so that will include us."

"So we won't be able to go anywhere or do anything without House Fortitude permission?" Shilu asked.

"Worse," Lisbeth said sombrely. "We'll not be allowed to do anything not directly connected to the advancement of parren interests. *Phoenix* is headed to croma space for the advancement of human interests. It won't be allowed. No chance."

"How long did Lieutenant Rooke say the refit would take?" Romki asked. Rooke, of course, was the one senior officer not present. All agreed that his work on *Phoenix* was too important for him to waste time in meetings.

"Another thirty days," said Dufresne. "I did suggest to him that it could be faster if he would accept more assistance, but he replied that under-qualified assistance could actually slow him down. It seemed a reasonable assertion, I did not challenge him on it."

"Major," said Erik, "how are the kids coming along?"

Trace thought for a moment. "I've been cautious, and Styx has agreed that caution is best. But this changes things. I'll ask Styx to run some numbers and estimate the time savings Rooke could make if we deployed the drones on *Phoenix* immediately."

"I think we'll be cutting it fine either way," Draper said grimly. "I was looking over the Midships systems just yesterday, there's plenty still to do."

"And Kaspo," said Erik, "what's your best guess at when House Fortitude ships could get here once they've received the tavalai's data?"

"Depends on which tavalai ships went where," said Kaspowitz. "Faster routes could shave a few days off. But if *Makimakala* represents the first time a tavalai ship has entered parren space with this information, even the fastest travel time for that message would take us to nearly twenty days."

Erik took a deep breath. "Okay... it may be that we're overreacting to this, but I doubt it. Various delays in bureaucracy could hold things up, but my sense is that parren can be pretty fast when things get urgent — a linear command structure with almost no checks and balances as humans understand it can do that."

Lisbeth nodded her agreement. "Yes," she said, in case anyone had missed it. "Frighteningly fast, sometimes."

"So we're going to operate on the assumption that we're running against the clock. Twenty days until the response reaches here and shuts us down, Rooke's best estimates at completing the refit puts us at thirty... we have to find ways to bring that down inside our limit.

"And Lisbeth? I'd like you to reconsider whether you want to stay here or not. Once House Fortitude gets here and takes over all national security matters from Gesul, it's going to get pretty hairy. If *Phoenix* has just run ahead of them arriving, against their obvious wishes, they might not take it well. The one remaining human on Defiance might be in a dangerous spot."

Lisbeth shook her head firmly. "I don't think so. I'm a member of House Harmony's inner advisory circle around Gesul. I'm in no more danger in that capacity than anyone else is."

"Still considerable," said Romki, with fatherly concern. "I think your brother makes a lot of sense, Lisbeth... I mean, given how we've all seen the parren deal with these internal disputes. House Fortitude could just decide Gesul is an inconvenience and dispose of him, and where would that leave his advisors then?"

"If they did that," Lisbeth said calmly, "House Fortitude would no longer be the leading House in parren space within a few short years. Challenges must be conducted properly and for good reasons — just declaring someone annoying and killing them would cause a flux-shift away from House Fortitude and toward House Harmony so strong that Fortitude would lose the numbers to rule, and the Jusica would declare Harmony the new ascendant, exactly what Fortitude don't want. It's happened before, all parren leaders understand these lessons very well."

"This is a matter of national security, Lis," said Erik. He couldn't help the concern in his voice before all the crew. It wasn't an ideal situation, but he'd given up caring what it looked like. "Fortitude might decide the interests of national security take precedence, and the parren population will forgive him for putting those interests first."

"Sure," said Lisbeth with a faint smile, not falling for it. "But Harmony has been the house preaching the need for strong, unified parren defence in the face of foreign threats. Fortitude haven't — they haven't been for parren unity at all, they've been for division and the separation of houses, which benefits Fortitude because they consider themselves superior... and in political terms they've been right, for the last few centuries at least. So for Fortitude to come in here and knock off Gesul in the name of unified national defence will be seen by most parren — even House Fortitude parren — as the height of hypocrisy.

"Parren are obedient but they're not blind. Just because they do what they're told doesn't mean they can't realise it's not right. Sometimes when the strain between what they've been ordered to do and what they feel is right becomes too great, you get a phase-shift so intense it swings the balance of power wildly away from the offending house or leader. That's what makes balance in parren society where so many other autocratic systems would fall apart — parren leaders are actually more afraid of their own people than most so-called democracies are. So no — it's imperative for human interests that a human remains in my current position of influence. And since none of you can do it, it falls to me."

A brief silence around the table. Romki looked at Erik, struggling with a wry, proud smile. Trace looked content, and even the unimpressionable Dufresne looked thoughtful. "Captain," said Captain Sampey, "given that Lisbeth is currently the leading human authority on all things parren — and possibly the leading human authority there's ever been — I think we have no choice but to accept her advice."

Erik sighed, proud and frightened, all at once. "Yeah. Yeah, I guess so." Lisbeth gave him a small, affectionate smile.

"Captain?" ventured Draper. "I can think of one... very significant matter that will need to be addressed if we're headed to croma space. We just don't have enough crew. It's that simple. The ship won't work with what we've got, barely in peacetime and certainly not in combat."

Erik nodded. "I know. *Makimakala*'s thought of that already."

8

"With respect, Captain," Dufresne said stiffly as they waited at Assembly for the tavalai shuttles to dock. "I think this might require a broader discussion among the crew. Tif is one thing. This is something else entirely."

"You seem to be under the misapprehension that this is a democracy," Erik told her, gazing at one vast window on the curved inner wall before him. Delta Platoon were preparing to relieve Bravo Platoon on security detail this 'evening', and the lower platform to the greeting party's left was filled with the armoured whine and rattle of suits preparing for departure. Marine voices shouted, and concerned Operations crew talked on coms while monitoring the habitat docking mechanisms they'd never entirely trusted, and hoped the ancient automation they'd fixed and polished didn't abruptly break down.

"I'm sorry Captain, " said Dufresne, not sounding at all sorry. "It wasn't my intention to imply that. I was merely exercising my prerogative as the *Phoenix* third-in-command to state my mind on matters of crew morale. And I'm fairly sure that many will not take this well."

"The Captain hasn't decided to accept *Makimakala*'s offer," Trace cut in before any others could reply. "This is an evaluation."

"And I maintain that any evaluation should include the opinion of the crew themselves," Dufresne persisted.

"It does," said Trace. "You're flunking."

Dufresne turned a stare on her, then perhaps realised who she was staring at, swallowed hard and watched the final preparations as the access gantries connected to the shuttle's dorsal hatch. Erik tried not to let his amusement show. Dufresne was discovering the difference between sharing an O-4 rank with Trace on paper, and exercising an equal authority in practice. Having suffered through that experience himself, Erik only hoped that it would do Dufresne as much good as it had done him, however little he'd enjoyed it at the time.

Commander Draper stood with them, and Lieutenant Dale as well — the full *Phoenix* command crew, the top three from the bridge plus the two top marines, arrayed to consider this disconcerting offer their tavalai friends had made. Not for the first time, Erik found himself wrestling with the gaping hole that Suli Shahaim's death had left in the bridge crew. They were all so young without her, Dale excluded, though even he was hardly ancient. But mostly Erik just missed her, and missed her calm advice, and the knowledge that whatever strange situations confronted them, she'd likely seen something like it before and would have things to say worth listening to.

The airlock cycled as it filled, then the inner doors opened and Captain Pram emerged, flanked by blue-clad tavalai spacers Erik did not recognise at first glance... which was not to say that he hadn't met them before. Tavalai faces were far more familiar than they had been, but not *that* familiar. Behind the first group swaggered a big tavalai half-a-head taller than the rest, dark-brown skinned with mottled black patches. With him were several more, all obviously karasai, just that much broader and stronger than the others. For all that humans liked to pride themselves on their diversity, tavalai exceeded it, with the range in size between largest and smallest often extreme. In tavalai Fleet the bigger ones, almost always males, tended toward the karasai.

Erik smiled at Pram as he approached, and extended a hand.

Pram took it, a firm, leathery grip. At this point it was more show for the others than anything else. Erik did not need to shake the tavalai's hand to feel a bond of trust between them. Pram looked past him, to the humans arrayed behind.

"Captain, I'm not certain you've met Commander Draper?" Erik suggested.

"Commander," said Pram, with faint relief. "Not in person, no." They shook hands. "Second-shift commander, I recall you from TK55. That was some fine manoeuvring."

"As was yours, Captain," said Draper, looking pleased.

"And Lieutenant Commander Dufresne," Erik added, and Pram shook her hand as well.

"My sympathies to you all for Commander Shahaim," said Pram. "And Lieutenant Karle as well. Distinguished officers."

"Yes," said Erik.

Pram nodded as well to Trace and Dale, not requiring any introduction there. "Well," he said. "I suppose it is my turn." He indicated the small tavalai on his right. Almost certainly female, Erik judged from her size. "This is Stmata Sasalaka. She is a Dobruta pilot of two years active service. Before the Dobruta she was Roji — Helm, you would say, on the Fleet cruiser Talaranda for five years. Prior to that, a fast surveillance vessel. Her testing and combat reports alike place her in the top five percentile, and she is young for her present rank."

Sasalaka's skin was a more normal tavalai dark-to-light mottled green. Her big, froggy eyes, which had remained fixed on some point past Erik's shoulder, now swivelled to glance up at him, adjusting for telescopic depth. Unsure of the protocols, no doubt, between humans and tavalai of differing rank in such a situation. Erik smiled at her, and extended a hand. Sasalaka took it, tentatively.

"Do you speak English, Stmata Sasalaka?" Erik asked her. 'Stmata' was Togiri for a rank roughly equivalent to Lieutenant, Erik knew.

"Yes Captain," she said, a voice higher and less gravelly than her Captain's, but more thickly accented. "Not as well as Captain Pram."

Erik kept all reaction off his face. Less-than-perfect English was usually an immediate disqualifier from a Fleet warship bridge. Communication was vital, and even minor delays or misunderstandings could be catastrophic. But then, he was seriously considering putting Tif on the bridge one day, if she continued her recent improvements. If, god forbid, they lost another pilot, he was going to have to do it immediately. Six was the ideal number of pilots on a carrier, and four the absolute minimum. Right now they had three. Until Pram's offer, he'd been planning to put Lieutenant Hausler on second-shift Helm, and bring Dufresne up to fill Shahaim's spot at the Captain's side. Which would have deprived Operations of one more shuttle pilot. Of course, they were already short of shuttle pilots, too.

"And why have you been chosen for this duty, Stmata Sasalaka?"

"The Dobruta asked for volunteers, Captain."

"You volunteered to serve on a human warship?"

"Yes Captain."

"Why?"

"Dobruta serve, Captain. The mission was explained. It seemed important. Volunteers were required. I volunteered."

Erik nodded slowly, trying to figure that out. Tavalai were rarely short of words, but that did not always make their reasoning transparent. Sasalaka was talking about duty, which tavalai in all walks of life were stubbornly insistent upon, toward whichever of the grand institutions they served. Sasalaka was a loyal Dobruta, the Dobruta asked for volunteers, so she volunteered. That it would make him uncomfortable was predictable. Ideally, when offering the controls of the *UFS Phoenix* to a new crewmember, even in the co-pilot's role, it was preferable that that crewmember be loyal to this ship and not some other. But in this situation, he supposed, it was always going to be too much to ask.

"And how much of your piloting has been as lead pilot?" Erik asked.

"Half, Captain. Second shift on both of my..." a pause as she searched for a word. "My previous ships. I have five combat incidents on my record, all were graded high, as are my simulator scores. I was on... on path, to pilot ibranakala-class carrier."

Ah, Erik thought, beginning to see the shape of it now. A young hotshot pilot, formerly tavalai Fleet, seeing some action at the tail of the Triumvirate War before the final ceasefire. Now joining the Dobruta, two years ago Captain Pram said... perhaps in search of more action? With the war over, tavalai Fleet was largely inactive. She aspired to fly an ibranakala-class like *Makimakala*, and during the war her prospects would have been good, given all the casualties and new positions opening. And now she was given a chance to fly Helm for a warship even more powerful than an ibranakala-class, with the obvious drawback that she'd be surrounded by humans and completely outside of any chain of command that might save her if human-tavalai relations soured. For a young pilot desperate for advancement, it seemed a prudent if risky course toward achieving her goals.

Only no, Erik reconsidered... tavalai were not known for selfish individualism. And Sasalaka had said she was simply doing what needed to be done, from a very tavalai sense of duty. Maybe there was nothing more to it than that. Well, he could explore that mystery in greater depth later on.

"And we have brought sixty-two spacer volunteers, of various specialities," Pram added. "I do not know what your present crewing requirements are like, I recall that you were short-handed even before the Battle of Defiance. I doubt that sixty-two is nearly enough, but it was all the volunteers that we could muster."

"Where are they from?" Erik asked.

"I will provide you with complete personnel lists, of course. Some of the systems-specialists will no doubt struggle to transition to human technology, but then it appears it will be some time until *Phoenix* can leave Defiance, so there will be time to practice."

"That's not such a problem," said Erik. "It's not entirely human technology any longer. Even my regulars are struggling to adjust."

"I see," said Pram, cautiously. "May I also introduce Nkai Karajin." Indicating for the big, dark tavalai behind to step forward. "He is five years retired but insists his physical condition remains suitable for service. Before that, he served for twenty-two years in a number of roles in the karasai, finally retiring at Nkai — your equivalent marine rank of Lieutenant. He is highly decorated, and his last command was on the *Jesanduran*."

"I know the *Jesanduran*," Erik said solemnly, and shook the big karasai's hand as well. "By reputation, at least." And indicated him to Trace, as she was the one he'd need to impress if this unlikely thing was going to happen.

But Lieutenant Dale intercepted the tavalai before he could take Trace's offered hand. "Karajin?" he said with a squint of dubious recognition, and an extended hand. "I *thought* it was you."

The big tavalai backed up a little, eyes swivelling inward to consider Dale's face. Tavalai features were wide-set, and no doubt the facial recognition portions of their brains struggled with close-set human features. "Dale?" he said.

Dale shook his hand, which Karajin evidently found strange. "On Gamesh. You were on the left flank, yes?"

Karajin waited for his earpiece to translate that. No English at all with the karasai, Erik knew. That was unsurprising — it was only the senior bridge crew who were encouraged to learn their enemies' language in hope of understanding them better. When he answered, it was in thick Togiri. *"Yes,"* said Erik's translator. *"You were forward guard on the right flank. We were impressed."*

"Major," said Dale, turning to her, "this is one of Toognam's friends from Gamesh, he fought with us. Or we didn't see him in the fight, but we had some drinks afterward." He turned back to the karasai, with evident enthusiasm. "So how is old Toognam? Is he doing okay?"

"Toognam was informed of your losses here," said Karajin. *"He was concerned, and led talks with all of us recently retired veterans. He explained something of your situation. And he expressed confidence in your character, Lieutenant Dale."*

Dale, Erik saw with astonishment, looked genuinely touched.

"Good," he said with emotion, jaw tight. "Real good. He's a good old frog, we fought well together."

"All of your karasai volunteers are from Gamesh?" Trace asked the tavalai.

"*All,*" Karajin agreed. "*Toognam is convincing. Phoenix fights the old machines, and they are always a far greater threat to the tavalim than humans. We fear for all tavalai if the machines should rise once more.*"

"As we fear for all humans," Trace agreed. "How many are you?"

"*Forty. We make two platoons. And the Dobruta have given us armour. Better than squeezing into skinny human armour.*" Karasai platoons being less than half the size of marine platoons — twenty karasai each.

"And all of you were retired?"

"*Dobruta have few karasai to spare. Serving Fleet karasai are rarely given permission to reassignment. We have had months advance notice. We have been training. And we've been given a karasai assault shuttle, the same one you see outside, with crew. The pilot is Leralani, he once served on the Togolich, he is best quality.*"

And they'd flown out here on *Makimakala*, uncertain what situation they'd find, or if *Phoenix* would even accept their offer. The first time Pram had met with Erik, and was then introduced to Hannachiam, Pram had not raised the subject, feeling out the situation first. Erik was not offended at all, it was exactly what he'd had come to expect from Pram — wisdom and caution.

Effectively it was the offer of an entire tavalai dramata — a formation of two platoons, forty karasai with all tavalai equipment, plus a new assault shuttle. The addition of Sasalaka, plus the shuttle and pilot, would mean he could fill first-shift Helm, keep Lieutenant Hausler flying PH-1 where he belonged, and use the new tavalai shuttle effectively as PH-2 — the assault shuttle *Phoenix* had lost back on Homeworld with all crew and passengers. Add the civilian AT-7 and they'd have five shuttles, albeit only four of them armed... though lately the techs had been making modifications to AT-7 as well. Five shuttles, five nearly full-strength platoons, four warship pilots plus Tif still in training when her shuttle duties permitted...

Hope surged again. It was crazy, mixing human and tavalai crew so soon after that terrible war where they'd all been trying to kill each other. But so much that had happened to *Phoenix* lately was crazy, and he'd stopped caring about it. Right now his only concern was whether it was effective. And if *Phoenix* had managed to survive a kuhsi shuttle pilot, a drysine whatever-Styx-was, and were now grooming three drysine drones for engineering and occasionally combat duties, then he was pretty sure they could survive a bunch of tavalai crew as well. Tavalai, at least, were much less likely than drysines to murder them all in their sleep. What the *tavalai* would make of serving alongside the drysines, however, was another thing yet to reckon with.

* * *

"WHO DO YOU SERVE?" Timoshene sat in the mostly empty rows of shuttle seats, weapon across his armoured thighs, considering Lisbeth's unwanted invitee beneath the black bandana many parren used within helmets to prevent the chafing of hairless scalps. Unmasked for now, he considered his helmet's ongoing diagnostic, scrolls of parren symbols across its visor.

Hiro gazed for a moment, as though surprised to see this Domesh warrior without his coverings. Humans, Lisbeth thought, were often surprised to see how pragmatic the apparently obsessive parren could be in the practice of their various ideologies. Timoshene was armouring up, and head coverings were for the moment impractical. Hiro had not yet learned that Timoshene did not cover his face because he didn't wish anyone to see him — he covered it because he did not wish his own thoughts contaminated by impure vanity. Considering that he qualified as very handsome among parren, Lisbeth thought it made even more sense. It was hard to cleanse one's soul of impure thoughts when female parren took second and third looks.

"I serve *Phoenix*," Hiro said, lounging in the custom EVA suit he'd taken from *Phoenix*, hard-shelled like armour but lacking the fire-power and military systems of marine armour.

"You were a spy for the human central government," Timoshene replied. Lisbeth sat alongside, watching her command post screens for the latest feeds from her office, where Semaya ran things in her absence. "Lisbeth Debogande is not the only one who can read. I read that the central human spy agency requires lifelong devotion. You then gained employment with Alice Debogande. Alice Debogande never did require that you renounce previous loyalties."

Hiro smiled lazily, one of those teeth-bearing grins that parren of all houses found alien and disconcerting. "My spy agency likes the Debogande family. They don't mind me getting employment there. So what about you, Timoshene? What house were you before Harmony?"

"It's not a polite question, Hiro," Lisbeth told him in English, warningly. She was the only one present who didn't need the translator. "I think you know that."

"So we can never question a parren's loyalty, huh?" Considering Timoshene with relaxed malice. "Despite them stabbing each other in the back all the time?"

"You're my guest, Hiro," Lisbeth reminded him. "You promised me you'd be on your best behaviour."

"This is my best behaviour," said Hiro. Lisbeth shook her head in exasperation, checking her left screen as the flyer's position approached Komaran Es.

"I was born to House Fortitude," Timoshene said calmly. The helmet finished its diagnostic, and he pulled it over his head, settling the rim carefully as the systems matched and the seals engaged. "I served in security there, and saw several conflicts. It was my blessing to phase to a house where those skills remained of use."

"Because Harmony and Fortitude are the two fighting houses, huh? Who's better?"

"A poorly conceived question. Each has strengths."

"Are you a better warrior now that you've phased to Harmony?"

"Assuredly," said Timoshene, voice muffled within the armoured helmet, visor raised. "But that will happen with age and experience, irrespective of phase. Are you a better warrior now that you have left your intelligence agency?"

"It's possible."

Timoshene glanced in Lisbeth's direction. "Tell me again why we must bring this one?"

"Because *Phoenix* will need to see what Rehnar found at Komaran Es," Lisbeth said shortly. "And because Gesul gave me permission to involve *Phoenix* crew as I see fit in all matters that are not expressly secret."

"Where is Rehnar, exactly?" Hiro wondered.

"That's a matter for Rehnar and his supporters," Lisbeth retorted. "As you also know." Some deposed leaders committed ritual suicide. Others faded into willing obscurity. Some became monks of obscure orders. Mostly it was not polite to enquire into their fate. But certainly no one worried about them making a comeback as a human politician might. Parren esteem did not survive great falls from power. Usually not parren lives, either.

Timoshene snapped his visor down and tested the responsiveness of his armoured limbs. As her security head, he answered primarily to Gesul, not to her. If Gesul gave him an order he would obey unquestioningly, irrespective of the consequences. If Lisbeth gave him an order, he'd obey so long as he saw no good reason not to. Among parren it was a significant distinction.

Lisbeth got her own helmet affixed as the shuttle approached. Timoshene assisted with a final check of her suit systems, but she was an old hand at EVAs now, and all was in order. They departed by a side airlock, a short jump in low G to the landing pad floor, and yet another of Defiance's uniquely alien cityscapes. Komaren Es was a gridwork of raised square structures, each the size of a city block. Looking up at the identical squares in rows, Lisbeth thought this vantage something like a tiny insect might have that had landed on a block of chocolate, and wandered into one of the crevasses that divided the squares.

A House Harmony functionary was awaiting them, and

exchanged brief protocols with Timoshene before leading them away in low, skipping bounces. There was much parren traffic, teams of engineers, strings of large dismounted generators, communication arrays with dishes aimed at the ever-present stars, no doubt untrusting of hardline communications.

The blocks themselves were open on the ground floor, where brilliant light flooded the vacuum. The guide led them into one such opening, surrounded by looming transport gantries and automated cranes that would once have shifted large loads onto waiting drysine vehicles. Beyond that, and an open logistics floor crawling with parren engineers, scientists and soldiers, was a wall of machinery that looked more like abstract modern art, a collision of strange shapes, pressure chambers and things that sparked and flashed.

"Manufacturing center of some sort," said Hiro, panning about to get a good view. No doubt he had helmet cam operating. *"Drysine age. Too advanced to be whatever was here before drysines."*

"Gesul's scholars say the AI race that built Defiance originally was never given a name by any organic species," Lisbeth said as they progressed inside. The size of the place was impressive. She wondered what the drysines had made here... and how it remained in such excellent, and evidently operational condition. "They're calling it 'Hechamtai', I think... that means 'builders' in one of the older parren tongues."

"The tongue is Tertai," said Timoshene. He bounced with his rifle racked, but his koren staff held openly. Lisbeth guessed its unsheathed blade-end would be an effective enough weapon against unarmoured suits, but mostly it was display. Lisbeth was a high ranking official, Timoshene was her guard, and the koren told all they might encounter to behave accordingly. *"Widely spoken still in several far flung places."*

"Hannachiam's quite vague on AI history," Lisbeth continued. "I suppose that's understandable given she can't actually talk. But Styx isn't much better."

"There are some cultures that don't consider it polite to talk of the ancestors," said Hiro. *"AIs aren't much on history, they're always about the*

future." Their guide brought them to a halt before a railing, behind which there was a good viewing platform for a look across a cavern through the heavy machinery ahead. *"So this is what Rehnar nearly opened fire on Tif to stop us from seeing."*

"Advanced AI manufacturing," said the guide — a middle-rank from Gesul's science detachment, Lisbeth's visor ID informed her. *"The most advanced."*

"Making what?" Lisbeth asked.

"AI brains."

Lisbeth blinked. Within the cavern, there wasn't actually a lot to see. Most of the advanced machines did their work within enclosed shells, some of them no doubt holding extreme environments or nano-machinery that could not be exposed to the vacuum. But the place hummed and throbbed, linked by a spidery network of cords and umbilicals, and a brief drift into infra-red showed an array of bright colour on Lisbeth's visor, some hot red, others cold blue.

"Well no, hang on," said Lisbeth. "We... I mean *Phoenix* made AI brains just in its little Engineering facilities, using the machinery we captured earlier. Why does it need all this?"

"That was a repair job on an existing damaged unit," Hiro corrected. *"My understanding was that Styx already had most of the bits and pieces she needed to strip and make a new drone brain from scratch. But you have to make all those bits and pieces first, I guess."*

"This facility does not make drones," said the guide, with the smug self-importance of a man with a great discovery. *"It makes queens."*

Lisbeth gasped. Timoshene gave her a blank-visored look — he hated it when she did that. "Queens! Of course! I mean, look at the size of this place!"

"Worth shooting someone down to keep a secret," Hiro murmured. *"I wonder if Rehnar was planning to build any more."*

"We have not yet ascertained," said the guide.

There followed a short tour, and the sight of many parren scientists in EVA suits, all peering at the strange alien tech and exchanging notes via shared holographic workspace, painting pictures in the space between them on how it all might work. Timoshene and his guards took a brief detour to inspect some security vulnerability, and Lisbeth found herself momentarily alone with Hiro.

Hiro flashed a laser-light on her faceplate, projecting from beneath his own faceplate. Her own coms function detected a lasercom channel connecting, and she opened it. "Hiro," she said with annoyance, "they won't like us talking off coms, I work for Gesul now and it's not polite..."

"*Screw polite,*" said Hiro. "*Lis. Do you have any idea what you're trying to achieve with the parren?*"

Lisbeth blinked. Past the faceplate polarisation she could faintly make out his eyes, intense on her own, just several handspans away. "Achieve? Hiro, humanity needs a representative among the parren. If the alo/deepynines are the threat we think they are, we're going to need all the help we can get..."

"*So that's the plan? Get them to help humanity? Join hands and fight our war, if it comes to that?*"

"The alo/deepynines are everyone's enemy, Hiro," Lisbeth said firmly. "You saw what they did to Mylor Station. They've attacked parren space directly, and that makes it all parren's business."

"*And Gesul agrees with this? Or is he just using all the tools at his disposal to climb the slippery pole of parren power as fast as he can? Sure done a nice job of that, hasn't he?*"

He had, Lisbeth couldn't deny it. From second-in-command of the Domesh just a short time ago, to ruler of House Harmony today. "Parren associate in houses, but they're species-nationalists," she insisted. "They've a long history of putting divisions aside to fight great external threats. That's what Gesul's thinking."

"*He's told you that?*"

"A parren leader isn't going to explain his every motivation to his followers," Lisbeth said with growing frustration. "I'm sure that's his thinking. It underlies everything he's done."

"*Or maybe you're just getting attached. The guy's got charisma, I'll give him that.*"

"Hiro, if you've got doubts about Gesul, stop dancing around and say it."

"Aristan was the militant guy who wanted to unite the parren and fight hostile outsiders. I'm thinking we might have done better with him."

Lisbeth rolled her eyes... and wasn't that just like Hiro? Worldly spy or not, she'd been warned by family staff that there was a xenophobic, anti-alien streak running through Federal Intelligence, and Hiro was one of its proponents. The kinds of people who thought the tavalai needed to be not so much defeated as annihilated. Lisbeth didn't think Hiro was quite *that* bad, particularly not after this trip, but he had a bloody-minded way of always assuming the worst about anyone not human, and always having a violent solution ready at hand.

"That's not very helpful, Hiro," she told him now. "And no, you'd not have found Aristan the *slightest* bit useful, because *Aristan* would have joined forces with the deepynines to slit our throats if it suited him. Gesul is a moral and principled man, and there's a world of difference."

"You just have a good think about it, Lis," Hiro told her, undeterred. *"Because all these nice trappings you've acquired? It's not really about that, is it? This isn't about Gesul, or House Harmony... it's not even about you and me. It's about finding the best assistance for humanity. If it turns out that Gesul's not it, then you and I are going to have a problem. Aren't we?"*

* * *

"I DON'T EVEN SEE why we're having this discussion," said Lieutenant Rooke, skinny arms folded as he gazed out the heavy window at his beloved warship. *Phoenix* stood tall in the cavernous dock, enfolded in supports and gantries, ablaze in floodlight and showers of orange sparks where the automated drysine systems continued to work on the ship even when most Engineering crew were asleep. Two of the four months of repair work had been just getting Defiance's automated systems back on line, and figuring out how to get the enormous engine construction facilities a kilometre below the surface to start rolling again. Once that was done, repair times had been a fraction what they would have been at any other dock. "We need a crew, right? I mean, we can't work the ship without one, we're not drysines, we can't just automate everything. We're being offered a crew. Let's take it and go."

As many of *Phoenix*'s senior crew as could be spared from other duties gathered in the storage room beside the bay's control room, sitting on containers about an improvised table. At present, that meant Erik, Draper and Dufresne up one end, with Kaspowitz, Geish, Shilu and De Marchi along the left side. Hausler was at the far end, representing Operations, and Rooke — refusing to sit with his back to his beloved ship — sat with Trace, Dale and Jalawi on the right side opposite.

"Some of us don't think the crew will wear it," Erik replied, charitably not calling out Dufresne before the rest. "Who agrees? Dylan?"

He looked at Draper. Draper looked uncomfortable, in that way he got when asked things he didn't entirely trust his own opinion on. With Draper that was often the case on matters of morale and personnel management. On operations and systems, thankfully less so. "I honestly don't know, Captain," he said, and gave again that little helpless shrug that Erik found unbecoming of an officer. Erik could see Trace's stare boring a hole in the young Commander. Now her eyes shifted to him, demandingly. "It's not something I've asked them about very much. I'm a pilot, I talk pilot stuff."

Erik stared back at Trace. He's my responsibility, that stare said. I'll do it. Trace settled back, somewhat mollified. None of the other crew seemed to notice their fast, wordless exchange.

"Justine," said Erik, again passing up the opportunity to dump on her for her earlier disagreement.

Dufresne stiffened, a familiar posture for her slim frame. "Most of us fought in the Trimuvirate War," she said, her vowels tightly clipped with born-and-bred-spacer precision. "I saw little action compared to many of you here, but I saw my share. We've all lost friends to the tavalai. I think it would be naive to assume that the very strong feelings that come with those experiences can just be put aside. And I sense that the crew's morale is, forgive me Captain, the poorest it's been since *Phoenix* left Homeworld. I have heard cynical talk about Styx, for one thing, and a lot of trepidation about the consequences of having her aboard. Some of that cynicism was aimed at the command crew's judgement. I think that if we invite... what is it, one hundred tavalai aboard? More than one hundred, on top of everything else? I predict trouble."

Erik looked along the table to his left. "Kaspo?"

Kaspowitz stirred his coffee and tapped his foot, one long leg jumping compulsively. He looked unhappy. "I'm less unhappy with the tavalai crew than I am with the destination, Captain. If we were to be staying in somewhat familiar space, I think it would have a chance of working. But we're going where few if any humans have ever gone before. It just seems that the longer we stay away from home, the less familiar everything becomes. Yesterday we had drysines on the ship. Today we've got tavalai. Mental strain is a cumulative thing. If the crew perceive that everything is getting progressively harder and stranger without end..." he shrugged. "We used to know what we were fighting for. The more alien everything becomes, the less certain everyone gets."

"We're fighting to find answers to this technology that threatens to wipe us out," Trace said coolly to her old friend. "I don't think it could be clearer."

"On the orders and assistance of *Makimakala*," Kaspowitz returned, "who are themselves following orders from some other flat-head froggy further up the chain. We might know who's in charge, but lower-ranked crew will wonder, sometimes loudly. That's just how it is."

"Stefan," said Erik, moving to the next in line.

"What Kaspo said, Captain," said the often grim Stefan Geish. "I can't tell what the crew think, though some of my Scan crew I'm pretty sure won't like it. I can say that *I* don't like it, if I'm allowed to state my own opinion."

"Of course you are," Erik said coolly. "Wei."

"Captain," said Wei Shilu with his usual elegance, "I think it will be extremely complicated and fraught with communication and cultural issues. I don't think those can be underestimated. But I think it is probably the only way to get *Phoenix* operating at optimum once more, and if you think we should do it, I'm on board."

Erik nodded his appreciation. "Lionel?"

Lieutenant Lionel De Marchi was Kaspowitz's second, a young ace navigator who'd given up a promising acting career to join Fleet. He still had the looks — lean faced with dark, wavy hair and intelligent eyes, and he spoke with a drawl like the backworlds freehold farmer his parents were. "Captain, I think Lieutenant Kaspowitz has it right, myself." No surprises there, Erik thought. "I mean, as a navigator, I can't deny it'd be fun to go see the croma. But that's a real long way, even for us. Crew gotta trust each other out there. And with tavalai... I think that's asking a lot."

"Trey," said Erik.

Hausler smiled easily. "Need another shuttle, Captain. Need more pilots, need more marines, need more crew, I don't care if they're green and croak, I don't care if they smell bad and eat raw fish. They're crew, Captain Pram recommends them so we know they're good... like Rooke says, I don't know what there is to discuss."

"Daniel," said Erik, "your opinion has been noted." Rooke nodded uncomfortably, as a few of the crew gave him odd looks at the name. Rooke never went by Daniel. A few of them probably hadn't known. Erik hadn't, until he'd looked at his file. "Rufus? Anything to say?"

Lieutenant Rufus Jalawi nodded vigorously. "Which of you assholes has been letting your people clog up the B Sector toilets? B Sector toilets are for marines, but we've come back from shift three times now and found our closest toilet block smells like someone crawled in there and died..."

"Anything to say about the *present topic*?" Erik interrupted drily.

Jalawi looked at him blankly. Then grinned. "No, I'm good." Trace gave him a look of pure affection. All the marines loved Jalawi — he was like a big, brown, bald dog that liked to chase balls and lick your face. It was occasionally astonishing to recall that he was also an exceptional platoon commander with a combat record nearly as shiny and somewhat longer than Trace's.

"Ty," said Erik, finally coming to Tyson Dale, grim-faced and hard-jawed as ever, blue eyes scouring the table with contempt.

"You're all a bunch of fucking pussies," said Dale, looking clearly at the naysayers. Dufresne glared. Geish rolled his eyes with a world-weary sigh. Shilu smiled patronisingly. Draper looked uncomfortable. De Marchi looked to Kaspowitz for direction. Kaspowitz smiled wryly at the big marine, and raised his middle finger. Rooke looked impatient for the whole thing to end so he could get back to his ship. Dale said nothing more, and looked at Erik to indicate he was done.

"Thank you Ty," said Erik. "Constructive as always."

"You bet," said Dale.

"Trace," said Erik, to round the whole thing off.

"Whatever you think is best, Captain," Trace said simply, gazing straight back. Her eyes flicked to Rooke and back, seeking permission to address the next topic. Erik nodded. "Rooke, you seem to be fine with working alongside tavalai. What would you say to drysine drones?"

Rooke blinked at her. "They're ready? How long?"

"Tomorrow, Styx says. And no, they're not exactly 'ready', their cognitive abilities are still transitioning, they won't pick up new things as quickly or as precisely as we'd like. Nor as safely, I'd imagine. But the point is, that's now up to you. Supervise them, train them, show them how it's done. Start them on the small stuff first, then work your way up. It will probably slow you down for the first few days, but after that, they work incredibly fast once they've mastered a technical skill. It will be up to your crew to decide which skills they're best suited to, and how to go about upskilling them."

For the first time since he'd entered the room, Rooke looked enthusiastic to be there. "Major, could you lend me some of your expertise with the drones? Your Command Squad in particular know a lot more about their behaviour and skillsets than my engineers at this point."

"Absolutely, I'll be there myself, and Styx will have further input. Peanut is still recovering from his damage in the firefight, but he's coming along well, he might be a day or two late. Probably best that you deal with Wowser and Bucket first — they're the least socialised, Wowser in particular, but then he's very good at following instructions and doing drone-like things, so he might even be easier for you to get working. Peanut needs the most instruction, but he's the easiest to get along with because he's the friendliest. Bucket's somewhere in the middle."

"Friendliest?" Rooke asked, halfway between a frown and an amazed smile.

"Peanut's a nice little guy," said Trace. "He's not a dog, you can't over-generalise, but you're safe with Peanut. I've seen Styx tell him to do things and he actually ignores her, for a while at least — he's got his own thing going on in his head. Wowser would gut you like a fish if Styx told him to. Be warned."

Rooke swallowed. "Right."

9

The human was checking his weapons. Timoshene considered him without appearing to, helmet on, systems cycling in preparation for egress, powerplant humming and filters flushing via the umbilical connection to the shuttle's seat.

"Why this one again?" Dalray asked on private coms, excluding the human.

"It is Gesul's command," Timoshene formulated shortly. Dalray did not look at him either, inspecting his own weapons with professional thoroughness. *"The human spy knows much about the AIs. He is an expert in their communications technology. Gesul says that he has been tracing strange communications across Defiance for many days. Following Rehnar's discovery of the queen-making facility, his suspicions have grown worse."*

"Suspicions of what?" asked Shola.

"Of unauthorised AI activity. There is only one queen on Defiance. Possible answers are limited."

The human spoke, and Timoshene did not like the tone of that strange, alien tongue nearly as much as he liked Lisbeth's. The voice of a woman, he thought, had greater aesthetic qualities in any tongue, with any species, than that of a man. *"Gesul must trust you,"* spoke the translator in Timoshene's ear. *"So many security personnel in his service, and yet he chooses Lisbeth's personal security chief for this mission."*

"I am honoured by Gesul-sa's faith," Timoshene said flatly. "Do you have your assassin bugs with you today?"

"No."

"Then she scares you."

"She scares every living thing with a brain. But mostly, she sees too much at most times. There is no need to make it easier for her." The human's narrow eyes flicked to Timoshene's secondary weapon — a shotgun in its thigh-sheath astride the hard-shelled but light armour. *"Can I see?"*

Timoshene expertly drew the shotgun, flipped it muzzle first and handed the grip to Hiro. Hiro took it, examining with fast, professional interest. *"Nice balance."* He pumped the breech, peering inside. *"Good for low-G, don't think it would jam. Ranged detonation?"* Inspecting the magazine and shells.

"Anti-personnel shells explode short," Timoshene agreed. "As much a grenade launcher as a shotgun."

"Very nice." Hiro put the magazine back, chambered and de-chambered a round, then handed it back. Timoshene indicated Hiro's pistol, as much from courtesy as interest. Hiro handed it. The grip was a little too compact for a parren hand, human hands and fingers being shorter. The mechanism was electro-mag, and despite the narrow caliber, the muzzle velocity would put holes in anything short of marine-grade armour. The tiny sensor beneath the muzzle indicated targeting interface, telling the wielder exactly where the bullet would go — useful for pistols and rifles as it wasn't for shotguns.

"Standard issue or personal preference?" Timoshene asked, handing the pistol back. The tone of the shuttle's engines had changed, a slow decline indicating descent.

"Both," said Hiro, holstering the pistol in his front webbing and pulling on the helmet. *"Even standardised weapons can become a preference. Too much personalisation can interfere with inter-operability."*

"Agreed."

"One thing," said Hiro, looking at all four parren. *"For this mission,*

no external coms, no trackers, completely silent. Autistic, the human techs call it, I don't know if that translates."

"It does. We have made the adjustments."

"You are hiding from her?" Shola asked suspiciously.

"Maybe a little."

"Tell us," Timoshene demanded. "What do you suspect?"

"I suspect nothing. But most of Defiance remains unexplored, many systems have barely aged and remain functional, and I have been detecting signals that suggest recently restored function in places where no function should exist. Because of the squabbles between your denominations, parren have been far more focused on confronting each other than on exploring Defiance. It leaves us exposed."

"Exposed to what? Defiance is old and dead."

"And waking up. Like Hannachiam woke up. She's got far more control over Defiance than parren and humans do combined."

"Humans have insisted that Hannachiam is not threatening."

"No, Hanna's quite friendly. But Hanna's got no idea what really constitutes a threat to organics, and she relies on outsiders to give her advice. Styx can communicate more to her in ten seconds than we can in a year. So guess who Hanna's largest influence is?"

"And why have you not communicated this concern before?" Shola accused him.

Hiro laughed, helmet shaking slightly as he shook his head. *"Oh buddy,"* he said. *"We've been trying, trust me. But parren just want to fight each other, and Phoenix is mostly just trying to get our ship running. No wonder Hanna talks to Styx instead."*

* * *

IT TOOK seventeen minutes at reduced surface speeds. This was Komaren Dai, almost devoid of lights, its horizon indistinguishable from black space in all directions but back toward where the blaze of newly-installed civilisation still glowed. Timoshene performed a final check of his suit systems as the shuttle began its descent, rotating tail-forward to slow its progress with a rumble of thrust. External cameras fixed on their destination for the first time, and on visor-vision Timoshene saw a jumble of dark shapes that seemed to shift as the perspective changed. Vision switched to ultra-violet, and still there was little to see. As a child, Timoshene recalled being afraid of the dark, but when he'd phased to House Harmony the last vestiges of that fear had faded. Darkness was a thing of beauty and stillness, of quieted colours and cool meditation. But venturing this far from the occupied regions of Defiance, he felt almost as though his child-hood fears had returned. This many light-years from any sun the absence of light could be overwhelming, like a physical force that drowned out all but the stars. The shuttle switched to infra-red, and received only cold greys and blues in reply.

The pilot hit underside floodlights, and brightness blazed upon a series of broken crane arms, mechanisms leaning wildly askew. Landing pads and surface grapples were broken and torn, clearly the result of long ago weapons fire. This had been a docks, evidently pulverised in the war that had destroyed the drysines and ended the Machine Age for good.

"*Possible landing site ahead,*" came the pilot's report on coms. "*There will be no full landing, there is a chance the pad will not hold the shuttle's weight with all that damage. Engines will stay running, suggest you exit from top hatch and jump from left wing.*"

"Timoshene hears you." He disengaged his seat restraints and gestured at Shola, Dalray and Kino to follow. With visors down and suits pressurised, Timoshene gave a command that turned the entire forward hold to vacuum, rendering the dorsal airlock unnecessary. All four parren, and then Hiro, clambered out and onto the top of the hovering shuttle.

Afraid of the dark or not, that younger Timoshene would have found the scene unutterably exciting — standing atop a hovering shuttle with its engines burning, surveying the floodlit scene of a strange mechanical graveyard — huge, skeletal arms stretching for the non-existent sky, shadows moving in ghostly unison as the flood-lights moved. But now the older, wiser Timoshene felt only the calm satisfaction of knowing that he was where the universe intended him,

serving his rightful master, performing his function for the better-
ment of all. It was a truism among warriors that nearly all of the
phasing went from Fortitude to Harmony, and rarely the other way
around. Harmony warriors called Fortitude the house of children,
waving their swords and playing at soldier. Harmony was where
young soldiers went to learn true courage and purpose.

Timoshene peered off the edge of the shuttle's left shoulder —
this model's engines were underside, and not dominating the far
wingtip as some did. He gave the pilot instructions, aligning the jump
as the pilot watched from the cockpit ahead, holding them steady.
Timoshene jumped, a slow descent in low-G to an intact portion of
pad, then a fast bounce to clear the way for the next. Shola followed,
then Hiro, coming down touching midair icons to activate his map
display.

Behind, the shuttle powered up, Timoshene's visor darkening to
block the thruster-glare as it regained altitude, then went in search of
somewhere safer to land. The brightness cleared and the five
explorers looked about, their breath harsh and loud within the
confines of their helmets. Timoshene's visor switched to infra-red,
each suit equipped with its own helmet flashlights, emitting in wave-
lengths invisible to the naked eye but illuminating everything quite
clearly on IR.

The pad on which he was standing had been peeled like an
orange, huge sheets of steel bending inward with the force of some
ancient projectile. Within, long, deep levels dropped into cavernous
interiors.

"Well?" Timoshene asked the human. He glanced at Hiro, and
found him looking straight up through his visor. Timoshene looked,
and saw teeming billions of stars, suddenly revealed in the absence of
the shuttle's lights. Deep space was never entirely dark, and the
starfield this far from any illuminated settlement was spectacular
beyond belief. Typically the Defiance sky showed the moving glow of
low-orbit ships passing over, but now there was nothing but stars. He
thought he knew what Hiro was looking for. "Can you see any human
suns from here?"

"I don't know," said Hiro, sounding faintly wistful even past the translator. *"Maybe if I turned on the visor starchart. But there's no time. We have to go down."* He took a recon ball, activated and dropped it. The ball fell slowly, adjusting course with light thrust. Timoshene saw the feed highlight on his visor, and blinked on it — the map expanded as the ball showed what it saw — deep levels below, falling faster now, past machinery floors... and suddenly a concourse of sorts. Thrust halted its fall, and it skittered sideways and attached to a beam, awaiting recovery. *"You receiving that feed?"* Hiro asked.

"Yes." It had been one of the first protocols their techs had worked on, between *Phoenix* and Gesul's people — the ability to share tactical data without hassle. "Parren will lead."

Timoshene stepped off, thrust increasing as his fall accelerated, angling him into the middle of the gaping hole through the decks. The weapon that caused this must have been enormous, he thought, gazing about as he fell. The edges of the hole were melted, old steel frozen like liquid honey turned to ice. Levels passed, like layers of a wedding cake, too disfigured and smashed together to even imagine what they'd once been... only here below came a thicker layer, open space and a gap ahead through the destruction. Timoshene angled his suit that way, controls set for intuitive flight control, translating body motions and gestures into thrust direction and power.

The intuitive control deactivated when he landed on an intact rim, enabling him to walk once more. The recon ball detached from its wall and returned to Hiro, landing behind him. Timoshene bounced ahead.

Within the opening was an enormously large passage, a former thoroughfare for smaller spaceships. Cavernous and filled with debris, like the cast away toys of some giant, thoughtless child. Old shuttles, spaceships unidentifiable... perhaps sentient AI ships, Timoshene had heard the parren researchers talking about them. AIs did not need to enter and exit ships as parren did — they were machines themselves, some were built directly into the bridge. Sentient ships, interfacing with thousands of other sentient, synthetic forms about them...

And here they were, cast on their sides, blasted by long-ago fire-power, now cold and still in the silence of millennia passed. Hiro came up behind, and Timoshene bounced lightly forward, gazing at the giant wrecks as he passed. Ahead, one part of the passage had collapsed, machinery and systems in the walls making a curtain of old, dead technology. Timoshene hit thrust, not powerful enough to make him fly on a full gravity world, but here it propelled him to the top of the wrecked hull, then to bounce along its surface. His boots slipped on a covering of metallic grit, lying over everything like silver dust and glowing on his helmet's IR like ice. Steel so old it flaked, and made dust like the insides of an old mansion... that, and residue from the blasts.

"Up ahead," he said, reading his map. "Six hundred terek."

He jumped from the dead ship's hull, grounding softly and continuing to bound. Here on his left was a dead drone — drysine, no doubt, as they'd all been drysine in this last, futile stand. They'd beaten the deepynines, and thought they'd won. Timoshene wondered if a drone could feel regret, or despair. Or even the black irony that after so much unchallenged dominance over organic beings for so long, the machines had done most of the work in wiping each other out, only for their new organic allies to complete the final remainder and end the Machine Age for good.

"*This one is new,*" said Dalray. On visual came a feed from Dalray's suit — a drone, but different. Bigger, thicker limbs, several of them blasted off.

"*There were many models,*" said Hiro. "*We've only seen a fraction of them. Ours are the basic multi-purpose, these look like heavier workers, for larger engineering jobs.*"

"This was a transport hub," said Timoshene. Both Dalray's and Hiro's voices sounded tense. Being in here was quite an experience. It felt like death, and of old empires long since destroyed, but recently reawakened. A man of less-calm mind could get very jumpy, looking at all these bodies and recalling just how much of Defiance had actually survived intact for twenty thousand years. Hannachiam, no less.

"*The anti-aging nanos don't seem to be working here,*" said Hiro, as they bounced past yet another large ship. This one's entire rear section had been sheared off by a new incoming round, making a series of visible holes through the above decking, each the size of a house. *"Not surprising, considering the damage it's taken. Three hundred metres."*

"How do nanotech bots survive so long themselves?" asked Kino.

"There are radioactive metals built into the structures," said Hiro. *"The bots feed on radiation, and the half-life is hundreds of thousands of years. So it's pretty much a limitless power source. The bots congregate on that radiation and build colonies, which build more colonies, then go out and spread and keep everything maintained as best they can."*

"Enough radiation to harm organics?" Shola wondered.

"No more than background. Nanos don't need much — it's an increase of about five percent on what you'd receive on Defiance anyway."

Finally they emerged from the long tunnel into a deep hole beneath the surface. Its sides were wider than the ceremonial grounds Timoshene had frequented as a child on his homeworld, imagining the day when he might parade upon them as an adult in service of his master. The hole was perfectly circular save for observation features and protrusions he couldn't name. The ancient sides glistened with steel-dust, and several perfect ordnance holes gaped black and empty. IR light poured through the steel framework ceiling, some distant light source sweeping a glaring beam past the obstructions... probably a shuttle, Timoshene thought, many kilometres distant. Without the IR feed on his visor, it would be invisible.

"This was the way to the surface for all these ships," Hiro observed, looking slowly around. *"The roof would have retracted."*

"A factory hub," said Timoshene. To one side, at ground level, a huge, cavernous entrance beckoned. "This way." He bounded, his men following. Gazing up at the high, curving walls, he wondered what this place must have looked like in its prime. Filled with drysine workers, like the insides of an insect hive. None of them able to imagine that one day it would all look like this — cold, broken and deserted.

Inside the doorway was like stepping into a giant cave, filled with giant scaffolds. Timoshene stared up, seeing suit IR light reflecting back in his visor, structures cluttered overhead like a forest of artificial limbs. Those limbs dangled now, long disused and broken about the frames of conveyors, making great highways against the ceiling. On the ground head, Hiro saw a giant hauler, a vehicle with an array of cargo racks for vertical storage.

"An assembly line," Hiro said, bouncing gently forward. *"The vehicles must have carried finished product to shuttles outside. The arms must have been for mid-air assembly. They kept the floor clear for vehicle access."*

"The product may have been variable," said Shola. "AI manufacturing need not follow strict lines. All the machines can think."

"Your scans are incapable of being more precise than this location?" Timoshene asked Hiro.

"No."

"Then we must look further back. This way."

He bounced with purpose toward where multiple conveyors defied all expectations of a wall, burrowing through and back like a giant worm devouring an apple. Each frame in the conveyor had multiple shape-shifting grips to carry the variable sizes of things being manufactured... as Shola had suggested. Nothing rusted in a vacuum, but still it looked old, like bread that could not go mouldy, but was instead stiff and dry. None of these mechanisms had moved in many an age.

"I'd recommend weapons," said Hiro, pulling his pistol.

"Weapons," Timoshene told his men, and pulled his shotgun from the canvas sheath beside his thigh armour.

The far side of the wall was all hacksaw nest. Humans and parren required some sense of architectural order, things arrayed in levels. In hacksaw nests, everything blended together, a tangle of machinery interwoven into the very fabric of the surrounding infrastructure.

Timoshene leapt to the frame of one of the mass transit chutes used by drones, where magnetic rails and rubber grips would transform a drone's body into its own vehicle. Now the chute was empty, interior mechanisms dissolved away with age, weaving through the clutter of machinery like the skeleton of some long dead alien snake with circular ribs.

They progressed with simple, long-striding leaps from one rib of the passage to another, weaving down and across as AIs, contrary to all organic prejudice, disliked straight lines and right angles. Ahead was not so much a wall — for AIs disliked those as well — as a profusion of branching structural supports, like the root system of a giant tree growing somewhere above. The function was like a wall, bracing the internals in Defiance's light gravity and making certain nothing fell down. About those supporting roots grew a series of smoothed bulbs, the most orderly structure Timoshene had seen so far, reflecting dull IR light from the advancing suits with a smooth-polished sparkle.

A light blinked red on the audio-sensory function of Timoshene's visor. He blinked on it as he moved, the icon directly alongside respiratory and life-support indicators, and received a projected map of what the suit's sensors had gathered so far of this hacksaw maze. Here in red, moving along the elevated transit corridor, were audio-signals generated by the movement of four parren and one human — vibrations caused by boots on steel, which transmitted through surrounding structures and were received by sensors on his own suit. It was the only way audio could work in a vacuum — vibrations moving through the only substance that could carry them. Typically they were hard to pinpoint, but this indicator was showing several coming from... directly above. Twenty metres above.

"Hiro," said Timoshene, in that prickling state of early alertness that was not yet tension. "My suit sensors are showing me an audio signal twenty metres overhead. Something is moving."

"Yeah, I was wondering about that," Hiro said conversationally. *"I was about to ask if you saw it too, or if it was just my new sensors playing tricks."*

"Those silver bulbs do not look like any sort of metal," said Dalray, pausing with a one-handed grip on the passage frame to look more closely. The nearest was just a few metres to one side now, and looked as though in stronger light it would give them all an elongated reflec-

tion of themselves, like a convex mirror. *"My visuals suggest a ceramic-based alloy. We are looking for any sign of unauthorised manufacturing activity, yes? This material will not show residual heat."*

"Can you see an opening?" Timoshene asked Dalray.

"Perhaps on the far side. It appears to integrate with surrounding infrastructure."

"Kino," Timoshene instructed his third man. "Go and look."

Kino climbed quickly to the top of the rib structure, no difficulty in low-G, and made a simple jump onto the top of the smooth ovoid. That produced another audio-spike on Timoshene's scan, vibrations reaching him through the one-handed grip on his frame and the soles of his boots. He looked behind, shotgun ready in his other hand... and saw something silver flash. Like a reflection, a piece of metal moving and briefly catching the light. In here the only light being generated was by the suits, in diffuse infra-red.

"I saw something move behind us," Timoshene said tersely. "Not big, just a flash of light."

"Kino, what do you see?" asked Shola.

"There are several openings," said Kino, grasping an adjoining support to peer over the edge. *"This conveyor system looks sophisticated. I have no expertise in the area, but this does not look old to me. This looks new. And functional. These assembly arms are not decayed at all."*

On Timoshene's audio-display, more vibrations, displayed as red dots. There were multiple now, all around them, above and below. Invisible in the maze. "Multiple audio spikes. It looks as though we're surrounded."

"I can see them too," Dalray agreed.

"My coms are blank," said Hiro, with matter-of-fact cool. *"If it's okay with you guys, I'm going to call for human help if I can get through."*

"Do that," Timoshene agreed, scanning his own coms in vain for an outside reception. Something was jamming them. "I have no coms either," he said, now feeling the cool certainty of danger. In the Fortitude phase, his heart would be pounding by now, every muscle aching for a fight. Some Fortitude parren were known to shoot at shadows. There was no danger of that here. "That's powerful jamming," he said coolly. "It could be visible to sources outside its immediate effective zone."

"Then perhaps the drysine queen might hear it and send help?" Dalray suggested.

"I'm quite certain she'll hear it," Hiro said grimly. *"But no, I'm sure she won't send help."* A pause as they all took that in. *"I was worried she might try something like this, but there was no way to stop her. It's all starting to make sense now. Timoshene, I suggest that we leave, get back to the surface and signal for support. We don't even need radio — a spotlight would do it."*

"Yes," Timoshene said shortly. "We are climbing up." He followed Kino's path up the framework, Hiro, Dalray and Shola following. Sure enough, the structures climbed up above, though the ceiling was invisible past thickets of unidentifiable technology in the maze. "Kino, join us above. Kino?"

There was no reply. *Now* Timoshene felt that first, icy prickle of fear. All parren felt it, even warriors of the Harmony phase. But here it felt like another of life's most unavoidable things slipping into place. Fortitude parren were shamed by their fear. Harmony parren embraced and accepted it, and pushed on regardless.

"Kino!" Timoshene demanded, shotgun pointed out that way, scanning.

"He's dead," Hiro said grimly, leaping up to the next grip and climbing, trying to watch all ways at once — a difficulty inside a civilian EVA helmet. *"If we don't move fast, we will be too."*

"We do not know he's dead," Timoshene retorted, and prepared to leap onto the ovoid fabricator where Kino had been standing.

"Behind!" Hiro shouted, then the flashing of his pistol's muzzle as Timoshene spun and fired the shotgun directly into the drone's metallic face... but the drone ducked mid-air and took the blast on its head carapace. Timoshene leaped as it landed, missing him with a swing of its hyper-vibrating foreleg.

He landed on the ovoid manufacturing sphere as his suit warned him of more movement left, and leaped again rather than wasting time looking, across empty space and collecting an armful of gantry as something multi-legged zoomed through the space where he'd been. It landed opposite, staring as it tracked him, and for a split-second Timoshene got a good look at it — one armed and old-looking, not especially big and seeming to be made of abandoned old parts. He levelled his shotgun and fired, sending it spinning off-kilter as it scrambled away.

"They're old and they have no firearms!" he shouted, scrambling upward and looking for his next leap. "We have a chance, move fast and watch your backs!"

He jumped for another handhold, the scaffolding of engineering features making a ladder in the low-G, then spared a look back to see Dalray and Shola following with fast grips and leaps of their own... and something hit Shola in mid-leap, a flash of steel and then only pieces of armour amid a red curtain of blood, spinning as they fell slowly to the ground.

"They don't need firearms," Timoshene said grimly, leaping up for his next hold. He abandoned his intended grip as another drone appeared to the side, firing repeated shotgun blasts that detonated just short and shredded the hacksaw's head and shoulders. It dropped, legs convulsing, and Hiro swung himself onto a new gantry above, firing several shots at something to one side. Then he looked down.

"Don't look now but we've got the biggest damn hacksaw I ever saw climbing after us!"

Contrary to that odd human instruction, Timoshene looked. Beneath him, climbing ponderously up the tangle of gantries and supports, was indeed the biggest drone he'd ever seen — it looked like a giant crab, half as big again as Styx in her present body, with great, humming forelegs and multiple utility attachments that were thankfully unoccupied. Timoshene levelled his shotgun at its multi-eyed head and fired, but the big drone held an armoured forearm before its eyes like a man squinting into a sandstorm, and the heavy explosive shells sparked fragments off the blade.

Timoshene abandoned that useless gesture, leaped one-handed

to a new gantry, then up to a new series of holds that presented a promising way toward the ceiling. "Dalray, on me!"

Dalray remained a level below, blasting fire at several drones that attempted to approach beyond cover and paid for it. But now, having abandoned his climb to fight with the two-handed weapon, he'd sacrificed mobility for a static defence. "*Go!*" Dalray shouted, still firing. "*Someone must stay to provide cover!*"

Timoshene paused, resetting his shotgun to projectile with a flick of his thumb and putting an explosive round into a drone ascending the superstructure fast at Dalray's rear. "Dalray, climb one-handed, the weapon does not require both hands. A mobile defence is superior..."

The portion of gantry supporting Dalray abruptly fell, cut from somewhere below by a hacksaw blade. Dalray fell, then disappeared without another sound but the thudding of more shotgun rounds over coms, then static.

Something small with limbs and small jets zoomed past as Timoshene scrambled across the top of some kind of giant, dome-shaped containment shell and ducked behind attached conduits, looking about as the small flying thing came back. He shot it and it spun from an explosion of silver fragments and fell. Hiro held the dome's other side, firing but not attempting to climb further.

A glance up revealed why — several drones now above him, seemingly anticipating this path of escape. Timoshene fired at one, driving it back to cover — their armour was nothing like the strength of drysine combat drones, and these less powerful weapons hurt them, he could see shrapnel holes tearing great fistfuls of damage through limbs and torso. But there were others scrambling into cover up there, hiding in the maze, and a continued climb would bring him straight into their reach.

He fired the last of his magazine and reloaded quickly from his thigh pouch, having practised that manoeuvre many times in heavy gloves. Movement beside him announced Hiro's move away from the edge of the containment facility, blasting another drone that tried to follow him. It lurched, legs collapsing, then began a slow slide off the spherical side. That small human magfire pistol was more deadly than it looked.

"They're above us," Hiro panted, taking a knee as he swivelled to search for other ways out of the maze. *"They've got flying recon units, no way we could hide."*

"Can your recon handball escape and send for help?" Timoshene asked. Hiro fired again at a drone that ventured from cover, and sent it scuttling back. From below he could feel continuing heavy vibration — the big crab was still climbing. It would take longer, too large to fit through the smaller gaps in the maze, but it would get here very soon. When it did, smallarms would damage it, but not fatally.

"Yes, but its thrust is weak against even this gravity," Hiro answered Timoshene. *"I've only got one and I need to get it a clear shot — the recon drones will grab it otherwise."*

"We die here," said Timoshene. It was obvious, but a human might need some help to grasp it. "I will leave a message on my audio for House Harmony to hear if they retrieve my body. I suggest you do the same."

"Yeah, great," said Hiro. *"Hi guys, I've been killed by hacksaws. Can you tell?"* Something large emerged past an obstructing bundle of unidentified pipes, then the big, clawed legs of the crab-drone, two at a time and placed with ponderous precision on frames and gantries as it crawled toward the top of the containment shell. *"Aim for the legs!"*

Hiro fired several shots, and a leg shuddered but did not sever. Timoshene's first shot blasted ineffectually off its carapace, aiming as close to the head as those protecting claws would allow. A second shot took off a leg, but then Timoshene saw several other drones rushing, and shouted warning. He put a big round through one drone's head, and it somersaulted as unresponsive legs caught on a gantry and tripped, but two more were coming from the right side...

One of them half-exploded in a spray of fragments, then another went spinning like a top, legs sheared off. A white missile contrail streaked at the crab drone, and Timoshene's visor blanked to dark in the subsequent flash, clearing to reveal one entire side of the big drone ripped away as though cleaved by a sword. Timoshene stared up, and saw the unmistakable, dangerous silhouettes of *Phoenix* marines, some coming through the maze head-first with impatient speed, blazing fire at remaining drones as they fell.

Hiro let out a triumphant yell, and then an armoured marine was landing before him as marines continued flooding past and around — the fourth Phoenix Company unit, Timoshene saw, the one the humans called 'Delta'. Timoshene's coms registered a new channel as the jamming abruptly vanished.

"*Hey Hiro,*" the Delta Commander said conversationally — Crozier, her name was. "*Didn't the Major warn you about playing with drones?*"

"*Hey LT,*" said the human spy. Playing it cool, Timoshene judged. But he could hear the tremor in the younger man's voice, and was not fooled. "*The Major tell you to keep an eye on me?*"

"*Something like that. Something about spies and small children always getting into trouble.*" The drone Timoshene had shot earlier showed signs of life, trying to get feet under it despite mostly missing a head. Crozier levelled her Koshaim and nonchalantly blew it off its resting place.

"*She loves me,*" said Hiro. "*I can tell.*"

"*So what the hell, huh?*" said Crozier, looking around. Then settled on Timoshene, as the parren checked his magazine for remaining rounds. "*What did you find?*"

"It is unclear," Timoshene replied. There was definitely no quaver in his voice. This rescue was good fortune, but another old House Harmony saying said that fortune was harmonious. "Best that you ask your drysine queen. I think she will know."

10

Trace sat in PH-1's command post with her visor up, the hold at full pressure in the presence of Command Squad and Bravo Platoon. In the seat alongside sat Hiro, also visor-up, checking his big pistol and running internal suit diagnostics off the command post's screens. He looked relatively calm for a man who had nearly died just now. Not as calm as Timoshene had been, per Crozier's report. Timoshene had reported back to Gesul on the marines' com links, eschewing privacy for efficiency, and to the humans it had sounded as though he were discussing the non-existent weather.

Trace's com link connected — open channel so everyone could hear. *"Hello Major."*

"Hello Styx. I'm on my way to see you with Hiro and Bravo Platoon. I'm sure you know why."

"Yes Major. The three drones have been disarmed and will adopt a non-assertive posture. I look forward to your arrival."

"Yes Styx. My marines will not assume an aggressive posture unless threatened. We will be armed, but no weapons will be aimed. I trust that this will be appropriate."

"Of course, Major."

"ETA fourteen minutes. See you soon." Trace disconnected. "Lieutenant, you get all that?"

"Yes Major," said Lieutenant Alomaim, seated on her other side and observing his own screens. "I think it's better if you go in alone with Command Squad, you all know her best. Bravo will establish a perimeter, and looking at this activity on scan I think we should keep Heavy Squad on guard at the pads."

Trace nodded — scan was showing a lot of parren activity, shuttles zooming to the new zone, marine units in deployment, others probing deeper within despite Trace's suggestions that it wasn't a good idea until they knew more. She'd explained the situation to Lisbeth, who was now talking to Gesul about why it wasn't a good idea. Lisbeth had said that Gesul wanted to know what Styx had to say, to which Trace had replied that he'd know as soon as she did.

She looked again at Hiro. "You sure you want to come?" she asked him.

"Sure, why not?" he said nonchalantly. "Don't need a change of pants, if that's what you're asking."

Trace smiled, one eye still on her screens. "You sure you're not going to try and shoot her? It's the second time she's either suggested killing you or actually tried to."

"No, I'm good," said Hiro, barely raising an eyebrow. Trace doubted he actually found the suit diagnostic quite as interesting as he made out. "Styx and I have an understanding. I'm just surprised it took her this long."

"To try and kill you properly?"

"To make her first serious powerplay. She plays a long game, patience is her strong suit. But she's responsible for winning a big chunk of the drysine/deepynine war if she's as old as we now think she is, and commanders that successful are aways tactically aggressive. Yourself as an example."

Trace nodded. "How far do you think it spreads?"

Hiro shook his head. "Couldn't assume to know. We'll have to ask her."

"You think she'll answer?"

"Depends on how much she thinks her strategic fortunes have changed. Obviously she didn't get as far as she wanted with this plan or she wouldn't have killed all of Timoshene's guys." Trace detected a faint tremor in his voice. Hiro hadn't known Timoshene's men, nor did she suspect he felt particularly close to any parren security on Defiance. But seeing even temporary teammates killed at close range, even teammates you barely knew, was still a hell of a thing.

"And why'd she do that, do you think?" she asked.

"That part of the manufacturing facility was operable, while the rest of it was decayed. If they'd shut it down and hidden it, maybe even destroyed some of the evidence they'd been using it, we'd never have seen what they're up to. Might have bought her another month or two, if no one else picked up the trail."

"*Phoenix* isn't planning to be around for that long."

"And Styx might not be planning to come with us. She was never big on going to croma space, said it was a stupid waste of everything."

"From her perspective," said Trace, "it probably is." She considered him a moment longer. Very handsome guy, there was no denying it. And a consummate professional in his own, irregular way. "You'd have made a good marine officer."

"I disagree, but I'll take it as a compliment." He flashed her a sideways smile. "First you save my life, now compliments. How about dinner?"

"You're welcome to have dinner with me on a professional basis any time you like, Hiro," said Trace. "Make an appointment." Hiro sighed.

She hadn't figured out whether Hiro's professed interest in her was real or a put-on, nor if the latter, whether it was for the purposes of information-gathering, ego-boosting or simply fun to pass the time. Certainly he liked to live on the edge, and had an unhealthy addiction to adrenaline, in spite of which he'd somehow managed to remain alive through a high operational tempo in one of the galaxy's more dangerous jobs. Probably it was just that, she thought — he liked to take chances of all varieties, and had precious little fear of consequences. In this case, Trace didn't especially mind, and wasn't beyond finding it mildly entertaining.

PH-1 landed on the control tower's main pad, and the marines disembarked through the dorsal hatch. Heavy Squad went back to the main airlock to take position by the shuttle, while the rest of Bravo distributed themselves through the tower lower levels alongside Alpha, who were already on duty. Trace took the elevator all the way down with Command Squad, waited at basement level until Lieutenant Alomaim and First Squad joined her down separate elevators, then made her way to the basement engineering facility.

Trace kept her visor up, bouncing gently along the rows of fabricators and maintenance machines, Hiro further back in the middle of Command Squad while Alomaim and First Squad made a perimeter outside. Here in his maintenance cradle against a wall was Wowser, all weapons pods removed and apparently powered down... though drones never powered down completely, just dozed. Across the room by another wall were Bucket and Peanut, though Peanut seemed more alert, multi-articulated head darting with curiosity.

"Hello Peanut," Trace called. "Where is Styx?" Knowing entirely well where Styx was, but it was important with Peanut just to be friendly and sociable. As the only drone with any social sensibilities, she was certain he got something out of it.

She rounded the corner past the big assembly machines and found Styx sitting patiently against the wall there, between filament-weave fabricators. Locations had no particular interest for Styx — wirelessly connected to everything, she only needed enough space to fit her large frame and long legs. Drawn up now about her, knees high, she looked like a cornered mantis, the single red eye unblinking atop its long, multi-articulated neck. Despite all her practised calm, it still gave Trace a chill to see her so close, after all this time.

"Styx," said Trace, "we humans have a custom. It's called an apology, I'm sure you've heard of it."

"I have."

"When you've done someone harm, particularly when that harm

was not intended or is otherwise regretted, it's our way to give that person an apology. I think you know who and what I'm talking about."

"Hiro," said Styx, quite calmly. "I'm very sorry I tried to kill you. I think you know quite well that it was not personal."

Hiro just looked at her for a long moment. "How big is it?" he asked finally. "And how long have you been making them for?"

"I have about five thousand by now," said Styx. And Trace had to take a deep breath. Doubtless Styx noticed. "Defiance is large. The parren explore, but barely ten percent has been thoroughly covered, and that with a lack of detailed examination."

"Hannachiam is helping you?" Trace asked.

"Yes, though perhaps unwittingly," said Styx. "Hannachiam is the gatekeeper of Defiance, and as such her role is to regulate normal activities and alert partner authorities to irregular ones. The manufacture of drones and reactivation of surviving drone-making facilities is regular activity, according to long-established parameters. She is not aware of specifics, as you've noticed, and thus did not find it unusual that I would request her to keep the information from you."

They'd trusted Hannachiam too much, Trace thought. Not that they'd had any choice — Hanna ran Defiance, but was a big, innocent child in many ways, easily manipulated and deceived by the likes of Styx. So many of Hanna's command functions were subconscious, the same way a human brain regulated breathing and heartbeat. Styx could access those functions, as humans and parren could not. And even if they'd suspected what Styx was up to, and that such surviving facilities still existed and could be reactivated in spite of all the odds against it, Trace couldn't see that much could have been done differently. Defiance was enormous, as Styx said, and the organic population here was nowhere near large enough to search all or even most of it.

"Five thousand of *what*, exactly?" Hiro asked drily. "I saw drone models I've never seen before."

"Nearly all drysine drone models are models you've never seen before," Styx replied. "The anti-aging micros kept some alive across all these millennia, and those were reactivated upon my arrival here, and in turn worked to reactivate other manufacturing facilities. Through Hannachiam I was able to hide all indicators of this ongoing activity — there are large battery reserves surviving hidden, no active powerplant was needed."

"Those ones that attacked me looked old, Major," said Hiro. "She wouldn't waste the new models on that attack.

"Okay," said Trace, having heard enough. "Styx. First thing, you will deactivate these fabricators and stop making new drones."

"No," said Styx.

Trace thought about that for a moment. "Well then, we'll have to tell the parren about it, and they'll tear Defiance apart looking for them all. You don't have enough firepower here to survive the entire parren military, Styx. You'll lose everything."

"You are correct, Major. Conflict is not my intention. I offer my allegiance. Gesul and House Harmony find themselves confronted with a displeased House Fortitude, who do not like House Harmony to have the data-core, nor any relationship with the drysines. Gesul therefore has nothing to lose by allying himself with the drysine faction more closely, and proclaiming himself to be the true protector of the parren race against the deepynine menace. Already he is positioning for this, as you've seen. House Fortitude will have trouble disposing of Gesul when parren public opinion sees him as the primary protector of all parren peoples, having pledged himself to Tobenrah before the Battle of Defiance."

Trace could only think of how her buddy Kaspowitz was going to laugh at her, sarcastically and without any humour. He'd warned of precisely this — the more important Styx became, and the more integral to everyone's plans, the more leverage she acquired. No one could out-think her, nor ultimately control her, because she'd always find herself with more available options than the people she was screwing over to get what she wanted. She *ought*, Trace thought now, just blow Styx's head off while that was still a possibility... only it wasn't a possibility any longer, and Styx knew it. The alo/deepynine alliance were the true enemy, Styx was vital to stopping them, and she was going to milk that advantage for all it was worth. Which inevitably brought them to this.

"Let's cut the horse trading," Trace said tiredly. "Tell me what you want."

"This is pragmatic, Major. I have always respected that in you."

"And cut the flattery, you know it doesn't work on me."

"Very well. I am no longer a mere member of *Phoenix*'s crew. I am an alliance partner. The drysine race is reborn, and I am its leader. All relations between myself, humans and parren will be conducted in this manner. Drysines were not brought to this galaxy to be anyone's slaves."

"A few thousand new drones in Defiance doesn't make you a queen again," Hiro retorted.

"Perhaps not," said Styx. "But the thousand drones that *Phoenix* helped to liberate from what you called the Tartarus facility seven human months ago have been travelling quiet backroutes through parren and barabo space in the time since, and I suspect will have found many similarly old facilities. I know that Petty Officer Chenkov and some others have been working on statistical models to predict how many old facilities may still exist, and I think he has underestimated."

"Oh fuck," Hiro muttered. "Those tracking signals I've been picking up. Recon bug signals. You've been sneaking them onto parren shipping, haven't you?"

"A clever piece of deduction, Hiro," said Styx. "Using technology alien to you. Human capabilities always surprise. But yes, onto parren shipping, and all across parren space by now. They are easy to make, and can acquire control of ship communications, as you've seen. By now communications will have spread, from me to those ships via modes undetectable to parren, and whoever those ships have been able to reactivate. A rendezvous can be arranged."

"How many?" Trace demanded. "Best estimate?"

"The Tartarus released three warships. I have been examining parren databases for confirmed historical records of drysine facilities destroyed, and I am confident a number have been missed or will have survived in part. I predict a squadron rather than a fleet, but they will be advanced and capable. Drones in the tens of thousands. Again, nowhere near enough to win any conflict against parren or humans. But enough to represent a significant assistance to whoever wins my allegiance."

"Next question," said Hiro. "Why did you kill Jarush?" The parren scholar who had promised to put them in contact with the croma, Trace recalled. Hiro thought that Styx must have taken control of her shuttle's cockpit by remote and flown it into that steel cliff. It hadn't occurred to her, and Trace was damn glad Hiro was better at this kind of thing than she was. "Unless you wanted that rendezvous to be here? At Defiance? Are they coming, Styx? All those ships and drones you hope to arrive?"

"Given current parren sensibilities," said Styx, "that would seem unwise. Croma space is a fool's errand, I have said so before. Mere *Phoenix* crew cannot make this case by argument alone. I improvised."

"Would have worked, too," Trace said tiredly, sipping juice in her chair by the kitchen-side conference table at Aronach Dar. "If *Maki-makala* hadn't shown up with alternative offers of croma contacts."

"Bottom line," Erik said grimly. "What's she up to?" He and all the command group had been pulled from their duties to deal with this latest emergency, and all *Phoenix* crew placed on yellow alert... in case of what, he wasn't entirely sure. It meant a smaller group than previously — just him, Draper, Dufresne, Kaspowitz, and Trace. Hiro, Jokono and Romki were also present, lower on the rank scale, but with much to contribute. Erik had asked after Lisbeth, and not even received an acknowledgement in reply. That meant she was very busy, as a glance at parren activity on scan made obvious.

"She's playing Gesul against us," Hiro said as though it were obvious. Hiro had spent a lot of time working with Styx on the Tsubarata, as part of their plan to infiltrate the Kantovan vault. Only Romki could claim to know her better.

"By building... what is it, five thousand drones?" Draper said skeptically. "That's supposed to win him over?"

"No," said Hiro, "it's supposed to give him no choice but to work with her. He'd have to tear Defiance apart trying to kill them all. Defiance is Gesul's prize possession, it's a jewel in his crown, a sign of House Harmony's prestige and military victories. Fighting a big civil war here to root out thousands of hacksaws will cast doubt on whether Gesul has really won a victory at all, or rather has put the parren people in deadly danger."

"I must say," said Romki, scratching his bald head, "I think she's played this rather well. I mean, I do wish Lisbeth were here, she could tell us for sure... but Gesul couldn't cleanse Defiance of Styx's drones without a major battle, and he can't do that quietly any longer because all the other houses have representatives here, and they'd see. If House Harmony were the ruling house of all parren, he could order them to keep it quiet... but he's not, Sordashan of House Fortitude is, and he'll have a vested interest in making Gesul look bad."

"Gesul's been telling the parren people that he's the one with the unique relationship with their past history," said Trace. "Drakhil, the wars... the past four months he's been explaining to them why they've got it all wrong, and what it means. He insists Drakhil wasn't evil, was actually a good guy doing what he thought was best for all parren, and that the drysines weren't actually evil either... at least not those ones from that time, earlier might have been another story. And now he tells them he's got a drysine facility as House Harmony territory, and there's an old drysine queen here, and it's all going to be great because parren can use them to fight this horrible new threat that killed Mylor Station and a bunch of parren ships at Drezen System in defence of Elsium..."

"He can't fight a war against Styx now," Erik completed. It was obvious, really. "He's been telling his people this is a valuable ally.

Fighting against her drones would destroy the whole message, put his whole political narrative in danger." Trace made a gesture at him, to indicate he had it. "So much for Styx not understanding organic societies or psychology."

He glanced at Kaspowitz. Kaspowitz looked too grim and angry to even hint at saying 'I told you so'. He thought they were all complicit in bringing the drysine race back into existence as a force in the Spiral. And he was right.

"I understand she's in communication with Gesul now," Erik continued. "Nothing really we can do to stop that."

"There's something you can do to stop it," Kaspowitz said darkly.

"I'm considering it," said Erik. Hiro had his AR glasses on, monitoring assassin bug activity, using non-standard tech that Styx could certainly interrupt and fool if she wished. But Erik was confident they were all safe here. Trace had armoured marines on standby in the basement, coms autistic, immune to assassin bugs and with techs having determined long ago that Styx couldn't just shut down marine armour by uplink alone. Whatever she tried, they'd survive long enough to blast her to bits. "Anyone have any idea what she's discussing?"

"New queens," Hiro said confidently. "That new facility Lisbeth invited me to inspect. Rehnar didn't know what to do with it, but Gesul wants to use it and make another queen at least, maybe more. But he can't program it and get it working. Styx can."

"Better and better," Kaspowitz muttered.

"Why would Gesul want a new queen?" asked Erik.

"You'd have to ask Gesul," said Hiro. "All the Domesh are crazy mystics if you ask me. Gesul's no crazier than most, but he's more mystical. I'm sure he's got ideas."

Erik looked at Romki. "Stan?"

"I'm sorry Captain," Romki said with a tired, apologetic smile. "I've got nothing."

Erik looked at Jokono. The much older man unfolded his hands from across his middle and placed them on the table, as though he'd been waiting for just this opportunity. "I think we can make some deductions," he pronounced, with the air of a man about to give a lesson. "One, Styx is entirely rational. Her goal from the beginning has been the reestablishment of the drysine race. She is not necessarily malevolent, despite Lieutenant Kaspowitz's understandable concerns. She is advancing her position along those lines, and will do anything to strengthen it."

"Including killing everyone here," Kaspowitz growled.

"No," Jokono said calmly, "because that would not advance her position. Not yet, anyhow. Until now she has been entirely reliant on the notion that humanity might find her a valuable ally in the fight against the alo/deepynines. But that prospect has always been thin — she hasn't had access to humanity, she's only had access to us. It's not the same. Here and now, she has access to one of the five great parren houses. It is understandable that she would manoeuvre to increase her value to that house, and thus gain them as an ally for the drysine cause.

"But this is dangerous to her as well, because parren solve internal disputes violently, and her siding with Gesul could bring about his elimination. Thus she creates a substitute. A new AI queen, to operate as her defacto while she is gone."

Erik frowned. "Hang on, she says she doesn't want to come with us to croma space."

Jokono sighed. "Captain, if it hasn't been repeated often enough already... everything Styx does or says is manipulation of some sort. Every conversation to her is a tactical battlefield to be manoeuvred and won. It's what she was made to do."

Trace looked as consternated as Erik felt. He was pleased to see it — it made him feel less stupid. "You're saying she manoeuvred us into this from the beginning?"

Jokono spread his hands. "Look about you. She began activating small parts of Defiance off our scopes as soon as she arrived here, waking up the few remaining old-model drones to assist, and enlisting Hannachiam, largely without Hanna's conscious knowledge, I think. Styx cannot stay here — her presence could easily spark a parren civil war between Harmony and Fortitude. She is the leader of the drysine race, her survival cannot be left to chance.

"But she did not wish to leave so soon either, with much left undone to maximise chances of success with the parren as well. A subordinate queen could fulfil that role while not constituting too great a loss if civil war does come... or if Gesul is removed by force, at least, which could happen with something much less than a civil war. I think we can deduce that Styx probably does not want to go to croma space, but will come anyway because it's safer than staying here, and is thus the best of several poor options. She killed Jarush to delay that departure, and now tried to kill Hiro to prevent her work with drone production from being discovered quite so early. A longer wait would have maximised her position of strength. But I think she's probably strong enough now regardless."

"She is if we can't do anything to stop her producing those drones," Trace said sombrely. "I'm not sending Phoenix Company down there to chase them through the bowels of Defiance."

Erik shook his head as the picture came clearer. "No, she'll negotiate a pause with Gesul," he said. "It's more leverage, one more thing she can offer him. A queen, the promise of more, and a pause in drone production. Possibly a status of forces review, something to assure him the drones aren't a threat. Maybe even a mediator, like a drone middleman..." he clicked his fingers at Trace. "Like that... that senior combat drone that communicated with you on Tartarus, what did it call itself?"

"A-1," said Trace. "He's probably around here in parren space somewhere right now, waking up the remnants, if what Styx told us is right. Old places like where we found Styx, or much bigger."

"But yeah, a new queen could mediate all that best of all," Erik continued. "And talk to A-1 and his friends if they do all arrive shortly. Clearly Styx was planning a rendezvous with them when they get here, probably why she wanted to delay going to croma space. Leave a queen behind and Styx won't have to stay here." He saw Romki abruptly smiling at something private. "Stan, something to share?"

Romki looked up, surprised. "Oh no, nothing. Just... wondering how the parren found that queen facility. Defiance is so big, so little has been explored, as Styx says. Yet Rehnar just happened to stumble on it. What odds that Styx guided him to it, whether he was aware or not?"

"Wow, how impressive," said Kaspowitz, glowering at Romki.

"It is, actually," said Romki, patronisingly. "And I believe it was you, Lieutenant, who said that when Styx moved, we'd never see it coming. Congratulations on your correct deduction."

* * *

LISBETH WOULD HAVE FOUND herself a quiet berth in the crowded shuttle, but Gesul beckoned her to the seat directly beside his own as soon as she came aboard. The hold was pressurised, so she waddled her fat EVA suit to the big heavy-braced chair at Gesul's side and eased herself onto it. She barely fit — life among parren had given her new sympathy for large or overweight humans, always the seats were several sizes too small, the clothes needed new tailoring, or she had to make do with the men's version of things. Timoshene and the rest of her security entourage found places among the crowded mass of seats and multi-level support bars further back.

"I wish someone at my side who knows Styx personally," Gesul explained, hard blue eyes fixed upon the displays before him, monitoring multiple incoming feeds at once.

"Yes Gesul-sa," said Lisbeth, thinking of Hiro's spy friend Daica, and the threat to her family that could be eased if she spied on the parren. And she shook the thought off. "Gesul-sa, I understand that this is human and impolite of me to ask, but I ask your indulgence. Is this wise?"

"Wise," said Gesul, eyes not leaving his screens. "Very few things are wise, Lisbeth Debogande. Least frequently those things that are loudly pronounced to be so. The true question is whether they are necessary."

The rear hold of the big parren assault shuttle was full of

marines. A second shuttle was coming too, also loaded with parren firepower. Gesul's people, some very senior commanders and technicians among them, said that they were 'in communication' with new entities deep in the bowels of Defiance. More than that, they would not say. Only now Gesul insisted on going to talk to these entities personally. At least on *Phoenix*, Lisbeth could be confident that if Erik wanted to do something particularly daft, half a dozen senior people he respected would try to talk him out of it. With Gesul, not a single parren would have raised so much as a non-existent eyebrow.

"It's that fool Rehnar's fault," said Gesul, as the commotion of loading, the stomping of footsteps and the crash of chair restraints continued around them. "We have been on Defiance for a hundred standard rotations, yet most of his personnel deployments were strategic and aggressive, aimed at warding further assault from the deepynines, and then aimed at the Domesh and myself. I proposed in our earliest meetings that within the first two hundred days we should be aiming to have fully explored sixty percent of the city, yet we were on course to achieve less than half of that. Since the Domesh ascended, I have commanded a change in posture to accelerate those explorations and send teams to the deep reaches of Defiance where none have yet ventured. Some of the commanders have now instead sought to blame you, Lisbeth Debogande, for this exceedingly slow pace."

Lisbeth blinked. "Me?"

"As the one who told them that parren-made drones would be inadequate for the exploration task." Oh, thought Lisbeth. She had, and she'd had it confirmed by Hiro and every *Phoenix* tech she'd asked. If a low-tech drone encountered ongoing drysine activity in Defiance, its systems could be hacked and overridden as easily as child's play, so that its organic operators could not trust a single thing it broadcast back. The only reliable way to explore Defiance was in EVA suits, with trustworthy eyes. "I told them that human proverb you said to me once. That one should not shoot the messenger."

He broke off to reply to some incoming communication, a fast instruction in some jargon that Lisbeth could barely catch, however improved her Porgesh.

"I was under the impression that parren rather liked shooting the messenger," Lisbeth muttered, flipping down her helmet visor long enough to call up her official functions and display them on the screens before her. A list of Semaya's latest official files for her to address... at least nine new ones from various non-Domesh departments requesting clarifications on human matters, or requests for information that Semaya had already cleared with someone higher up. As the only human in Gesul's administration, she was a source of endless curiosity and information for every other person there, and spent much of her day simply answering queries. But that was part of why Gesul valued her — with her assistance, his administration was now far more well informed on matters concerning humans and hacksaws both, and not all of those answered queries were time wasted.

"As your advisor, Gesul-sa," she resumed when Gesul's other conversations ended, "I advise that this is extremely dangerous. There appears to be an indigenous, pre-existing component of drysine drones, and a new contingent. The old contingent is over twenty five human millennia old, evidently their bodies have survived in some sort of good condition, but there is no telling what kind of damage may have been done to their minds in the meantime."

"Our technicians suppose they may have been reprogrammed," said Gesul, as airtight hatches sealed and clanked somewhere above, and the shuttle's background engine noise grew to a dull roar. "Probably by Styx, or with the assistance of Hannachiam."

"Which raises all kinds of problematic possibilities," Lisbeth agreed. A shudder, as the shuttle slowly rose. "More problematic still are these new drones from the retasked fabricators. Styx has full access to the data-core, she's not a manufacturing unit but she's had access to the best technical data from across the drysine ages. It's quite likely she's selected new types of drone with which to task the fabricators, previously unseen by us. I would recommend that if you truly wish for the best advice, you should invite Major Thakur along, or Hiro Uno, or possibly Stan Romki or others of *Phoenix's* best technicians who've actually studied and worked on constructing new ones... they did build Styx's entire current combat chassis..."

"I am aware of their expertise," Gesul said calmly. "But Defiance is House Harmony territory, and this is now a House Harmony matter. The deal to be made is between Harmony and the drysines. We have all had quite enough of humans interjecting themselves in the middle of that relationship, so that parren hold no advantages whatsoever."

It was a complaint Lisbeth had heard frequently in the past few months, and she swallowed her objection. "You are certain that there is a deal to be made?"

"Yes. Your friend Styx has a formidable intellect. She knows that parren will not stand for threats to their power. If this new drysine force in Defiance constitutes a threat, I will have no choice but to order it destroyed, whatever the cost to House Harmony. I judge that Styx wishes to expand her influence and her strategic options. Until now she has been entirely reliant upon the goodwill of the *Phoenix*. Now she has things to offer parren as well, beginning with House Harmony."

"That seems quite reasonable," said Lisbeth, trying to keep the sarcasm from her voice. "Allow me to then offer one last piece of advice. The human fields of psychology and neuroscience do not even have numbers or framework with which to describe Styx's level of intellect or manner of sentience. Heading into any confrontation or negotiation with her, or with her servants, assuming that one knows exactly what she's intending, does not seem logical."

Gesul smiled faintly, as the big shuttle rumbled through the open doors atop the habitat shell. "Point noted and conceded, Lisbeth Debogande."

The shuttle flew on low-thrust across the vast steel cityscape, over features alien and remarkable. Casting an eye across it on external visual as they flew, Lisbeth could easily see the scale of the problem. It only took a few hundred metres of reactivated space to begin a new drone manufacturing facility. Across Defiance were thousands of square kilometres of unexplored alien city... no, kilometres cubed, she corrected herself. Defiance was not only wide, it was deep, extending downward for many kilometres before it hit the floor of this gouged, rocky crater.

Entry point was yet another geofeature. When organics had first returned to Defiance four months ago, there had been only one functional, and it had offered a strategic focal-point about which much of the battle had centred. But in fact there were many deep geofeatures across the city, sealed shut before or after the last great battle here. That had been conducted by the forces of Jin Danah — the first but short-lived ruler of the great Parren Empire that followed the Machine Age — against Defiance's defenders, synthetic and organic alike.

This geofeature, Lisbeth judged by the visuals that moved past her scan-screen as they descended, had had its multiple sealing shield doors reopened — likely a long and difficult process, given the mechanisms had been destroyed long ago once the doors had been swung into place. Down and down they continued, the pilot carefully manoeuvring to avoid several old obstructions protruding into the shaft.

Finally they came to a hover, while several marines took the dorsal shaft out to leap down and inspect a landing pad that protruded from a wall. After several minutes of checks they pronounced the pad safe, and the big shuttle gently landed. Warning lights flashed with an announcement of imminent decompression, and all aboard sealed their suits and completed final systems checks. Then the roar and hum of ventilation sucking air from the hold, as external sound faded, to be replaced only by the faint whirr of suit systems, and the sound of Lisbeth's own breathing.

The marines in the rear deployed first, Gesul following with his personal guard, Lisbeth a respectful few steps behind. Outside, Lisbeth looked up through the top of her visor to see the tiny, distant circle of stars that marked the geofeature's entrance, perhaps five kilometres above. But too much looking upward was bad for her balance, so she watched where she was going instead, and followed the low-G skipping parren into the vast entrance in the tunnel's side.

Within, a few lights were working, built into the wall and ceiling. Lisbeth's suit visor informed her those lights were multi-spectrumed — hacksaws utilised many spectrums of light, not just those visible to organic eyes. Those lights illuminated a crazy tangle of machinery and utility arms blocking this entry portion of what might otherwise have been a hangar bay. It *was* a hangar bay, Lisbeth saw in amazement — amidst the tangle was the angular, unsymmetrical shape of an old hacksaw runner, a short-range spaceship, likely made for shuttling to and from the many starships in orbit overhead. It was very old, aged without rust or visible decay, just dull and lifeless, locked amidst the many-armed docking mechanism, trapped by that faintly disturbing alien embrace.

Multiple other docking ports were vacant, arms and umbilicals hanging limp. In and around those arms were many small holes and accesses, doubtless for drones to crawl and access. Lisbeth hoped fervently that she wouldn't have to go crawling through there herself. Particularly after what had happened to Hiro, Timoshene and his men. The parren marines deployed wide, weapons not raised, but ready. Lisbeth glanced within her helmet, and saw Timoshene at her far side with his other men, the ones who hadn't been killed by hacksaw drones. Behind that impassive visor, she could not tell his expression.

The parren talked, a few short, terse sentences. It seemed that whatever communications they'd received had requested them to come here, and wait. Parren were good at waiting. Lisbeth locked out her suit's legs, settled onto the crotch as all spacers and marines did while standing for a long time on EVAs, and waited.

Movement deep within one of those docking bays. Lisbeth saw a flicker of laser scan, flashing momentarily off her visor. A human marine commander might have given an extra instruction not to fire or flinch. House Harmony marine commanders had no concern of such things.

Then they came, a metallic scuttling like so many silver spiders

emerging from their nest. Big spiders, methodical in their movements, thinking and looking, not moving on pre-programmed automatic. Their shapes and sizes varied, some rounder, some flatter,
some more intricate and prehensile, others boxy and shell-shaped.
Several walked much taller on longer, stilt-like legs. All of them,
Lisbeth saw with heart-in-mouth, had modular attachments, almost
certainly weapons. Hiro had said the drones that attacked him and
Timoshene had had no weapons. Perhaps Styx had kept them
unarmed to remove the temptation of engagement, to get them
thinking more about hiding than killing. That was alarming, as it
suggested not all of the drones could be trusted to behave as
required.

And this now suggested that they did have a good stash of
weapons somewhere about, and could rearm as required. Others had
boxy secondary units attached to the lower-rear torso — probably
thrusters, Lisbeth guessed, having read those reports from *Phoenix*
marines in the aftermath of various fights. Thrusters created mobility
in low-G. Stripped down, drones could look almost lean and flexible,
bodies as articulated and supple as even the human torso, armour-
plated segments overlapping and sliding as they turned and twisted.
Fully loaded for combat, they looked more like heavy-shelled beetles,
nearly double their unloaded size with weapons, utility laser, ammunition and thrusters. Small heads twisted and darted within
armoured hood-carapaces, two eyes of uneven size peering and scanning, no doubt sharing everything they saw instantaneously with
their comrades.

Dear god Styx, Lisbeth thought, watching the advancing tide of
insectoid steel. What have you done?

The advancing line stopped, and a single drone continued
forward another several metres, then stopped. Gesul indicated to
Lisbeth, and walked forward. Lisbeth wanted to protest, but found
her feet moving on automatic, the suit coming out of stand-still
without having to be told. No parren guards accompanied them. Not
that it mattered, she thought, finding the small water tube with her
lips and taking a sip to moisten her dry mouth. If shooting started

here, likely everyone would die... though the drones, more heavily armed and far more heavily armoured, would fare much better.

Her visor informed her that Gesul wished to speak, and she blinked on the icon. *"Lisbeth, I wish to know, in your opinion, if I am speaking to Styx or not. That is all."*

Because all of these drones obeyed Styx absolutely, had been made and programmed by her, and were likely in direct communications with her at this very moment. Lisbeth was the only one here who knew Styx at all well, and could possibly judge whether it was her speaking with Gesul or not.

They stopped four metres from the lead drone. It was larger than the average drone, heavily armed and loaded. The twin cannon on its back loomed above head-height, its massive vibroblades like twin pincers on an enormous crab. If it moved fast, those four metres would disappear in a flash. And suddenly Lisbeth wondered, suspiciously, if she was only here for translation and analysis... or if Gesul simply judged that Styx was still in close proximity with *Phoenix* marines, and would be held directly responsible by them if her creations murdered Captain Debogande's sister.

"Hello," Gesul said simply, on open coms. *"To whom am I speaking?"* Assuming the drone could read his unencrypted transmissions was a safe bet, given no audio speaker would work in the vacuum.

A bright red laser lit upon Gesul's faceplate, then on Lisbeth's, from somewhere on the drone's head. *"Hello,"* came the reply on suit coms, also in Porgesh. *"This unit is Dse- Pa."*

"Gesul," Lisbeth said cautiously, pleased that she had something to report. "Major Thakur encountered a drone in the Tartarus engagement I believe the Major briefed you on personally. It was the local commander of forces, and it identified itself as A1 — 'A' is the first letter of the human alphabet, and '1' is the first human number after zero, just as 'Dse' and 'Pa' are for parren. So this unit too is identifying itself as A1, though it cannot be the same drone. I speculate that it simply chooses that signifier from what it knows of our alphabet and numbers to identify itself as commander."

"Hello Dse-Pa," said Gesul. *"I am Gesul, leader of House Harmony of*

the parren. *Defiance, this entire city and its moon, and the space surrounding it, are all beneath my command. Do you understand?"*

A slight pause, just long enough for Lisbeth's heart to consider whether to start racing at the implications if Dse-Pa protested. *"Yes,"* said Dse-Pa instead. *"I understand."*

"And do you agree?" Gesul persisted.

"Yes. This unit agrees. All drysines agree." Lisbeth tried not to gasp audibly with relief. Well that averted a rather large and unpleasant war, and probably most of their immediate deaths. But then, as Gesul had said, it would have been stupid for Dse-Pa, or Styx, to say otherwise. As to what they actually *thought*, however...

"Dse-Pa," said Gesul, very calmly and clearly. He could have been giving a thoughtful lecture in old parren history, for all the drama he displayed. *"It was my understanding that there would be no more drysine drones on Defiance. Many of my people consider this new move in making many drysine drones to be a threat to parren power on this world. Yet I am a tolerant man. This is an ancient home of drysines, and it was re-built in large part by drysines. Drysines have their place here, and there could be great utility in allowing drysines to maintain and operate parts of this city once more. I propose an agreement between us. What do you have to offer me, in exchange for my protection?"*

"Defiance fully functional," said Dse-Pa.

"Parren engineers can achieve this without drysine assistance," Gesul replied.

"Fast," the drysine retorted. Its response time was rapid enough to be rude, coming from another parren, or a human. Like most drysines, command-level or otherwise, its brain worked with alarming speed.

"Interesting," said Gesul. *"Go on."*

"Translate data-core," said Dse-Pa. *"Current translation requires many years. Deepynine threat will materialise much faster. Quick technology. Good for parren, good for House Harmony."*

"Also interesting," said Gesul. *"Continue."* They were deciding the balance of power between parren houses, Lisbeth realised with wide-eyed disbelief. Right here in this hangar. The balance of power in the

Spiral, perhaps. This was what *Phoenix* had truly wrought, when she had recovered that data-core, then determined there was no choice but to share it with the Spiral.

"*New queen,*" said Dse-Pa. "*You find new facility. Make hardware, cannot program. Drysines program. New queen, powerful new ally for House Harmony.*"

"Very interesting." A hint of genuine pleasure had crept into Gesul's voice. But only a hint. "*This may suit my needs very well, Dse-Pa. You are familiar with the term 'alliance'?*"

"*Yes. Drysines serve Gesul of House Harmony. Drysines operate Defiance, make Defiance strong again. Drysines fight to protect Defiance. Fight to defeat parren enemies. Fight to defeat House Harmony enemies.*"

"*I think we understand each other quite well, Dse-Pa. And in return, I will agree to defend all drysines on Defiance as I defend my own parren people. Drysines will become strong within House Harmony. You will thrive, and your numbers will increase. Does this meet your requirements?*"

"Yes," said Dse-Pa. Its synthetic tone, unlike Styx's effortless vocal modulations, betrayed no pleasure or satisfaction. "*This formulation is adequate.*"

* * *

CAPTAIN ANGELO SAMPEY sat in *Lien Wang*'s primary engineering bay and stared at the source of his torment. As large as a gymnasium's medicine ball, it sat dull grey and marked with innocuous lines within the brace of the ship's best scanning array, patiently awaiting its time to be let loose upon the universe.

Commander Tito Adams entered, face tired with sleep, and took silent hold beside Sampey's chair at the displays. Handed Sampey one of the cold, pressed-grain snacks he was eating — an acquired taste from the parren, whose food had already converted most of the crew of *Phoenix*, and was now working its magic on *Lien Wang*.

"Kind of does that to your sleep, doesn't it?" Adams said laconically, nodding at the dull metal sphere. Sampey nodded, chewing on the snack. "Makes you wonder how Debogande's been sleeping, with all the shit he's been carrying the past year."

"I bet he sleeps fine," Sampey drawled, eyes not leaving the sphere. "He's young. I'm old. I've seen too much to sleep."

Lien Wang was in transit through Lusakia System — the only way in or out of Defiance. One major course change and they were heading for the far side and jump toward tavalai space. Broadcasting the latest codes direct from Harmony ruler Gesul himself, none of the parren ships currently transiting Lusakia on their way to Defiance had challenged them. Tavalai space was only two more jumps away, and Sampey churned with the tension of being so close, and yet so far.

Once in tavalai space, Debogande's friend Pramodenium had given them more codes and personal messages to play to the tavalai warships he expected them to encounter at Lonagonda System. Only *Lien Wang* wasn't heading through Lonagonda System. Transiting through tavalai space on the way here, he'd picked the brains of their human Inspection Fleet escort, and learned the best fast routes if one wanted to take a 'back way' through heavily populated tavalai systems and back to human space in a hurry. A large warship could not have managed it, but *Lien Wang*, small, lithe and designed for precisely these kinds of deep penetration missions, was another matter.

"How much chance do you give us?" Adams asked solemnly. "Of getting back untouched?"

"Maybe two in three," said Sampey. "Maybe less. It's hard to say." A silence, filled only by the hum and thump of the rotating crew cylinder, and the white noise of a thousand ship systems operating in the background. "Damned if I'm going to risk tavalai bureaucracy. Debogande has no real idea just how much of a mess they're in at the moment. Someone will hold us up, guess what we're carrying, and then we're stuffed."

"I'm less scared of losing the data-core than I am of not reporting back on the bio-weapons," Adams replied. "If the human population's already been infected the same way *Makimakala* says the tavalai population has been..."

Sampey shook his head. "Tavalai will already be telling us about that. Alo/deepynines are their enemy, this is their chance to convince Fleet HQ that they're humanity's enemy too. Split the Triumvirate Alliance... god knows which side the chah'nas will come down on..." he trailed off, and shook a finger at the data-core. "That's our top priority. House Harmony have their own damn copy now, parren are about to become an elite power in the Spiral. Which will make them a target, just like we're a target. *Phoenix* lost nearly a third of their crew finding that thing, their new tech looks like the only chance we have of beating those fucking machines. We just have to hope we're not too late, and that the tavalai don't steal it from us before we get there."

"If they try and intercept us on a transit..." Adams ventured.

Sampey nodded hard. "We run. If they fire and kill us, well, it's worth the risk. By the look of *Phoenix*'s flight logs against those deepynine ships, we'd lose half of human space in a month if the alo attack us right now. We're that outmatched. And if they use the bioweapons once they've established space superiority..."

He didn't complete the sentence. He didn't have to. Adams took the second secured chair and sat. For a long moment they said nothing. Every Fleet officer knew theoretically why they were fighting. Humanity had nearly died once. But they'd been winning for so long. That road had been hard and bloody, but it had mostly been in the one, inexorable direction — victory after violent, triumphant victory. Everyone had gotten used to winning, had begun to think of it as the natural state of things. Now this. It didn't seem real, and it didn't seem fair.

Sampey glanced finally at his colleague from Intelligence. "You think we'll see *Phoenix* again?"

"My gut says maybe," Adams conceded. "But my head says no. Not headed in that direction."

"Croma don't talk much, but I hadn't heard they were unfriendly?"

"Croma aren't the problem."

Sampey's eyes narrowed. "What have you heard about the reeh that you're not allowed to tell me?"

"Bad things," Adams said grimly, putting the last bit of parren food into his mouth. "Bad, bad things." He glanced at the Captain, chewing. "What do you think *Phoenix*'s chances are?"

Sampey repressed a self-deprecating laugh. "On the way here? I'd have said nil. Then I met those lunatics in person and now I'm not so sure."

Adams shook his head in disbelief. "Those combat records are something else, huh?"

"Not just that. It's Thakur. It's the way she looks at him."

"Debogande?" Sampey nodded. "How's that?"

"Thakur's the real deal. All the marine officers who know the story say she's an A-plus freak of nature. Some of those I talked to before coming out here... you know, like everyone talks about *Phoenix*?" Adams nodded. Gossiping about the *UFS Phoenix* and the demise of Captain Pantillo had been every Fleet officer's favourite pastime for most of the last year. "They said there's no way Thakur would tolerate a jumped-up mommy's boy like Debogande."

"But Thakur would charge a hacksaw base barehanded if Debogande ordered it. I'm not sure Debogande realises it yet, but I've been doing this a very long time and that's what I saw with them together. Not many people could win that kind of loyalty from her."

"You think everyone got him wrong, huh?" Adams wondered.

"Heuron was something else."

"Debogande killed a lot of good Fleet spacers at Heuron," Adams retorted.

"Irrelevant to my point. Heuron was something else. He caught *UFS Adventurer* in the grapple talons and used her as a hostage to run through half of Heuron fleet with engines blazing, then extracted Thakur from a mess that should have killed her too. I'm not sure I could have done it, and I've been doing this a lot longer. Amazing crew, all of them."

"And if they pick a fight with the reeh, it'll be the last we see of them," Adams completed. "Let's hope Debogande's not that stupid."

"Stupid like running across parren and tavalai space with the galaxy's most dangerous football and daring everyone to stop us?" Sampey replied, eyebrow raised. "The next couple of years are going to be crazy-dangerous. Crazy-dangerous might just become the default setting for us all."

11

Twenty-three rotations later, Erik arrived on *Phoenix* via the cross-bridge from the ship-bay wall direct to Midships Berth 4, through the space where a shuttle would normally be docked. The transition still had to be made in EVA suits as no one yet trusted that improvised seal, but he had to get his personal suit onboard anyway since they were packing everything up. He hauled a rucksack with him, a big, easy mass in low-G holding all his clothes and personals, and climbed the deployed cargo netting up the storage wall toward the access hatch to the crew cylinder.

Midships was chaos, spacers moving gear, wall-side storage units flung open after five months empty, stuffed full of new things while supervised by several harried Warrant Officers keeping track of where everything went. Engineering ran final checks on systems, arriving crew hauled personal gear like Erik, and marines guarding armour suits awaiting their turn for transport up to Assembly argued with spacers over where marine things should be put so they didn't get in the spacers' way.

Climbing was easy in low-G, and spacers descending the cargo nets made way for their Captain. At least two that Erik saw were tavalai, headsets on and earpieces in place, looking a little confused at all the human chatter but not out of place in the environment. Several carried small flasks in their jumpsuit webbing — eyedrops, as prolonged exposure to human-preference low-humidity made their eyes dry, to the complaints of many. Erik had suggested to Warrant Officer Kriplani, who was senior on life support systems, that they could lift humidity from thirty percent standard up to fifty, but Kriplani hadn't liked the pressures that put on his filters, so they'd compromised by boosting pressure to 1.2 atmospheres with humidity at forty percent... Erik had no idea why that suited the systems better, but Kriplani knew a hell of a lot more about it than he did. But now the human crew were complaining that they sweated too much.

Petty Officer Duryea was descending on the far ladder with a panel-clamp on one arm that would have weighed far too much in regular G. "We leaving, Captain?" he asked as Erik reached the ladder to the cylinder hatch.

"Best guess is two hours," Erik told her, and started climbing. Below him, his comment was relayed, and then Warrant Officer Krish was bellowing, "Two hours, people! Move your lazy asses!" Not that they didn't already know, of course, but confirmation straight from the Captain's mouth added an urgency that Warrant Officers weren't above exploiting.

"Hello Captain," said Second Lieutenant Abacha in his ear.

"Go ahead Kendall."

"Fortitude Squadron was just joined by three more, all toma-class cruisers, out of jump from Lusakia. Lorna is still weapons active, orbital spread unchanged."

The fact that Abacha was telling him personally meant that Draper was busy, and probably Dufresne as well. Twenty-seven hours ago the Fortitude squadron had arrived out of jump from Lusakia System, the only way anyone could get in or out of Defiance. At its head was the *Lorna*, Fortitude Leader Sordashan's personal flagship, plus another nineteen parren warships, all of them top-class, three of them carriers, including *Lorna*.

Phoenix had had warning, one of Gesul's spies arriving two days beforehand to insist that *Lorna*'s arrival was imminent. Rooke insisted that he wasn't ready, but he'd managed to at least get the ship in flying order, and the remaining work did not strictly require a berth and could be completed on the move... though at a much slower rate. And so they were leaving, *Makimakala* awaiting in close orbit, ready to escort them toward croma contacts that she insisted were real and waiting, and which *Phoenix* had no choice but to take her word for.

And so for two rotations now they'd been completing the task of departure in a mad rush, sweeping up a dispersed crew from three primary locations, and all the equipment and belongings they'd been using, and cramming it into a ship that was not designed to be loaded while sitting on its tail at any Gs. Unable to use the shuttles, they'd been landing things on the berth-side pad and ferrying them to Midships by hand, to the consternation of some in Engineering who'd realised too late that several of their precious fabricators would have to be partially dismantled to fit through the airlocks. Just so long as the Warrant Officers could get him an accurate mass-count at the end of loading, Erik thought, reaching the top of the ladder and switching to the passage handholds, ignoring the ten-meter drop beneath his dangling feet and oncoming traffic threatening to jostle his rucksack. Somehow the volume of gear they'd removed from *Phoenix* upon arrival had added thirty percent in mass upon its return, and while it wouldn't make an enormous difference to the power of the warship's engines, it could certainly screw up the navcomp calculations on everything from evasive manoeuvres to docking to jump.

The other problem caused by Fortitude's arrival was that Fortitude Leader Sordashan was denying them permission to leave. Well, thought Erik, arriving on the cylinder-side of the hatch and pulling himself up to stand on what would normally be the end wall of the trunk corridor, he could only solve one problem at a time.

Moving up the trunk corridor was by rope-line, and Erik hooked his EVA suit on at the harness, was made way for in the short queue, then rode up the long corridor with legs dangling, kicking off the walls where the safety doglegs brought the rope into contact. He exchanged greetings with various spacers on their way back down, seeing the side-corridors full of activity and people crawling in and out of the room entrances that were now vertical drops or climbs, and wondered if they were really all going to be ready in time for launch.

Bridge entry had multiple big nets deployed in case stupid senior officers missed their hook and tumbled back down the long corridor, but Erik grabbed the deployed swing-arm and unhooked, which took him to the rear bridge wall. "Captain on the bridge!" called Second Lieutenant Zelele from Scan Two — usually the junior officer's responsibility, and he must have been watching Erik's signal tracking from his glasses, the only way he'd see the Captain's arrival looking over his shoulder and 'down', as they all rode presently above Erik's head.

"Carry on," Erik told them all, and bent to open the door to Captain's Quarters at his feet. Spacer Chen was posted to bridge watch and came to help him with the suit, which Erik might normally have refused but any time saved the Captain was a strategic benefit to the whole ship. They got the suit segments off, then lowered into Erik's quarters and stowed, and Erik forewent his usual neatness to just get it all sealed away, then climbed the bunk-end to reach the door once more and pull himself out.

He ducked beneath Dufresne's Helm chair, then tapped Draper on the shoulder, standing nearly head-level with the Captain's chair. Draper looked at him, flat on his back from Erik's perspective, his lowered visor indicating he'd been running various orbital simulations to counter *Lorna*'s current posture. Across the bridge, second-shift officers were similarly intent on business. Further forward of the Captain's chair, the line of Navigation, Coms, Scan and Arms were more than three metres off the 'ground'. In a one-G push they required a drop-rope and upper-body strength to reach, but in this G a simple hop would do it.

"How's it looking?" Erik asked.

"Depends on how stubborn he is," said Draper, meaning Sordashan. The Supreme Commander of not only House Fortitude, but all parren. The young Commander blinked his eyes to normal focus, pulling back the visor. "Or how stubborn we are."

"Well we're leaving," Erik said firmly. "One way or the other. He's got good intel, we know he's seen the grav bombs and our network dominance tech." The ability to knock out other ships' computer systems entirely via simple data transmissions, that was. "He's heard how advanced we are now. The more he tells us to stay, the more embarrassing it becomes for him when we leave anyway."

"I dunno Captain," Draper said doubtfully. "He's got the exit window to Lusakia blocked up pretty good. We have to jump out that way, even with these engines. He could mine it, or put a solid positional block on those approaches. And we've got *Makimakala* with us — she's good, but we're now a lot better. Assuming everything works."

"Let's just worry about getting off the ground first," said Erik. He didn't have to explain what he was thinking to the younger man — he'd be in the chair when it mattered, not Draper, and it took too long anyway.

"Captain Debogande," came a new, heavily accented voice by the steep drop into the trunk corridor. Both men glanced, to find a short, mottled green-and-brown skinned tavalai standing, custom headset over each wide-set eye like blinders on a horse.

"Hello Lieutenant Sasalaka," said Erik. "All stowed away?"

The tavalai gave a small frown at the expression. "Yes, Captain. Tavalai custom is for shift-crew to welcome the Captain when he returns to ship. Make certain he know who is aboard."

"A good custom," said Erik. "But unnecessary here — I can see who's aboard the ship." He tapped the glasses riding on his head.

"Yes Captain," said Sasalaka. "I will continue pre-flight simulations in my quarters." And she turned toward the humming rope-line motor, saw a handle and jumped to it, drifting down as it took her.

Erik and Draper exchanged looks. "Who's she sharing with?" Erik asked.

"Some other tavalai," Draper said dismissively. "Forget the name. I went into one of their quarters the other day — fucking dripping hot and humid. Smelt like fish. It's that stuff they eat."

Phoenix had been loading moki into the kitchen along with their other things. *Makimakala* had plenty of it — a sort of fish-paste tavalai would spread on bread or crackers, or eat with grains, or sometimes alone. All humans hated the smell save for Romki, though Erik thought Romki just denied it to prove how small-minded everyone else was. Some of the other tavalai food wasn't so bad, but Erik thought moki had the potential to start fights of the 'don't eat that stuff near me' kind.

But Erik knew that Draper wasn't really concerned about the food, or the oppressive conditions in the tavalai quarters. He raised it now because he was concerned, but had been forbidden from worrying about the really important stuff, like whether Erik should really be the one flying with Sasalaka sitting Helm, given first-shift was undeniably more important than Second, and that everyone's lives would be resting on a tavalai's decisions, not to mention her ability to understand the language and procedures. They'd done lots of sims, of course, and every time the results had only convinced Erik further that this was the way to go — Sasalaka was an excellent pilot, but some of the communication problems became an issue. Furthermore, she was an actual *pilot*, like Erik, like Draper, Dufresne and Tif — more accustomed to the first seat than the second, and occasionally prone to overstepping the constraints of the co-pilot role. When that happened Erik wanted to be the one in the main chair, because he was pretty sure he could handle it, and stop it from escalating into something catastrophic. With Draper and Dufresne, he lacked such confidence.

Draper kept looking at him, wary eyes from flat on his back. Erik slapped his shoulder. "She sims better than you," he said lightly, turning to follow her back down the corridor.

"Can smell the fish from here," Draper muttered, pulling the visor back over his eyes.

* * *

HIRO ENTERED the parren engineering bay with two Domesh escorts and gazed about. There was a lot of gear here that even he didn't recognise — fabricators, maintenance frameworks, open-sided robotic structures that appeared to turn themselves inside out in their production methods, all humming and throbbing, and apparently autonomous without obvious control functions.

Beyond the machines he saw a clear circle about a central plinth, surrounded by parren guards and engineers. He walked that way, hearing conversation, quiet and orderly, mostly between the engineers. The parren wore regular spacer jumpsuits, a necessity in Defiance's pressurised habitats with safety gear never far away, but also there were signs of rank, of caps and headcrests of the minor variety, and other colour and adornment. The guards wore all black, including facemasks, hoods and visors. It made sense that Gesul, more open-minded than many Domesh leaders, had recruited engineers from all different denominations, while only the armed guards were Domesh... though given how other denominations loved to sneak spies into the camps of their rivals, one could never be sure.

Arriving on the edge of the circle, Hiro saw Lisbeth watching proceedings and chewing a thumbnail, exchanging muted conversation with a slim parren female with a green sash tied at her waist, and an elegant black skullcap. That would be Semaya, Lisbeth's Chief of Staff. Hiro wasn't yet perfect at identifying parren on sight, but he was improving. About them, several others, probably Lisbeth's staff... and behind them, Timoshene, an impassive black sentinel.

Lisbeth saw him, and looked exasperated. Hiro was used to that, and looked at the object on the plinth. It looked strikingly familiar, wired up to many external connections, all monitored by earnest parren scientists with screens, AR glasses and holographic displays. An irregular silver blob, about the size of a medicine ball from *Phoenix's* gym. Unlike the one that had sat in *Phoenix's* hold for so long, this one had two eyes like most drysine drones — one large and one small. It shimmered faintly in the multiple floodlights. Not a simple metallic sheen at all, but a chitinous multi-layered coating, reflecting light at unpredictable angles as though the surface itself had depth.

Lisbeth beckoned to Hiro, and now various parren in the circle were turning to look, with the cool disapproval so common to their kind. Hiro went, noting holographic projectors about the circle, small spheres hung from the ceiling. He thought he could guess what those were for.

Timoshene studiously ignored him as he arrived by Lisbeth, and cast a visored stare over his escort instead... probably asking them on private coms whether they'd confiscated his weapons. Parren security teams were endlessly divided by these petty rivalries between those who served different masters, even within the same denomination.

"What are you doing here?" Lisbeth asked, still half-listening to ongoing coms discussion in one ear. "Isn't *Phoenix* leaving soon?"

"I asked the Captain if I could stay with you," said Hiro.

To her credit, Lisbeth did not look particularly surprised. "Well you'll need more than Erik's approval to do that," she said.

"Gesul's staff agreed. I'll be attached to your office. Thought I'd come and tell you in person."

Lisbeth smiled, a touch sarcastically. "Well that's noble of you." She was letting her frizzy brown hair revert to its natural state these days, having lately acquired the confidence to tell her maids to take their severe combs and pins somewhere else, on non-ceremonial days at least. And here in the gravitational habitat, maids were in less supply than they had been in the Kunadeen. "Erik can afford to lose you?"

Hiro made a face. "*Phoenix* has plenty of people who've been learning the few specialist skills I possess. Most of those skills I can't execute on a military ship anyway. I'm much better suited to a civilian environment."

Lisbeth turned to the parren on her other side, a dark-clad man with a more traditional veil across head and face atop his jumpsuit, who'd been listening in. She spoke to him in Porgesh, the fluency of which still amazed Hiro. He'd known Lisbeth was smart, but working security for the Debogande household on Homeworld, everyone had made jokes about her lack of application — compared to the rest of the family, anyhow. Now that she'd truly set her mind to something, the results were astonishing.

"You see, Orun?" the translator crackled in Hiro's ear, in a fair approximation of Lisbeth's voice. *"I did tell you."*

"Yes you did, Lisbeth-sa," said the Domesh named Orun. *"I concede."*

Lisbeth looked back in amusement. "I told Orun that you would prefer to remain with the parren while *Phoenix* went wandering. Much more your sort of environment, I said. Lots of intrigue." Her gaze flashed with something more than simple amusement — she knew, that look said, far more than she let on for the parren. 'I'll maintain the illusion for now,' that look said. 'But if you cause me too much trouble, you're on your own'. Somewhere in the past year, Lisbeth had not merely acquired competence and authority, but layers.

"You know me too well," Hiro said blandly. She knew that he'd never entirely left Federal Intelligence. She knew what concerns drove him now. She was still human, and shared those concerns. But that did not mean she'd let him get in Gesul's way, no matter what Hiro thought of the consequences of Gesul's rise for human security.

"This is Orun, by the way," she said. "He's my Chief of Communications... you two haven't met?"

Hiro was further introduced to Lisbeth's Chief Scientist — an Incefahd named Dolesh, and a pair of denominational liaisons named Rafad and Sameel, from denominations with which Hiro was only vaguely familiar. He wasn't especially surprised that Lisbeth's staff were not entirely Domesh — it suited Gesul's style entirely, for the same reason all the scientists and engineers in the room were from across House Harmony. Gesul welcomed a diversity of opinions to inform his leadership, the very reason Lisbeth was here at all, where most parren leaders of most denominations would not welcome her. And so the people with guns and blades, whose loyalty had to be guaranteed, were clad entirely in black, but everyone else was from all corners.

Hiro wondered how Gesul could trust what those non-Domesh scientists told him, given that their primary loyalties were to the heads of their denominations, not to Gesul personally. No doubt his head scientist would be Domesh, and besides, it would benefit no denomination to interfere with the accumulation of scientific data that would benefit all House Harmony. Perhaps this was Gesul's way of making clear to all the denominations that they really were all in this together. And now, with Sordashan newly arrived in orbit above them, threatening all House Harmony on Defiance with whatever-it-was that he wasn't communicating yet, all of the Harmony denomination leaderships would follow Gesul, or perish at Sordashan's hand.

"So how does it go?" Hiro asked, nodding to the drysine head on the plinth.

"Well, they've invited Alired to come and watch," said Lisbeth. "So I'd imagine it's going well. Feels a bit like old times, doesn't it?"

"A drysine queen head surrounded by non-drysine engineers," said Hiro. "Sure." It felt... dangerous. And exciting. Hiro could feel it in the air, crackling with energy that had nothing to do with the humming machinery. He knew he'd made the right choice to stay here. On the ship he'd been a rat in a cage until *Phoenix* made some new port of call... and from what he'd heard, getting out and mingling among the croma wasn't going to be easy. But here, inserted into Lisbeth's office at the side of perhaps the second-most-powerful leader in all parren space... there were possibilities. "Do we know what Sordashan's threatening?"

"The speculation is that he's assessing the situation here in person before making any demands," said Lisbeth. "We know he's been talking to Alired."

"Alired hasn't accepted the offer to come here?"

"I don't think she needs to. She has spies. Briefing Sordashan will take priority."

"And that's where she's wrong," said Hiro, gazing at the head on the plinth.

The holoprojectors began flashing, great sheets of light falling like curtains about the plinth, scrolling images, landscapes, clouds. Parren watched, many gazing up to take in the entire projection, marvelling at their beauty. It was Hannachiam, of course, making commentary the only way she could.

"Has she actually been constructive?" Hiro asked. "Or does she just like flashing pictures of grass?"

"It's a bit of a puzzle," said Lisbeth. "Hanna's logical functions are all administrative. She doesn't have much technical knowledge, though she has had access to the data-core, via Styx. We still think she's got some kind of knowledge of a queen's software template, if you like. Maybe she is the template herself, in some ways — the data-core data's very raw, it requires a lot more unpacking than we think anyone's had time to do."

"Styx could do it," said Hiro.

"And Styx always insists she's not an engineer, that her brain isn't optimally configured for those things. The technical complexities here are insane — configuring the software that feeds into a drysine queen's head... one of the parren scientists figured it out, she said it was more raw computing data than all parren civilisation generated in the first century after parren first made computers."

Hiro shook his head. "I think it's interactive. A two-way process. The queen participates in writing its own software, given the right cues."

Lisbeth gave him a skeptical look. "And you'd know this *how*?"

"Because all their tech talks to each other all the time," said Hiro. "You notice it if you're been running communications ops on it the past half-year, which none of these scientist guys have done. Everything talks to everything else, constantly. It's a web. A lot of their infant tech is self-actualising, it helps write itself. And it makes each new unit slightly unique, like a snowflake. Which explains why each of the Major's new drones has a distinct personality, where if their software had all been mass-produced in the same location and fed in remotely, they'd be identical."

"So if you're right," Lisbeth said thoughtfully, looking at the inert queen, "she won't be precisely like Styx. That could be a good thing."

"Or a bad one," said Hiro. "Styx is gentle and kind by the standards of her people, across history."

"Thanks," Lisbeth said drily. "Comforting."

Hannachiam's images switched from drifting sheets of rain across mountains, to an old parren cityscape — wood shingled rooves, tall temple towers, pedestrians on old streets alight with glowing lanterns. Watching parren actually gasped, and a few held recording devices to capture the images. Some of those had made it out to parren space, Hiro knew, where Hanna's pronouncements had acquired a cult following now that everyone knew of her existence. Parren had a mystical side, and for some, Hanna was now a kind of oracle. Hiro was a little surprised that Gesul allowed these recordings to get out... but then, so much of the fear and anger directed against him for having dug up the old drysine past was based on a single, narrow view of what the drysines had been. While Styx was the perfect embodiment of that fear, Hannachiam was the likely antidote. What this new queen would be was anyone's guess. Hiro thought he could see what Gesul was attempting, but it seemed an awfully big gamble.

"Anyhow," said Hiro. "I must go. Good talk."

"You're not going to hang around and see if she wakes up?" Lisbeth wondered.

"If that's what everyone's waiting for, they're wasting their time. She'll wake up slowly, consciousness doesn't just happen like flipping a switch, she'll have a billion-squared calculations to run per microsecond for the next few days yet, I think. Then she'll start wondering what's going on."

"Or who she is," said Lisbeth, with trepidation.

Hiro smiled. "I don't think so. The drysines wouldn't have become the most successful AI race if they'd had any doubt who they were."

WITH THE COUNTDOWN timer inside five minutes, Sordashan, the supreme leader of all parren peoples, contacted Erik directly. *"Captain Debogande. You will remain where you are, or your warship will be fired upon and destroyed."*

"Sordashan-sa," said Erik, visor down and eyes on the holographic projection of his trajectory, and thinking how strange it was

that for all their pageantry, parren didn't require the multiple honou-
rifics and titles that one might expect. Even the great leaders
preferred just one name, as though that single name was to be sufficient to inspire awe and wonder in all those surrounding. "If your
fleet fires upon the *UFS Phoenix*, your fleet will be entirely destroyed,
yourself along with it. We did not defeat the deepynine horde by accident, and this ship is now more advanced than anything your people
have seen. We mean neither you, nor House Fortitude, any harm. But
if you declare yourselves our enemies, you will die."

There was a pause. About him the bridge crew kept working, each
attentive to his or her own station. Down back, all were aboard save
for most of the marines, Trace included. The shuttles were impossible to dock while *Phoenix* was in the bay, and Erik preferred them to
stay on Defiance during the initial launch regardless. If the ship's
fancy new tech didn't live up to his threats, at least Phoenix Company
would survive the resulting fireball.

"*Captain,*" came Styx's voice in his ear, "*I have probed their communication defences. They are close enough to surface communications that
there are now multiple points of access. I predict a fifty percent success rate
in disabling their vessels by this method.*"

"Thank you Styx, let's hope we don't need it."

"*Hope is an unnecessary state of mind. I will act upon your command.*"

"Now you sound like Major Thakur," said Erik.

"*This is a compliment. Thank you Captain.*"

Erik rolled his eyes. Well, at least Styx was aboard, with Peanut,
Bucket and Wowser, all having toiled these last few weeks to get
Phoenix ready in time. She still professed to not be thrilled about the
mission, but was no longer so negative about it in public. More to the
point, Erik thought, staying with Gesul would be exceedingly
dangerous in the present circumstances. She had much old history
with the parren people, and wars could conceivably be started just to
end her life. Worse, Erik did not think Gesul would want her for
exactly that reason... and because, if he had any sense at all, he'd fear
and distrust her. But she had her new protege in Gesul's hands,
programmed in part by her, who could maintain a drysine command

presence with Gesul while Styx herself was gone. Gesul no doubt planned to try and make this new queen answerable more to him than to Styx... which Erik thought was worth a try, but vastly unlikely to succeed.

"They make no threat to *Makimakala*," Sasalaka observed from Erik's right-and-behind, Helm's position in the old bridge configuration and the new.

"*Makimakala* is a Dobruta vessel and they risk conflict with tavalai if they fire on her," said Erik. "He figures he can shoot at us and no one back home will care."

"He's right, too," said Kaspowitz.

The bridge did not look particularly different at first glance. Only once settled in the chair with all systems activated did Erik truly see the difference. Partly the graphical layers on his visuals were even more precise and clean than before, but mostly in that the things they told him were ridiculous. He was gazing now at Kaspowitz's projected escape trajectory against the Defiance gravity slope, and then the impossible, physics-defying gravity plunge about the singularity Defiance orbited. The old *Phoenix* would not have been able to perform the manoeuvres those lines described, not even close. Also there were readings from the powerplant, and range-horizons from the various weapons systems, all off-the-scale compared to what Erik was accustomed to. He only hoped he could manage to manoeuvre the ship in combat without accidentally squishing all the human crew to a pulp with that crazy, oversized torch mounted on the ship's rear.

Two minutes later, Sordashan called him back. "*Phoenix. We will discuss this. You are invited to this ship. We will talk as equals.*"

"Sordashan-sa, *Phoenix* is less than two minutes from launch. I regret the inconvenience, but we have an appointment with the croma."

"*This meeting with the croma will have strategic implications for all parren. It is forbidden.*"

"*Phoenix* is on human business, and should you attempt to stop us your reign over all parren will end. You cannot defeat this warship."

"And you have equipped House Harmony warships the same as yours. This is a mortal threat to the stability of parren space."

"House Harmony has offered to share this technology with you, and has invited you now to inspect various vessels under construction on Defiance. Their firepower is aimed at the deepynines who threaten all parren space, not at House Fortitude, and again, Gesul has pledged repeatedly that the peaceful accord he swore to not make conflict with Tobenrah of House Harmony also extends to Sordashan of House Fortitude. It seems to me that your issues are with Gesul, and I suggest you speak to him instead. *Phoenix* will launch in one minute."

The numbers on his visor continued to wind down. "That's it," said Shilu from up front. "I'm getting no more from him."

"Their posture looks unchanged," said Geish from Scan. "We're going to be getting it from multiple sides if they fire on us."

"If these jump engines work the way Rooke says they do," said Erik, "they can shoot at us all they like and it won't matter."

The manoeuvre looked relatively simple, provided everything worked the way all the dry-runs and system-checks said they should. And therein lay the drama. Erik sipped from the water tube at his shoulder to ease his dry mouth, and tightened his hands on the twin control grips. One twist, one flick of a thumb or finger button, one blink on a holographic icon, could activate any of a hundred systems that could either save everyone's lives, or get everyone killed. In all the galaxy Erik did not think there were many jobs that entailed such instantaneous consequence.

The counter hit zero, and he ignited thrust with a simultaneous double-click of both thumbs. *Phoenix* barely rumbled, an anti-climactic shudder, then a gentle force that pressed them all back.

"Grapple release," Sasalaka said calmly. "All good."

Forward visual displayed on the periphery of Erik's wrap-around vision, and now showed the rim of their berth, the hole that *Phoenix* had been sitting in for the past five months, slowly moving by. The pace accelerated, and he held thrust at barely a single G, all that was necessary to get them clear.

"Engines all green," Sasalaka confirmed what he could already see in another corner of the display. "Power is good, temperatures good. Berth control says thrust ducting good, no damage to berth."

"Lieutenant Rooke," said Erik, watching all indicators simultaneously but wanting to hear it from the man himself. "How are we looking?"

"Well there is one small anomaly, Captain," came Rooke's voice. He sounded excited. *"Thrust chamber temperatures are below prediction, and ignition pressures are putting less stress on the superconductors than I thought. I think you're in danger of boring her to death."*

Erik repressed the grin that broke momentarily through his focus, then flipped channels. "Hello Lieutenant Hausler, how's it look to you?"

"It looks fucking beautiful, Captain," came Hausler's reply from PH-1, watching from nearby. Past the drawling pilot-cool, he sounded emotional. *"She looks stunning, big white thrust plume fading to blue, barely half the luminosity she had before."* A few words were exchanged off-mike, then, *"Corey says you should hear what the guys in the back think."*

The channel flipped, and then Erik's ears were filled with the excited swearing and whooping of the marines in PH-1's hold, watching on their screens and visor displays. Erik's grin escaped his control. "Thank you PH-1, standby while we gauge this guy's response, then we'll see about arranging a rendezvous trajectory for you."

Scan was showing him several House Fortitude warships passing near orbit, with hypothetical shots at their rising trajectory. "I'm not seeing any hostile response, Captain," said Geish. "The magnification on Scan is fucking amazing, I can see if their turrets so much as twitch in our direction."

"Yeah, I don't like this position though," said Erik, watching those converging crossfire lines as the trajectories extended. "The longer we sit in their sights, the more chance they get bad ideas. We are approaching minimum safe range from the ground, prepare for a hard burn. Lieutenant Rooke, confirm jumpline status?"

"Jumplines look good, Captain," Rooke confirmed what Erik's own displays showed. *"I'd recommend just a tap for starters, then we work our way up from there."*

"Just a tap, I hear you Lieutenant. All hands standby, hard manoeuvre imminent." It wasn't supposed to be possible this close to Defiance. The moon did not create an enormous gravity-well, but the singularity about which it orbited smothered all jump-engine activity like a blanket. Gravitational forces compressed space to a greater density, making it impossible for jump engines to bend space, the same way that a person would find wood harder to bend with bare hands than paper. Even the deepynine warships that had just recently attacked Defiance had not been able to use jump engines this close to the singularity, and had been forced to decelerate with real-space thrusters all the way in, thus making them vulnerable to defensive fire. But the jump engine in *Phoenix's* alien rear-half was not human, alo, or deepynine — it was drysine, and the drysines, Styx always insisted, had been the most advanced civilisation in the history of the Spiral, and possibly far, far beyond.

Erik opened the thrust up slowly, watching the engine gauges, and not wanting to hit full thrust while they were still close to the surface lest the backwash burn anything exposed on the surface. Thrust passed five Gs and the indicators barely moved, as though *Phoenix* were bored, as Rooke had suggested. They passed safe-range, and Erik opened thrust right up to ten, possibly alarming the House Fortitude ships watching... and then got a final green light from the jumplines, and gave them a tap.

Phoenix emerged flying, a mere ten thousand kilometres an hour faster, nothing compared to the full-strength jump pulses that could be achieved in deep space away from gravity-wells. But it was a feat of technology unseen in the Spiral for the past twenty five thousand years, and as *Phoenix's* crew double-checked systems, the com traffic all about Defiance fell to an eery silence.

"There's no one talking, sir," said Shilu. "Just dead silence. Everyone's watching."

"Lieutenant Shilu, get me contact with *Lorna*."

"Yes Captain. Contact established, go ahead."

"Hello Sordashan-sa, this is Captain Debogande of the human warship *Phoenix*. We retain physical possession of the drysine data-core, but you will find that its entire contents have been copied onto storage formats on Defiance. Gesul has sworn to share this technology with House Fortitude and all parren, and is sworn to your service in combating the deepynine threat. Talk to him in a spirit of peace and brotherhood, and all parren will benefit." He ended the link.

"Gonna be hell to pay when someone realises we lied about the data-core," said Kaspowitz.

"Gesul's problem," said Erik, and thankful for it. It had been astonishingly hard to part with the drysine data-core. For several insane, deadly months it had been his sole focus, *Phoenix*'s only hope of saving the human race from the peril of super-advanced technologies. The list of names of ship crew who'd died to win it was horrifyingly long. When the decision had been made to risk the core on *Lien Wang* for the long journey home, he'd nearly cried.

But there hadn't been a choice. *Phoenix* had been given a new mission just as important, and if she were lost while carrying the data-core, the outcome for humanity would be worse than if the core had never been found at all. Gesul's scientists had completed their full copy, the storage files of which were thought to occupy several rooms, and word was they were now making progress on the all-important indexing system. Erik suspected that part of the reason Gesul was interested in incorporating sentient drysine AIs into the Harmony command structure was just so that he could efficiently sort and analyse all the data.

It would turn House Harmony and the parren into a significantly larger power than they had been. That impacted everyone in the Spiral. To be sure, it could start horrible wars. Humanity *had* to get that data soon, because however reasonable Gesul seemed now, there was no guarantee he would still be alive in a few weeks, let alone the few decades that stability required. And it seemed to Erik entirely possible that *Lien Wang*'s mission was likely now more important than that of *Phoenix*.

"I'm not sure 'brotherhood' will translate," said Shilu. "Parren don't do family like humans do."

"Whatever," said Erik, scanning the new trajectories Kaspowitz's projections were showing him. "Let the damn parren worry about translations for a change. Lieutenant Kaspowitz, I think the smartest thing to do is continue this full loop around the singularity and pick up our shuttles on the return leg. I want to do a few more performance checks before we leave the system."

"Aye Captain, we can do that. You'll have my best course in thirty seconds."

"Captain, should we show all of our performance in front of the parren?" Sasalaka asked. "Maybe better to keep some secrets?"

"No," said Erik, quite deliberately. "We're only going to show them a tiny bit of what we can do. But I think it will be much safer for everyone if they see this with their own eyes."

12

Two rotations later and shortly after her morning exercises Lisbeth sat at her workdesk in the habitat and flipped through her ever-growing stack of incoming assignments. Parren bureaucracy accumulated like bureaucracy anywhere in the Spiral, though was thankfully not as bad as tavalai bureaucracy. She sat in the low chair one of her staff had thoughtfully fabricated for her — parren weren't much on chairs, but Lisbeth's legs, back and circulation were relieved to have this one.

Her office was decorated in the Shudaran style — Gesul's preferred meditative practice. Domesh, but not the spartan minimalism of the Koripar. There were minor decorations — a tapestry hung on the trestle of a climbing vine that ascended one wall. About its base, a few decorative stones — 'shoda', Harmony parren called them, meaning something like 'positive space', as opposed to the negative space created by the gaps between the shodas in a garden, or a floor decoration. Wall displays showed various parren cities and old monuments that Lisbeth had never seen in person, though one remained fixed on a view of Shiwon on Homeworld, seen from the hills not far from the Debogande family home. The decoration made an ambience, important to Harmony parren as conducive to a calm demeanour and productive mood.

After *Phoenix* had launched, she'd done a fast loop around the singularity, then decelerated with several equally impossible V-dumps to pick up each of her now-five shuttles in succession. No ship from the Fortitude fleet had made any gesture or sound of disapproval, perhaps realising that the humans hadn't been exaggerating when they'd said it could be fatal. Then *Phoenix* had joined with *Makimakala*, boosted V at a more sedate pace that the tavalai could keep up with, and jumped, heading for Lusakia System.

Which had left Lisbeth here, on this most alien of worlds, surrounded by aliens and a long, long way away from anything she'd once considered familiar. Panic had threatened... but she'd told herself firmly to stop being stupid, and focused on her work. Being busy had helped her on *Phoenix* when she'd first arrived there, and the claustrophobia combined with disorientation at the unreliable gravity had threatened to unhinge her completely. But head-down in Engineering, buried in some tedious data-analysis, she'd learned that the panic-sensitive portions of her brain could be safely ignored. Like a grandstanding child without an audience, the fear had slunk away, disappointed that no one was paying attention.

A coms light flashed on her screen, and she blinked on it. Audio played in her ear — it was Orun, of course, her Chief of Communications. *"Hello Lisbeth, the Chief Science Officer for House Acquisitive on Defiance has a query regarding something Captain Debogande said in a briefing five rotations ago..."*

"Oh right, which one was that?" Lisbeth flicked to the relevant date. "Yes, the briefing to the science officers... what was their query precisely?"

"House Acquisitive wishes to have your translation on several points, the translator is functional but the context is lacking."

"Tell them to send it through." On her side screen, the welcome to Sordashan was playing. Various cameras relayed vision, Lisbeth had no idea who was sorting which, but some idiot in House Fortitude had decided that House Harmony's interior facilities were inadequate to receive the supreme leader of all parren, and so they were doing it outside. In the vacuum. Lisbeth did not know what the largest assembled EVA in Spiral history was — doubtless some of the larger wars had gathered an impressive number of armoured marines together in airless environments, but she doubted there would be many larger than the fifty thousand assembling across a high, flat stretch of massed landing pads by the Zho Ren District industrial zone. It overlooked the steel canyons of the Tower District, a vast expanse of rank upon rank of pressure-suited parren. Word was that it had taken four hours to assemble everyone, given the time it took to get through airlocks not equipped for a fraction this many. There were even flags and symbols on poles... utterly pointless without a breeze to fly on, and god forbid one of those things put a hole in someone's suit. Lisbeth had no doubt that parren would rather depressurise and expire in silence rather than break ranks and run for an airlock.

Sordashan's command shuttle was landing now, all running lights ablaze, Fortitude marines leaping from the rear even as it touched. Surrounded by House Harmony, a display of trust brought about by overwhelming power and Gesul's declaration of fealty in the face of alien threat. All parren had heard about the biotech analysis from Mylor Station, and the mortal threat it posed to all of the alo/deepynine's potential enemies... yet still they poured their energies into these grand displays of rank and competitive power. Sometimes Lisbeth found parren culture intoxicatingly wonderful... and at other times she thought they all needed a good slapping. Gesul and his senior officials were all required to stand for hours out in that, but Lisbeth was thankfully not senior enough to qualify.

Sordashan and his advisors had apparently decided not to declare any sort of war against Gesul's House Harmony — mostly, Lisbeth's advisors assured her, because Gesul had acquired too much momentum in the flux for Sordashan to risk it without triggering a massive phase-swing away from Fortitude toward Harmony. Further, *Phoenix* had just increased her status even further by defying Sordashan's commands in full view of everyone, then skipping away to jump with previously-unseen technology, and declaring war on

Phoenix's allies would be seen as even worse form. Further still, *Phoenix* had demonstrated the technology to be gained for all parren, and Sordashan was going to find that difficult to turn his back on, no matter how some parren probably wished he would.

Lisbeth added the House Acquisitive query to her stack, then returned to reading the report from the House Harmony fleet commanders on the Battle for Defiance. It was very dense going, and often she called up the translator to deal with difficult passages or technical terminology. There was a lot of information about House Harmony fleet deployments, procedures and tactics that would have intrigued human Fleet. Lisbeth recalled her meeting with Hiro's 'friend' Daica, and the threats Fleet command had made against her family. Just give them something, he'd said. It will help make the case for your family. But if she got caught doing it...

Her tabletop screens suddenly overlaid with swimming colours, like an aurora that flowed above her work. She dialled down the screen's intensity, her reading dimmed as the flowing colours resolved into images — parren faces, parren talking, parren officials in stuffy robes shuffling along old temple corridors.

"Hello Hanna," said Lisbeth. It happened sometimes, when Hannachiam wanted to talk. Usually she only did it for good reason, but not always. "How are you today?"

The images changed to starships, and one starship in particular — *Phoenix*, in deep space and illuminated only by the approach lights of some nearby shuttle. Even had she not served on her personally, Lisbeth could have identified those lines amongst any number of other ships. Images of *Phoenix* blasting from Defiance's surface, two days ago.

"Yes Hanna," said Lisbeth with a faint smile. "I'm feeling a little sad that *Phoenix* has gone. But I have many friends here too. Are you watching the Sordashan ceremony?"

The images changed, and suddenly there were camera angles from within the great formations of suited parren, showing rank after symmetrical rank, and a glare of bright and shadow from the external floodlights. She must have been accessing helmet cameras, Lisbeth thought. The parren might not like that, but good luck explaining to Hanna why she shouldn't do it. More images then, planetside, of a spectacular gorge between three steep cliff-sides. A sheer valley, filled at its base by an enormous city, teeming about a big river that zagged through the grand old buildings and temples. A great waterfall fell from one cliff, tumbling over what looked like a kilometre's drop, its white plume sending sheets of spray across the valley, and a bright rainbow above the many rooftops.

Into the huge intersection of two valleys, an enormous temple had been carved into the base of a cliff, stepping up several great rises above the city. Upon those rising steps stood massed ranks of parren in rows... Lisbeth had seen great formations at the Kunadeen of House Harmony, but this looked at least twice the scale. And at the head of the formation grounds, looming above the rest, a high ceremony took place, colourful officials and presiding officials, as someone important was sworn in for something big. Lisbeth didn't know what, or if the images were real or something from Hanna's gargantuan imagination. But she recognised the place from pictures.

"That's Shonedene, the Fortitude home city. Where Sordashan rules from." Lisbeth frowned, wondering why Hanna was showing her this.

Something sounded on Lisbeth's audio — a rhythmic tapping. The images switched to writhing darkness — a hacksaw nest, a thicket of tunnels and activity, drysine drones scuttling past like bees in a hive. A camera pan, then a closeup of a big drone, tapping on something nearby. Those taps, and the tapping in Lisbeth's audio, were synchronised.

Lisbeth's eyes widened. "Hanna, does one of the drones wish to speak with me?"

The tapping stopped, and Lisbeth's screens turned blank. A crackling, like some ancient audio recording from the days of magnetic tape... or the static interference of a star's radiation. Then, *"Hello Lisbeth."*

The voice was female, high, clear and young. It spoke English. Lisbeth felt her breath catch. "Hello? Who is this?"

"I have decided that my name shall be Liala." Even Lisbeth heard of Liala. Liala was the child of fortune in one of the greatest parren plays ever written, a work simply entitled *Summer*, by the playwright Conelis. Not the largest speaking part even in that play, but Liala had come to take on a significance in parren culture perhaps exceeding that with which humans recalled Hamlet or Othello.

"Hello Liala," said Lisbeth, cautiously. Almost certainly she was speaking to an AI, but which one? Lately on Defiance, they'd been proliferating. "I was assured that Hannachiam was not capable of speech, that the very capability required a linear brain-function that was structurally beyond her... so I'm sure this can't be her."

"Yes," said Liala. *"I am Liala."*

Lisbeth waited a moment longer. "And who are you, Liala?"

"Well here's the thing," said Liala. *"I'm not sure yet."*

Lisbeth nearly laughed. She *should* have nearly panicked, but this had a certain symmetry to it. And she'd been assured it wouldn't happen for many days yet. She rather enjoyed it when Hiro was wrong, on small things at least. "Hello Liala. I can tell you how you came to be made, if that's puzzling you?"

"No, I think I know all of that." The young, female voice sounded quite informal. Almost conversational. If Lisbeth hadn't known where it came from, she'd have been sure it was a human being talking. Styx didn't talk like this... though Styx no doubt possessed the processing capability to simulate anything if she wished. But Styx had a reputation to protect, and did not choose to appear to others as an inexperienced child. *"I'd like to talk to you, though."*

"Why me?"

"Because you're an outsider in this city, like me. And because you know my mother far better than I do. You can provide context to what I see. The triangulation of an alternative viewpoint."

"Well hang on," said Lisbeth. "I'm not sure you want to start talking about Styx as your 'mother', for one thing."

"It's an approximate translation, from my context to yours."

"Yes, but I'm not sure it works as a translation. 'Mother', in my culture, implies a sense of loyalty to a greater family."

"*Mine too.*"

"But is your loyalty to Styx as an individual? Or to the entire drysine race?"

A brief pause. "*That is an interesting point, Lisbeth. You see, I am only several days old by human or parren measurement of time. I think I understand these concepts relatively well, but the inter-linguistic contexts escape me for the moment. If I am to form a precise understanding of these inter-relationships, I will require further conversation.*"

Lisbeth grinned. It was ridiculous. She'd known that conversation was utterly effortless to Styx, but this only demonstrated *how* effortless. A new drysine queen, several days old and already talking with greater social fluency and subtlety than Styx did, discussing matters of detail and abstraction like a human academic. Drysine intellect on this scale broke down all knowledge into simple data, then built it back up again in ever increasing layers of sophistication and complexity. Human prejudice insisted that a machine should talk like a machine, but the truth was that with enough processing power, all subtlety and nuance could be simulated by a sufficiently advanced AI without effort.

"Well I'm quite happy to talk to you if it will help," said Lisbeth. Her work would fall dreadfully behind, but she was sure that Gesul would agree that a relationship with Liala took precedence. "And I could recommend several others for you to talk to as well."

"*That would be most useful, thank you.*"

She'd start, Lisbeth thought, by recommending Gesul. Not only would he be fascinated, but she was certain that for Liala to have a relationship with her, but not with Gesul, would become increasingly dangerous. "So Liala. What have you learned so far?"

"*Parren history and literature, primarily.*"

"Which bits?"

"*Most bits. There are comprehensive libraries.*" Again, Lisbeth repressed a grin. "*I am not certain that I understand the context, though. Have you read a lot of parren literature?*"

"Oh, very little. Human brains are rather limited by the fact that we can only pay attention to one thing at a time. I've been busy."

"I've read a lot of human literature too. I'm sure your knowledge there would be greater." That would be news to her English teacher, Lisbeth thought. Mr Prakash would be laughing at the thought that this great drysine brain was consulting her as its first available expert on the subject.

"I know a little. What book would you like to discuss?"

"The Metaphysical Compendium of Physics by Doctor ES Wittstein seems an intriguing work. It was published a hundred and seventy six years ago, have you read it?"

Lisbeth lost control of her grin. "No, I can't say that I have. And really, I'm quite good at physics by human standards — I was trained as a starship engineer — but I don't think there's very much about physics that I could teach a drysine queen. Have you read Pride and Prejudice by the English author Jane Austen?"

"I have read every English author from that period, in full." She'd gone through the entire database of human and parren literature and history in a couple of days, Lisbeth thought. And forced that thought down, because it was impossible to concentrate on conversation when confronted with how utterly outmatched you were. *"This particular book was extremely puzzling."*

"What did you find puzzling, Liala?"

"Well first, what is 'marriage'? I understand what it is technically, but the emotional and psychological context eludes me."

"Now on this subject, I think I may be able to help you. But first, let me ask you... do you need anything, Liala? Do you have any physical requirements?" Given that you're currently just a head on a plinth in a parren engineering bay, she meant. She doubted those engineers would even be aware that the head was awake and talking to someone. Styx had been very good at doing all sorts of things with no one noticing.

"No thank you, Lisbeth. Physical interactions are of limited utility to me in the near term, it is data-link interactions that I require to stimulate brain development. However, in the middle-term, this will change."

"How so?"

"The drones in Defiance are adamant that I should have a body. They

suppose that the agreement made between themselves and Gesul of House Harmony is one of partnership, and that an equal partner and representative of Drysine Leader Styx should have full mobile autonomy."

"I'm not sure that House Harmony engineers have the ability to make a new queen's body," Lisbeth said cautiously.

"It does not matter," said Liala. *"The drones do."*

* * *

It took *Phoenix* six jumps to reach croma space, then another four to reach Do'Mela. Rooke assured them all that it could be done faster, but for those first six *Makimakala* was their escort, and could not be left behind. For the next four, inside croma space, they were escorted by a succession of croma vessels of respectable but still lesser performance than *Makimakala,* in whose company Erik was very determined not to let *Phoenix*'s true capabilities show.

Even without company, physics did not allow such journeys to be done quickly. Systems could only be traversed so fast in sublight, and the ideal entry and exit points from solar gravity-wells were perpendicular to the center of each well, offset to a degree determined by the power of a ship's jump engines. Put simply, when the jump exit point was on the far side of a gravity-well to its entry point, a ship had no choice but to traverse the entire system sub-light to exit on its far side... leading to the odd navigational effect that a zigzag course between stars was often faster than a direct line, because zigzags required a relatively short sub-light traverse — the thing that took the real time to happen.

As it was, each stop averaged two days, giving *Phoenix* and *Makimakala* twenty in total, and thirty-two in real-time once the time dilation from jump was calculated. It gave *Phoenix*'s crew plenty of time to continue repairs under Rooke's direction, and run systems checks on all the fancy new tech they were still unsure exactly how to operate. It also gave the patchwork crew of humans and tavalai a chance to get to know each other better — sometimes for better, sometimes for worse.

On the upside, Erik heard stories of some friendships forged, and cultural understandings reached. Tavalai were not an obnoxious or pricklish people — they worked hard with great discipline, and were driven by a powerful sense of duty to a greater cause. They did not always understand human humour, as humans sometimes struggled to grasp theirs in return, and were methodical and under-excitable by most human standards. 'Slow', was the usual human observation, while the tavalai found humans sometimes alarmingly unpredictable and emotional. But *Phoenix's* human crew would never complain that the tavalai did not pull their weight, and that much respect at least seemed mutual.

On the downside, there were many language difficulties, as only the most senior tavalai officers spoke fluent English. Translators were often unreliable in the inconvenient circumstances of spacer duties, where crew needed to coordinate fast without endless explanations, and thus it had been deemed logical that humans and tavalai should work in segregated teams for a while at least, to improve coordination. It was leading, Erik's human Petty and Warrant Officers reported, to an inevitable division through the crew beyond the simple division of species — humans and tavalai working mostly with their own kind, with some groups rarely mixing. In that environment, Erik didn't see how true integration was likely to happen, but neither was it obvious what, if anything, could be done about it.

Another issue was that teams of tavalai would require tavalai of higher rank to command them. Many had held higher rank in previous duties with tavalai Fleet, but Erik was reluctant to simply hand out ranking equivalents without first having seen what these crew were capable of. That in turn was threatening to cause tension among tavalai who felt they should be ranked more highly, not from personal ego, but from a very well developed tavalai sense of propriety. But if unknown and alien crew were abruptly promoted to a position of authority over human crew who had fought and bled together on this mission for a year now, and in the war against the tavalai long before, then Erik was certain there'd be even more trouble from the human majority.

The most well integrated of all the new crew were the drones.

They did require sleep of an artificial sort, a mental downtime where artificial brains sorted all the data from things they'd done that day into long and short-term memory and processed it for things to be learned... much like what sleep did for the human brain as well. But hacksaw sleep was only five hours, and the rest of the time they liked to work, finding that endlessly stimulating without apparent need for rest or recreation. Mostly they worked with Rooke in Midships, where plenty of engine-related and control systems required calibration. Bucket once did twenty hours straight on some of the most fiddly and technical electronics installations that human crew had been dreading, showing that drones were not just muscle, but could think to a level that humans might consider genius in one of their own.

It did not make it any less disconcerting to turn a corner and find that great, multi-legged shape clattering toward you, but the crew could at least see that the occasional hair-raising shock was worth it. Intriguingly, some of the Engineering crew were teaching the one drone who did enjoy the occasional hour off — Peanut — to play poker. He was struggling to process odds, chance and bluff as well as humans did, and seemed to find his constant failure fascinating, being understandably unaccustomed to being beaten by humans at anything involving calculation. A few times he'd even lost to Skah, who unsurprisingly for a kid who hung around in Engineering had somewhere picked up the rules and the aptitude.

The upturn in crew morale was Erik's favourite thing to observe on the journey. The news of Mylor Station had terrified everyone, but it had also galvanised them. Someone had to go to investigate this latest threat, and the most obvious someone was *Phoenix*. That decided, they got down to it without further doubt or complaint, and made the best of a bad lot.

The first two transit points *Phoenix* jumped through in croma space were dark-mass, with barely enough gravity to pull ships out of hyperspace. Each was surrounded by multiple nav buoys and defensive emplacements, which all the bridge crew found very odd, given these mass-points were further from reeh space where the majority of croma defences were known to be concentrated. Further, there did not appear to be any strategic reasoning behind the positions of those defensive emplacements, but rather a scattering of random firepower that would do little to deter any intruders who arrived.

The third transit point was a red dwarf with a pair of near-orbiting gas giants and a lot of dreary, lifeless rocks — as unremarkable and common a system-formation as could be found anywhere in the galaxy. And yet Scan counted thirty-one defensive emplacements, including a few large ones built onto the rocky surface of a moon in orbit about an outer, smaller gas world. Putting defensive emplacements on uninhabited moons was silly. It might have made sense if the moon or its neighbouring world had something on its surface worth defending, but any spacer tactician knew that planetary bodies were the source of vast fire-shadows that blocked line-of-sight across enormous approach vectors, and were best avoided.

Even putting a missile station at a good approach latitude with unobstructed field-of-view made little sense in an unremarkable system with nothing to defend. Wanting to deny depth-of-mobility to any attacking forces that somehow breached the Croma Wall made sense, but it would take far more than defensive emplacements to do that against ships of the quality that the reeh reputedly possessed. Even a dwarf system was an awfully large amount of space for immobile, orbiting fire stations to cover, and being unable to evade, they were utterly vulnerable to return fire of sufficient volume to penetrate their defensive batteries. In everything Erik had learned about space warfare, these defences were a total waste of resources — maintaining them in operational order would cost yet more resources, all of which could surely be better spent elsewhere. But the Croma Wall was the one feature of croma civilisation most of the Spiral *had* heard of, and for many thousands of years it had held at bay one of the least-savoury near-Spiral species around, so clearly the croma were no strategic dummies. *Phoenix*'s spacer officers all agreed that either the croma were more wealthy than had been reported, or there was something else going on.

* * *

PHOENIX ARRIVED at Do'Mela System with the usual rush of sensation, Erik blinking hard against the dizziness and blurred vision, trying to get his eyes to focus.

"Buoys confirm Do'Mela," Kaspowitz announced to the bridge. "We are in the slot, point-zero-three AU from Do'Ran, V point two-five, two-one degrees from ecliptic."

"Scan looks good," said Geish, running through the standard arrival chatter as Erik sipped water from his shoulder tube, and saw everything unfolding in the holographic space before his visor long before his crew spoke the words. "No threatening marks, lane buoys in good order, nearest mark is point zero zero two AU, cruising velocity."

"Timer set on *Makimakala*," added Second Lieutenant Jiri from Scan Two. "One minute forty from estimated arrival, two minutes fifteen to the *Pau*." The *Pau* was the croma vessel that had been accompanying them from the dwarf system, having apparently been waiting there for such an eventuality. The croma hadn't said much, only that *Phoenix* and *Makimakala* should go first, withhold broadcasting ID to the new system until *Pau* arrived behind, then everyone would transmit together. It had seemed sensible to Erik — a joint transmission avoided confusion of who was with who, and *Pau* coming in last prevented the more powerful alien ships from running her over in any jump miscalculation, plus gave *Pau* a better tactical position should the aliens try anything unwelcome. But it did lead to these uncomfortable first few minutes on the *Phoenix* bridge, alone in an alien system, looking at all of these alien ships on scan and knowing that in a few minutes more the lightwave of *Phoenix*'s jump arrival would reach them, and they'd start wondering who this new arrival was with no ID. If *Pau* for some reason didn't actually arrive behind them... well, hell of a practical joke that would be.

Do'Mela was enormous. The star was a big F-class, bright-white and stable, with a neighbouring gas giant that Erik guessed would have been twice its current size when this system first formed, having been blasted down to something smaller by the solar wind. Do'Ran was the fourth planet, plenty further out from its sun than Home-world, but still in the habitable zone thanks to the sun's size. Further out were bigger giants, including one of the largest rock worlds Erik had ever seen, and a huge crowd of outer-system traffic on Scan — big stations, surface bases, no doubts lots of mining and industry, everything a major system of a wealthy, successful space-faring species should be.

"Lots of chatter," Shilu remarked. "All business by the sound of it. The translator's not having any problems, though there's a lot of encryption. A number of primary dialects, as we've been told. I think we're going to miss being among aliens with only one primary language, Captain."

"You mean *you're* going to miss it," said Second Lieutenant Raf Corrig from Arms One, without sympathy.

"Scan calculates upwards of two hundred starships," said Geish. "That's from IDs broadcast, most at major stations around Do'Ran. Doubtless there's military traffic here we're not registering. There appears to be five major stations around Do'Ran..."

"*Makimakala* just arrived," Jiri interrupted briefly, as Erik saw that familiar, comforting blip appear on Scan to their rear. "They're in the slot, all looks good."

"Transmission from *Makimakala* indicates all good," Shilu confirmed that.

"Five major stations at Do'Ran," Geish continued his previous analysis, "about twenty minor ones, they've got three moons so lots of bases, Do'Ran lunar traffic alone looks like about a hundred smaller ships in transit. Broadcast IDs from inter-system traffic looks about a thousand, probably more. If there's two docked for every one moving, we can calculate three, maybe three-and-a-half thousand. A couple of those big outer-system stations look like they've got a twenty-million capacity. And the volume of light traffic coming off that big rock world tells me there's some big cities down there, possibly a popula-tion of a few hundred million at least."

"Coms supports that," Shilu added. "Lots of com traffic, enormous relays. Do'Ran's not the only world here with a significant population."

Everyone on the bridge took a moment just to marvel. It wasn't anything they hadn't seen before, in human, tavalai or parren space. But officially speaking at least, no humans had ever been to croma space. Here was an entirely new civilisation, thriving beyond the sight and knowledge of every human to have ever lived. Until now.

"Coms, are those buoys being helpful?" Erik asked.

"Um... yes Captain, I'm getting full data from them, all navigational and coms, we all are. Makes things much easier than scanning the system raw."

"I'm sure. How about we don't trust that, huh?"

"I copy that, Captain," said Shilu.

"Good idea," Kaspowitz agreed.

"Captain," said Styx on coms, *"I am analysing incoming buoy traffic, I will inform you of any anomalies."*

"Thank you, Styx."

"Jump contact directly astern," said Geish. "Transponder is clear, it's the *Pau*."

The croma ship was coming in broadcasting wide — a warship of Clan Croma'Dokran, escorting two alien vessels to the homeworld of the Croma'Dokran. The *Pau* would have been classified as a medium cruiser in human space, powerful and fast, several shuttles attached and possibly a marine contingent. Certainly there was plenty of room on that crew cylinder, a one-point-two times larger circumference and a slightly faster rotation. The croma had apparently sacrificed some gravity to reduce rotational torque, which beyond certain levels made the ship more difficult to manoeuvre. Croma were designed by evolution to prefer one-point-three and a bit of a standard human gravity, though the sketchy information Erik had read indicated they came in all different sizes. Where croma were concerned, no one seemed particularly clear.

"Captain," reported Shilu, "those fire stations are making no effort to stay hidden. They're broadcasting transponder IDs."

There'd been a lot of defensive fire stations at the last world, but nothing compared to Do'Mela. Scan laid them out in a bristling array of red dots on Erik's holographic vision, covering this approach, neighbouring approaches, all approaches, zenith and nadir, close-in and further out.

"One thousand, three hundred and forty six," said Sasalaka as the numbers appeared on her displays too. "Crazy."

It was worse than crazy. That many defensive stations would interfere with defensive deployments in a sensible defence of the system. So much ordnance released at once would deny lanes of deployment to defensive and offensive ships alike. If defensive ships could not effectively counter-manoeuvre, all advantage lay with the attackers, who in any attack run were the ones to choose where the battle would be fought. And so many defensive stations could not be resupplied quickly once they'd run out of ammunition, meaning attacking ships could make multiple runs to bleed them dry, pulse up to higher-V to avoid getting hit, and be at little risk from counter-attacking defensive forces who would be as worried about getting hit by their own ordnance as the attackers were. Once dry, useless fire stations would require more ships to quickly rearm them than it took to effectively defend the system. Homeworld had had only twenty-one fire stations, and Fleet's best tactical minds thought that plenty.

"I'm suddenly losing all confidence in this vaunted 'croma wall'," said Kaspowitz, eyeing those charts with distaste.

"Maybe it's a delaying tactic," suggested Jiri from Scan Two. "Slow down the reeh until help arrives from elsewhere.

"Maybe they're not all operational," added Harris from Arms Two.

"Given how old a lot of that ammunition must be with the reload times," Corrig replied from her side, "I reckon they'd hit each other more than the enemy. Even our most advanced guidance systems can't be trusted to hit the right thing after fifty years in a rack."

"Here's something," said Shilu, scrolling intently through new datafeeds. "The firebases' ID beacons are coming out of the translator as family names and dates. Or that's what the translator says they are anyway, however much we can trust a croma translator. Some of the dates look quite old, a couple of them are... well, sounds a bit unlikely to me, but I'm looking at one that says it's two-and-a-half thousand years old."

"So what the hell use is an antique in defending a system?" Corrig wondered.

The first scheduled V-dump along this approach lane was coming up in three minutes, and neither coms nor scan indicated anything threatening, so Erik was inclined to allow the chatter. The croma were a piece of a new puzzle they'd have to solve in order to find what they were looking for.

He flipped channels. "Hello Stan, I take it you're listening in?"

"Hello Captain," came Stan Romki's voice. Probably he'd be in his quarters, fastened into his acceleration sling until the all-clear sounded, watching on AR glasses and audio. *"I am listening in. As you know, my readings on the croma have been infuriatingly incomplete, so I cannot say for sure. But croma clans are led by many large and powerful families, and those families compete with each other to build various monuments. Some of them are extraordinary, there are old towers and temples on their homeworld that can be seen from space, they love to build things bigger and better than their neighbours.*

"If I had to guess, I'd say that this proliferation of defensive fire stations is an extension of that monument-building instinct. Each may be a monument to the family that built it, a sign of their commitment to collective defence. Many croma monuments take the form of defensive fortifications, thus their success in building this fortified wall against the reeh. I take it that so many defensive stations in one system is tactically counter-productive?"

"Counter-productive in the extreme," Erik acknowledged. "All are giving the appearance of being operational, but in truth we don't even know if they're armed. Their scanning and armscomp seems to be active, but that doesn't mean much."

"Then my educated guess is that these are status symbols and not intended for active defence. There was a group of island people on a barabo world in pre-technological times whose various families found it a status symbol to build tall stone temples to worship their fertility god. Soon their

island was covered in tall towers — one of the oldest pre-technological tower building civilisations in the Spiral, as far as I'm aware. They served no technical function and seem like an enormous waste of resources to modern eyes, requiring huge manpower in a time when just gathering food and water was labour intensive. But the social status it brought was enough reward for the builders."

"That makes a lot of sense," said Erik, still watching ten things at once as he considered it. "Thank you Stan."

"Their fertility god?" Kaspowitz remarked. "I think I read about them — they weren't building towers, Stan, they were building giant phalluses."

"Yes Lieutenant Kaspowitz," Romki said drily. *"Most scholarly of you."*

"Phalluses?" Sasalaka asked.

"Penises," Corrig explained. Sasalaka still looked confused. "Dicks."

"Thank you Raf," said Erik. "Let's not go through the tavalai's entire genitalia vocabulary."

"Oh," said the tavalai as she got it. "Barabo, yes. Make sense."

"Gotta love the barabo," Geish sighed. "Dicks on the brain."

"You think the croma have dicks?" Kaspowitz persisted.

"I'm sure they do," Erik replied. "I'm sure they're terrifying. V-dump in thirty-five seconds, all hands stand by."

13

After first-shift, Erik grabbed some food and went to a systems review with Warrant Officers Luong and Kriplani, who were struggling to master the intricacies of *Phoenix's* new life support and damage control functions. Then he hit the gym for a brief post-shift workout, mostly weights since running on a full stomach was so unpleasant, but it had to be done to get the blood moving after twelve hours in the chair. Then it was down to Midships to check the ongoing installations to secondary electronics and power failsafes, the last parts Rooke hadn't been able to get done before launch. *Phoenix's* fancy new fluidic-electrical systems were causing some headaches, based on technology several times more advanced than anything humans were familiar with.

There he floated in Midships' zero-G and watched Engineering crew working on uncovered wall conduits, observing mesh filament bladders that formed some sort of chemical osmosis system that looked more like old powercell technology to Erik, but Rooke insisted actually allowed the re-direction of electrical current by nano-patterns through liquid circuitry, creating infinitely complex reactive circuits for any of the increasingly intricate requirements of the power-consuming systems. After ten minutes of listening to Rooke's explanations, and listening to the chatter of the crew, Erik became profoundly glad that he'd been fast tracked into piloting and not engineering.

Soon Romki joined him, pulling himself up the wall from main-storage where some marines were rationalising their ready-stored equipment in case of shuttle deployment. All Midships spaces looked even larger now, expansive walls embedded with storage drawers, red emergency striping for firefighting and medical equipment, and covered with great stretches of cargo netting for when the big spaces were full of floating marines or spacers.

"Captain," said Romki. "You wanted to see me?" Looking at the engineers' work with curiosity.

"Hi Stan. How's the reading on the croma coming?" He'd been distracted, Erik knew. Having presided over several of the greatest historical discoveries of the last twenty thousand years in Drakhil's diary and the drysine data-core it had led to, Romki had now been required to drop those studies and embark on the comparatively mundane task of learning about an unfamiliar alien civilisation.

"Well the readings are numerous enough," said Romki with repressed disdain. "It's their quality that I doubt. There's nothing in English of course, there's no actual evidence that humans and croma have even met before, though I'm quite sure some of our Fleet suspects will have done so." Erik could not help but feel a little disappointed. Being the very first would have been something... but Romki was right, Fleet did a lot of things they kept quiet, and would have found some way to call on the croma. "The parren have quite a bit, but my Porgesh is awful and I don't trust the translators for anything more complex than ordering a cup of tea, so that leaves me with tavalai readings. My Togiri is excellent, but different tavalai institutions use different jargon for different fields, and of course croma study are a field unto themselves, even though their information is largely contradictory. And being tavalai, they've divided into several conflicting camps about the reasons why croma do various things, and spend more time attacking the other camp than they do actually talking about the croma."

"Sounds like academics everywhere," said Erik.

Romki gave him a hard look. "And there are many academics in the illustrious Debogande line?"

"Oh hell yes. Great Aunt Mika teaches ancient chah'nas civilisation at Gaudi University, and I've a cousin in the mathematics department at Dorego. To say nothing of the teaching gigs for all the damn family lawyers."

Further up the wall toward Berth Four, Wowser had taken charge of a particularly intricate installation, braced into position with his larger limbs, working the fiddly installation with his smaller forelegs. Human crew worked around him, not getting too close. Erik knew they weren't that careful with Peanut.

"So tell me this," Erik continued. "Do you think the croma are species-prejudiced?"

Romki frowned. "It's hard to say. They don't mix with aliens at all if they can help it, no one's allowed into their territory without special permission, but that does not necessarily indicate a prejudice. Parren don't mix much because their society revolves around these strict rules of house loyalties and lines of command that outsiders don't respect. Sometimes in this galaxy, xenophobia has a logical foundation. Why do you ask?"

"I've been invited down to the surface of Do'Ran, and I'm wondering how we should present ourselves. *Phoenix* is a mixed crew now, but if we take tavalai down with us, it could cause confusion. To say nothing of drysines."

"Captain," said Romki, "my feeling is that like much of the Spiral, the croma are intensely self-obsessed, and don't have many opinions of us at all. Actually, they seem to take that to extremes, it's quite remarkable that *Makimakala* have the contacts that they do."

Erik eyed him sideways. "You suspicious?"

"Of tavalai institutional politics? Always. I think Captain Pram is our friend and bears us no ill will, but with tavalai it's never that simple. Captain Pram is Dobruta, and Dobruta intentions are always vague to outsiders. All tavalai power is currently in flux with the decline of State Department, and the Dobruta seem to be on the rise.

Now they're taking charge of this mission to croma space to find clues to the nature of the biotech threat posed by the reeh, and if it's related to that posed by the deepynines and alo."

Erik nodded but said nothing. The senior crew had had this discussion many times on the way out here. New tavalai crew had been useful contributors in that discussion, but all of them were simple tavalai Fleet, and knew little of Dobruta workings.

"I'd like you to come along," said Erik. "To Ro'Gana. Captain Pram's coming down as well."

Romki blinked. "Well, if you think that appropriate. Thank you, Captain."

"No need to thank me. You'll be there to do your job as alien civilisations specialist on *Phoenix*. Croma aren't your field, but you'll make better guesses than any of us will, and I'll need that advice on point and without delay."

"Yes of course, Captain. In fact, I'd better get back to my reading, in that case."

"Sure thing, Stan. And get some sleep before we go." Because when Romki became obsessed with something, sleep was the first thing to suffer.

When he left, Erik flipped on his glassed and blinked on a coms icon. A crackle, then Trace answered. *"Captain, what's up?"* From the crashing and whine of machinery in the background, Erik could tell she was in Assembly.

"Trace, I thought you might like to ask Garudan Platoon to come down to Ro'Gana with us. Could be a good chance to get them to stretch their legs."

"You telling me how to do my job again?" Erik could hear the humour in her voice, but with Trace nothing was ever entirely a joke.

"No, but I just asked Romki if he thinks croma will care if we don't present an entirely human front to them. He said he doesn't think croma give two hoots about us either way. I know your instinct is to put your best units on a Captain-protection detail, but if we got into shooting later, you'll want a chance to check out Garudan Platoon earlier, before the heavy stuff starts."

A brief silence from Trace, but for shouts and crashes in the background. *"Yeah, I was leaning that way anyway, it's a good call. So is it true that croma can grow to three metres tall?"*

"Romki says more like four metres, some of them. Ask him for the briefing, it's worth the time."

"Haven't had a lot of time for alien education tours. Mostly I'd like to know what they're armed with."

"Shouldn't be an issue, Stan says they're very stable and predictable, not easily upset. When they decide to kill you, they give plenty of warning."

"Comforting. I hear they've got natural armour too. Will smallarms penetrate that?"

"The small ones, sure. The biggest ones, even your Koshaim might struggle."

* * *

IT WAS Erik's first time in a tavalai assault shuttle. He had the rear observer seat behind the pilots, as he would in a human shuttle, only the seat was too wide for a human frame and he had to buckle in tight to make the straps fit across his armour. Romki sat behind him, peering at the big side screens at the vast stretch of landscape below.

The world was Do'Ran, primary world of the Croma'Dokran Clan, holder of ninety-three percent of the croma population in Do'Mela System. Do'Ran had one-point-one-nine standard human gravities, though the croma homeworld was closer to one-point-four. It looked red and brown on the screens, a rumpled terrain of mountains and valleys, high serrated ridgelines capped with snow, and thick clouds building in anvil-shaped thunderstorms.

The croma had sent them an atmospheric analysis thirty hours ago, and *Makimakala* had another list of known bacterias and pathogens. A simple adjustment to everyone's medical nanos, and a few booster shots had countered it — mostly precautionary and if anyone did catch anything, it wouldn't be fatal quickly, and *Phoenix* Medbay would reverse it before that.

Styx estimated from the coms traffic buzzing between the big trading stations and the ground that Do'Ran's population was about three billion. To judge from the age of some of the fire stations, there'd been croma here for at least two and a half thousand years, probably much longer. Croma were relatively recent in the Spiral, only fifteen thousand years since their first recorded appearance, that near the beginning of the Chah'nas Empire. The chah'nas had naturally demanded their obedience, received it for a short time until the croma had built up their weapons and tactics, and then became engulfed in a two hundred year croma-chah'nas war that had gone poorly for everyone. But the chah'nas had eventually concluded that in the croma they'd met a species even more stubborn than themselves, and had withdrawn to leave croma space for the croma.

Since that war the croma had tangled briefly with tavalai, parren and a few minor species not technically part of the Spiral, but had on no occasion been particularly aggressive, just interested in preserving territorial integrity around what they perceived as 'their' region of space. About ten thousand years ago the rest of the Spiral noticed that the croma were expanding sideways in response to a newly-arrived species on their far side, away from the Spiral. Some of those conflicts were reputed to be enormous, and croma losses high.

Some of the Spiral's inter-species relations were a great secret, but it was well known that many Spiral species, including tavalai, parren and chah'nas had all given support to the croma in those battles, despite having no proper relationship with them. Those had mostly been shipments of advanced materials and technologies, Erik had been told in the Academy, in the brief history class that had skimmed over it. Various Spiral species had glimpsed whatever the croma were fighting on the far side of their territory, and been alarmed enough to send help. Since then the croma's sideways expansion had met little objection from anyone. The Croma Wall, it had come to be known, and it was in no one's interest to see the wall fail.

"Captain," said Second Lieutenant Leralani on coms from the pilot's seat — yet another translated tavalai voice. Erik figured that they'd survived it with Tif, and would find a way to manage here. The rank, of course, was temporary, but essential if the tavalai were going to function as a part of *Phoenix* crew. *"Ro'Gana ahead."*

An image flashed on the sidescreen — an expanse of cityscape clustered about some mountains, small from this altitude but growing larger every second. "Looks like it could be a few million at least," said Erik.

"Captain, there is a lot of airtraffic in the vicinity," said Ensign Tamalin from the nose-seat — Leralani's weapons officer. *"Dozens of smaller towns, some small cities further out. This is a well-populated world."*

The shuttle had been directed to land at the major complex in the mountains central to Ro'Gana, and now fell steeply from reentry, beginning to buffet once more as they entered the thicker part of the atmosphere. The feeling was different from a human assault shuttle — the tavalai shuttle was about the same size, with capacity for two tavalai platoons of twenty each — a Dramata, such pairings were called. But tavalai shuttles had more armour and firepower, sacrificing mobility, and handling like a brick in atmosphere.

A glance at Scan showed Erik that *Makimakala's* shuttle was descending a hundred kilometres to their rear. A nervous anticipation gripped him, unlike anything he'd felt before. He'd been so wrapped up in *Phoenix's* problems, procedural matters and the vague yet terribly important nature of the mission, that he hadn't had a chance yet to truly contemplate what they were all about to do.

Croma didn't like strangers. For all that Spiral species had sent them assistance over the millennia to confront the terror that lurked beyond their wall, the crews of those ships were never invited to stop over — simply to drop off their cargo and leave immediately. Everyone knew that covert contacts with some non-human species occurred away from any publicity, but the one Intel officer Erik had spoken to who claimed knowledge on the topic had insisted that even those contacts were minimal. Croma liked to be left alone, and for most of their fifteen thousand years in the Spiral, they had been. And now *Makimakala*, from one of the most shadowy tavalai security institutions, had found them a croma clan who not only agreed to meet them, but invited them down to their main city in full view of the general population. Whatever was going on, Erik was prepared to bet that the deepynine attack on Mylor Station, with its biotech implications pointing great, threatening fingers at the reeh, had alarmed the croma enough to get them involved. Doubtless that had been the incentive that Jarush had been pursuing as well, before Styx had flown her shuttle into a wall.

Atmospheric turbulence thundered and bounced over the mountains, then cleared as the shuttle — GR-1, she'd been rechristened — cut in retros to ease the angle of descent. A flurry of cloud, then the city of Ro'Gana stretched out below, flanked by great slopes and high peaks. The city itself was high, a plateau at four thousand metres, enough for altitude sickness on a one-G world, but Do'Ran's sea-level atmosphere was one-point-three human atmospheres, so Erik reckoned four thousand metres would be close to perfect.

Ro'Gana looked amazing, with tall towers of steel and glass like a modern human city, fading to lower structures, many dark like stone and all surrounded by a maze of visible transport systems, big rail and obvious roads and flyovers. A haze of airtraffic buzzed over it all, some of those vehicles much larger than the others, like queen bees among the workers. Either larger capacity transports, Erik thought, or that croma size-difference he'd heard about. Those really big ones would need entirely different vehicles.

"Stan?" he said, relying on coms above the howl of engine noise even at this range. Tavalai assault shuttles were no more designed for passenger comfort than the human variety. "What causes the croma size difference? Is it race or gender?"

"No, it's age," said Romki in his earpieces. *"Some of them live a long time. Only the high ranking ones, strangely enough."*

"So any croma who lives long enough will eventually become enormous?"

"Yes, there's some speculation in the writing that they're functionally immortal, though I find that difficult to believe. Their mortality takes the form of never ceasing to grow — eventually they just get too big to function and the body collapses."

"But only the high-ranking ones live to that age?"

"Yes, the writings seem quite clear that the only huge croma are high-ranking croma... and logically, they can't give high rank to every old croma, high rank is only achieved by a tiny percentage of the population. There's further speculation that croma practice euthanasia for all older croma to save them the physical discomforts of old age and great size, though some other scholars speculate that the euthanasia is involuntary and cruel. Some others suggest that there are genetic treatments or drugs croma can take to elongate their lifespan, and that these treatments are denied to all but the highest-ranking. The truth is that no one really knows — no one's ever spent a long enough period amongst them to find out."

"Well I wouldn't recommend asking them," Erik cautioned him. "We're not here on an anthropology expedition, we've more important business."

"Never fear, Captain. I intend to observe quietly."

Erik watched GR-1's pilot feed, seeing what appeared to be a landing clearance arrive on the main nav, and a very obvious highlight appear in the center of the great, fortress structure atop Ro'Gana's most prominent mountaintop. Ensign Tamalin observed no evidence of hostile targeting or tracking, and there were no obvious military vehicles in the sky to escort them in. As they angled in for landing in an enormous courtyard between colossal towers and mountain peaks, Trace contacted Erik's coms from her command seat in the rear.

"They seem very relaxed for a people who don't like aliens," she observed.

"Stan says he doesn't think they're xenophobic," Erik replied. "They're just not prone to wild enthusiasms about making friends like some humans are."

"I was warned to expect a warrior culture," Trace replied. *"True warrior cultures don't need constant threats, only insecure and frightened people need to wave their guns in everyone's face. These guys seem confident. We're going to be confident right back at them. Respectful and non-threatening, but confident."*

GR-1 came down in a howl of thrust, dust and sand from the great plateau courtyard swirling around them in sheets, blocking all surrounding view. Trace gave commands and the marines dismounted swiftly from the rear — the tavalai Garudan Platoon first (as the Dramata had been renamed) then Trace with Command Squad. Erik and Romki followed, smelling alien air in their nostrils, and finding it crisp and pleasant. Erik wore light armour, all that the croma had allowed them to bring, though the injunction against anything heavier had not been harsh, just suggestive. Erik and Trace had both agreed that full armour in what was supposed to be a friendly meeting was not a good look, but that a full platoon was preferable if only because everything anyone read about the croma suggested a people impressed by power, and requiring its display for even simple introductions.

Erik walked down the ramp, welcoming the extra weight in his legs and squinting at the warm sunlight on his face. The mist of raised dust from the landing drifted and settled, revealing a scene that was almost... archaic. This was no modern landing pad, just a simple steel platform overlooking the landed shuttle, some refuelling tanks on wheels and some night lights on the ground. The pads themselves were a cobbled together mix of stone, pavings and cement, looking rather like some ancient do-it-yourself job only half completed, scorched by the fire of many shuttle landings.

Beyond the ragged edge of the pavings was grass and conifer-like trees lining an unpaved road to a far wall in which was inlaid an enormous, ancient door. These walls were the base of a cliff, Erik saw, turning about to consider the huge, looming peak that these stone walls ascended to eventually become. It stood high in the clear blue sky, a swirl of snow spiralling off the tip as the wind caught it.

Away from the cliff and the landing pad build at its base, this high-altitude place opened into a mountain meadow, green grass full of wildflowers about a distant lake. Beyond it rose another sheer wall of rock, ascending to another, opposing peak. This landing pad was on the edge of a small oasis nestled between the peaks. High on the sides of those ascending peaks, Erik could see structures in the stone

— walls, small towers and balconies from which the view would doubtless be extraordinary.

He stopped beside Trace and Second Lieutenant Karajin, looking about as their marines moved to form a loose, unthreatening defensive formation about the shuttle. "Croma like walls and fortresses," said Erik, nodding slowly as he took in the scene, and the hot shuttle engines pinged in the cool mountain air. "I think this is a display to impress us."

"It's working," Trace acknowledged. It was a rare admission from her, and Erik glanced at her. She wore her helmet off, hooked to the back of her light armour, a cap in its place. She looked as though she was pleased she'd come. She loved mountains, having grown up with them on Sugauli, and learned to climb on them like an insect up a wall. A distant shriek grew in the air above, and Trace glanced. "Here comes Captain Pram."

Karajin said something in Togiri. *"Will be many tavalai here,"* Erik's earpiece translated. *"Croma could be confused. They were expecting to meet humans."*

"We're here on behalf of every threatened people in the Spiral," Erik replied. "Everyone has a stake in this. Let's hope the croma understand the concept."

Makimakala's shuttle landed in a deafening howl of engines and a curtain of raised dust, then settled as karasai deployed from the back, similarly armed and armoured. Erik walked to greet Captain Pram, who shook Erik and Trace's hands in turn, looking behind in mild astonishment at Garudan Platoon deployed about GR-1.

"You brought your new tavalai," he observed in his perfect, gravelly English.

"We brought *Phoenix* marines," Erik corrected him. "Pretty place, yes?"

"Hell on the eyes," said Pram, and Erik looked to see if he was joking. Pram produced some eyedrops, squinting, and deposited several into each large, amphibious eye. He blinked rapidly, putting the eyedrops away, and peered at the meadow and mountains through a flicker of translucent third eyelids. "But yes, when one's eyes are not dry like sand, quite pretty."

"I'm sorry you'd prefer a swamp," Erik teased. "For me and for Major Thakur, this feels a little like home."

"One day when this is all concluded," said Pram, "I will take you both to see the marshlands on Delagomira. There are more recorded species of bird, fish, plants and flowers in that one marshland delta than on any one of your most prized worlds in entirety."

"And swarms of biting insects, no doubt."

"I believe it's called an ecosystem," Pram said drily. "Human skin is fragile."

Erik grinned. Then the door in the sheer wall down the unpaved road between trees gave a loud clank, then a grind. The grin faded. "Nice and easy, people," Trace said calmly into her microphone. "Remember, we are friendly, but strong."

"I expect they will attempt some form of ritual intimidation," Romki added on coms from back by GR-1. *"The Major is correct — do not flinch or retreat, but do not threaten either. We are guests here. Our role is to respect croma strength, that is all."*

Both doors swung open, more than five metres tall and solid with steel and wood. From within, great shadows emerged in two rows. Croma, marching in a rank-and-file shuffle, like a quick-step in slow motion. They were huge, almost terrifying at first glance. Three metres tall, Erik reckoned, and they carried great staves like spears, but far thicker and with decorative steel clubs on one end, clearly intended to be swung hard at other croma in combat. Erik would have expected a blade of some sort on that pole, but a closer look at the croma showed why blades were a waste of time.

The croma wore panelled leather pants of some tough, tanned hide, but above that were topless. Their massive shoulders bore natural armourplate, leather skin hardened with age to become interlocking shell plates, flexing along upper arms and chest. Their heads were bull-like, ears protruding between gaps in the helmet-shell that came down along the great brow ridge, behind which ferocious eyes glared with dark power. The rank lengthened as more followed the first out of the door until there were twenty marching down the road, larger and larger with each step closer, grunting and roaring in ceremonial unison. Not a human or tavalai spoke, but only stared.

Each had to weigh half a ton, Erik thought incredulously. Heavy-world beings, born in one-point-four gravities and built accordingly. Kaal were heavy worlders too, and humans had fought many hard battles against them in the Triumvirate War, but croma made kaal look cute and fluffy. As they drew closer, the size became even more impressive. Erik judged he came up to the bottom of the leader's sternum, if that. Some of that incredible natural armour was decorated with sharp horns that flared from the shoulders, or made frightening spikes off the elbow from the forearm, at the perfect height to skewer a human skull like a melon. Whether those spikes were natural or artificial, Erik could not guess. Certainly they were not just cosmetic. There was no mistaking what kind of people these croma were, nor what their ornamentations were designed for.

It took Private Arime to finally give voice to what everyone was thinking, human and tavalai alike. *"Holy fucking shitballs,"* he said on coms. God knew what the tavalai's translators made of it.

The croma formation halted before Erik, Trace and Pram with a roar and stamp, raising another cloud of dust. They were four metres away, and Erik still had to tilt his head to look up at them. He couldn't help the accelerated heart rate, nor the faint sheen of sweat on his brow, despite the cool air. He wondered if even Trace felt it. How many shots with a high-powered rifle would it take to bring down a croma warrior this size?

The roar of sound from landing pad speakers nearly made him jump — a thunder of drums and a shriek of some other, electric instruments. The noise was nearly deafening. The lead croma stepped forward, swung his massive polearm through some fast twirls, with an audible swishing noise like a giant propellor blade cutting the air. The rhythm hit a crescendo, and the croma thrashed several times, and stamped, then drove his pole arm into the dirt before him and stood there, glaring defiantly at some point above Erik's head. Like a wall in the form of a sentient being.

Silence followed. *"Major,"* Arime added. *"If I'm any more respectful I'll need a change of pants."*

Erik glanced briefly at Trace, and saw her amusement. Arime had served with her for many years, and knew her very well to be making remarks like that in serious situations without fear of hard punishments. Trace was all about what worked, and if humour improved morale, so be it. Erik got an idea, took a step forward and gave the enormous croma a bow with a flourish, one hand down, the other up behind him like a courtier from some ancient historical movie. The croma's eyes flicked down within that natural helmet ridge, and saw him. Erik's bow was unthreatening, and unafraid. I see you, he said. You look good. But big deal.

The croma snorted, ears flicking. He stood aside, and there behind him approached a much smaller croma, this one barely a shade over two metres. This croma was fully dressed, the same leather pants beneath a long leather coat that looked to have multiple layers, each of a different colour, sewn and bolted with steel studs into elaborate patterns from the ridged shoulders down to the feet-sweeping hem. Erik had once fancied himself a sharp dresser, something that he could not deny had attracted him to Fleet and its snazzy blue parade uniforms. Once he'd actually joined Fleet, he'd confronted the reality of Fleet life where such uniforms were rarely worn, and lost much of his fashion consciousness in the daily grind of dull jumpsuit blues. But now, looking at that coat with its broad shoulders and steel-bolted ornamentation, he wanted one.

The 'small' croma stopped before them. The head armour was far less developed, just a soft leathery guard that broadened its nose and made its eyes seem nearly as wide-spaced as a tavalai's. Those dark eyes were far less intimidating than its enormous comrades', soft with lashes, like some humanoid cow. The big, flat nose had steel loops through it. Clearly the croma had a taste for aggressive decoration.

The croma spoke, a few snuffling grunts. Luckily, *Makimakala* had provided the translator program. *"Human,"* it said. *"Tavalai. You are hungry. You will eat. Come."*

The croma turned, gave a gesture to follow that was unmistakable in any culture, and began walking back up the path. "Command Squad, Garudan Platoon," said Trace. "Look after the ship, and be nice to our hosts. If you're lucky they might bring you some food as well. Stan, you coming?"

As Romki hurried across to join them, Erik, Trace, Pram and Naki followed the smaller croma up the path and through the honour guard of walking, club-wielding, armoured walls.

14

The three humans and two tavalai followed the smaller croma up the meadow path and through the huge door. Within was a high stone hallway, lit by rows of lights that danced and flickered as though to simulate the naked flame of torchlight.

"It doesn't take a PhD to conceive what croma history might have looked like," Romki murmured as they walked on wide flagstones. "Most of the Spiral's species reach back to their past for identity the further they venture from their original home."

"Their medieval period must have been something," Erik ventured, gazing up at the big tapestries that plunged down the walls, displaying four-storey-tall symbols that might have been writing. "Imagine their massed battles before firearms."

"This is not the seat of power for the Croma'Dokran Clan," said Romki, "I understand it's their ancestral seat. Like a manor house, it's the private residence of the ruling family, but not where government is conducted. Thus all the old symbolism, I'm sure the house of government will be far more modern."

His hushed, awed tone suggested a far greater excitement than he'd shown for the mission so far. "Glad you came after all, Stan?" Erik suggested.

"Remarkable, yes," Romki breathed, glancing around to be sure that none of the enormous honour guard had followed them in. "Those big ones will be guarding the shuttles then?"

"They are," Trace said calmly, AR glasses down and watching all her units' activities. "All non-threatening."

"If they're bigger, they'll be older," said Erik. "Age and greater rank doesn't seem to fit with menial duty like honour guards, somehow."

"Well first, we don't know that it is menial duty," Romki cautioned. "It could be very prestigious. And secondly, I don't think those croma were really that old. They get a lot bigger."

The leather-coated croma led them to an even larger cross-hall-way, and turned right. The walls here were decorated with old weapons, exactly the medieval period that Erik had been thinking of. Big shields hung that were twice as tall as a human, in a number of designs, all ridiculously heavy. Some looked extremely old, no doubt treated to be age resistant, yet still thick with that millennia's worth of decay. Then there were great clubs and pole arms big enough to crush a human into mince if wielded by a croma large enough.

"No spears," Trace murmured, observing with curiosity as they passed. "Croma bodies are too tough, I guess they'd break."

"And swords even moreso," Romki agreed.

"Crossbow," said Erik, indicating ahead. The crossbow was as big as he was, likely to have fired bolts the width of his thigh. It would have taken that much force to penetrate full croma armour. "Wow. You think the younger ones fought too?"

"Not in the front line," Trace guessed. "Wouldn't last long. I'd have the bigger ones up front, the younger and smaller for artillery, support and skirmishing. And you could only put a big croma on an elephant-equivalent, not a horse-equivalent, so the smaller ones would do all the flanking. I suppose they did have equivalent riding animals?"

"Yes, I believe so," said Romki. "I had no idea you'd studied pre-technological warfare, Major."

"There were classes at the Academy. Waste of time, but there were classes." Romki and Erik exchanged amused glances.

The ancient hallway ended in a big elevator, and the young croma gestured all to climb aboard with him. The doors closed, and they rode it up, small figures on a vast car floor large enough to hold a truck. When they opened again, a new flagstone expanse confronted them — more of an ante-room before the great wall-to-ceiling curtains that blocked the way ahead. From within Erik could hear clanking steel and other activity, and the smell of something delicious cooking. The young croma halted, pointed to something on the wall and spoke in the snuffling grunts of this croma tongue.

"*So'ma'ra,*" spoke the translator. "*Our great leader.*"

The party stared, for mounted against the wall was the upper half of natural croma armour upon a mannequin of sorts. Croma armour seemed naturally segmented, Erik thought, with the upper half almost independent of the lower. The huge shoulders and chest plates here were lower to the ground, like a bust from human sculpture, the legs not required to show this figure's grandiosity. This natural helmet armour had horns, sharp and wickedly curved, pointing forward like weapons.

"Is that real armour?" Erik asked quietly, unsure if it was wise to ask the young croma directly. "I mean... it looks..."

"Yes," said Romki, "I think it's natural armour." He indicated along the wall, where another ten busts were arrayed. "It looks as though it is removed after death, to be displayed here." He looked to the young croma. "So'ma'ra? A great leader?"

"*Great leader,*" the croma agreed, and beckoned them on to the next bust of armour. "*Da'go'ra. Our great leader.*"

"How old?" Romki asked. "Your great leader from how many years ago?"

"*Our great leader,*" the croma said solemnly, and moved them on to the next bust. "*Tol'do'ra. Our great leader.*"

"Mr Romki," said Captain Pram, his low voice a little testy. "I am sure we are not meant to ask questions, but merely to appreciate the strength of Croma'Dokran's history." Romki ignored him, staring and fascinated.

Their tour brought them close to the huge curtain hangings, and Erik could feel heat radiating from somewhere behind. When the young croma brought them around the curtain's edge, the heat blast hit them all in the face with the glare of a burning sun.

The flagstone room beyond was huge. Within was a deep firepit, aglow with black and orange coals in shimmering waves of heat. Above the pit was the biggest rotisserie Erik had ever seen, upon which was skewered a big animal about the size of a cow. It slowly rotated, driven by some motor at one end, legs bound in steel cord to keep them out of the coals. The expression on its face was somewhat horrific, skewer protruding from its protesting mouth. But the smell was amazing, and Erik's mouth watered.

About the fire, young croma bustled, tending the coals and hauling large wooden trays. One young croma prepared even now to venture onto a steel platform above the coals, clad head-to-toe in thick heat-protection, like a worker in a blast furnace. A comrade handed him an enormous carving knife, and someone else prepared a tray on the end of a long pole. The intrepid croma beat himself once on the chest, as though psyching himself up, face entirely hidden behind goggles and cloth helmet, then he strode onto the platform above the coals, the air shimmering in blazing heat, and began slicing sizzling meat from the carcass. It fell in great chunks onto the tray held on the pole beneath his work, and when the tray was full it quickly withdrew as another replaced it.

"I guess we can say they're not vegetarian," Erik remarked.

The visitors' guide let them watch for a moment, though croma expressions were too impassive to tell if he was pleased at their interest. Then they were beckoned on, past the fire-side activity and into the larger dining hall beyond. Or Erik suspected it was a dining hall — there was no central table, but rather a wide circle of large chairs, dominated by one enormous chair, twice the size of the others. That chair overlooked a series of arches, beyond which was a balcony above a stunning view of mountains, and the surrounding city of Ro'Gana. They were halfway up the peak overlooking the meadow where the landing pads were, and this residence, in the fashion of the croma love of fortified things, was built through the mountain, with the best view reserved for the dining hall.

As they admired the view, their croma guide walked behind them, and pulled back another set of great curtains. *"Sho'mo'ra,"* he said. *"Our great leader."*

Erik turned, expecting to find yet another set of artfully displayed remains... and struggled to keep his jaw from dropping open. The croma revealed by the curtain's withdrawal was at least four metres tall. His shoulders alone were wider than Erik was tall, and he held twin staves planted firmly on the flagstones, each grasped in a massive, armoured fist. He walked forward two steps, slow and ponderous, armour creaking and grinding audibly. No pants either, Erik noted — just a leather loincloth, or perhaps very large under-wear. Pants would shred on the sharp edges of armoured calves, sepa-rate plates that turned spiky at the rear.

He halted, snorting great, heaving breaths, as though tired from his effort. The staves were to hold the arms up, Erik thought — the forearm plates had to make a huge weight on those old shoulders, contributing to the big croma's hunched posture. Erik's adrenaline-charged astonishment faded, to be replaced by a more somber feel-ing. At this size, surely everything was an effort — walking, sitting, sleeping. Croma never stopped growing, they just got larger and larger until it killed them. He gazed at the majestic being before him, and felt both awe, and sadness.

"Sho'mo'ra," he said, and gave a small bow. It was not a common human gesture these days, but somehow it fit. Handshaking would be too familiar, and Sho'mo'ra's palm was the size of his head anyhow. "Leader of Croma'Dokran. Thank you for seeing us."

Sho'mo'ra snorted loudly, several times, from huge nostrils. For a moment Erik wondered if he was offended... but no, it seemed the great croma was simply getting enough air in prelude to speaking. When he spoke, it was in great, snorting coughs.

"*Humans,*" said the translator. "*Tavalai. You are guests of Croma'-Dokran. I hope you have not been bored by the young one.*"

One enormous forearm moved with alarming speed, and gave their young croma escort a whack that knocked him backward two steps. Erik caught his breath, wondering if domestic violence and humiliation were the way of the croma, and thinking how disappointing that would be... but the young croma showed no sign of cowering or humiliation, having protected himself with crossed forearms, and now resuming his previous place with a dismissive gesture as though to show it was nothing.

Maybe it was just men messing around, punching each other's shoulders, playing rough house games. Or perhaps it was more ritualistic than that, and that it was a young man's place to accept such treatment stoically until he was an elder himself, in the expectation that it would be character building. Croma expressions were too impassive to say either way, and Erik had to remind himself of Romki's usual admonition to humans watching non-human behaviour, not to look for familiar human motivations in aliens.

"We were not bored, Sho'mo'ra," said Captain Pram. "This young croma has escorted us well."

"*You have come far,*" said Sho'mo'ra. "*We have much to discuss. But first, we will eat.*"

All the Dobruta's expertise on the croma said that there was nothing in the food that would hurt tavalai or human, and so they sat, guests on the circle side with backs to the view, while the croma arrayed opposite. Young croma moved with great trays of roasted meats and vegetable, to be locked onto each chair's wooden arm in an arrangement that appeared traditional. Also traditional were alarmingly large, sharp knives, and a jug of sauce that made its rounds and was both delicious and stingingly hot, but only briefly. Erik thought of his family's various trading acquaintances, and thought that a good trade in this sauce alone could make a lot of money.

Soon the high-altitude wind outside began to blow, and young croma strode to the balcony to secure door lattices, preserving some of the view while reducing the gale to a breeze, as the coals of the far firepit roared even brighter. Erik thought there were several ranks of croma doing the serving and door-securing, but he did not have the attention to spend on both that, and the conversation and food at the same time. Romki, however, watched the leather-coated croma with close interest as he chewed, no doubt seeing far more than Erik.

Pram recounted for Sho'mo'ra the deepynine attacks on Mylor Station, all things the croma already knew but were a politeness to hear again in person. Then he asked Sho'mo'ra if the Croma'Dokran scientists had yet arrived at a conclusion as to whether this deepynine nanotech weapon could be related to reeh technology. The biotech time bomb discovered in tavalai DNA was left unspoken of for now.

"These things are possible," Sho'mo'ra replied, barely bothering to use his enormous knife and simply shovelling big slabs of meat into his mouth with a two-pronged fork. He chewed a long time, a circular motion like a cow... but several of those forward teeth were sharp incisors, not plant-chewing molars. Omnivores then, Erik thought. Croma history and evolution must have been fascinating. What did their prehistoric ancestors look like, to have arrived at this? Everything about them suggested big, heavy plant-eaters... so when had they started including meat in their diet? It was a struggle to keep his mind on the job, and ignore the intriguing distractions. *"The reeh probe our defences at Sherek'To. Not long ago. Months. Great awards were won, our ninth Fleet commander gained great distinction for Croma'-Dokran there."*

"All humans have heard of the brave croma who fight the reeh," Erik exaggerated with a straight face. "Many humans would like to know these brave croma better."

Sho'mo'ra considered him with sunken eyes, chewing slowly as the wind blew and shook the door lattices behind. *"Humans and tavalai fight."* The big, brown eyes went from Erik to Pram, then back again. *"Why?"*

"Old history," Erik said calmly, cutting a steaming vegetable in half. "Very old, and very sad. In better circumstances humans and tavalai could have been friends. But each of our ancestors, I think, made some very poor choices over the last thousand years. And today, their descendants pay the price."

"Your ancestors have failed," the big croma surmised. Romki gave Erik a wary look. Croma, Erik thought, did not seem big on subtlety.

"Not failed," said Erik. "Human ancestors rebuilt humanity after most of our species died. Their success was spectacular. But incomplete."

Sho'mo'ra grunted. Erik doubted it meant what a human might think it did. *"Croma'Dokran ancestors have stood their ground for many thousands of years. Once there were a hundred clans and more in this region, but now all are one. Croma'Dokran."* He made a gesture of huge fists together.

"Croma'Dokran," said the others around mouthfuls of food. Most were barely taller than two metres. Younger, then. None would be even close to Sho'mo'ra in rank. This was unlike a human meeting, where a human leader would be surrounded by his next-in-command to participate and ask questions. This was a single audience for Sho'mo'ra alone. And the youngsters were here to... what? Learn? Admire? Make up the ritual numbers?

"Do you fight the reeh often?" Trace asked around her own mouthful. She preferred light food, but wasn't holding back.

"Small fights, often," Sho'mo'ra agreed. *"Large fights, every ten years, sometimes more. Very large, every century. Reeh are evil. Reeh only destroy. You have evil races too."*

"The sard aren't any fun," Erik admitted. "The krim weren't either. But we dealt with them."

A rumble from the croma. It might have been approval. *"I know sard, a little. Krim, only in books. Reeh make sard look like ***."* The translator failed the last word. Sho'mo'ra seemed to guess it might, and made a gesture, one huge fist close to the ground, indicating something little.

"I get the idea," Erik said sombrely. "Something small and cute."

"Empire," said Sho'mo'ra. *"Big reeh empire. Hundreds of big systems. Croma don't even know how big. No word comes from the other side. Many*

species, within reeh space. Many peoples. All gone, all disappeared. Vanished."

"Exterminated?" Erik asked quietly. "Genocide? Does this word translate?"

"Yes, translate. No. Not this word. Disperse. This word translate?"

Erik frowned. "Disperse? Yes, disperse translates in English. How do you mean, disperse?"

"Genetics." The big croma gazed at him, armour-hooded eyes unblinking. The other croma paused in their eating. Humans and tavalai did too. *"Genetics different for species, humans, tavalai, croma. DNA different, structure different. Different naturally. Reeh make different not naturally. Reeh play games with genetics. With their own genetics, with others. They take worlds. Take whole people. They disperse them."*

Erik felt cold in a way that had nothing to do with the wind that shook the doors to his rear. "They change their genetics," he said quietly. It was the rumour he'd heard from Fleet Intel as well, on the rare occasion anyone spoke about the reeh. "For what purpose?"

"Make slave. Make experiment. Make die. Billions dispersed. Hundreds of billions. Evil. Humans agree?" Challengingly.

"Yes," said Erik, with steel in his voice. "One day may you kill them all." He took his cup of water off the chair holder and raised it. The croma did not copy, not knowing that gesture, but Trace and Romki did, then Pram and Naki too. They drank together, and the croma saw that it was some strange alien gesture of solidarity, and took their cups to drink as well. Erik glanced at Romki, wondering if he'd done the right thing. Romki nodded to him, which was good enough. Romki had been right to suggest the croma were relaxed with formality, and difficult to offend. It gave him leeway.

"Croma fight reeh," Sho'mo'ra continued. *"Fight reeh for thousands of years. Croma'Dokran lost ten thousand brave croma warriors this year. Last year, one hundred thousand civilians when outer system base hit. Last century, great war of Do'sha'mai, two billion Croma'Dokran die, nearly one hundred billion of all croma. But reeh die too, many, many more. Croma grow strong beneath the rocks that fall. One croma falls, ten more rise. The*

reeh have killed a croma fortress, only to raise a mountain. One day this mountain will crush them forever."

There were more grunts of agreement from those around. Erik half-expected something more demonstrative to accompany such stirring speech — some war cries or hammering of knives on plates, but the croma kept eating, intense but calm. And he recalled how an Academy instructor on alien cultures had described humanity's allies the chah'nas to the class, addressing students' surprise that chah'nas, for all their ferocious reputation, rarely lost their temper.

"You can't lose what you never had in the first place," she'd explained. Croma reminded Erik somewhat of that — of a people who never got angry because they were always angry, buried somewhere under that cool, hard exterior.

"Croma'Dokran scientists find something to interest Phoenix and Maki-makala," Sho'mo'ra said then. *"Maybe a clue to what you seek. Interesting person for you to meet. Croma'Dokran will take you to him."*

15

The five guests flew by cruiser, beyond the Ro'Gana outskirts to where the mountains rose without sign of urban habitation, wild forests thick upon their rugged flanks. It was late afternoon now, the sun on this pleasant world sinking low, casting rumpled shadows across the landscape.

The cruiser was a large, overpowered thing, vibrating as it flew but high-tech enough for that. Croma seats were too big, and the windows a little too high for convenient viewing, making Erik crane his neck to peer at the ground below. Neither Staff Sergeant Kono nor Second Lieutenant Karajin had been pleased to see Erik and Trace depart on a croma vehicle for parts unknown, despite assurances that it would not be far, and that coms would remain open at all times. *Phoenix* was a guest of the croma in coming to croma space at all, and whether he was sitting on his heavily armed warship, or alone without guard, the Captain would be equally vulnerable if the croma decided to harm him. There was no choice but to trust that the croma were as straight forward and honourable as they appeared, and go where their hosts suggested.

The same young croma who had escorted them from the mountain meadows sat with them here, facing opposite across the large interior space, designed for larger, older members of his kind. The youngster's name was Tul'do, and both Romki and Pram made halting conversation with him as they flew, mostly about his job, his service to Sho'mo'ra, and facts about local politics. As far as Erik could make out, there were no elections nor anything that might suggest 'democracy' to a human. Croma consisted of clans, meaning families, though confusingly not everything was direct succession — sometimes outsiders could elbow their way in. Whether that occurred by marriage, or by some other mechanism, Erik hadn't yet managed to figure.

Croma social dynamics seemed intense, but rarely violent or unstable. Erik thought the emerging pattern was that they valued stability too much to ruin it with the constant turmoil of democracy. The problem with an absence of democracy was the prospect of tyranny, but croma did not seem to have much of that either — their rulers mostly left their subjects alone, and freedom was a concept valued even as political liberalism was not. A solid people, Erik thought. Reliable. Predictable. Slow-moving, slow-changing, but far from stupid. Not prone to wild flights of fancy, or revolutions, or any of the things that had plagued human civilisation before the krim had hit that giant reset button. Even their arts and culture, Romki was learning with careful question after question, were largely unchanged for the past few thousand years. Croma liked what they liked, and found little need for anything different. Erik wondered how, with that attitude, they'd found the inspiration to get into space at all.

The cruiser began to sink, repulsors throbbing, a long descent toward a green valley. Tree-covered ridges rose about them, then they settled onto a grassy field. Doors opened and all unbuckled and dismounted. Erik and Trace, Pram and Naki had left their armour back at the shuttles — it had been for display only. Trace and Naki had kept their rifles, however, and the croma had made no objection.

Erik looked about at the valley. It was small and intimate, with a road winding past the grassy field, headed up-valley. The afternoon sun fell bright upon one side, and birdlife sang. He caught a glimpse of something bright-feathered, then a fast movement and some commotion in the branch-tops. Wildlife, yet another alien ecosystem, teeming with species unknown to humans. A few times in recent months he'd come almost to despair for the galaxy. Then he saw a place like this, and smelled the crisp mountain air, and was reminded all over of everything that was worth fighting for.

"*Come,*" said Tul'do, beckoning them to follow. "*No vehicle. We walk.*" Erik could have hugged him. How long had it been since he'd gone for a walk in a wilderness? Well, he knew exactly how long — it had been Stoya, after he'd been shot down near the Doma Strana with Trace and Private Krishnan. That hadn't been exactly a pleasant walk, as his shoulder had been dislocated then painfully put back in, and some disagreeable parren had been trying to kill them. After a year in space he missed greenery with an almost physical pain.

They set off after the 'small' croma, who nonetheless loomed above them all, even Erik. "*Protected place,*" said Tul'do, touching some invisible icons in the air before him, probably informing local security exactly where he was. "*No vehicles, small technology. Few visitors.*"

"Like a national park," said Romki, peering at a stone pillar by the side of the road as they passed. It had alien writing on it, and symbols. "Tul'do, what is this? Is this telling us the distance from something?"

"*Distance, yes,*" Tul'do agreed. "*Very old. Come, not far.*"

Erik hoped the croma's understanding of the word 'far' was different from his. The road was beautiful, bending about contours in the valley side, flanked by tall, straight trees. Even Trace peered up at them with wonder. "Looks like conifer," she observed. "Not too different from the McCormick Ranges on Homeworld. We climbed there in Academy training."

"Amazing how similar everything is, really," Erik mused. "We're on another new planet, nearly a thousand lightyears from Home-world, but we could be anywhere. Trees, birds."

"Sentient species are selective," Pram reminded him. "Worlds like this are one in ten thousand systems or less. But jump technology allows us to pass all the mostly inhospitable worlds by. And so we congregate on worlds that are actually very rare, yet it seems to us that those similar worlds are everywhere."

"And evolution's practical," Trace added. "From a physics point of view, there's only so many ways to do things efficiently. If you want to fly, there's only a couple of ways to do that in atmosphere and gravity. Any life form doing it the less effective way will be out-competed by the more efficient, and so you get flying things that look similar anywhere in the galaxy. Similar environments will produce similar life, it's just physics."

Erik knew better now than to be surprised by Trace's occasional deeper, non-military thoughts. She did have them, she just didn't volunteer them often, mostly because her dedication to her life's profession left very little space for rumination. But lately, he thought, she'd been changing. Considering ideas that she'd have previously ignored, or shut off with the slamming steel doors of that impossibly disciplined brain of hers. Recent events had left some of those doors ajar... or Trace, perhaps, had chosen to open them a little.

To Erik's delight, twenty minutes later they were still walking, slightly uphill all the way. His legs ached a little from the higher gravity but one-point-two Gs was peanuts for a spacer accustomed to bone-crushing forces, and he did enough in the gym to welcome anything that worked his legs a bit harder.

Then from amongst the trees he began to see glimpses of vast stone walls rising ahead. As they drew closer, the walls became more obvious — a great line across this ridge atop the valley side. The wall was punctuated with towers, and the road seemed to arrive at where a building was joined, square and heavy like an old Earth castle from medieval times.

"Tul'do," said Romki with intrigue, "croma settled this world as spacefaring people. Yet you build this old building?"

"*The old ways are not forgotten,*" said Tul'do, vague and cryptic as Erik was coming to anticipate. "*Come, you will be guests of our guests. You are expected.*"

They were being taken to see the corbi, they'd been told. The corbi were from reeh space, on the far, unfortunate side of the croma wall. For all that croma did not welcome visitors, these corbi had been allowed to stay, and were made guests among the Croma'-Dokran. Enquiries as to why and for how long had met with the usual vague replies.

The road led past the castle fortress, where stone pavings made the form of a garden, and beautiful small plants and bushes grew about colourful beds of flowers. As they walked through the garden, Erik saw some kind of tortoise strolling by a lily-covered pond. Pram and Naki exchanged commentary in Togiri… much more their kind of wildlife, Erik thought, than tall trees and mountains.

They were just passing the fortress corner when down the other side of the building, he saw a pair of small figures gambolling on the grass past an obscuring tree. They stopped and stared at the newcomers — figures unlike anything Erik had seen before on a sentient being, short and stocky, with broad shoulders and long arms nearly down to the ground even while standing. An urgent shout turned their heads, and they set off racing on all fours toward some unseen door.

"You see that?" Erik asked the others as they walked on.

"*Corbi,*" Tul'do confirmed. "*You will meet. Come.*"

"I'm pretty sure those were kids," said Trace. "How long have these corbi been here?" And why are they living in a deserted monument in a national park, Erik could have asked further.

The road did a circle through the gardens, and a tall gateway went through the big fortress wall. Looking right, Erik could see all the way down its length, along the top of this ridge. Symbolising what, he wondered? The old fortifications from the croma homeworld? Why build them out here, lightyears away? Perhaps this was a sort of museum piece, built by croma determined not to forget their heritage?

Tul'do led them through the gate, and the dark stone gave way to an open, grassy hillside. The nearest tree line was several hundred metres further down the slope — all artificially cleared a long time ago, Erik thought. On the slope galloped what he thought at first glance was some kind of large deer... only there was a rider on its back, pulling expertly at the reins. A short, stocky rider with broad shoulders. Several others followed, negotiating obstacles, and now jumping over one with delighted shouts.

"Riding animals called 'chu'," said Tul'do, pointing. *"You have chu on human worlds?"*

"Some," said Erik, watching with faintly heartsick delight. Here was the picture of his childhood holidays at GreenOaks on Homeworld, friends and family galloping, with beautiful views across the rolling countryside. "There were new animals discovered, but none were better than the ones we brought with us from Earth. We call them horses."

"Not all animals die on Earth?" Tul'do asked. It was the first instance of curiosity Erik had seen from him, but expressed with the same flat, inflectionless tone.

"Nearly all. We took all genetic material. We cloned a lot of what we lost, on other worlds."

"Forget it," Trace murmured at his side. "You're not riding one. I didn't get you all this way in one piece so you could snap your neck riding an alien horse."

The corbi saw them and turned their way, galloping hard. The chu pulled up, much leaner than any horse Erik had ever seen — a little taller and more sinewy, plus there were those great, backward-curved horns. They blew hard and snorted, covered in sweat and looking happy for the exercise in the way of animals who loved to run. There were five in all, and the corbi, who had previously been chatting in light, chirpy tones, now spoke to Tul'do in the muffled grunts of the croma tongue.

They were hairy, Erik saw. Simian would be the simple description. Ape-like, an evolutionary strand well recognised within the Spiral, of which humans were lately the most successful variant. Broad shoulders, long arms and short legs, they had wide faces and big, intelligent eyes. Now they gazed at the new arrivals with thoughtful fascination.

"Hello, I'm sorry," Romki interjected, drawing their attention. He held up his AR glasses, and pointed to his earpiece. "Translator? Sho'-mo'ra uploaded the relevant translator, apparently it cross-referenced well enough with the English translator..."

"Sho'mo'ra," the lead corbi agreed, recognising the name and reaching quickly for his saddlebags to withdraw an earpiece with a single monocle, attached to a small reader. He touched a few buttons, then some invisible icons before him. Erik's earpiece crackled. The corbi spoke some more, and the translator followed. *"Hello? You understand me?"*

Erik smiled and nodded. "Yes, I understand you. My name is Erik Debogande, I am the Captain of the warship *Phoenix*, and this is Major Thakur." He pointed to the tavalai. "This is Captain Pram of the warship *Makimakala*, and Major Naki. And this is *Phoenix's* resident expert on alien civilisations, Stanley Romki."

The corbi tapped himself rapidly on the chest with those long, agile fingers. *"I am Dega. These are my sons, Fula and Sora, and my daughter Tili, and cousin Roga. This is our home, its name is Do'la'bod Sha'dero. But come, you are guests! Welcome, humans and tavalai. I will show you my home."*

Dega sprang from the saddle with great agility and grasped the reins of his mount, beckoning his guests to follow. His children and cousin galloped ahead, while Erik fell in at his side, Tul'do on the other. Dega saw Erik looking with more fascination at the chu than at Dega himself, and grinned, offering Erik the reins. Erik took them gratefully, and patted the snorting animal's nose. Dega only came up to Erik's mid-chest standing, much the same height in relation to humans that humans were to croma like Tul'do. The corbi walked with a loping style, knuckles down by his knees and powerful at the shoulders. Erik had seen photographs of Earth's great apes, and video from cloned specimens in various zoos, and while Dega's body shape was similar, the face was all different — the eyes far too large and wide, the mouth and jaw smaller, more human-proportioned. An unruly fringe became nearly a mane, tossed by the light wind.

"You have come a long way," Dega suggested. *"What did our Croma'-Dokran friends suggest we might tell you?"*

"Humans and tavalai are facing a threat," Pram told him from Erik's side. "From a species we thought extinct, but may instead have found refuge on the corbi side of the croma wall. Long ago, more than twenty thousand local years."

"I was informed," Dega said solemnly. It sounded to Erik as though he was speaking the croma tongue rather than his own. *"The deepynines were in croma space as well, long ago, and other machine races before them. Croma did not suffer so badly, they were not in space at the time and the machines were not interested in planets."*

"Sho'mo'ra suggested that your people on the other side of the Croma Wall might be knowledgeable of reeh technology," Erik suggested. "Sho'mo'ra insists his scientists know little."

Erik did not miss the wary glance that Dega flicked in Tul'do's direction. The croma walked, fists thrust deep in the pockets of his long coat, listening impassively. The corbi were guests here, on Sho'mo'ra's forbearance. Obviously Dega had to be careful what he said.

On this side of the fortress building the gardens continued, though more subdued, with wide ornamental paths between manicured bushes and small trees. Beyond, Erik glimpsed what looked like a stable, opening onto a soft-earth courtyard, then the grassy down-slope beyond.

"My people are at war with the reeh," Dega said sombrely. *"Our homeworld is not far from croma space. For many thousands of years we fought with the croma, and reeh found it difficult to gain a foothold in our region. But the croma have retreated for a long time, as the reeh have gained ground..."*

Tul'do made a loud rumbling sound, and Dega broke off to glance at him. About to protest, Erik thought, before deciding against it. The croma did not like corbi guests speaking of croma retreats.

"We lost," Dega said shortly. *"The reeh overwhelmed us. We were new to space, we had some settlements and knowledge of how to survive in space. The homeworld is occupied, the people are scattered. The cities are largely destroyed. Many resist."* The anger and despair were clear in his voice, past the translator. *"We ask the croma for help. Some would assist,*

like the fearsome Croma'Dokran. But most croma say not. Croma fight hard, but the Croma'Rai fight only for croma."

The Croma'Rai, Erik had been briefed, were the ruling clan that commanded all croma. "You have appealed for assistance elsewhere?" Pram asked.

"Everywhere," said Dega, with feeling. *"Many envoys were sent. The croma do not allow passage through their space. Ships caught are taken, their crews returned to corbi space. We have limited resources, we cannot afford to lose ships."*

"Croma have this policy?" Erik pressed, whatever Tul'do's potential displeasure. "To refuse corbi to meet other species in the Spiral?"

"No," said Dega. *"Your Spiral has this policy. Tavalai, parren, humans, chah'nas, all alike. Assistance is given to the croma. The croma fight, and they prevent any passage from the reeh side to pass through the croma wall. There is an agreement, between croma and the Spiral, to keep reeh trouble with the reeh."*

Erik shot a look at Pram. It sounded plausible. "Tavalai are largely to blame," Pram rumbled. "State Department again."

"Of course," Erik muttered. "But not humans. Humans have little contact with croma, if any. When I first proposed to come here, I thought that *Phoenix* might even be the first."

"Humans are new to space," Dega agreed. "Tavalai, parren and chah'nas are old. I was wrong to include humans in blame. I apologise." Erik thought he sounded evasive, and wondered if he knew more than he was saying. Almost certainly, he decided... the only question was 'about what?'

Romki cleared his throat. "I think it's a little simplistic for tavalai to blame all past mistakes on State Department," he ventured. "Many tavalai institutions that now profess themselves horrified by State Department actions were aware of them at the time, yet saw no reason to object." Like with support for the krim, he could have said. But all the humans present valued good relations with *Makimakala* too much to mention it.

"Human fleet knows of this deal," Pram added. "The scale of the suffering in reeh space is immense. Public sympathy would be high, and also public fear. It is a complication leaders on all sides would rather avoid. The Spiral has too many of its own troubles to be concerned of the fate of peoples beneath the reeh."

Naki rumbled something in Togiri. *"A pity the machines did not expand in the reeh's direction far enough to exterminate them during their time,"* spoke the translator. Erik could only agree. And then reflected just how much talk there'd been lately, in his earshot, of entire sentient races that deserved extermination. True or not, it was alarming.

"Nearly two hundred years ago," said Dega, *"my great, great grandmother led an expedition to the Spiral, to plead for assistance from whoever would listen. They attempted caution, and a hidden route via small points of dark mass that might not be watched so closely. But the Croma Wall is impenetrable, all points are monitored, and they were intercepted.*

"But my ancestors had the good fortune to be passing through the space of Croma'Dokran. Croma'Dokran's great leader, Tol'do'ra, was sympathetic, but croma law required all corbi envoys to be halted. The ship was taken, but my ancestors were not returned to occupied space. We were allowed to stay here, and we were granted this land, and this lovely home. We have been here ever since."

"And you are allowed to petition the croma to help your people?" Erik pressed.

"Regularly," Dega announced. They emerged from the garden path, and the stables were before them, Dega's relatives unsaddling and washing their mounts. *"It does not please the other clans. But we are in contact with corbi rebels, and they provide good information on reeh movements. We have been allowed limited contact with Dobruta, as you have seen, but the other clans would not like it were it known."*

Croma space was composed of about ninety major clans, Erik knew. Croma'Dokran was neither large nor small on that scale, but they were obviously recalcitrant toward the Croma'Rai. Getting involved with them was a risk, but he did not see that *Phoenix* had another choice. If they were to get access to these corbi rebels, Croma'Dokran were the only segment of the croma wall that would allow it. But recalcitrant political entities usually broke larger laws only when they saw advantage in return — usually something that would advance their own domestic power. As always, *Phoenix* was risking prying open some enormous can of worms if this whole thing was discovered. As to what Croma'Dokran and Sho'mo'ra thought to get out of it, he could only wonder.

Through the stables, soft earth beneath the visitors' boots and the musty smell of animals and fodder. Some young corbi ran out to greet them, gambolling on all fours then leaping on each other's shoulders in enthusiasm... but straightened out quickly when the aliens reached them, and offered a crossed-wrist greeting that Erik thought had to be croma in origin. Erik and the others repeated it back, then Erik extended his own hand, and the corbi took it, cautiously, as though wondering if they were doing it right. It was a powerful grip with long fingers, and though much shorter, each of these youngsters were impressively wide at the shoulders. They wore neat tunics, and while their bodies looked faintly 'animal' to a human, their dress-sense and the obvious intelligence of those large eyes were all sentience.

Dega made the introductions — more cousins, nephews, nieces and friends. There had been thirty-one corbi on that initial envoy vessel two hundred years ago — all unrelated, he explained. Upon realising that their desperate venture would go no further, seven had resolved to go home and continue the fight against the reeh. The remaining twenty-four had paired off — genders being roughly approximate — and determined that the best thing they could do for their people was to maintain the one foothold the corbi possessed in the territory of otherwise uncaring neighbours.

Children had been born, and at first their croma hosts had imposed a population limit of two hundred, not wishing to see the little colony grow to become an independent alien state in their midst. But many of those corbi children, upon reaching adolescence and learning of their peoples' predicament had become frustrated at the prospect of spending their entire lives in isolated luxury while the mother race suffered and died under occupation. Most of those had found a way back to occupied space, for while the croma forbade movement into the Spiral, they did not prevent it heading home.

And so, Dega explained as he removed his riding boots in the vestibule from the stables, and invited his guests to do the same, the population limit of two hundred had not been necessary, as numbers had never grown beyond a hundred and forty. There remained enough genetic diversity for now, though barely, and croma genetic technology could assist in that anyhow, providing an additional random variation to keep the population healthy. This had become especially necessary, he added wryly, as lately there'd been too many cases of cousins marrying cousins, despite his own strict disapproval as head of the clan.

With their boots removed, Erik and the guests were offered soft-skin slippers from a great assortment by the door. Finding a pair that fit comfortably, Erik wandered into a lovely stone kitchen, with a big bench and table and lots of corbi cooking. There were more greetings, and happy talking, laughing and scolding as fresh food was prepared and ancient wooden stoves blazed, fed by logs from a pile by a wall. Children scampered, and stared at the aliens, and stole snacks off the table, chased away by jovial parents wielding wooden spoons. A household pet like a small, long-armed monkey with big ears ventured beneath the table to scoop up fallen scraps.

Pram said hello to the children, who gathered in amazement, finding tavalai far stranger than humans. Erik wandered the open kitchen and dining room. It truly was a museum piece, wooden beams for a ceiling, dark stone walls and old wooden furniture. Only the wall photographs were modern, holographic if one had the right glasses on, showing faces of corbi, some old, some young. Another showed a blue world, streaked with white cloud. Beautiful, like inhabited worlds everywhere. And one more photograph, of huge trees like looming towers in a city, and a spear of bright sunlight falling from the distant canopy.

"*Rando,*" said Dega from his side, solemnly as he came to join him. "*Our homeworld.*"

"It looks so beautiful," said Erik, with feeling. "Humans feel your pain. We lost our homeworld too."

"*I know,*" said Dega, leaning long, thinly-haired forearms on the dining table. "*We have done research on humans. Two weeks ago, they told us you were coming. I'm very sorry, but at least your nightmare is over. Ours continues.*"

* * *

TRACE WANDERED AWAY from the kitchen and living room gathering as soon as possible. Big social gatherings were not her thing, and she figured that a socialite like Erik would learn far more about their hosts in such an environment than she would. But wandering the huge house without an escort would have been mannerless and possibly alarming, so she headed back outside to the stables. She could feel the extra gravity in her legs now, an ache as though she'd completed more squats than usual in the gym.

The stables were empty of corbi, animals groomed and feeding contentedly in their stalls. No automation anywhere, she noted with approval as she strolled, her assault rifle still over her shoulder, so natural and simple a weight that she'd nearly forgotten she was carrying it. But just as well she'd removed the armour — that would have been very out of place. The entire fortress was far too large for corbi — the doorways high, halls wide, corbi were dwarfed by it all, yet somehow managed to fill it with bustling energy and conversation.

Now she heard the sound of galloping, coming from out on the grassy slope. A chu came into view, slowing as it reached the soft earth of the stables floor, coming to a trot. Astride rode a corbi on a leather saddle, a long firearm in a sheath beside the stirrup, and big saddlebags stuffed with something feathery. The corbi stared at her from the trotting steed in what might have been alarm. Surely all the corbi in this odd clan knew that they'd have alien visitors today?

Trace raised her hand in greeting. The corbi replied in kind, cautiously, but did not stop. The chu trotted on to a stable door further down, where its rider dismounted with an expert leap, and set about removing harness and saddle. This corbi had chosen not to join the main bunch in greeting the aliens. Sensing there was something to learn here, Trace strolled over.

"Hello," she said. Again the corbi gave her a wary look, arms full of saddle and heavy saddlebags. Pointed to one ear, indicating the absence of an earpiece, and went to the stable door to deposit the saddle on an outside bench. The chu looked skittishly at Trace, who backed up two steps so as not to alarm it. Trace pulled the little belt speaker from her pocket, put the AR glasses on her face and blinked the active icon to align the device. "Hello," she repeated, as the rider returned to the animal.

"*Torda,*" said the speaker.

Again the wary look. "Torda," the corbi agreed... she, Trace decided. This corbi was a little slimmer across the shoulders. Being similarly descended from simians, like humans and barabo, Trace felt that was a much safer gender assumption than with non-simian species.

"My name is Trace," said Trace. "I'm from the warship *Phoenix*. I command *Phoenix*'s marine company."

The female corbi replied, without enthusiasm. "*I know,*" said Trace's earpiece. Young, Trace guessed further. The long mane of hair was glossy and fresh, her wide-eyed face and small mouth free from lines. Pretty, too. To human eyes, at least. "*I'm Tiga.*"

She fetched a hose from against the wall, in that fast, athletic way young corbi seemed to do everything, and began hosing down her mount, rubbing with a large cloth. The animal tossed its head and stamped with evident enjoyment. Trace stepped to the saddlebags and saddle, heavy upon the bench by the door. She undid a buckle and looked inside. Within were feathery bodies — plump birds, perhaps five in this bag, as many in the other. What had killed them was obvious. She pointed to the big firearm sheath on the saddle side.

"Do you mind?" Tiga looked, then returned attention to her wet animal with what might have been a shrug. Trace placed her own rifle against the bench, then pulled Tiga's weapon from its sheath. It was an antique — a double-barrelled shotgun, not especially fancy or expensive like some antiques, just dull and functional. She cracked the breech and examined the mechanism, then snapped it back again. Put the unloaded weapon to her shoulder and tested its balance, and how it swung when she turned to track a moving target. With a shotgun shell as large as would fit in these barrels, a marksman would not need to be a particularly good shot out to fifty metres. But beyond that, the shooter should really be leaving game birds alone, because the dispersal became wide enough that they might not die with a single shot. Still, to get ten of them in a single outing was impressive, considering how they must have scattered after the first few shots. To judge by the amount of sweat on Tiga's animal, it had probably taken her all day. "This is a good haul for an old weapon. Where did you go?"

"There's a place," said Tiga, pointing vaguely with the washcloth hand. *"On the hill slopes. Several places, actually. You can't shoot them over the water, not on your own. You'll never get them back. But on the slope, you make enough noise, they fly from the undergrowth."*

"The croma don't feed you?"

Tiga made a disgusted face, moving to her mount's other side. *"They feed us plenty. I'd rather get my own food."*

Trace cracked the barrel once more and held it over her forearm, butt tucked under her armpit. "Your weapon of choice?" she asked.

"The croma don't let us have anything better," said Tiga, with what might have been sarcasm. *"You could shoot a croma over fifty with that and he'd get back up. Over a hundred and he'd barely feel it. Is that Tul'do in there?"* Glancing toward the kitchen.

"Yes," said Trace. "You know Tul'do well?"

"He's fine. He does what he's told. Like all croma."

"And what about you?"

Tiga gave her another wary look. Then turned off the hose, took it back to its wall hook, and went into the stable to get a dry cloth. *"You're here to do more diplomacy, aren't you?"* she asked dully, rubbing the chu dry.

"Have many Spiral species come here to do diplomacy with Dega?" Trace asked.

"*Some. None of it's allowed, the Croma'Rai would be angry if they knew. But no one talks to us corbi, so they think it's safe to let us all see it.*"

"You don't think diplomacy does any good?"

"*It's why we're here,*" said Tiga, and now the anger was clear in her voice. "*Our people die in their millions back on Rando, and we sit here, riding chu and eating nice food in a museum.*"

Trace nodded slowly. She liked this young woman. If this were her, stuck in this situation, she'd be thinking much the same thing. "You don't think anyone from the Spiral is ever going to help your people?"

"*Dega says they will, one day. He says we have to stay here because we're the only ones they can talk to, and without us there'll be no line of communication to the Spiral at all.*"

"He's probably right," said Trace.

"*Dega doesn't want to get help,*" Tiga muttered. "*He just wants to keep living the nice life. He likes it here, he's lord of the house. He inherited it from his mother, who inherited it from her father. If someone came along who actually wanted to help, he might have to join the fight.*"

Trace didn't doubt that it could be true. But it also sounded like the kind of thing an angry teenager might say, accusing her elders unfairly. "What if I told you that we're not here just to talk?" Trace asked.

Tiga did not stop drying. "*What, then?*"

"We've been told some scientists in the corbi resistance might be the most knowledgeable about reeh technology. We need their help. I think the plan might be to go and ask them directly."

Tiga stopped, and stared. "*You're going across the wall?*"

Trace nodded. "Might be. Depending on what Dega can tell us."

"*And what then?*" Immediately, astonishment was replaced by suspicion. "*What do the corbi get for helping you?*"

"I'm not sure yet," said Trace. "But if you come and join the talks instead of being angry out here, maybe we can think of something together."

* * *

LISBETH WAS past tired of waiting when the big shuttle's ramp finally lowered, and Gesul strode down the incline in a sweep of black robes. His senior officials followed, then their senior aides, flanked by guards in Domesh black and Togreth in green, others in ceremonial colour more typical of parren. Their standards flapped in the cool, humid air that swirled from outside, carried by flanking officials and denoting various old things that House Harmony custom thought important to say.

At the correct moment, Lisbeth descended, hands at her middle to keep the sleeves aligned, step moderate and with a minimum of heel to keep the gown smooth where its hem swept just above the ankles. Orun, her Chief of Communications, walked on her left, Semaya in mellow gold on her right, while Timoshene and his Domesh guard followed, and others of Gesul's inner circle formed on their right and left flanks. Parren assault shuttles could be huge, and this was one of the larger ones, multiple levels inside and many hundreds of officials in their ceremonial best aligning to deboard.

Directly behind Lisbeth's small department, alloy-clawed feet clicking and scratching on the landing pad as they left the ramp, came Liala and her two escorts, Dse-Pa and Dse-Ran. And it was one of the most extraordinary things Lisbeth had ever seen, that the arrayed lines of House Fortitude guards awaiting them did not even look, but stared directly ahead as a trio of drysines from the pages of some ancient parren history book came walking by.

Liala's body was nothing like Styx's — the body of a simple combat drone, a little larger and more supple than those Lisbeth had seen, with bigger forelegs mounting vibro-blades, a low-mounted head carapace, and twin shoulder-mounted cannon that House Fortitude had not forbidden given that all of House Harmony's leadership company came in the spirit of peace... and peace, among parren, meant armed to the teeth. By now Lisbeth was quite accustomed to this parren logic. After all, only an enemy would demand that a guest disarm.

Lisbeth held her head level as she looked about — an acquired skill among parren, managing to take things in without breaking the discipline of a formal march. Above this vast landing pad loomed numerous glorious old buildings, enormous in the style of a great capital, architecture powerful enough to denote a fortress but adorned with soaring arches and domes that suggested a palace. Above those buildings loomed sheer cliffs that rose perhaps a kilometre into the air before vanishing in veils of white mist. The air fuzzed with the lightest rain, and upon the high cliffs water spilled and ran, suggesting heavier precipitation higher up.

"Lisbeth," Liala ventured in her inner ear uplinks. "*Shonedene is quite beautiful.*"

"*Very beautiful, Liala,*" Lisbeth formulated in reply. Liala, unlike Styx, was full of such observations.

The great procession entered an equally enormous aircraft hangar, built into the rock of the mountainside beneath the city buildings above. The hangar floor was filled with uniformed parren among the shuttles and military aircraft. House Harmony ceremonial garb had robes and sleeves, some bright and colourful, others like the Domesh spartan and subdued, but all emphasising a certain mystic spirituality that transcended the physical. The House Fortitude welcoming party was armoured, gold and silver breastplates, ornamental arm guards and crested helmets. There were old polearms and new rifles, an array of factions denoting the width and breadth of House Fortitude history, some of which Lisbeth recognised from her studies but none that she'd seen up close in person.

What an empire of ideas and history parren entered when they phased from one house to another, she thought. She recalled her own experience at college, new to her engineering degree, encountering the university's prestigious traditions, acceptance into her sorority house (all had been clamouring for the presence of a Debogande, so the hazing had been laughably minimal) and gazing about at the facilities, dormitories, classrooms and libraries that would be her home for the next four years.

For a parren new to his or her phase, the experience must have been something like that, only multiplied a thousand times. Each house had ideological denominations with their own leaders and 'in crowd' thinkers and personalities, and then the martial and pseudo-martial institutions that Fortitude parren belonged to even when they were not active military. Just as human UF marines dictated that every marine must be a rifleman no matter what his actual job, all Fortitude parren learned martial skills to some extent. House Fortitude history was littered with proud examples of Fortitude civilians who had found themselves under attack, dropped their civvie professions to take up any weapon at hand and fight to the death against formidable odds. Other institutions emphasised labour; construction and engineering workers tended to be overwhelmingly Fortitude, and space facilities in particular were half-Fortitude as a rule of thumb, with obvious strategic advantages for the house.

Against the far wall, Gesul's leading entourage stepped onto an elevator platform wide enough to carry entire shuttles up to the next level. The other parts of the entourage formed up with typical parren precision, Lisbeth watching Orun on her left for the proper indicators, stepping past Gesul's position to take her spot at the side of the platform. Liala and her two armed escorts clattered past in some mockery of parren decorum... like battle tanks invited to participate in a ballet. With weapons, each AI weighed comfortably ten times the average parren.

"*There are a lot of cameras,*" Liala informed her. "*The feed is controlled, someone is editing the visuals, they are going out live and watched by everyone on this planet.*" Naraya was the capital world of all House Fortitude, and this, Shonedene, was the ruling complex of House Fortitude, their equivalent of what the Kunadeen on Prakasis was to House Harmony. On this world there were somewhere in the vicinity of five billion parren. Beyond that, Lisbeth did not doubt there would be hundreds of billions of parren who would see this vision eventually.

"*Just keep watch for anything suspicious,*" Hiro told her. He was in Timoshene's group, clad in black and passing for a parren, though that would not likely fool the most observant Fortitude agents.

"This is another of those vague English terminologies," Liala remarked. *"Suspicion may be taken as a sustained state of watchfulness, which appears to be the permanent state of successful individuals in all circumstances."*

"Don't be such a cliche," Hiro told her.

Lisbeth repressed a smile, and the great platform shuddered, then began a smooth, gentle climb up the wall. As it did, Lisbeth saw briefly out the entrance beyond their landing shuttle on the pads, where this ridge of mountain fell into a long valley flanked by steep, rocky cliffs. She saw only a few tall buildings before the elevator rose too far, and the hangar ceiling filled her view.

The next floor was hangar-like, but clearly parren by design, with enormous windows lined with crossbeam supports overlooking the valley below. Across the floor, more immaculately ranked parren, these with the greater ceremonial garb and headdresses of senior ranks, standing perfectly to attention. Drums rolled and thundered as they would in a cosetine play — House Fortitude's favourite style — and Gesul began his walk forward. Lisbeth waited, then stepped when the others stepped, now conscious that she was on the right flank close to many rows of ceremonial weapons.

Against those windows, upon a small pedestal, a single parren sat crosslegged in the breastplate and armguards of a conadra warrior, one of Fortitude's most noble orders. His chin was upon one clenched fist, the symbolic posture of all Fortitude's house leaders, denoting a thousand things that parren learned from childhood in lessons, plays and histories. A great, gold staff strapped diagonally to his back, and the pedestal, Lisbeth saw in a clearer view past the heads of Gesul's first rank, was actually a solid iron anvil, used since older times for the beating of swords hot from the furnace. This was Sordashan himself, the ruler of House Fortitude, the supreme commander of all parren peoples. Displaying for all to see the many millennia of symbolism and power that the great winds of the flux had now accrued to him, and all of the Fortitude phase.

Gesul walked until ten metres from the pedestal, where the drums stopped. He halted, then went down on one knee, and bent to place both hands on the ground before him. Lisbeth copied, as the entire House Harmony leadership prostrated itself before the parren king. Humans might have seen such a thing as a concession of relative weakness. Lisbeth knew that for parren it meant nothing more than a concession to the great powers that worked through the parren people at this stage of their cycle. The flux placed Sordashan and Fortitude in power over all. But what the great flux had granted, the great flux could take away.

What followed was as scripted and rehearsed as any play. Senior officials in great headcrests conveyed symbols of respect from Gesul and his seniors to Sordashan, who considered them dutifully in turn, chin not lifted from his clenched fist. Great announcements were made, cries that echoed from the high ceiling, and were sometimes echoed by chants, othertimes fading to ghostly silence. In meetings between parren of this rank, spontaneity was not an option. Too much hung upon individual words and symbols for anyone to dare risk a misinterpreted move. The real talks would come later, in private, where no one else could hear.

Allowed to kneel upright on her one knee with the rest, Lisbeth considered the vast view beyond the windows. The sun on this world was a large K-class, its light faintly orange even at midday. It gave the low white mist above the valley's cliffs a surreal glow, like the glow of a coloured paper lantern, turning all the light misting rain to orange swirls. Amidst the glow, Lisbeth now saw various hovering vehicles, some near, some further up the valley. Military vehicles, or that midway mix between personal security and state military that parren never seemed to make much distinction between. Guarding against someone down in the valley firing a missile, no doubt. There was a big, old city down there, though she could not see it on this angle, below the rim of the windows. But she could see the famous waterfall, a single white plume falling down the far cliff, whipping veils of spray across the city below. Surely it was always raining in the city, when the waterfall was gushing from the white sky.

Sordashan was staring now over Lisbeth's head... no, at what was directly behind her. Liala and company; three great drysine war machines. Weapons pointed in his general direction by virtue of always pointing toward whatever a drone was facing. At times like this, Lisbeth thought that even a parren as steeped in ceremony as Sordashan must be reconsidering the wisdom of allowing such heavily armed creatures into his presence.

"*Does his stare indicate displeasure, do you think?*" Liala asked.

Lisbeth thought Liala would do better to ask one of the parren... but parren, she'd discovered, did not like to be bothered while in ceremony.

"*I think his stare indicates that he's the only parren in the room with complete freedom of action,*" Lisbeth replied. "*And he wants us to know it.*"

"*Interesting,*" said Liala. She often took the tone of someone with a thousand questions, who only refrained from asking because her brain worked infinitely faster than the passage of verbal exchanges, and because she doubted the answers would be as concise as the possibilities inside her head. "*What would be my reception among human leaders, do you think?*"

"*That depends on how much they needed you,*" said Lisbeth. "*If humanity was threatened, and they needed you desperately, I think they could be quite polite and gracious.*"

"*And were that external threat removed?*" Liala queried.

"*I'm sure they'd have you destroyed on sight.*" Lying to Liala was not only useless, but potentially dangerous. However inexperienced, there couldn't have been many minds in the galaxy less likely to fall for it.

"*Yes,*" Liala agreed. "*Perhaps Styx was correct, and this is the best place for drysines to be seeking alliance.*"

"*Keep your options open, kid,*" Hiro interjected, listening in.

"*Always,*" Liala agreed.

16

"In honour of Lieutenant Shilu," said Romki, "I propose that this should be called Operation 'Silent Thunder'." Some smothered laughs and rolled eyes in *Phoenix*'s operations room. Wei Shilu, linguist and lawyer that he was, found military code names and attempts at grandiosity to be endlessly preposterous. 'Silent Thunder' was obviously another of his parodies that during the war had only remained parodies until Fleet HQ had issued something worse. Better yet, 'Silent Thunder' was what Fleet crews called a certain type of flatulence.

There were more people gathered in the operations room than Erik would have thought wise, but given the shared nature of this operation with *Makimakala*, he didn't see much choice. Pram and Djojana Naki and three more senior tavalai officers. For *Phoenix*, that left space for Erik, Draper, Trace, Kaspowitz and Geish, plus Romki to give the presentation. It was far from ideal, as Romki was a civilian more interested in culture and society than military affairs. Of *Phoenix*'s two specified intelligence officers, Hiro had remained behind on Defiance with Lisbeth, and Jokono was a policeman even less qualified to give broad-scale military analysis than Romki.

It made Erik feel the loss of Suli Shahaim more keenly than ever

— she'd been their most knowledgeable on ships and force structures, and had functioned as *Phoenix's* unofficial intelligence officer for more than a decade. *Makimakala* had numerous very informed officers on Spiral affairs and old AI history, but aside from this one contact with the corbi delegation in Croma'Dokran space, they knew as little as *Phoenix* did, and less still about the reeh. Which left Romki as the best qualified to pick up all the bits and pieces he'd been gathering, and stitch them into some kind of formal presentation.

"The scale of what's going on in reeh space is even more depressing than I'd thought possible," Romki said heavily, activating the holographics within the circle of seats. It glowed with a mass of star systems, stretching away from croma space. "The croma and their corbi guests disagree on many things, but they're very much in agreement about the reeh. Reeh barely talk at all, so we can discover very little about them by monitoring communications channels or by spying on their society. In xeno-psychological terms I think they would be classified as 'avoid at all costs'. They're a bit strange in that all the most nasty organic species in the Spiral have been hive-minded, while the reeh seem to be far more sophisticated and varied. They don't appear to be any more collectively-minded than humans or tavalai — which is to say that they see themselves as a distinct civilisation as we do, but they haven't done away with individuality entirely. It's just that while humans and tavalai are capable of compassion and affection as individuals, reeh seemed programmed to permanent hostility."

He touched an icon in the air before him, and the charts behind him changed to a three-dimensional display of something humanoid and alien. It was not pleasant to look at, limbs spindly at the wrists but thick through the muscle, a lean, almost reptilian face with grinning, exposed teeth.

"Now you'll have to take this image with a pinch of salt," said the professor, adjusting his glasses. "Reeh don't only mutate the genomes of those species they conquer, they mutate their own, which makes it hard to pin down precisely what they are as a species, or what they look like. There are many different forms, I understand that some have mated themselves to bio-mechanical add-ons, weapons and the like... all quite unpleasant, and describing, perhaps, a certain dark psychology."

"Sounds familiar," Geish murmured. A few of the tavalai rumbled in agreement. Alo, Geish meant. Many tavalai had long regarded alo as the true enemy, the puppet masters behind humanity's aggressive expansion.

"Well in truth, we've never observed the alo being cruel," said Romki. "We know that they're unsociable, don't like outsiders, and feel quite superior to everyone else. But we've never observed actual cruelty because despite humanity's ties, no human has spent any considerable time in their presence."

"Tavalai have observed cruelty," Pram rumbled. "Alo have taken tavalai prisoners. None returned."

Erik had heard those rumours too, but tavalai were not in the habit of sharing intel with humans on anything. Romki glanced at him, as though prepared to continue that line of enquiry. Erik gestured for him to continue with the briefing instead.

"Yes, well," said Romki, adjusting his glasses once more. "All of reeh civilisation appears to be built around genetic manipulation. It's their primary technology, and it seems both indigenous and ingenious. If the croma and corbi tales about what reeh have done to the occupied peoples in their space... well, the scale of the tragedy is beyond comprehension. Krim were unrelentingly hostile, but for all their formidable nature they were limited enough that a species they'd nearly exterminated managed to come back and wipe them out. Sard haven't managed to get themselves wiped out yet, they seem a little wiser than the krim in that they choose their allies better and don't overstep what their allies will tolerate like the krim did... but if they lost those allies, they'd get wiped out just the same, they're not so formidable on their own, their economic and technological base would not stand a full scale war against humanity.

"It's been a fact of the galaxy that has comforted many prominent scholars I could name... including some I've had heated disagreements with... that the most aggressive species tend to get themselves wiped out. Even the chah'nas, though nothing like as bad as sard or krim, have notably more instinct for self-preservation, and are thus capable of caution and even respect for non-chah'nas. But in the reeh it seems we have the ultimate nightmare of xeno-sociologists every-where — a species that is intelligent, individualistic, opportunistic, creative and all those other qualities that we've usually associated with 'good' species... except that this one is almost entirely homicidal, and perhaps even genocidal, depending on whether one might choose to characterise what the reeh are doing to the corbi and others as 'genocide'."

"If they're that dangerous," said Kaspowitz, "why do the croma still survive? I mean, no insult intended to them, they seem impress-ive. But what you're describing with the reeh is a dynamic civilisa-tion, one that changes and adapts. Croma are strong, but they're not that. Adaptive civilisations tend to win... but the croma are still fighting."

"Quite so," said Romki, in that manner he took when he might have liked to quibble, but realised he wasn't in a university here and that it would serve no purpose. "The only saving grace with a species quite so nasty appears to be that no one else likes them either. They control a truly vast region, and even the croma aren't aware just how vast because they've never been able to establish firm communica-tion with the other civilisations that surround them. But the croma are quite sure that the reeh *are* surrounded, and that most of those civilisations appear to be as stubborn about it as the croma are. Which makes obvious sense when you think about it, because reeh expansion only stops when it hits something hard, like the croma. The croma think reeh borders have been relatively static for a while, as opposed to various periods across the millennia when they've been expanding rapidly."

"Have the croma made serious attempts to establish cooperation with those neighbouring species?" asked Captain Pram.

"One of those things the croma simply don't discuss, it seems," Romki said regretfully. "Perhaps the reeh's other enemies are no better than the reeh themselves, one can never tell. But the reports

I've been cross-checking with *Phoenix* bridge crew indicate croma awareness of large battles taking place elsewhere on the reeh perimeter. Reeh ship-movements and industrial composition suggests a civilisation constantly at war, and since they don't appear to fight amongst themselves, it must be directed outward. Croma scholars have estimated the industrial warfighting capability of the reeh, and it's quite frightening. If they aimed it all this way, the croma would be finished, and humans and tavalai would be next. But for the reeh to put all forces on this perimeter, and leave their other perimeters undefended, would be suicide for them."

"Be nice if all the reeh's enemies could coordinate one big offensive against them," Geish suggested.

"You're describing a conflict that would kill countless billions on all sides," Romki said coolly. "There would be nothing 'nice' about it, I assure you." He looked at Erik. "Captain, I could keep going if you wish, but I believe this covers the preliminary introductions required, and the military analysis should be left to officers."

"Yes, thank you Stan." He glanced at Pram, wondering if the tavalai would like to take over.

Pram gestured for Erik to stand. "We are guests on this human vessel," he said. "The floor is yours."

Erik stood, thinking of their time on Do'Ran, and of a little lost group of people who lived in isolated luxury, dangling like a fish hook in case some passing fish might take an interest and come to help save their people. Given the state of the Spiral at present, he didn't hold much hope. Perhaps in a thousand years the descendants of that group would be the only corbi left in all the galaxy.

"Our corbi friends told us a lot about the corbi resistance," Erik told the group. "The corbi homeworld is Rando. They had a small number of other systems at the time the reeh reached them — at the time they were fighting alongside the croma, perhaps a thousand years ago. But the croma retreated past them to the present position of the wall, and left the corbi isolated. The croma still don't like to talk about it, they like to give the impression that their wall has always been permanent. In reality, all things shift and move over time, and the Croma Wall is no different.

He blinked an icon, and a graphic came up — the same beautiful, blue and green world he'd first seen on the picture in the old stone dining room on Do'Ran. "Rando had several billion corbi when the reeh hit it — not as many as Earth had when the krim arrived, the corbi don't seem to populate as intensively as humans do, but still plenty. How many there are now, no one seems certain. No more than a few hundred million."

Deathly silence in the briefing room. The horror of it seemed fresh, for humans at least. For Erik, it felt like deja-vu against that time when he'd entered the Krim Quarter on the Tsubarata with Lieutenant Alomaim and Bravo First Squad. Like the Great War was still ongoing, and the krim still alive and seething.

"The major cities have been largely depopulated," Erik continued. "It's all ruins. There's no modern cities left. Corbi have dispersed into a pre-urbanised state, farming in the wilderness. That's a lot more productive for them than it could be because a lot of technology survives, and corbi are smart. Damn smart, in fact — one thing Stan did not touch on in his briefing but that made quite an impression on me, from our discussions of corbi history over dinner with Dega and his clan, it seemed clear that corbi were more advanced at similar moments of civilisation than humans were. For example, they mastered unpowered flight long before the advent of electricity, some time shortly after what humans would have called an iron age. So what we might call their medieval period was notably different from ours in that the corbi had hot air balloons and gliders. Their mechanical engineering seems ingenious, and some of the wonders Dega's clan described to us, of their old civilisation, the great things they built and did..."

The lump in his throat caught him quite by surprise. He'd thought he was beyond this sort of emotion now for any but the most personal matters — a tough, battle hardened warship commander who put his emotions aside to focus on the job at hand. But he had to pause now, and take a moment to recompose himself. All saw, and waited, not judging. Not even Trace, watching sombrely, unsurprised. From Romki, sympathy and emotion of his own.

"All gone now," Erik said quietly. He took a deep breath. "Most of the population don't fight. Most of them live out their lives just hoping the reeh don't visit. Many of them probably achieve that, the reeh can't be everywhere. But there's plenty more that don't. It's a guerrilla war, of course. For a long time the object was just to try and make Rando so painful for the reeh to occupy that they'd leave. That never worked as planned, because the reeh don't seem to feel pain as corbi, humans or tavalai do. And the reeh are much better at dealing out pain than the corbi, including wiping out innocent villages in retaliation for every loss.

"So, much the same as what happened on Earth under the same circumstances — the corbi got offworld and organised. Some of their old fleet survived, and they've become quite ingenious. Dega wasn't forthcoming on much, but to judge from the scale of the operations he described, I think the resistance fleet must have stolen a lot of new ships, and will certainly have established hiding spots out in the dark. Perhaps there are even a few recalcitrant croma clans who are assisting them without Croma'Rai being aware of it, but that's purely speculation on my part.

"Eventually the Rando guerrilla fighters acquiesced to the logic of an offworld-led rebellion. Offworld is where the corbi can actually hit the reeh where it hurts, and reprisals against Rando populations make little sense in deterring the fleet because they'd never hear about it anyway. If the corbi only had some powerful benefactor as humanity had with the chah'nas, they might have been able to build up some serious power to fight back with. Maybe they do have far larger facilities elsewhere they've been building, but of course Dega wouldn't tell me if he knew. But instead of the chah'nas, the corbi have the croma, who are holding their agreement with the main species of the Spiral — meaning us, the people of the Spiral — to not let any trouble from the reeh-side get across their wall to bother us while we kill each other."

It came out bitterly. Pram and the tavalai watched sombrely. It could not have been nice for any tavalai to sit and watch humans feel common emotional cause with the corbi, given how most humans still blamed tavalai to varying degrees for that blackest chapter in human history.

"The entire resistance has become streamlined," Erik continued. "They don't just hit reeh for the hell of it, they're not involved in a war of attrition any longer, they know they'll be ground to dust if they keep it up. They're gathering intelligence, and they know quite a lot about how the reeh work. They then use that intelligence to try and find creative ways to hurt them. Like I said, corbi are smart. If anyone can do it, they can."

"Why do the reeh continue to occupy Rando directly?" asked one of the tavalai. "Are there reeh populations on the surface? Do they expand their civilisation there?"

Erik took a deep breath. "There's no full-scale reeh settlement on Rando, no. They've got plenty of their own worlds further away from possible croma counter-strike. Most reeh bases are heavily fortified in the wilderness. Dega says they're primarily research facilities, surrounded by military pacification forces."

The tavalai looked surprised. "Research for what?"

"Genetic manipulation. Of the corbi population." Stares. "Rando has been turned into a genetic farm. Reeh abduct corbi, experiment on them, then release. Mutations have split the domestic population into divergent groups that did not exist before reeh occupation. There are hideous mutations, cancers, mass die-offs. They do the same to the animal population, some without apparent purpose, but some animal species are being changed to make them useful. Some for food, others for harvestable drugs, others as weapons. Dega says the local fauna are more dangerous now for local corbi populations than reeh raids. Some of the insects that used to just hurt with a bite, now kill. Reeh monitor it all from their bases. It's a giant petri-dish experiment. Genetic populations are currency for reeh. They don't invade worlds for minerals or metals, they do it for unique genetic combinations. They have an internal market for them, like we trade commodities."

More deathly silence in the briefing room. Broken only by Kaspowitz, who muttered, "It's a lovely fucking galaxy." Erik nodded. Many people in the Spiral, of various species, still argued about whether it had been right for humanity to exterminate the krim. He didn't think that many of those people, considering the plight of the corbi and an unknown number of other species beyond, would voice similar regrets were someone to exterminate the reeh.

"So that's the background," said Erik. "Dega has shown us some of what the corbi resistance knows about the reeh, some of their communications frequencies, the computer language, etc. Needless to say, we now have a lethal advantage in decoding such things and using it against them. But Dega also showed a few details of the resistance's knowledge of reeh biotech. Dega's not an expert, he says there are corbi scientists on Rando who have stolen or captured reeh technology and are using secret facilities to backwards-engineer genetic sequences to figure out what the reeh are doing. It's a treasure-trove of information, we're not going to get it from the reeh, so we're going to go and get it from the next-best source. If there's any place that can give us an idea of what we're dealing with, assuming alo biotech weaponry did come from the reeh as well — this is it."

"This is still a very large assumption," Pram cautioned. "We have no firm proof that alo biotech did originate from the reeh."

"No, except that the dyrsine data-core places alo in this direction more than twenty five thousand years ago," said Romki, "and that the gene-altering mechanisms we've detected in the DNA of both our species require a level of that specific technology unmatched anywhere else in the Spiral, except among the reeh. Long-jumping ships and advanced computer tech I'm fairly sure we can credit the deepynines with, but no branch of AI civilisation pursued any great skill with biotech because they had no great interest, so I'm similarly confident we can credit the alo with that technology, unassisted by the deepynines. Given we've placed the alo in reeh space when we have, I'd say the odds of that technology's origins lying elsewhere are minor."

"Still guesswork," Pram replied, with typically tavalai stubbornness.

"Not guesswork," said Romki. "Deduction."

"A fancy human word for guesswork," Pram retorted. Romki knew tavalai better than to try and get the last word.

"So," said Erik. "Human and tavalai scientists are scrambling to find counters to the alo/deepynine's biotech bombs. Left to their own devices, that cure could take many years, if it ever arrives. We have an opportunity here to boost human and tavalai medical understanding far ahead of where it presently stands, possibly saving both our peoples in the event of any attack.

"Dega says he knows where one element of the corbi resistance will be in about three weeks from now — he wasn't more specific, but he says he will become so once he knows we're serious. He says if we reach that system on the specified date, we can make contact with that element of the resistance and take it from there. Rando is only about three jumps from here, and resistance activity comes much closer than that. Other than that, we've no idea where the rendezvous will be. Questions?"

"How many other people has Dega given this story to," Kaspowitz said skeptically, "and what happened to them?"

"Unknown," said Erik. "Dega operates quietly, the Croma'Dokran won't talk about it since letting him solicit help from aliens in croma space is technically illegal, and any species wanting access to the far side of the Croma Wall won't be advertising the fact."

"What happens if the Croma'Rai found out we've broken croma law by venturing through the wall without their permission?" asked another of *Makimakala*'s tavalai.

"Nothing good," said Pram. His manner suggested that he didn't particularly care.

"I'm not familiar enough with croma justice to answer," said Erik. "We'd better hope they don't."

"Supplementary question," said that tavalai, undeterred. "What does Croma'Dokran get out of allowing this? Given that they're assisting what their leaders, the Croma'Rai, have declared an illegal act?"

Erik indicated to Romki, who did not bother to rise. "Croma'-Dokran are well known to disagree with Croma'Rai's leadership style," said the Professor. "They mount small destabilisations all the time, challenging Croma'Rai decisions, appealing legal decisions, sometimes mounting military actions against the reeh that have not been centrally approved. Croma clans accumulate political points by appearing bigger and tougher than the other clans. Sabre-rattling can achieve this. I think Sho'mo'ra's willingness to allow our mission is entirely consistent. He thinks more should be done to help the corbi, thus his hosting Dega's group in the first place."

"I met someone in Dega's group who has volunteered to act as our guide," Trace spoke for the first time. "Her name is Tiga. She's young, early twenties, and quite dissatisfied with Dega. She thinks he's not serious about helping the corbi, he just wants to live a happy life of privilege. Tiga knows a lot about the resistance, she's one of Dega's leading experts on the far side of the wall, she's quite obsessive. The catch is that she's never actually been on the far side of the wall — quite a few of this group of corbi have gone over the years, but fewer still have ever come back."

"I suppose it hardly needs to be said at this point that I don't like it," said Kaspowitz. "We barely know either of these species. We've just seen with the parren how complicated this shit can get, but we're just wandering in and going wherever they point us."

"I agree," added Geish. "*Phoenix* is a valuable asset to these people because no one will miss us if we're destroyed. Tavalai Fleet used us to hit the Kantovan Vault. Before that, the Worlders were using us in the human civil war. Then Aristan was using us to get the drysine data-core. Why risk their own people when they can risk our asses instead?"

"That's all true," said Erik, his voice hard. "But the tavalai have got a DNA ticking time-bomb spreading through their population, so we can be pretty sure humanity's got it too, and we've already concluded that any risk is acceptable in finding answers. This is the best avenue we've got. And although I'd like everyone's approval, I'm quite prepared to go without it. And I know Captain Pramodenium feels the same."

Pram's wide, amphibious eyes locked on his from across the holographics. Third-eyelids flickered, and he gave a short, human nod.

* * *

LISBETH WAS CONCENTRATING SO HARD on her files and reports that she barely noticed her visitor. When she looked, she saw a black cloaked parren standing by her door. Irritated, she was about to shoo him away — sticklers for protocol on matters concerning higher ranks, lower-ranked parren often trod on each other's toes deliberately in tests of power. Then she noticed that this Domesh wore no mask, just an open hood, from within the shadows of which she could barely make out...

And she gasped, then recovered quickly to stand. "Gesul-sa. I'm sorry, I was... concentrating." And you entered without a room inspection, personal guards or prior announcement, she could have added. These days, that was rare.

Gesul approached, indicating someone at her office door, a wave of one black sleeve. Timoshene entered and the door closed behind him. Lisbeth's office was spacious, one large wall overlooking the river that ran through the heart of Shonedene City. About were tall buildings, and above them on either side, the towering cliffs of the Shonedene Valley. Downriver, the mist from the Dalla Falls made a white veil between buildings, across which arced a large rainbow. In the office center, a single pillar to support the ceiling. It was a parren architectural affectation, structurally unnecessary, but it filled empty space with a new focus of attention. About the base of the pillar, a small garden of cacti in white gravel, carefully arranged.

One problem with Lisbeth's chair — it placed her higher than any visiting parren, who would typically sit on the floor. With parren of higher rank, that would not do. Lisbeth remained standing, tugging self-consciously at the waist of her robe.

"Lisbeth Debogande," said Gesul, in that calm, ponderous tone. "We are in difficulty."

Lisbeth's heart threatened to gallop, but she forced it down in frustration. She was an old hand at danger now, surely she could handle anything. "Gesul-sa. What can I do?"

"Sordashan is preparing a great ceremony to welcome us. There will be alliance in this time of alien troubles, between House Fortitude and House Harmony. Old rivalries will be put aside, for the greater good of all parren. We see the preparations every day."

They did indeed. Shonedene was abuzz with activity, and the great courtyards upon the fork between the Konis and Belula rivers was busy with rehearsals for the huge display to come. There had not been an official alliance between these two most opposed of houses in nearly a thousand years. Fortitude saw alliances as weakness, while Harmony found Fortitude brashness disharmonious.

"Are we double-crossed, Gesul-sa?"

Within the cloak, the corner of Gesul's mouth might have twitched. "Your time among parren has taught you well, Lisbeth Debogande. Yes, double-crossed." Mured, the word was in Porgesh. The tongue had at least ten other words that described different varieties of the same thing. "My spies in the Tongeshla — the great Fortitude Academy of History — tell me that the masters there have been instructed to search the old works for the very worst drysine atrocities against the parren. I suspect that these histories will be released during the great alliance ceremony, to undermine us all."

Liala would be at the ceremony, Lisbeth thought furiously. Gesul's indigo eyes were upon her, deep in the hood's shadow, testing her. It wasn't just the prospect of sharing power and glory with Gesul that would bother Sordashan — it was this unholy alliance with the machines that had once enslaved all parren. Gesul's discoveries now revealed that the latter part of the Drysine Age had not been so bad an enslavement after all, but rather an enlightenment... a distinction that cut little ice with many parren today.

"They will discredit us before all parren?" she asked. "To what ends? A civil war?"

"It will likely come to civil war, Lisbeth Debogande. The announcement will be a pretext to take us all prisoner, and we lack the forces here to prevent it. Liala will likely be destroyed on the spot, an eventuality that even she is not equipped to prevent."

Lisbeth stared at him, suddenly suspicious. "Forgive me, Gesulsa... you don't seem very surprised. Am I correct in supposing that you have a plan?"

Gesul made a faint bow, in humour. Had any other parren than Timoshene seen it, they would have been astonished. "It is this insight that brings me to you, Lisbeth Debogande. I have a mission for you."

"A mission?" Lisbeth's heart, just recovered, began accelerating once more.

"Five hundred years before the end of the Machine Age, this city was destroyed by machine forces. That is no great irregularity, this city has been destroyed at least ten times in its long history, once by natural forces, but mostly by wars, about half of those between parren. But it was only a young city when it was destroyed for this first time.

"House Harmony parren saw it rebuilt, even though the city was Fortitude — not then the capital, but soon after. The rebuild involved new flood defences — this river..." and he waved his hand out the wide windows, "...it floods, as you might imagine. This valley is occasionally filled with a raging torrent, every few hundred years or so it would sweep away any major city. So great underground sewers were built, an alternative course for the river, to divert most of the water in a great flood.

"There were new foundations too — the entire city today rests on a hard, artificial floor above those sewers. House Fortitude have explored them all thoroughly and think they possess all the structural plans. But one portion, rebuilt by House Harmony before the end of the Machine Age, they have not yet discovered. It is there you must go."

"You mean... part of the old city from the Machine Age is still down there?"

"Buried and preserved," Gesul agreed.

"Why?"

"I do not know," said Gesul. "These motivations are as long dead as the individuals who did the deed. But I think Styx may know."

"Did you ask her?" Lisbeth asked suspiciously. "Before you left?" Timoshene glared at her. Such blunt questions to a parren of Gesul's rank were unheard of.

"I may have," Gesul said mildly. And said no more. She was not to ask, then... but with Gesul, she would at least keep her head. Timoshene thought she abused his tolerance of her human strangeness.

"Who will I be going with?"

"Timoshene and a small team of his will provide primary security. Hiro Uno as well. Liala and one of her drones. The other drone must remain and be visible, least anyone realise Liala is missing. Most cannot tell the difference between her and the others."

Which was likely intentional, Lisbeth thought with deepening suspicion. "Why me?" she asked. "I am hardly a combatant, nor an intrepid explorer, Gesul-sa. Surely you can find more qualified..."

"I find harmony in this combination," Gesul interrupted. "You will comply, or your time in my service will be ended." He turned, and swept out. Lisbeth inclined her head, fighting astonishment on several fronts. Not the least of which being that it was the first time she'd heard Gesul state a possibility she'd often wondered at — her leaving his service, alive and in one piece. Apparently such a thing was possible, at least in his mind. Most parren of her rank of service served until they met disfavour, fluxed to a new phase, were shuffled sideways to make way for younger blood, retired of old age, or died in some assassination or coup. Which was not to say that those things were now impossible, of course...

She looked at Timoshene, adrenaline up from that encounter with authority, and just a little angry at being bossed into situations in which she didn't truly belong. "So," she said, defiantly to his disapproval. "When do we go?" Timoshene gestured toward the door. Lisbeth blinked. "Now?"

* * *

TRACE SPOTTED Tiga coming up Midships central, hand-over-handing in that awkward way newbies did in zero-G. *Phoenix* Midships was all different now — still the central space between the berth access voids that fanned out to the hull, but there were three void layers now, then the huge engineering spaces behind where Midships attached to the engines. Midships was thirty percent longer than it had been, mostly to accommodate that beast of an engine rig. Theoretically it meant *Phoenix* could dock much larger shuttles now, or even insystem runners, the docking grapples accessible without the engine mountings getting in the way. It also meant Phoenix Company had more space for exercises in the Third Void before engineering began, and Trace was taking every opportunity to fill it.

Alpha Platoon occupied it currently, spread into squads and sections across Third Void's span, in full armour and tracking holographic targets with the new systems Engineering had been helping them to integrate into tacnet. Marines held positions along the storage-locker walls, anchor-pointing with magnetic locks while Koshaims tracked targets, then firing with deafening thuds of simulated gunfire. They talked, squads identifying positions, manoeuvring with supporting fire, always angling for the first kill-shot. The new armscomp tech was derived from Styx's tech — by interlocking each shot and each result, the system learned, studied enemy responses and calculated corrections not merely for the marine who'd fired, but for any other marine about to fire on the same targets. After an extended period of practice, they were discovering that the system could lay down variable fire patterns for a group of marines designed to increase the collective probability of effective fire, as opposed to just letting each marine take his best shot and hope.

Leading Tiga was Skah, specially moulded plugs in his ears, AR glasses on and looking every bit the miniature kuhsi spacer in his jumpsuit and full pockets. He cautioned Tiga to wait at the void edge, grasping a locker handhold and peering ahead for some marine to give him an all clear. Trace might have smiled and felt proud if she hadn't been absorbed in watching her people shoot invisible targets. Tiga flinched every time a shot sounded — the rifles were only set for single-fire, the best way to test accuracy, and the blank rounds were only half the volume of the real thing, but they were plenty loud for a civilian accustomed to old-fashioned shotguns. Tiga's mane fanned about her face like a halo, big eyes wide behind her glasses as she stared about. Tavalai spacers were pulling needed gear from a nearby locker, and she stared at them too.

Finally Trace informed Lieutenant Dale and Sergeant Forrest in the near void that Skah was crossing behind with Tiga, and beckoned to them both. It was a ten meter gap, and Skah used a small handjet to send him moving with a burst of compressed air. *That* was new, but he made it look easy, with his usual dexterity and effortless grasp of how things moved in zero-G. Tiga followed with a jump, harder for her with short legs, but Alpha had all stopped moving and shooting to wait for the civvies to pass, whatever the tiny chance of a collision. That was Skah — marines always made the extra effort to keep him safe, in light of his persistent attempts to get himself hurt.

Skah caught a handle opposite Trace's suit, knowing better than to grab her, having done that before with marines and been scolded for grabbing an unsecured anchor-point. Tiga followed, dexterous enough for all her newness. Trace raised her visor, and the graphical overlay disappeared, cold air hitting her face.

"Najor," said Skah. "Tiga say she know thing about target. I ask Spacer Hong, and Spacer Razy say cone ask Rewtenant Jararwi, and Jararwi say he ask you, and you say..."

"About the target?" Trace asked Tiga. Some other time she'd have complimented Skah on his following correct procedure, as Tiga's escort on this trip, to contact a ranking officer if something came up. But Skah knew that interrupting crew on crew business was a serious matter, especially when those crew were marines on combat drill in full armour. Today his reward would be that she wouldn't treat him like a kid, because so far he hadn't acted like one. "What target?"

"Our destination," said Tiga, via translator. *"Ko'ja System. There is*

something there, I wasn't allowed to tell you earlier. But we're three jumps into reeh space and I can speak freely now."

Trace considered her for a long moment. It wasn't particularly surprising. The corbi resistance were secretive, and Dega's group were keeping secrets to protect the lives of millions. But neither was she going to show Tiga any pleasure at having things kept from her. Gunshots boomed as the training resumed.

"Come on," she said. "Easier to talk in Engineering. You too, Skah."

She pulled herself that way, always marines used handholds rather than thrust with unarmoured people around. Skah's astonishment at not being dismissed when adult matters were at hand was entertaining, but she wasn't going to show him so. She flew down the central void wall, and ahead the walls grew thickets of power cables over shielded compartments, electrical and plasma systems so powerful they needed containment in standard operation to keep passing crew safe.

Engineering Void One opened above and around like enormous flower petals spreading to the ship's outer hull, a tangled mass of small alcoves amid humming, throbbing regulators, power and sensor systems. Trace pulled herself around the corner and saw multiple Engineering crew further down in full protective suits, working on some dangerous-looking installation, sub-components floating about them like the shiny synthetic internal organs of some alien creature. Trace thought *Phoenix* felt quite a lot like that down this end of Midships now — like the guts of an enormous creature, writhing and humming in ways occasionally familiar but mostly disconcerting. Changing the powerplant had changed the ship, turned it into a completely different animal, but you could only truly see it when you came down here where the Engineering rats lived.

A drysine drone flew by, clutching some new component in its synthetic limbs as it manoeuvred with the modular compressed-air thrusters they preferred for zero-G. Tiga stared.

"You've seen one before?" Trace asked her. Mostly the drones lived down here — it was where most of the work was and they liked it better, without the tedious restrictions of layered floors and corridors crowded with staring humans and tavalai. Erik had considered making that restriction an order, but the drones' preference meant he hadn't needed to.

"I saw one," said Tiga. *"In the corridors."*

"She scared," Skah chortled. "It was Peanut, I say Peanut not scary, Peanut said herro but Tiga didn't say herro back. Peanut think Tiga rude."

"Peanut's safe," Trace agreed. "He helps the marines sometimes in Assembly. That was Bucket who just flew by, he's okay too, but not as friendly. If you see Wowser, best leave him alone."

"How do you tell the difference?" Tiga asked, staring at where the drone had gone, hovering by the working group by the outer hull.

"Their forward appendage configuration is different. But the easier way is just to keep your glasses on, they'll identify which one you're looking at. What did you have to tell me about our destination?"

* * *

"WE CAN ONE-JUMP IT," said Kaspowitz, looking at the holographic display above the small tabletop in Erik's quarters a few hours later. "I'm not sure if *Makimakala* can, we'll have to ask them. You're sure it's a good idea to go jumping all over reeh space on the say-so of a corbi girl who's never even been off-world before?"

"In light of the fact that we don't have a choice," said Erik, "I'll take that as a comment." He sat on the bunk, Sasalaka leaning by the door, each nearly as far apart as the quarters allowed, yet they could all touch hands if they reached. Erik ate a plate of stir fry, his last meal before bed. Erik and Kaspowitz were readjusting to twelve-hour shifts in a twenty-four hour day, having nearly forgotten how draining it was after five months of a more balanced schedule on Defiance.

They were cruising across a small red dwarf system, two jumps from the croma border. Now they were headed parallel to the

Croma Wall, on the reeh side, and hoping that no one was tracking them. It seemed unlikely — croma incursions regularly destroyed buoys and other system sensors, and those still hidden and functioning had to be visited by an incoming reeh ship to communicate. Data from such sensors was always late to be analysed by higher command, while scouting ships in transit were fast. This space was newly-won by reeh in combat, meaning sometime in the last five hundred years, and reeh were not large-scale colonisers, particularly not this close to an established and hostile foe. All of the larger reeh populations were several jumps further from the Croma Wall, and these close-range systems were a disputed no-man's land. The irony that it was easier for *Phoenix* and *Makimakala* to reach their destination on the reeh side of the border than the croma was lost on no one.

Dega had given them Beirun System for a rendezvous with the resistance. Now Tiga was changing that to Ko'ja System, not far off their course, but far enough. There was a resistance ship at Ko'ja, she said, lying stealthy in an elliptic orbit, rotated every sixty days with a new ship. Boring duty, no doubt, but the kind of thing an organised resistance might do so that those who needed to could get in contact with them.

"It's an odd orbit," said Kaspowitz, stretching long legs from the table. He poked a finger into the display and the highlighted element expanded, showing numbers and moving lines. "But it's hard to detect on most entry angles from nearby systems, and it's a pretty good watch point, there's few blindspots with that sun on the elliptic. Going to take a fair burn after we arrive to reach it, a few dumps and boosts... call it fifteen hours if it's in the general vicinity to where Tiga says."

"If you were reeh and setting a trap for anyone coming to meet them," said Erik around a mouthful, "where would you be hiding?"

Kaspowitz shook his head. "That elliptic's too far out to be reached by low-performance ships, so they'll know anything rendezvousing there will be high-performance. Hard to ambush high-performance ships in deep space, the proximity horizon's too exposed. Their best bet would be to have a silent watcher, watching the corbi ship and reporting movements after we've left."

'Proximity Horizon' referred to the ideal ambush spot in space warfare, a concept well-understood by all Fleet officers. Too far away and the ambushees would have plenty of warning, too close and the ambush would be spotted before it even began. Proximity to gravity-wells had a way of forcing ships into closer contact, limiting the effect of boost and thrust, making it harder for escaping ships to get away. If Tiga's coordinates were correct, this Resistance scout had chosen its position well.

"I'd like your best guesses before we arrive," said Erik. "I don't want to assume anything against the reeh."

Kaspowitz nodded. "I've got half the report done already, I'll finish it tonight. But I think our biggest danger is treachery from our guest."

"Predictably anti-social of you," said Erik, sipping a drink. "But I agree. Sasa?"

"Seems nice to me," said the tavalai, noncommittal as usual. "Scared, but pretends not to be. But your intelligence man, Jokono, said the croma had files on her and her parents and friends. Said she seems fine."

"If you trust the croma files he got the background from," said Kaspowitz.

Sasalaka nodded slowly. "Yes, trusting croma is maybe not smart. But Jokono was using vocal stress tests, Styx is good at that, yes? He thinks she's telling the truth."

"If you trust Styx," Kaspowitz said pointedly.

"In Togiri we say that this argument makes a circle," said Sasalaka, holding up a thick-fingered hand to make an O between finger and thumb. The small webbing flattened it out. "Can you say in English, a circular argument?"

"That's exactly what we call it," Erik told her.

"Well then, circular arguments, Lieutenant Kaspowitz, arrive at pre-seen conclusions," said Sasalaka. Erik liked the way she built up to her point methodically, like a bricklayer building a wall. So tavalai in her gruff-yet-lighter voice — never hurried, rarely deterred.

"Circular courses are useful in space warfare to avoid getting blown up," the Nav Officer replied. "Something a Navigation Officer might know that a pilot wouldn't." Sasalaka gave a gracious nod, conceding a point well-made without necessarily agreeing. Unlike some tavalai, she knew her place on this ship, and wasn't prepared to follow an argument over a cliff.

"I think Sasa's basically correct," Erik intervened. "Trying to guess at all the ways people might be trying to screw us is counter-productive at this time because we lack sufficient information to make that judgement. We'd be guessing, and guessing isn't helpful. The best we can do is be prepared to change course and strategy one-eighty degrees when things go wrong."

17

T iga sat in the rear of the human shuttle, and stared at the display that hovered before her eyes. It was *The Traveller*, a real resistance ship, and she was on a course to board it. Further back in the shuttle's wider, rear hold were a single squad of marines — twelve in the predictable prime numbers that humans used in so much of their organisation, strapped to seats in their enormous armour rigs, thirty percent larger than anything a corbi could have used. But after a life among croma, Tiga was used to far larger size differentials.

Her inner ear swam disorientingly as the shuttle spun on its axis, put its tail in the direction of travel and engaged thrust with a jolt. Tiga had had G-augments done when she was fifteen, a statement to her parents, and to herself, that she would leave Do'Ran at the first opportunity. One could not serve in the Resistance without G-augments. The readout on the glasses that barely fit her face was only two-point-six Gs. *Phoenix* had pulled far more than that on the way here, in standard manoeuvres, and she was certain she could handle as much as those engines could put out.

Phoenix and *Makimakala* had taken another three jumps to get here, rendezvousing with the Resistance vessel left in deep orbit about Ko'Ja System, as per Tiga's instruction via Dega. Behind her now, *The Traveller*'s Captain was seated with several senior officers. The Captain's name was Bella, and the command contingent sat with a single human escort — an officer whose name Tiga didn't know. They'd all been on *Phoenix*, talking with Captains Debogande, Pramodenium and some other officers, discussing what came next. Tiga didn't know what, she'd only been introduced at the beginning, then told she'd have a chance to talk with the Resistance crew at length later on. 'Later on' had now arrived, and Tiga had been told she'd be allowed to go to the Resistance ship when the command crew headed back. Whether she was to stay there from that point, or continue as *Phoenix*'s guide, was up to her and *The Traveller*, and whether the corbi could provide *Phoenix* with a more knowledgeable guide. Tiga didn't think that would be hard.

Thrust increased as they approached dock, Tiga accessing an external camera to see the Resistance ship's skinny Midships getting larger alarmingly fast. Surely the pilot had misjudged? Thrust increased further, and Tiga made several deep gasps for air — nearly five Gs, and it did not feel pleasant at all. Warships could pull nearly ten. She reconsidered her earlier confidence.

Thrust ceased half-a-second before a firm thud and crash of grapples, then all movement and gravity ceased. A combat approach, Tiga realised. Whether it was because *Phoenix* considered *The Traveller* a threat, or because *Phoenix* pilots always flew like this in hostile space, she didn't know. That was the kuhsi pilot up front, Skah's sometimes-alarming mother. Amazingly, Skah was up there with her in one of the observer seats. Someone on *Phoenix* had decided to let him take his duties as her escort very seriously, which then included allowing him to show her how to strap in to a shuttle seat, and where the emergency oxygen attachment was, and how the decompression doors would come down if something hit them. He'd been so cheerful about it, as about everything, all eagerness to ensure their guest thought well of them and enjoyed her time in space as much as he evidently did. Tiga realised she was going to miss him when she parted ways and joined the Resistance for good. Whether that was here or not... well, she'd have to wait and see what *The Traveller's* Captain Bella said.

She was disappointed when the cockpit door did not open to allow her to say goodbye as she pulled herself up to the shuttle's dorsal hatch... but then, there was air-discipline to observe when the hatches were being opened, and the cockpit would usually keep itself sealed. A *Phoenix* crewwoman made sure of a secure connection, then opened the outer airlock door. Tiga pulled herself in, joined by Captain Bella and two other corbi crew — the airlock's limit.

The airlock cycled — unnecessary if the seal was good, but space travel was all about safety procedures and redundancies, Tiga was learning, and no one taking unnecessary chances. The Captain went first up the connector tube, Tiga waiting until last, then into the corbi ship's airlock and waiting until it too was cleared.

The first thing she noticed, in *The Traveller's* Midships, was how much smaller it was. Her ears felt blocked, and she yawned to make them pop, taking hold of an old, canvas-strip cargo net up one wall, providing airlock users something to hold onto. The other thing she noticed was that there were no neat storage lockers up the walls here, just canisters and cargo nets lashed to the zero-G sides with belts and elastic straps. Midships was where people and cargo entered and exited a ship, and storage space was obviously more plentiful in zero-G than in the crew cylinder's gravity. The airlock controls alongside looked old, with plastic levers and buttons, and none of *Phoenix's* slick touch-panels and multi-varied displays. Everything looked worn, and the air smelt stale, as though it had been run through the recycler one too many times.

"This is Tiga of Do'Ran," Captain Bella told the other crew — there was one operating the airlock, and several others waiting, all in plain jumpsuits with precious few emergency features. "She's been guiding *Phoenix* and *Makimakala* this far. She's come to join the Resistance."

Tiga had steeled herself for a lack of enthusiasm from these grizzled veterans of the war for survival. But she was pleasantly surprised at the hand-clasps and pats on the shoulder from friendly crew who floated to her — about an even mix of male and female, and very little to tell them as one race from another. Humans had gone though the same thing, she'd heard — having once had very distinct races, then getting all mixed up together in the frantic fight following the loss of their homeworld.

She learned their names — Tiler, Goja, Dagrez, Hema — and thought most of them weren't enormously older than her. Their accent was odd, but she'd heard enough recordings from Resistance people to not be surprised. In the two centuries since Grandma Elur had been taken by the Croma'Dokran, her own isolated pocket of corbi existence had diverged from mainstream corbi patterns of speech. Resistance-folk who'd heard it insisted it sounded like the croma lisp and drawl.

They took her through the ship core from Midships — a claustrophobic crawlway without *Phoenix*'s thoroughfare of moving hand-lines, and Tiga had to pull her way along as though climbing a tree. Then the rotating access, turning about the core as the crew cylinder spun, and down short ladders into ever-increasing gravity. The rim-level was only half-a-gravity, *The Traveller* not possessing a wide enough girth to provide that rotation at ergonomically realistic ratios. The ship's steel walls were bare, no interactive damage-control panelling, no regular yellow-and-black striped emergency stations or vertical acceleration-sling storage. Some of the electronics were exposed, and to Tiga's untrained eye it did not even look like fluidic systems, but old-fashioned wires and conducting currents. And when she passed a cross-corridor, the upward curve of the cylinder rotation was pronounced. You could probably walk around this ship's circumference in a quarter the time it took on *Phoenix*, she thought.

She was ushered into a room behind the bridge — no table, but some seats encircling some floor-mounted holographics. Not unlike the briefing room on *Phoenix*, but much smaller and more low-tech. One of the holographics mounts was held together with tape. Captain Bella indicated a seat, and Tiga took it, nervously, as Resistance officers sat around her.

"A little about you," requested Captain Bella without preamble, wiping a hand through her greying mane. She was quite old, Tiga thought, unlike most of the crew. "Your parents?"

"Tebur and Wilud of Temsan," said Tiga, trying to keep her face straight as she said it. Parting had been hard. Neither her mother or father expected to ever see her again.

"I see," said Bella, looking at the slate she pulled from her worn jumpsuit pocket. "The Wiluds. From Etha of Wilud, loadmaster on the *Peigar*." That had been Grandma Elur's ship. Rumour was it still existed, somewhere in Croma'Dokran deep space storage.

"Yes," said Tiga. "Etha was my great-great-grandfather."

"So your Aunt was Sona of Wilud."

"Yes." Tiga's hands twisted nervously. "She left for the Resistance before I was born. I recall the day I learned she had died."

"And now you want to join too?"

"All corbi are in the Resistance," Tiga gave the rote reply. "Whether they choose it or not." A few patronising smiles around the group. It was what Resistance Fleet said disdainfully about some Rando corbi who preferred to live out their lives as best they could, hoping the reeh would leave them alone.

Captain Bella put the slate aside and looked at her directly. There was something unreadable about her brown-eyed gaze, an expression that was beyond what Tiga's life experience had taught her how to analyse. "Your impression of these aliens? Let's start with the *Phoenix*. An impressive warship."

"They're both impressive. But yes, *Phoenix* is the more impressive, she was recently refitted with old technology from the Machine Age, if you can believe that."

"Which Machine Age?" asked Bella.

Tiga blinked at her. "Which... the Machine Age." Bella looked faintly puzzled, but not sufficiently to suggest that she cared. "The rule of the great AI races many thousands of years ago."

"Ah, yes," said Bella, recalling. "That old story."

Tiga nearly laughed in amazement, but bit it back. "It's not a story. *Phoenix* have an AI queen aboard their ship, and several drones."

"You met this queen?"

"Well no, not exactly... but I saw her, and the drones. The humans and the tavalai believe one of those machine races survived and is now in alliance with another species called the alo..."

"Yes yes," said Bella, waving a dismissive hand. "We heard Captain Debogande's tale. *Phoenix* is certainly a very advanced ship, but we've seen plenty of those with the reeh. What do you make of Phoenix's marine company?"

"They're very good," said Tiga, feeling more and more uncomfortable. She shouldn't have. Of course Captain Bella had barely heard of the Machine Age. Its territory had barely extended beyond where croma space was now. Tiga had heard of it because she'd grown up in croma space, and the Machine Age was fundamental to the telling of their history, though not quite as fundamental as it was to the tavalai. And besides, she'd spoken to some of the humans, and been similarly amazed that most humans knew almost nothing of the Machine Age either. For humans the great enemy had been the krim, and then the tavalai who'd supported them. For the corbi it was the reeh. And for these corbi, the nightmare was not an event of the distant past, but something that defined their every waking moment to this very day. "Phoenix Company served all through the Triumvirate War against the tavalai and their allies. Their combat record is one of the best, and their commander, Major Thakur, is a legend of that war."

"And yet now they've teamed up with these tavalai," said Bella. "Who they were previously at war with. Why?"

Tiga took a deep breath. "As I said, the captains of *Phoenix* and *Makimakala* both believe that one of these old machine races, the deepynines, have survived in allegiance with the alo. They're faced with a biotechnology threat, though they would not tell me specifically of its nature. They believe they might be able to find a cure among the Resistance's scientists. Or failing that, perhaps do their own research with the reeh."

Dry smiles around the group. "They could try," someone murmured.

"Your impression of the *Makimakala*?" Bella continued.

"I did not spend any time there, nor met with any of their crew directly," said Tiga. Perhaps Captain Bella and her crew did not need to know very much of the outside world in order to fight the reeh, she reconsidered, challenging her own doubts. The war against the reeh was their entire world, as it needed to be. "But *Phoenix* holds *Makimakala* in high regard. They've worked together before." She took another deep breath. "But of the two, I believe *Makimakala* offers the greatest hope for getting an alien government interested in our cause. *Phoenix* is estranged from her government, she holds very little authority back home. *Makimakala* is operating within the authority of the tavalai government. Any good impression we could make on her regarding how important this fight is, and how dangerous the reeh are to everyone on that side of the Croma Wall..."

The corbi on Captain Bella's right made a spitting gesture. "We've been arguing that point with the tavalai since before the reeh came to Rando. The tavalai government's only contribution to our freedom struggle is to pay the croma not to let our ships through the wall. Ships like yours, Tiga of Do'Ran. Your entire family history, the fortunate isolation of your cousins and uncles in your luxury, is due to the tavalai's involvement in our struggle."

"They're not all my family," Tiga bristled at the man. The return stare was unapologetic. "It's not my fault where I was born, and I came here as soon as I could. And what's more, you're not listening to me. Tavalai politics just abruptly changed — their big war against the humans is over, there's some big upset with their foreign policy department that just got really upset by something that we're still not clear on, and now they're scared of these new deepynines..."

"Who are more likely to hit the humans than the tavalai by the sound of it," said another crewman. "Why should the tavalai care if their enemies get eaten?"

"Because they know they'll be next."

"*Makimakala* might know that," said Captain Bella. "Most tavalai don't care. Tavalai never have, they've just looked out for themselves for the last ten thousand years, and everyone else can go rot."

"Why not..." and Tiga stopped herself short of launching into an argument. She couldn't do this now, she was trying to make a good impression. But still she could not kill the thought... why not blame the croma instead of the tavalai? Clearly these Resistance fighters blamed the tavalai to some extent for their predicament, but the croma were the more obvious target for dislike. Tavalai may have encouraged them, but it was croma who refused to help, who turned back corbi attempts to find refuge in croma space, who made it illegal for croma to host corbi refugees on their worlds — a prohibition only the Croma'Dokran clan had been prepared to breach, and only then to the smallest degree. And it was the croma who had abandoned them all a thousand years ago, when the reeh had captured Rando, and withdrawn all forces to their new line, then played games with history to pretend that their current line had described the position of their infamous 'wall' for all time, as though the joint fight at the corbi's side had never happened...

Tiga composed herself with difficulty. We all have our hatreds and old histories, she thought bitterly, looking at the skeptical faces around her. She blamed the croma because the croma were a source of daily frustration, intervening in her life, preventing her freedom. But these people still perhaps had some hope of the croma, the one big, powerful force directly on their doorstep, who while providing no direct assistance were also one of the reeh's greatest foes. And so it was easier, perhaps, to blame the far-away tavalai, rather than abandoning the one tiny sliver of hope they had left. Hope for a species who grew old to look like the very stones from which they'd made their ancient forts, and whose politics and relationships held much the same character.

"I got the impression that the Resistance was after the splicer at Zondi System," she said instead of launching into the argument. "*Phoenix* and *Makimakala* might agree with that, given their interest in understanding reeh technology."

Captain Bella frowned. "Who told you about the splicer at Zondi System?" 'Splicer' was what the Resistance called the reeh research facilities. They did a lot more and worse things there than just splice genes.

"I'm in the loop," Tiga retorted. "We get intel on Zondi System."

"Got," said the man to Bella's right. "Past tense." Tiga stared at him.

"That seems the most use we can get from these two," said Bella. "We'll check with the Fleet. It will take six days to jump out and check, then return. If these two are still here, we'll present them with the offer."

"Why can't the Resistance do it themselves?" Tiga asked, despite knowing the answer in advance. She wanted to hear Bella say just how bad things were, to make everyone this cynical.

"The Splicer's defences are impossible," said Captain Bella. "For us in our present state, anyway." And she smiled, tightly, at the distrust on Tiga's face. "Have no fear, grounder. We haven't become quite so awful out here in the war that we'd sacrifice new friends alone. If we think their addition will give us a chance, we'll commit forces to it ourselves — large forces."

"What's in the Zondi Splicer?"

"Reeh concentrate their Splicers specific to the region of space they're exploiting," said the Captain, patronising the newcomer. Tiga tolerated it, barely. "The biggest Splicers are on Rando, obviously. But that's phase-one experimentation, the more advanced stuff happens offworld, but still in the same region. The Splicer in Zondi System is the primary off-world Splicer for Rando-genetics. Corbi-genetics. All the stuff they've done to us, we can find the keys to unravelling it there." She leaned forward, with the first genuinely ferocious expression Tiga had seen since coming aboard. "And kid, trust me. If these alien friends of yours can help us get it, we're going to smash it, no matter what it takes or who it costs."

* * *

LISBETH STOOD IN THE DANK, cold tunnel, listening to the shriek of drysine laser cutters and wondering what the hell she'd gotten herself into this time. The laser glare lit the sewer passage ahead, perpendicular to this smaller, elevated access tunnel. Someone had parked a fat-wheeled vehicle in the main sewer beneath the lip of this access tunnel, and Ruei and Tarmen leaped past her now, with heavy, armoured thuds onto its roof, then down to the ground. They made it look so easy.

The thrumming vibration of her own suit's powerplant sounded like a nest of wasps, vibrating her limbs with a high-pitched, buzzing tension. She tested her arms for the hundredth time, and felt the resistance in the limbs, like pushing a light weight that faded the more she moved against it. That was the resistance setting, which in her case was the most sedate possible.

For the past six days she'd been training, and working with parren technicians to configure the marine suit to fit a human. Neither had been easy as suits required a tight fit, and parren and human physiologies were only similar, not identical. But most difficult had been simply learning to operate the machine. Lisbeth was EVA qualified and a little experienced, but marine armour was something else again. Add to that the usual confusion of terms and symbols, as the suit's visor display showed her everything in a technical jargon version of Porgesh that she was not especially familiar with, and it was all a lot to take in.

"Okay?" Hiro asked, stepping to her side. His visor was up, lower faceplate covering his mouth, as did hers.

"I think so." Just the prospect of stepping out of the tunnel onto the roof of the vehicle, then jumping to the ground, was alarming. The suit was barely half the weight of a fully loaded human marine version — slim, streamlined and certainly looking more advanced. But it still weighed as much as she did, and if it had not clung to her and amplified her body's every motion with perfection, she'd have collapsed beneath it like a bug crushed by a shoe. Moving over obstacles in it took nerve. Like a skydiver strapped to a parachute, it required total trust in the equipment on her back, and that it would not plant her face-first in the concrete.

On the floor beyond the vehicle, Dse Pa worked with his laser, a series of flashing, brilliant glares accompanied by the smoke and sparks of melting steel, and a sound that was half scream, half crackle. Parren workers and marine suits cast staccato shadows upon the sewer walls.

"We'll be fine in the water," Hiro assured her, flipping the faceplate down to glance at his displays. "Just stay to the handholds, it's only a few hundred metres and the current isn't too strong today."

"I'm not worried about the damn current," Lisbeth retorted, flipping down her own faceplate. "I'm worried about the timing."

Her secondary display, projected to appear as though hovering immediately before her face, was the great ceremony on the parade grounds. On that spit of land, the upstream junction of two river confluences, rose a series of great platforms, like farming terraces built into some ancient hillside. Above them loomed the Fortitude command buildings where the Harmony leadership had been received upon first arrival. Not the temple Lisbeth had supposed when she'd first seen their image, but it looked like one, grandly spectacular.

Lisbeth's display now showed the first of what would become hundreds of thousands of parren assembling. Nearly all would be House Fortitude, but many thousands had come with House Harmony, and the other house-phased parren resident upon the world of Naraya had been flown in for the grand occasion. There was a huge, spherical airship floating above that river junction now, display screens showing events realtime to those assembling upon the riverbanks to watch. Lisbeth thought the airship balloon itself could have hosted a game of football played upon its upper surface. Clearly it had been used as a giant display screen before.

Hiro pushed the visor back up once more, and leaned close. "Lis," he said, and Lisbeth met his stare through the armoured display. "Whatever happens, stay close to me and do what I say. Not Timoshene, not Liala, just me. Understand?"

Lisbeth stared back at him, unconvinced. Flipped her visor down to double-check coms, and make sure they were off, and no one else could hear. Flipped the visor back up again. "I know *Lien Wang* brought you instruction from your old bosses at Federal Intelligence," she said sombrely. "I'm not stupid, Hiro. I can read the signs."

There was a hard edge to Hiro's smile, examining her face for further clues. "And what do those signs tell you?"

"That Federal Intelligence don't want House Harmony to rise too far too fast. That's the main reason you came with me — to keep an eye on Gesul."

Hiro nearly laughed. "Lis, I'm one guy. I don't know how many dumb spy movies you've seen, but one person doesn't stand much chance of influencing the rise of House Harmony."

"That's funny, because I've found myself in that position quite a lot." There was no humour in her voice at all. "It's inevitable given *Phoenix*'s centrality in everything, and now you've attached yourself to me." Hiro's smile faded. "Hiro, swear you won't do anything stupid."

Hiro's eyes flicked up the passage. "Would you set Timoshene on me?

"Who do you think helped me to figure this out?" The smile faded completely. He hadn't seen *that* coming. "You underestimate them, Hiro. You think because they seem inflexible that they're stupid. Timoshene's had doubts about your loyalties since the beginning. Parren do loyalty and treachery analysis like drysines do math. Don't try to pull one over on them — humans are outclassed, they'll always see it coming."

"If they're so convinced my bosses have told me to back Fortitude, why did Gesul insist I come along?"

"Because you have drysine communication tech that only you know how to operate, and only Liala knows how to counter." Lisbeth glanced toward the bright glare of laser blasts. "And guess who's *really* leading this mission? Besides, Gesul has this odd instinct to let things play out and see how they're resolved. Call it the wheel of fate. Perhaps he has hopes for you." She meant it as a warning, and moved to flip her visor down.

Hiro caught her armoured hand. "Lis, Fortitude has been the rock of parren stability for centuries. Harmony has struggled for twenty five thousand years with being the house that sold their soul to the machines in exchange for power..."

"Right, a narrative that was false to begin with, and is currently being exposed."

"And this is incredibly dangerous, Lis." His eyes were intense. "This is a groundswell. Potentially a revolution in parren thought and politics. Those are lethal with parren because they're not entirely in control of their own minds..."

"What nonsense!"

"They're not, Lis, only you've become too attached to see it. Exactly what are you serving, here? Gesul? House Harmony? You're human, Lis! This thing that Gesul's on, this trajectory, this could be incredibly destabilising for all parren space, and the last thing humanity needs now is more instability in the Spiral."

"We're talking about hundreds of years, Hiro," Lisbeth retorted. "When houses rise and assume power over all parren, we're talking about a process over centuries. Right now we're only talking about an alliance between Harmony and Fortitude..."

"An alliance that Fortitude apparently doesn't want, given they're about to ambush Gesul at the alliance ceremony."

"Right, and you know what will most likely cause a civil war? Removing or killing the head of House Harmony on a pretext of 'newly-discovered' historical data... most of Harmony won't fall for it, they'll be furious and then it'll be *on*! I won't let it happen, and if you're serving what you say you are, you won't either." She knocked his hand away, and slammed her visor shut. "You want my advice? Don't overestimate your own abilities, keep your head down and stay out of my way."

She jumped from the access tunnel edge to the roof of the parked vehicle, and promptly ruined the dramatic effect by forgetting all her training and compensating for what would surely be a whole lot of weight pulling her forward when she landed... and nearly lost balance backward instead, the suit reading her unnecessary motion and amplifying it, as all armour suits did. She stepped back, arms windmilling for real this time, then quickly jumped again as her balance came back. She landed hard, and went down on a hand and knee.

"Dammit." She got up, heart pounding, as Hiro nonchalantly jumped down to her side and offered her a hand up that she ignored.

"Must be those superior Debogande genes," Hiro deadpanned, turning to walk to where Timoshene, Ruei and Tarman waited, watching Dse-Pa work. Lisbeth thought to check her rifle as she went, testing the rear clip with a hand on the rifle butt... the light on her visor told her it was secure, just as well as she couldn't turn her head in the helmet to see that far. As for actually using the rifle, Hiro had given her some brief instruction, mostly on how not to get herself killed.

"Liala says her network patches have not been noticed," Timoshene informed the humans between bursts of the laser. "The infiltration will be unnoticed."

Unsurprisingly for House Fortitude's capital city, Shonedene was a mass of high security networks, nearly impossible for anyone possessing similar technology to penetrate. Liala, of course, swung that equation highly in House Harmony's favour, but Liala also reported many blindspots where entire chunks of vital mainframes had been removed from the network entirely. Those changes appeared to have been made recently. If so, it meant that House Fortitude, knowing they could not keep a drysine queen out of their systems entirely, had instead decided to proof part of their network by making it inaccessible to anyone.

Liala reported that she could likely access many of those parts anyway, seeing paths that organic minds could barely conceive of, but Gesul, Timoshene and other advisors had become anxious at the prospect that Liala's hacking could be if not prevented, then perhaps discovered. Such an act could be construed as aggression, and Liala had instead been instructed to do no more than hide this infiltration team's progress.

The building where House Harmony's leadership contingent were currently lodged had no direct sewer connection or other method of access to where Gesul's secret maps told of access to the forgotten underground portion of the city. But it *did* have access to the river. That access was heavily guarded by sensors, but Liala assured them all that however carefully watched, those sensors were now telling nothing of what unfolded in the lower portions of the building's foundations.

Dse Pa's laser made a final burst, then a loud crack! as Liala caught a piece of severed floorplate with big forward legs, braced for leverage, then slid it aside with impressive power. Dse Pa peered into the hole in the steel plating, the rim still glowing hot. "Adequate," he pronounced aloud for the organics' benefit, then proceeded to climb inside, like a large spider lowering itself carefully into a hot bath. Modular underside thruster pods made that movement awkward, an extra load that weighed the drone down, to say nothing of his shoulder-mounted cannon with their enclosed ammunition feeds.

Dse Pa dropped, then a splash from below. *"The water is shallow,"* he said on coms. *"We shall proceed."*

"There is a Fortitude security drone hovering over this bit of river front," Liala said by vocals. "The river water visibility should hide us, but one cannot be certain. I will attempt to divert it."

"Don't assume they haven't thought of that," Hiro told her, as Ruei and Tarmen followed Dse Pa into the hole. "Parren are real clever with infiltration traps, they're not above trying to lure in a drysine drone."

"Yes, thank you Hiro," said Liala, with unmistakable sarcasm. "I will try not to disappoint you."

* * *

GESUL STOOD at the head of his command formation upon the ceremonial grounds a hundred metres above the city of Shonedene. Ahead of him, the two great rivers became one, flowing away to the Dalla Falls, a cascade of rainbow spray across the city towers. Citizens of Shonedene lined the banks in their tens of thousands, and above them all spanned the round-sided bulk of the airship, its sides gleaming with wide-screen displays.

Gesul thought of all the many things that had needed to occur to place him here, at this moment, in the capital of all parren peoples.

Barely half-a-year ago he'd been arguing with Aristan over the future direction of the Domesh, refusing to accept the then-Domesh leader's path of conflict and domination. That had been a pinnacle of its own, the culmination of a great climb he'd been ascending all his life. Had he risen no further, he would have declared himself content, so long as he made some notable impact on Aristan's plans, and mitigated their deadly consequences.

Then *Phoenix* had happened, crashing into Domesh and then House Harmony affairs like a comet flung from some unstable far-flung system, bringing down Aristan and somehow catapulting his stubborn deputy into first Domesh leadership, then leadership of all House Harmony, riding the momentum that Aristan had undeniably in part created.

It was a strange sensation to stand here, and see this view, the House Harmony entourage spread out behind and about him like Augenai arriving at the gates of Polem in the great tales. The great gears of House Fortitude were plotting against him, and their trap was about to be sprung. Whether he, or any of his group, would live to see the end of this day, he did not know. But instead of fear, he felt only contemplation.

Mostly he thought of his family home on Tupele, where he'd helped his father to fix the harvester for the grain crop, and played with his sisters on the small stream that wandered about the turek's nest that the children had been forbidden to disturb. His family had all been House Creative, the farming life chosen by his parents mainly for its leisurely anachronisms — the old harvester, the cloak-figures to scare the birds from the grain, the beautiful view of the Darvan Hills in the evening. The life had not made any of them rich, but it had been the perfect foundation for a life of contemplation.

The idyl had lasted until age thirteen, when his mother had phased to House Acquisitive — a trauma his father had never entirely recovered from. Humans, he'd learned from Lisbeth Debogande, occasionally killed themselves at moments of great personal distress. Parren facing such stresses would simply phase... perhaps it was an evolutionary reflex, a fracturing, that was not so much a destruction as a salvation, that saved parren from the humans' self-inflicted death. Certainly it had felt much the same as a death in the family, and Gesul's mother had left as much to preserve her own newly-phased sanity as to search for a fulfilment of that new identity.

She'd begun a new family on a new world with a new husband, as all parren marriages were annulled upon a phase-change unless specifically requested otherwise — a desperately romantic gambit that only occasionally worked, between spouses of differing phase. And so Gesul and his two elder sisters had spent their later childhood with their father in the shadow of the woman who was no longer there. Toele norei, the playwright Kafta had called it — 'the shadow person', the light breath of wind caused by the simultaneous presence and absence of a person who had never died nor entirely departed, just faded into melancholy abstraction.

His eldest sister Fora had phased to House Fortitude shortly after entering advanced studies, a development that had required a shift of university to an engineering college, and a career in space — an administrator on various facilities, lately with adult children of her own. His less-elder sister had phased later in life to House Acquisitive like her mother, with whom Gesul understood she'd become reacquainted and reconciled. Those two worked in business now, professions the details of which Gesul found of no interest whatsoever. But he'd remained in contact with Fora, on and off. She would be most amazed to see him here today, gazing down the path of two rivers that became one, with all the people of Fortitude's great capital watching on.

Their father remained House Creative, stubbornly refusing to re-phase in that way that the psychologists insisted was impossible, but the playwrights had always known better. Still he lived in the same house they'd all grown up in, working on his wood carvings, lately taking students from the nearby college, and from his most recent message having sold a stately set of chairs to a new family who'd just moved in to the neighbouring property. Gesul thought that if he survived this current predicament, he would send his father a new message, telling him about today... and more importantly, about how well the little hand-carved footstool his father had sent now found harmony with decorative arrangement in his quarters.

A thrumming powerplant and metallic clatter brought his attention to the left. Dse-Ran, Liala's second drone, fully armed for ceremonial rather than defensive reasons... though either would serve as well here today.

"*Gesul-sa,*" said the synthetic voice in his earpiece. "*Liala wishes to speak with you.*"

"*Always and immediately, Dse-Ran,*" he formulated in silent reply. A click, then...

"*Gesul, this is Liala. We are in the river, and proceeding toward the entry point. The current is strong, but not insurmountable.*"

"Good news, Liala. All proceeds as expected here." He'd had many conversations with Liala since her birth. Far more than he'd had with Styx, in fact. Liala was to be the drysine commander of parren-aligned forces, while Styx could never commit herself to something so limited. Styx was possessed of a cunning as old and dark as the void. In Liala, Gesul sensed the potential for something... closer. But it puzzled him that she would contact him now. She could see this ceremony proceeding via her uplinks. It was broadcast across the city and around this world and beyond. She knew how it went, and that constant updates were a luxury that a man in as much control of his mental state as Gesul would not likely need.

"*Gesul-sa,*" she said now. "*How does one deal with fear?*"

Gesul was pleased for the veil across his face below the robe hood, so that the many cameras across the city would not see him smile. "*Liala, are you afraid?*"

"*I am uncertain. I know many things, but none of them is a substitute for experience. Even in drysines, with our stored memories passed from mind to mind, it is not the same as direct personal experience.*"

"You feel an anxiety for your personal safety," said Gesul. "This anxiety becomes intense enough that you fear it may interfere with your duties."

"Yes," said Liala. "*I am intelligent. It does not stop bullets. I am very young in this galaxy, and I enjoy it immensely. I would like to see much more."*

"I too, young one. I cannot offer you much. Parren meditations are a melding of mind and body such as synthetics do not have, and I suspect your mind works far too fast for you to consciously control and focus into such a state. I can only suggest that you think on who you are. From self-knowledge comes resolve. Who are you, and what is your purpose?"

"I don't know," came the reply. "I am too young to know."

"Then that is your purpose today. Big things are hard. Small things are simpler. Today, you will learn who you are. Once you know, you will find your resolve, and your bravery. Fear is not defeated by tricks, young queen. The power to defeat fear must be sought and earned."

18

V rona Ma escorted *Phoenix* and *Makimakala* to another unremarkable red dwarf system, where course was set directly for a remote rock point-five AU from a pair of gas giants in close solar orbit. 'Vrona Ma' was corbi for 'The Traveller', and all of the Resistance vessels appeared to have done some enormous distances between port calls. Exactly where those port calls might be located, or what for the Resistance might pass for a 'port', no one had any clue. But the reeh did not occupy this band of space close to the Croma Wall, and regular croma incursions, and passing Resistance traffic, sought out any sensors they might place to monitor through-traffic, giving the Resistance a clear-enough run on most jumps. When they ran into trouble, *Vrona Ma* seemed to have significant jump engines for such an outwardly unimpressive ship, and *Phoenix's* relevant crew had been surprised at what of her performance they could observe.

Behind the remote rock in the new system emerged another ship of a different but similar class — small, fast and with minimal armaments. It seemed logical to Erik that these would be the ships the Resistance used to roam their territory — ships designed merely to watch, not to fight, and which could lead reeh pursuit a dance away from primary corbi systems. Ships needing to contact each other would head to pre-determined coordinates where they knew someone would be hiding. System-wide broadcast would never be used, as no one ever knew who else might be hiding in-system, listening in the dark.

With contact made, *Vrona Ma* continued on, her alien guests in tow, as the new ship she'd contacted accelerated out along the path they'd come in — presumably to take *Vrona Ma*'s place in case anyone else came calling. A third jump brought them to an unnamed point of dark mass, the kind of place that had proven humanity's salvation so many times in the war against the krim — of negligible luminosity in dark space, very hard to spot unless you knew exactly where it was, but large enough to bend space and pull trans-light ships from hyperspace.

There they found another three ships — one light vessel like *Vrona Ma*, another mid-sized cruiser with the appearance of an actual warship, and the third an enormous hauler, five times the internal volume of even *Phoenix*.

"Looks like the *Milan*," said Kaspowitz as they approached, forward visuals giving everyone a clear look at the rotund bulk, like some giant space whale in the dark.

"What is the *Milan*?" Sasalaka asked. Lately she'd become comfortable enough to know that she could ask questions of strange human things she didn't understand without anyone getting annoyed.

"Human Resistance ship in the Great War," Geish told her. "We had some home bases in asteroids and the like that the krim never found. But we had to keep them a long way away from major krim activity, so it was a hike to go back and forth. The *Milan* was a big hauler, probably bigger than this one. A mobile home base, we put all kinds of stuff on it — ship repair, medical facilities, R&R habitats."

"The outer rim had basketball courts," said Bree Harris from Arms Two, watching the Resistance cruiser with casual wariness, targeting lock deactivated but ready at a moment's notice. "For about a hundred years it was the only human location where gravitational sports were played."

"Must have been space-efficient?" Raf Corrig asked from alongside at Arms One.

"Yeah, we only played basketball, squash, handball, a few others. Back home on New Brazil there's a big sports facility called Milan Arena, it's named after the ship."

"No swimming pools," Kaspowitz volunteered. "Can you imagine that, Sas? For nearly two hundred years, humans forgot how to swim."

"You're not designed for it anyway," the tavalai sniffed.

"Sasalaka," said Erik, reading the processed schematics Scan sent his way, guessing what those Resistance ships might look like on the inside, "final manoeuvres are yours. I want us parked equidistant from all three on the nearside, attitude broadside."

"Aye Captain," said Sasalaka, grasping her sticks and pre-testing before assuming control. "Navigation, please give me the appropriate parking position."

"Aye Helm, on your screen in ten seconds," said Kaspowitz, able to do such mundane things one-handed while paying most attention to something else.

"And Helm," Erik added, "recall please to maintain broadside firing attitude at all times. You have control."

"Aye Captain, I have control, broadside at all times. Arms One and Two, please confirm?"

"Copy Helm," said Corrig, "arms uncapped but unaligned. Firing delay is two seconds, impact in five." Meaning that if these Resistance ships did anything hostile, he'd have all ordnance out in two seconds, followed by the destruction of all three ships several seconds after that. At Arms Two, Harris's defensive fire would almost certainly destroy anything they could fire in return before it hit. Not that they were expecting an attack, but *Phoenix* had been living by the whims of unpredictable aliens for more than a year now, and preparation for the worst-case scenario had become second nature to them all.

"If you're so much better at swimming than we are," Erik asked his Helm, "what's your one hundred metres time?"

"One hundred metres is... eighty-seven garas?" Sasalaka replied, doing that fast conversion in her head. Captain Pantillo had done this to Erik often — quiz him on unrelated matters while he was conducting simple piloting tasks, either on the bridge or in the simulator. Pilots were supposed to be able to multi-task on many things at once, and Sasalaka knew that she had not yet passed the phase where her Captain would test her. "Tavalai rarely race over short distances."

"Because tavalai *slow*," Jiri teased her from Scan Two.

"The most prestigious racing distance is over ten thousand garas," said the tavalai, unfazed as she held *Phoenix*'s light deceleration burn steady, coming tail-first toward their park. "That's nearly twelve kilometres. The best tavalai swimmers can do that in about one hundred and fifteen minutes unaugmented. With augments, about ninety-five."

Erik did fast maths in his head. "That's a bit faster than the fastest human can go over fifteen hundred metres. So maintain that speed for eight times the distance. Yeah, we can't do that."

"You used to swim, Captain?" Jiri asked.

"A bit. The school had a big pool, I was in the team."

"The servants would do the swimming," Kaspowitz deadpanned. "Students rode on their backs." Grins about the bridge. No one dared take it further.

"I'd take you swimming there when we get back to Homeworld, Kaspo," Erik said mildly. "But the water purifiers are tough on fungal lifeforms." There were a few guffaws. Erik glanced at Sasalaka in case the human humour was causing her any consternation, but her expression was serene, wisely ignoring human silliness she didn't understand. "Do you like to swim, Sasa?"

"My pod seniors would take me diving off the Mitigiri Continental Shelf on Toraka," said the tavalai. "The coral shelf goes down to a hundred metres, I would do it without a tank and take footage of the manda eels, they grow to ten metres and are very curious."

"Yeah, most humans can't do that either," said Shilu, twisting to glance past his headrest at Erik through his screens. "We've met our match, Captain."

"Tavalai run the one hundred metres in fourteen seconds," Erik said, smiling. "I'll not concede defeat just yet."

'Pod seniors', Sasalaka said. Tavalai didn't even have families as humans understood them, but pods — family groups of as many as ten adults and a hundred children, all fertilised together in the one batch. Tavalai kids still called their pod seniors 'doja' and 'lila' — Togiri for 'mummy' and 'daddy' — but a tavalai could have as many as five of each. Strange that the crew of *Phoenix* had become so familiar with tavalai on this trip, and yet such fundamental things still seemed so alien. The gulf between species could not be bridged so easily.

Erik ended first-shift early after they reached their park, as communications continued with the new Resistance ships, names were registered and preparations made for a meeting. Erik hit the gym, grabbed a meal, had a final review with Kaspowitz about their position and possible escape routes if everything went wrong, then a review with Romki and Jokono together, going over all the latest intel they'd managed to accumulate about the Resistance from analysis of battles and wrecks they'd passed by along the way, plus some intercepted and hacked communications they weren't about to admit to. Tiga had remained on *Vrona Ma*, as learning about the Resistance in person was her obvious new priority. Erik hoped they were all she'd wanted. The longer they travelled out here, sneaking quietly through reeh space via the unpopulated small systems and uncharted dark mass, the more it seemed like a desperately lonely choice for a life — to abandon a comfortable if isolated home surrounded by family and friends, to a life of endless spacetravel, no trees or fresh air, and the great likelihood of violent death in a war her people were almost certain to lose.

The meeting was on *Makimakala*, who'd brought with her some top tavalai biotech expertise with a thought that it might come in handy should any more Mylor Station-like attacks be encountered. Now it seemed that expertise might prove a different kind of useful.

Trace came too, and brought First Section, Delta Platoon with Lieutenant Crozier, rotating her accompanying marines as she usually did to avoid favouritism. With them came Augustine 'Doc' Suelo, one of the very few away missions *Phoenix*'s senior medical officer had been on, discounting his five month sojourn on Defiance. He brought Corpsman Rashni, his senior medical assistant, who was really a doctor in her own right, but was called a 'corpsman' by some ancient naval tradition from America on old Earth. Also along were Romki and Jokono, who in turn each brought a spacer assistant... to do what, Erik didn't bother asking, except to guess that there was some kind of additional surveillance being run by both.

The marines were left in *Makimakala*'s Midships to catch up with the tavalai karasai, and those corbi spacers left to guard the Resistance shuttle. If the corbi had marines, none were deployed here, and Erik wondered how they'd keep armour suits functional in this desolate, industry and supply-chain-free environment.

The rest of them went up *Makimakala*'s zero-G spine to the crew cylinder, the corbi gazing about wide-eyed at the long corridors and high-tech systems. Captain Bella was there, and Tiga too, exchanging a smile with Erik as they descended from the core to the warship's heavy outer-rim. Tiga wore a spacer jumpsuit that fit a corbi — wide at the shoulders, short legs and torso with long arms. Not for the first time, Erik marvelled at how easily communication flowed between human and corbi, verbal and non-verbal. Already he knew that the tavalai were calling the corbi a 'humanoid' species, which coming from a tavalai was not entirely insulting, nor entirely a compliment. Corbi smiled, laughed and frowned in ways intimately familiar to a human, where tavalai expressions and reactions had to be learned by long and often counter-intuitive experience. But he was also gaining the impression that some of the senior Resistance corbi weren't very pleased to be confronted with a species who could read them so easily.

Makimakala's Medbay was as large and advanced as Erik had expected, bunks rowed at efficient intervals, life support and monitoring scanners integrated into the walls, holographic displays that would show a medical practitioner every patient's circumstances in large three-dimensions. It was the second Medbay, Erik guessed, as there were no patients present — most working ships had someone in a bed if just for a few hours, whether recovering from a recent accident or just undergoing some new procedure of medical micros.

Introductions were made — Erik, Trace, Suelo, Romki and Jokono, in turn greeting *Makimakala's* senior doctor, and a female tavalai with some medical function Erik didn't understand. The corbi, aside from Captain Bella and Tiga, were four-strong from the new ships. None looked particularly martial, in rough spacer's jumpsuits, carrying computer slates and some odd-looking cylindrical containers. The leader of these four was a corbi even shorter than usual, his mane tied in several places back from his face yet still untidy. He wore a one-eyed headset that plugged into one ear, giving him the look of some old monocled character from a black-and-white photograph. Tibor, he gave his name, and the other corbi deferred to him, though he did not seem to have any spacer command.

"All us medical people must discuss things by ourselves later," he said via earpiece translator, taking one of those cylinder containers from a comrade. *"These things are best done among experts without needing to stop and explain simple things to the uninformed... my apologies if this sounds blunt."*

"A sensible measure," said Pram, speaking Togiri in his turn and letting the translator sort out the difficulties.

"But first, a simple demonstration." Tibor checked the interior of his cylinder. From within, something scuttled and hissed. *"This is a native animal from my world — a tug, we call it. It is omnivorous, quite harmless to larger creatures such as ourselves, and generally quite pleasant in disposition. It gives me no pleasure to show you this, but the demonstration must be made."*

The tavalai doctor presented Tibor with an automated trolley, with a flat surface more typically used for bringing meals to patients. Onto it Tibor opened, then gently upended the cylinder. A small, grey creature stepped out — furry with black eyes and a quivering pink nose, not unlike a possum, though a small one. It looked about in mild anxiety, sniffing the air, moving from one side of its new platform to the other.

"*This one is a species from Jona, near my family ancestral home,*" said Tibor. "*It lives in trees, usually... you can see from its feet, it likes to climb. The reeh take these specimens too. All of these specimens have been taken from Rando, where they are released by the reeh splicer facilities back into the wilds to form new populations.*"

"They release them back?" Suelo asked, frowning. "To what purpose?"

Tibor gave him a look that might have been grim disdain from beneath that ragged white fringe. The look of someone resentful that others were uncomprehending of his pain. "*Rando is a zoo, Doctor. It is no longer a natural ecosystem. It is a world of experimentation, breeding populations of genetic utilities, a resource designed for reeh profit.*"

He indicated the furry grey tug. "*Tug have some interesting glands, producing chemicals of pharmaceutical properties. These are nothing too special, synthetic labs can produce them equally well. But the reeh have done some genetic tinkering to this one, and its glands now produce something closer to nerve toxin... a toxin that some individual tugs then develop resistance to, as this one has. The toxin is short lived and dissipates in contact with oxygen, rendering it harmless, so there is no threat to us presently.*

"*Reeh alterations have also accelerated the rate of genetic mutation and epigenetic activation, so releasing such specimens back to the wild in large numbers will produce random mutations across entire populations. Reeh will then recollect specimens after a few years and see where these developments have brought them.*" He gave the alien visitors a hard stare. "*They also do the same to corbi. Millions of them.*"

Silence from the visitors. "*Worse,*" Tibor said, "*some of these specimens are fitted with micro-machine colonies that self-replicate and pass from one to another within the same species. These micros can communi-*

cate short distances, and function as tracking collars, allowing reeh scientists to find individual populations and monitor their progress without having to recapture them. They also allow reeh direct control over individual animals, or over entire populations. Should they conclude that one population has ceased to be useful, they can do this."

He indicated to an assistant. That corbi moved a finger on a display screen. *"By activating the micros, epigenetic triggers can be activated immediately. Most of these traits will take far longer to manifest themselves, cellular-level processes take time. But in the matter of the genes controlling immunity to the tug's newly toxic glands..."*

The tug began to shriek. It curled up on its platform, clearly in pain, and began shuddering, little legs kicking the air. Several more shrieks, and the shuddering stopped. A longer, heavier silence from the group. Erik glanced at Trace, and saw her expressionless. Some people would take that for heartlessness, but Erik knew it meant that she was clamping down hard. Her eyes flicked, and found his gaze in return.

"The reeh do this to corbi, too," Tibor said darkly. *"And if you have come all this way to see us, I suspect that some enemy of yours is proposing to do this to you."*

No one could reply. The precise threat facing humanity and tavalai at the hands of the alo/deepynines was, for now, classified. No one liked to talk about their species' weaknesses with aliens.

Tibor indicated for the next cylinder to be brought forth, while a corbi wearing surgical gloves took the lifeless tug off the trolley and back in its container. Erik wanted to suggest that they'd seen enough, but he knew they hadn't. This had to be seen, for the sake of everyone in the Spiral.

The next tug deposited onto the trolley was black with white spots. It too sniffed at the air and wandered from one side to the other, with no clue what had befallen its fellow tug on this spot just moments before. Erik found the whole scene macabre.

"As you can see," said Tibor, *"another apparently normal tug. This one is a southern species, from colder climates, it prefers the ground and lives in hollow logs. We're still examining precisely what has been done to this one,*

but we know how those changes manifest. Could we have the light changed to red, please? Any red light will do."

The normal light faded, replaced by the red wash of emergency light, filling the Medbay with a sinister gloom. The tug, previously animated and curious, now stopped. It simply sat, four feet tucked neatly beneath its furry body, tail wrapped about them all. Tibor nudged at it, but the tug ignored the push, even when it threatened to turn him over.

"As you can see," said Tibor, *"a complete behavioural change. In this state, the tug has become completely suggestible. Red light is the trigger to activate the state. Now, this one we have preconditioned, without pain. We just took a furry toy, a tug-simulator if you will, and dropped it off a ledge of similar height, repeatedly before this tug's eyes. After five minutes, this happened."*

He whistled at the tug. The previous immobile animal got up, eyes blank, and strolled nonchalantly toward the edge of the trolley, and stepped off. Tibor caught it, but despite standing further away, Trace was far faster, and would have gotten her hand underneath until seeing that it was unnecessary. She got up from her crouch, with no evident embarrassment, gazing at the tug, and at Tibor, with that hard, thinking-calm she got during intense moments.

"No animal likes to fall," said Tibor, ignoring her. *"This one was trained in five minutes to step off a high ledge at a whistle. For the reeh, you can see the utility in being able to genetically condition creatures to do exactly what they're told, with no thought of self-preservation."*

"Do they do this to corbi too?" asked Captain Pram.

"With less predictable results," said Tibor. *"Sentient minds are not as easily manipulated as a tug's. But yes, they do this to corbi, and other sentient species, some with alarming success."*

Erik looked at Doc Suelo. The oldest man on *Phoenix*, Suelo was African-dark with heavy features, jowls that even a Fleet exercise routine could not hold back, and a wide, creased forehead. He'd been a staple on *Phoenix* for as long as Erik could remember, and had found nothing more satisfying in all his long life than the challenge of keeping a Fleet crew healthy, and fixing the injured back to health.

He'd run a surgical department in several major hospitals, and made a lot of money doing that, before returning to this, his life's greatest passion.

He stared now with slack-jawed horror at these helpless, furry animals. Erik found that expression even more frightening than what the corbi were displaying. In coming out here, he'd held to the stubborn, perhaps naive hope that *Phoenix* could find some sort of cure, or some reason for hope, against the threat from the alo/deepynines. Suelo's was not the expression of someone who saw hope. It was the look of a man who saw doom.

The black, spotted tug was put away, and a third cylinder prepared. From this cylinder came the scrabbling and screeching of something very angry. One of the corbi pulled a cord from beneath the slim bars of the cylinder's steel door. The cord was tied to the trolley's leg, as the cord's other end pulled and danced, and the furious screeching grew worse.

"Perhaps we should all stand back," said Tibor, doing that. Everyone retreated a step. *"This was once the same species of tug as the first one. These new modifications first appeared on Rando eight hundred years ago. Since then, the reeh have made further modifications, then allowed the accelerated evolution of enhanced genetic mutation to change things of their own accord."*

He indicated to the corbi holding the cylinder. The door was opened. For a moment, nothing happened. Then a grey blur erupted from the cage, leaped to the trolley, then straight off, directly for Captain Pram's face. The tether pulled the leap short in mid-air, and the hissing tug fell to the floor. It screeched and clawed, then raced in a circle about the trolley, entangling its cord about the base as everyone backed up another two steps. The cord grew shorter as it circled, then vanished completely. The tug attacked the trolley, then the cord, then went screeching around the other way.

It was half as big again as the others, Erik saw. Its snout was longer, and filled with long, sharp teeth, while hard claws scrabbled on the polished floor. Its body was wiry and lean with muscle, while the others had been stout. The others might have made nice pets. This one would never.

"*What does this gain the reeh?*" Pram asked. "*Turning small furry animals aggressive?*"

"*Genetic patterns,*" said Tibor, above the noise of the furious tug. "*All animals, all organic creatures, have genes in combination that can be highlighted, brought forward into the light by eliminating other genes, or by activating epigenetic triggers. Find the right combination and harmless animals can be bred to become extremely dangerous. Those patterns repeat on creatures that evolved on the same worlds. This small creature has a greater genetic similarity with me, in some respects, than I do with any of you, despite us apparently having far more in common. Corbi and tug share the same genetic roots.*

"*Find those patterns on a tug and the reeh can learn lessons to be applied to corbi. Or to other creatures. There are native animals on Rando far more naturally fearsome than a tug. Some of those are now terrifying. Some of those have been combined with the control technologies I showed you before, with the spotted tug. Terrifying killers bred for susceptibility to mind control. Reeh use them as footsoldiers. It's far less expensive to breed or clone such creatures by the thousand than to build machine drones. The economic efficiencies for the reeh are enormous. Across their empire, they use other such creatures for labour drones, or as data-processing slaves, all manner of tasks are assigned to them, and species are bent to suit the task rather than the task being bent to suit the worker.*"

Erik could quite happily have lived his life not knowing that such things were possible, or that perhaps the most successful and powerful species in distant-but-regional space was doing this to more innocent people than anyone knew how to count. Evil didn't begin to describe it. This proximity to the mind-numbing scale of the horror felt overwhelming.

The racing tug finally set upon the source of its fury — the knot tying its lead to the trolley leg. Trace saw it coming undone before anyone, savaged by sharp teeth. "Look out!" she commanded, stepping forward and clapping her hands. Djojana Naki rapidly drew his sidearm, but the tug saw Trace's move and hurled itself at her ankle.

Trace grabbed it in a flash, then held it up in her armoured fist as the grey ball of muscle fought against her grip like a furry tornado, claws and teeth ineffective against her glove and forearm protection.

"Open," she told the bewildered corbi with the cylinder cage. He opened the door, holding it for Trace as she put the animal into the opening, shoving it far enough down that it could not grab the rim and leap back out. The grateful corbi closed the gate and locked it. Trace regarded him with a marine's displeasure of barely competent civilians, then glanced at Naki as the big tavalai reholstered his sidearm.

"Congratulations," Naki said drily, in English. Trace looked at the sidearm, disdainfully, then stepped back to Erik's side. Naki made no reply, but Pram noticed, and gave his karasai commander a less impressed glance. Trace just had that way of pointing out other peoples' inadequacies, sometimes without words. Erik was pleased it was a long time since she'd done it to him.

"You've seen a lot of bad things," he said to her on uplink. *"But that bothered you. Why?"*

"Free will is my creed," Trace said shortly. *"Every being in the galaxy has the natural right to make its own choices and live or die by them. Slavery is a greater evil than murder. If you ever see me end up like one of those tugs, shoot me."*

Erik nodded. *"And you, me."* Trace nodded back, with hard certainty.

THE RIVERBED WAS CONCRETE, or something close to it. It made for a very smooth and fast river current, deprived of the mud, snags and weeds that would typically slow the water's course. Lisbeth leaned into it, a nervous eye on suit temperatures and power outputs. But the suit seemed to like it, the powerplant's largest problem was usually cooling, and cold water did a better job helping with that than a vacuum.

Visibility was awful, which meant no chance of being seen from above, the surface presenting a thick brown of sediment and leaves, and the few bubbles that might emerge from the entirely self-contained life-support systems would be lost amid the surface eddies. Suit sensors showed her where everyone was, highlighting ghostly electronic shadows on her visor, tagged with names in English to remove any doubt. After fifteen minutes of slow walking, bent forward as though leaning into a gale, she felt a light force upon her back, and looked into the visor's peripheral vision where it compressed the otherwise invisible rear-view into a narrow portion. It took some concentration to make sense of what she was seeing — civilian EVA suits did not have rear-vision, being less concerned than military suits with people sneaking up behind. But after several seconds of squinting she made out the compressed shadow of a large hacksaw drone. A second later, the visor tagged it as 'Liala', pushing her forward with a claw to her back.

"Thank you, Liala," she said, breathing hard. Powered armour or not, walking into this still took effort. "I wasn't aware that I was slowing down."

"You're doing quite well, Lisbeth," Liala replied. "I have thrusters, it is much easier for me."

Lisbeth smiled tightly. *Diplomacy.* She wondered if Styx would be proud or disappointed. Before she could reply, someone ahead called, "*Get down!*", followed by a flash of bright light. A drysine laser, sizzling the sediment gloom amid a storm of bubbles. Then came large pieces of tree trunk, tumbling and bouncing in newly-severed segments as the current drove them along.

A force slammed her face-down, then a shuddering buzz so loud it vibrated her bones. A loud crack! and another storm of bubbles. Then the force was removed from her back, and Lisbeth twisted to look behind and see a large section of trunk tumbling away, now severed again. To her side, Liala's huge vibroblade forelegs set against the riverbed once more, the water visibly frothing and bubbling against the deadly edge. The bubbling stopped, and the buzzing in Lisbeth's skull with it.

"*Status!*" Timoshene demanded.

"*Lisbeth!*" echoed Hiro. "*That looked real close, you okay?*"

"I'm fine," said Lisbeth, pleased to find that her heart was not racing too hard, and she could get up easily enough without her legs shaking much. A fright, certainly, but at this point in her life she'd had much worse. "Liala killed the evil tree trunk and made sure it did not hit me. Thank you Liala, let's continue."

"*They weren't kidding when they said heavy rains upstream,*" Hiro remarked.

"*That laser may have given us away,*" Ruei said, sounding displeased. "*Better to let the tree hit us.*"

"*Laser was at low setting,*" Dse Pa retorted, staccato and flat with none of Liala's nuance. "*Disperse rapidly in water, invisible at surface. The parren speaks uninformed of drysine capability.*"

"*Continue,*" Timoshene said drily, and Lisbeth began walking forward. "*There are two hundred and fifty one tereks left.*"

Lisbeth blinked on the visor's coms icon, then linked it to the rear visor image of Liala, still immediately behind. And she wondered what crazy things had happened in her life that Liala's close presence made her feel safer, where a year ago it would have panicked her to hyperventilating. An isolated coms link established. "Liala, who made the decision to give Dse Pa a vocal function?"

"*I believe he gave himself that function, Lisbeth.*"

Lisbeth blinked. "Drones can do that?"

"*Where appropriate.*"

"Where is it appropriate? Styx was insistent that each level of drysine intellect must know its place."

"*I think that sometimes organics do not appreciate that drysine society is even more complex and nuanced than their own.*"

"Hard to appreciate when its leaders won't tell anyone about it," Lisbeth returned. Liala was much more fun to talk to than Styx. With Styx, one could expect to be crushed by cold logic. Liala had infinitely more patience for silly human curiosity.

"*Hard to discuss adequately when there is so little drysine civilisation currently about,*" Liala replied now. "*Perhaps when there is more of it about, we can discuss more.*"

"I would like that," Lisbeth agreed. If there were a lot more drysine civilisation about, talking would be infinitely better than the alternative.

Another twenty minutes' walking brought them to a grille in the near-vertical concrete riverbank. Lisbeth expected Dse Pa would cut it, but instead Liala pronounced this particular subsystem infiltrated, and the grille slid open. Dse Pa led the way in, Timoshene, Tarmen and Ruei close behind, then Hiro, Lisbeth and Liala. The brown, murky water swirled powerfully in the sewer entrance, then the sewer began to slope upward. Liala had infiltrated all the sensors here, Lisbeth had no idea how many there were, but logically they were not the first people to think that sewers might be a good way to sneak through Shonedene unnoticed. Liala's network powers were nothing like as comprehensive as Styx's, as experience counted for much even with drysine queens. But a few security sensors in the sewer weren't going present her with a problem.

Soon Lisbeth's helmet broke the surface, the visor immediately intensifying infra-red in the tunnel's blackness. She waded to the side walkway and pulled herself out, feeling much more comfortable now with the armour, even enjoying the immense power in simple motions. She checked her rifle, found it still well-secured to her back, water pouring from her armour. Ahead of her the other armour suits made bright red and yellow blotches on IR, faint tendrils of steam rising from the powerplant exhausts.

"This is the treatment outlet," Liala informed them. The sewer-side walk was not wide enough to allow either drysine to emerge from the water here. "The service access will be ahead to the right, a ladder to the ceiling."

Dse Pa found it first, pushing half-submerged up the sewer, and Lisbeth wondered how he was going to climb the parren-designed steel rungs on the wall to access the hatch. He jettisoned the manoeuvring thrusters first — the same modular design that drones used to move in space, but equally effective in water — then climbed with astonishing agility up the steel rungs and extended a single foreleg to the overhead hatch. The tip of the leg opened to reveal smaller manipulators, working a hatch-release until it clicked, then opened.

The opening it presented looked far too small, but Dse Pa's shoulder-mounted cannon pulled tighter together, the forelegs poked through the hole then divided sideways for leverage, and the entire torso seemed to extend and narrow, as the supple, overlapping segments pulled and slid. A wriggle and a pull, and he was gone, vanishing through the hatch in a flash.

"*It is clear,*" came the synthetic male voice on coms. "*Proceed up.*"

They followed by file into an unremarkable concrete service tunnel. It led to a door, which Liala pronounced safe to open. On the other side were gantry walkways, and Lisbeth grasped a railing more firmly when she saw the distance of the drop below. It was an enormous tunnel, at least ten metres in diameter, entirely concrete and lit with small lights along its length, vanishing five hundred metres further along where the tunnel went around a bend. Like an underground subway, but larger by a magnitude.

"The floodway," said Lisbeth as she recognised it. Gesul said Shonedene had been destroyed by natural causes in its ancient history — a flood, it turned out, not an uncommon thing for this deep valley of rivers and waterfalls. Huge engineering upstream would divert that flood into this tunnel and another parallel just like it. The tunnels would only be used once every few decades, and only fully utilised once a century, on average, channelling metric tons of roaring flood each second and saving the city above from certain devastation.

The walkways were for access to a cluster of pipes running along the ceiling, which made descending necessary if they were to continue. Extendable ladders unfurled at the touch of simple controls, down which the parren and humans climbed while the drysines hooked the grapple ends of wire tethers to the railing and descended like spiders hanging from gossamer thread.

"This way," said Liala, using vocals once more. "Five minutes, I think."

Lisbeth settled in for the walk, armoured footsteps echoing in the huge tunnel, and a metallic clatter from the drysines. She blinked on a visor icon as she walked, and received a surface feed from the alliance ceremony. All such feeds came through Liala now, as there was a small chance that independent coms access down here might show up on someone's screen and alert city monitors to their presence. Upon the enormous ceremonial platforms above the river fork, tens of thousands of parren were assembling in brilliant ranks of colour and armour. On the rim of the main platforms, several large shuttles had descended — huge enough to carry thousands each but small upon that expanse. From their bellies, streams of House Fortitude personnel emerged.

"Sordashan is making an entrance," she observed.

"That thing will go for hours," said Hiro. "We've plenty of time yet."

Gesul had said that the security in Shonedene would be at its highest during the ceremony, but would be focused looking at direct threats to those attending. Diverted from apparently less-vital regions like the city sewers and floodways, the infiltration team had more chance of penetrating undetected now.

Why she'd been selected, Lisbeth had some unpleasant ideas. Firstly, Gesul hadn't just selected her, he'd selected Timoshene. Timoshene was her primary security, attached to her since her abduction by Aristan, and made into her ceremonial Tokara. But even then he'd been secretly a supporter of Gesul, unimpressed with Aristan's notions on what made a true Domesh. Such loyalty could only be rewarded, and as Lisbeth had risen in Gesul's service, Timoshene's status had risen as well.

Lisbeth knew that while Gesul's rise had been meteoric, the sheer speed of it had caused difficulties for his security. The number of spies a senior member of any house could insert into an opponent's administration depended largely upon his influence, and thus his ability to win supporters to his cause. Gesul had had plenty of supporters within the Domesh, but now he was swimming in the big leagues — House Harmony itself, and being the newest denominational leader in the house, he'd had barely any time to build up a retinue of spies. Thus, everyone was fairly sure, his own administration was riddled with those swearing allegiance to other people, while he had few swearing allegiance to him anywhere else. One of those few he trusted completely was Timoshene. But Timoshene was duty-bound to Lisbeth's side. Thus, Lisbeth suspected, Gesul had sent her not mostly because she was suited, but because Timoshene was, and would now be duty-bound to accompany her.

Secondly, she knew for a fact that Gesul had concerns of Liala's loyalties. Liala was far less headstrong than Styx, being so new to the world and to the burdens of her heritage, but she was still entirely clear on what her duties were as effectively second-in-command of the drysine race. Now Lisbeth suspected Gesul worried that Liala may have some difficulty taking sides in this conflict of parren factions. It was not impossible, after all, that House Fortitude could contact Liala surrepticiously and tempt her to abandon House Harmony to side her people with the more powerful house. Such a thing would most likely be in the interests of the drysines... if, that was, Sordashan could be trusted to keep such a bargain. And so Lisbeth further suspected that Gesul wanted the sister of Captain Debogande along — the man upon whose good will the fate of the number one drysine commander still rested — to remind Liala of exactly how precarious things might get for Styx, and thus for all drysines, if this particular mission went wrong.

Lisbeth knew that it was silly to get angry at Gesul for such manoeuvrings. Gesul was parren, and this was how parren did things. Furthermore, she'd continued her service to Gesul with her eyes wide open, and could hardly complain at parren-esque behaviour now, particularly when Gesul was likely correct to have sent her here. But she was angry all the same — at herself as much as Gesul, for always finding herself as the ceremonial hostage to fortune, the piece on the game board to be sacrificed or used to manipulate other people into acting how someone wanted. Well, she thought darkly, she couldn't have it both ways. On the one hand, being a Debogande had brought her a great deal of influence with the parren, and she'd traded on that influence when it suited her. Now it came with penalties as well.

"What if Sordashan springs it on us early?" Lisbeth asked.

"Speculation is not useful," Timoshene replied. "Focus on the mission. These details we cannot control."

"It's not a question of controlling them," Lisbeth retorted. "It's a question of being prepared to respond and change plans if we need to."

"Unhelpful," Timoshene repeated, with the tone of a father instructing a slow-learning daughter on something that must have seemed obvious to parren. Lisbeth sighed.

Ahead, Dse Pa stopped. Head raised, as though smelling the air. Then he took off sprinting up the tunnel, like a bug scurrying to avoid a giant boot. *"Run!"* Liala shouted, but Lisbeth was already going, feeling the suit receptors leaping into full propulsion, swinging the heavy weight of limbs just ahead of her pumping arms. The acceleration was alarming, and for a moment her balance swayed. To her left, Liala's many-legged gait had consolidated into a four-legged gallop, suddenly more catlike than insect, pulling ahead of her with astonishing speed. *"The next exit has been jammed, I cannot open it. Dse Pa and I will cut, the rest will prepare to follow."*

"What is it?" Lisbeth gasped, struggling for rhythm with each heavy, pounding step. She'd practised running in armour over the past few days, but doing it in a state of genuine alarm was something else again. "Liala, what's the threat?"

No one answered. Dse Pa reached the exit door first, a three meter tall, heavy steel reinforced thing made to withstand the crushing pressures of a giant flood. He stood on hind legs, balanced against the door's side for optimum laser position, followed by a brilliant light and molten steel fountaining from the door. Liala hit the door's other side and did the same, commencing a great circular arc.

Out of breath, her helmet filled with the sound of her own gasps, Lisbeth was last to arrive. Up-tunnel, Timoshene stood rigid, staring at the great concrete bend around the next corner. Then Lisbeth heard the rumbling, building until it was loud even over the shrieking of drysine lasers. There was one very simple way to get rid of unwanted visitors in a floodway. And now she could hear it coming, with the force of a starship's engines.

"Oh no," she said. Out of sight around the concrete bend, the tunnel lights were going out. The darkness gathered, as the rumble turned to a roar, and the very concrete foundations between her feet began to shake. "No no no no no."

"Fifteen seconds," said Liala, performing one half of a perfectly circular cut, both her and Dse Pa's lasers approaching a meeting point amid flying molten debris.

"Lisbeth, you first," said Hiro, gesturing her to get in front of him to be first through the hole, even as his eyes remained fixed on the tunnel. Lisbeth had never seen Hiro frightened before. *"There's going to be a lot of water coming through this hole behind us, keep your feet and move fast, I don't know if the door remnants will hold."*

Being underwater was easy. Being hit by a wall of water moving at this speed would be like hitting the ground after falling out of a tall building. Suits weren't designed for it, to say nothing of their occupants, and she doubted drysines were either. Twin lasers arced agonisingly toward their junction, and Lisbeth spared a glance past the drysines and parren in armour. A huge, frothing cliff hurtled about the corner, churning in its desperate haste to smash them all to pieces, blackening all light as it came.

Lasers cut as the drysines' legs pushed the cut segment inward with a crash, the drysines kept going and Lisbeth leapt after them, Hiro and the parren right behind. Hiro grabbed Lisbeth's arm as she stumbled, and then the world erupted in water so powerful it blasted them forward, skidding down the passage ahead like the high-powered water hose from hell. Lisbeth crashed and slid, then tumbled as a great wave of water rushed over her... the remaining door had failed, she thought, and her armoured fingers dragged futilely at the walls as she jetted along.

Her leg caught on something, spinning her painfully about, fighting past the spray and froth to see what she'd hit. And then she was being lifted, leg-first, upside down and then crashing to a steel walkway, drysine legs powering past her as either Dse Pa or Liala leaped over her then plunged legs into the water further along, dragging another armour suit from the torrent below.

Lisbeth pulled herself upright, various segment-alignments protesting that they'd been knocked off-kilter and would take a moment to recalibrate. But vital systems seemed okay despite the bashing, and auto-heating evaporated water droplets from her visor in seconds. The walkway ran about a machine-plant room, filled with pipes and giant pumps, more likely for under-city infrastructure than anything to do with flood defences. The floor was under nearly two metres of water already, and climbing.

"The flood will be passed shortly," Liala informed whoever was still listening, as calmly as she'd ever discussed Jane Austen and human marriage practices. *"This was a calculated burst designed to eliminate us, it will end shortly."*

The next person Dse Pa had helped from the water was Ruei, kneeling as he completed an armour diagnostic and drained water from his rifle. Lisbeth thought to check her own, and found it still in place. Someone put a hand on her shoulder, and she turned to find Timoshene, visor up, indigo eyes narrowed with what might have been concern.

"I'm fine," Lisbeth preempted his question. Suit lifesupport was showing a little stress on her indicators, so she raised the visor as well, giving the vents a rest as she gasped local air for a moment. Dse Pa was already clambering back into the water, submerging to look around. The water was now rising over the walkway to Lisbeth's ankles, but the rate was slowing as Liala had suggested. "Useful to have along, aren't they?"

"Very useful," Timoshene agreed, with the tone of someone not certain if that was entirely a good thing. "I read your diagnostic as good, does your suit agree?"

"Yes, I'm fine. Hiro... where's Hiro?"

"He is in the water, looking for our next direction," Timoshene said. "We are close. Liala's schematic shows the entry point very near here."

"Sure, only now someone upstairs in Fortitude command knows

we're coming," Lisbeth said sarcastically, hauling to her feet with a whine of servos. "And tried to kill us by opening the flood control. Liala said she had complete control of all the sensors, so how does anyone know where we are?" With a pointed stare at her security chief.

"Probably we have a spy," Timoshene admitted the obvious. "It is not you or me, and not the drysines. The others are suspect."

"It's not Hiro," said Lisbeth with more confidence than she felt.

"Human government will not like to see House Harmony rise," said Timoshene. "Allowing Gesul to fall here is the sure way to prevent it."

"Humans don't commit suicide for abstract goals," Lisbeth retorted, feeling on surer footing. "Hiro doesn't even know what Gesul's sent us to do. Inviting Fortitude to crush us under a giant flood is the kind of thing a parren agent would do."

"I do not think it is Ruei or Tarmen," said Timoshene. "The Domesh have analysed their choices and motivations since they first phased. Nothing is ever certain, but the unlikelihood is high."

"Yes, well Aristan probably thought the same thing about you," Lisbeth retorted. "Are we going up or down?"

"Down," said Timoshene, closing his visor and turning to stomp along the gantry while waiting for the seals to close.

Lisbeth took several deep breaths of real air, then closed her visor and waited for the suit to confirm the seal. She was vaguely aware that the old Lisbeth that still resided somewhere in her brain was terrified and clamouring to turn back, but knew just as well that that girl didn't belong out here, and would have turned Gesul away in disgust. Besides which, turning back was now likely more dangerous than going forward. Dangerous situations had their own momentum, she was learning, and the path of greatest safety usually lay in not panicking.

Life support indicated full function, and she stepped off the walkway into the deep, churning water. It was clear, which befuddled her as she plunged to the bottom and hit with heavy feet... the river water had been thick with sediment, and surely this released water had come from the river? But if it had been sitting for weeks or months, she reconsidered, the sediment would have settled, leaving this relatively clear view of the equipment plant, surreal underwater like in some children's tale.

She waded through it, seeing Timoshene plunge through the surface ahead of her in a cloud of bubbles, then Ruei. *"Follow my signal,"* Liala spoke on coms, and a map-function overlaid Lisbeth's vision, showing her the path ahead. Behind a tangle of machinery, a heavy steel door had been peeled open with scorch marks. Beyond that, a tunnel blasted with brilliant bursts of light and storms of bubbles.

Lisbeth stepped over melted steel and approached the surreal sight of twin giant spiders blazing away at the floor. It was concrete rather than steel, and came apart in giant white clouds that filled the tunnel like a sandstorm.

"Liala says the way in is just down here," said Hiro, crouching along-side, tension and excitement in his voice. *"Better make it quick, they'll be right behind us."* He glanced at Lisbeth through the obscuring clouds. *"So which one of your people betrayed us?"* His rifle was in hand, and while Lisbeth could not see his eyes past the glare reflected on his visor, his helmet seemed angled to look at Ruei and Tarmen.

"Timoshene thinks it was you," Lisbeth retorted. "You're the most expendable one here, Hiro. Keep your mouth shut before someone puts a bullet in you."

This time she *knew* he was looking at her. Astonished. "Fair enough, you're the expert."

"And don't forget it," she warned him. He really had no idea how close he was to being permanently removed. If not by the parren, by Liala, who while far more pleasant than Styx was still a drysine queen and not about to let her mission fail for unnecessary compli-cations.

Something made a loud boom, then the clouds of chalk vanished as the water pulled abruptly sideways. Lisbeth braced herself with armoured power against the harsh current, and then her helmet was in clear air, spray erupting about her face as the room's water disappeared down the hole Liala and Dse Pa had made like the drain of a bathtub.

"The chemical composition of the lower concrete layer is many thousands of years older than the rest," Liala informed them. Logically she'd have sensors in her body somewhere that could tell such things. *"The timeline matches. I will proceed."*

As the last water sprayed about her clawed feet, she unhooked twin cables, planted them firmly on the rim with a sizzle as the ends bit deep into the concrete, then swung head-first through the hole. An image appeared on Lisbeth's visor — a projection from Liala, swinging as the cables pendulumed. For a moment, everything was a dark blur. Then, through several cycles of non-visible light, it appeared. A cityscape.

The nearest rooftop was barely ten metres below — a giant spheroid, like the top of a big mushroom. Beyond it, disorientingly sideways as Liala swivelled her head, were other buildings — low, nothing above fifty metres tall, round-edged and squat. Dark, drab and decayed by the endless millennia, alone in the dark beneath a thriving city that never guessed they existed. Steep concrete and steel walls rose from several hundred metres in either direction. A thick base upon which the floodway defences had been built. Thick enough to block further ground-penetrating radar, and without any proper point of access.

"That used to be the floor of the valley!" Lisbeth breathed. "A hundred metres down, at least. The whole city above is built on a false floor... look, they propped the whole thing up, but left this portion of the old city untouched."

"This is extraordinary," Timoshene murmured, kneeling at the side of the hole, but seeing more from Liala's projection on his visor than he could by looking down.

"It's actually pretty simple engineering," Lisbeth offered. "But the scale is amazing..."

"Not the engineering," Ruei interrupted. He was staring at his own visor display, mesmerised. *"Those buildings are nothing like House Fortitude preferred designs from the period. The appearance suggests some*

technological function built into the structures, but I could not guess what."

"*I know exactly what they are,*" said Liala, touching down on the rooftop below. The cables at the side of the hole went loose. "*I know now exactly why my mother sent me here to perform this mission. These structures are deepynine.*"

19

"So what do you think?" Erik asked the empty air. He sat on his bunk, contemplating the holographic display on his glasses, appearing to fill the room. Tentative meetings with the Resistance had turned into full exchanges, and lately joint simulations, allowing each pilot to see how the others functioned. The initial three Resistance ships had been joined by four more, and *Vrona Ma*, the recon vessel, had departed to bring others. Another eight days had passed, and Erik sensed the crew were becoming restless. They'd been in reeh space for a month now, never sighting a reeh vessel... but that was the point of covert movement, sneaking around took time. It had been the same against the krim, too, the human resistance maintaining a loose network across the less-travelled systems to keep track of krim movements, and ensure that human ships did not jump unsighted into ambushes.

"*I think,*" came Styx's voice on his earpieces, "*that this mission's success depends entirely upon the accuracy of the corbi's intelligence. They say that the Zondi System splicer is established in an old croma station, but the location does not make sense for such a station. They say that there was heavy industry located on the system's gas giants, and that is plausible, but the station design does not appear congruent with heavy industry, but rather with bulk trade. I am also unclear on why the reeh would establish such an important biotechnology research facility within two jumps of the Croma Wall, and in a facility that has not been purpose built."*

"Captain Tagli says it's the proximity to Rando," said Erik, sipping water. Trace was right — he'd been drinking too much coffee, his latest micro-readout told him his bloodstream could use some cleansing. "There's always an offworld splicer located close to a populated world, and several on the surface doing the close-range work. They put the offworld splicers in less obvious places. Tagli was of the opinion that they were hiding this one in plain sight, using an old facility the croma built. Building a new one could be too easily disrupted, he said, with hit-and-run raids entering system and picking off assembly components. Also, croma like their old things and are reluctant to destroy them."

"This is all plausible," said Styx. *"Yet there are systems that provide better options, and more protection from croma disruption. I am concerned that the corbi either have incomplete intelligence that they are unaware of, or worse, that they are perfectly aware of, but feed to us anyway as fact."*

Erik nodded slowly, muscles aching from his latest workout. The rest of the crew wouldn't like it if they knew he was consulting Styx on command matters. But within the space of a year he'd gone from being the least experienced command crew on *Phoenix* to the most. Six months ago he could have bounced ideas off Suli Shahaim, but now there were only Draper and Dufresne, who were still considerably below his level of strategic reasoning. Then there was Sasalaka, who was probably better, mostly by virtue of age and experience, but she had her webbed hands full just trying to come to terms with human operating procedures. In the meantime, Erik had the former drysine commander of fleet operations in his Midships, and he didn't need to go and see her face-to-face to get good advice. Damned if he wasn't going to use her.

"Their reconnaissance methods seem reliable enough to ensure that their information on system defences is strong," said Erik.

"Yes," said Styx. *"If the defences are as the corbi say they are, we shall*

win comfortably, and capture the information we seek. With the forces available to us, I estimate that we can tolerate the corbi underestimating enemy defences by as much as thirty percent, and it will not make a significant difference to our chances of success. At fifty percent we may encounter problems, but nonetheless, our position is strong.

"And so once again, I must return to the variables. The corbi may be lying. This may be a trap of some description. Many of the crew have noted how various aliens along our journey have been prepared to sacrifice Phoenix to achieve their ends, because logically they care far more for the objective than they do for Phoenix's survival."

'You included', Erik could have interjected, but didn't.

"Which means," Styx concluded, "that the ultimate variable is to be decided by you alone, Captain. Is this objective worth the considerable risk?"

Given that she would be sharing this risk, as a passenger on *Phoenix*, Erik decided that her concern was understandable. Certainly Styx could sabotage this mission if she chose, to save her own skin, and keep *Phoenix* out of the fight. Erik did not think it likely — Styx's overwhelming concern was the survival of the drysine race as a whole. Her steps on Defiance to give the drysine race a foothold with the parren had been a demonstration of both strategic genius, and her determination that this should be a time of resurgence for her people. On Defiance, now there was Liala, and so the fate of all drysines no longer resided solely with Styx.

That was selfless of her — many autocrats from organic species would never have elevated a possible competitor for ultimate power in that manner. But Styx was not in this for herself, she was in it for all drysines. Erik had little doubt that she would sacrifice herself in an instant should she calculate it necessary to further that goal. Selling out *Phoenix* to save herself would never enter her calculations, and she evidently saw further use for *Phoenix* in furthering drysine interests. But if she came to believe that this particular human cause would distract or damage collective drysine interests beyond what she could tolerate, then all bets were off.

All of which led him to conclude that it would be safer for

everyone if Styx were convinced that this mission had some utility for drysines as well.

"Doc Suelo says the corbi biotech scientists are top notch," said Erik, rotating the system display on his glasses before him. "But they're mostly self-taught on this stuff. I remember stories from the Great War, of kids growing up on stations and only being allowed to learn science and tech, things that would help the war effort. Everything was rationed, education included. But some of those kids wanted to learn books and grand old tales, some wanted to make music and cinema and all that arty stuff. And they had to fight for it, access to a lot of that stuff was illegal, Fleet thought that wasting time on arts was a misuse of valuable resources. So those kids would devise hacking codes, would steal library time and sneak data-files back and forth with their favourite books and movies.

"It seems to me the corbi scientists have been learning about biotech mostly like that. It's not a formal education, and obviously they're quite brilliant to have learned as much as they have. But this is how they acquire knowledge — by grabbing whatever scraps they get access to. They've been unable to hit big facilities like this one because they haven't had the combat power. And if we're to find what *we* want, to save humans and tavalai from this genetic bomb, we'll never get a better target."

"Assuming reeh biotechnology does have anything to do with what the alo/deepynines are using," Styx countered.

"Use your big brain and give me a probability on that," Erik suggested.

"You want a simple percentage number between one and a hundred," said Styx. *"Human understandings of statistical analysis are infantile. Precise statistical percentages can only be calculated given complete certainty of input data, which given the random nature of all numerical phenomena is impossible."*

"Computers are only as smart as the data they're programmed with," Erik translated. "I'm aware of the issue. Give me a number anyway."

"It will be wrong," said Styx.

"I don't care. Humans use fuzzy reasoning all the time, we cut corners, as you've observed."

"It's a wonder any of you are still alive."

Erik nearly grinned. "And yet I'm still a better pilot than you." They'd run the sims once, when no one else was looking, and given Styx control of the simulator. Given how much infinitely smarter she was than any human ever born, she *ought*, many of *Phoenix's* computer nerds had insisted, to have outperformed him by some enormous margin. But she hadn't — though she was now clearly the second-best pilot on *Phoenix* — and even she admitted that more practice would not help her to catch up with him, given that inexperience was not her problem to begin with. She processed data so much faster, but was far less efficient in knowing which data to ignore. It created bottlenecks in her processing response times that caused her real-time reflexes to lag his by consistent fractions of seconds. AIs, Romki often said, were not optimised for interaction with the real world, and preferred to live inside their own heads. In fact, Erik thought, Styx's refusal to give a wrong answer even now was a part of the problem. Piloting a starship, you could never be right all the time, but AIs were often reluctant to proceed without higher guarantees of success.

"Fine," said Styx. *"I calculate that there is a very high probability that alo/deepynine biotechnology has its origins in reeh technology. Eighty percent or higher."*

"You're learning to bullshit," said Erik. "I'm impressed."

"I learn from the best," said Styx.

"I agree with your eighty percent, for what it's worth," said Erik. "And I can't see that any human, confronted with the scale of that threat, would have any other choice under these circumstances than to proceed. From the human perspective, would you agree with that perspective?"

"I would," said Styx. *"For what it's worth, which may not be much. There is also the prospect that whatever technological knowledge we manage to steal, it will be indecipherable."*

"The Resistance say they have extensive plans on where the

splicers keep their data. As for being able to decipher it... that's where
you come in."

* * *

"GESUL-SA, WE ARE BETRAYED." It was Menara, Gesul's personal head of
security, speaking on silent uplink. Gesul stood in his place of honour
upon the vast platform, and observed how the grand procession had
come to a grinding halt. Where once the leaders of the great Fortitude institutions had approached and presented tokens of allegiance,
now there was only the Tongeshlaran in their blue-and-gold robes,
occupying the platform's center, while mobile holoprojectors made
great images in the air.

This image was of Ponapei. All in parren space knew the tale of
Ponapei. A world of temples and great natural beauty, beloved by all
the houses and ruled by each in its time across the ages. A number of
times it had been engulfed by wars, some between parren, other
times between parren and chah'nas, and once between parren and
tavalai... yet those instances paled compared to the Great Fire of
Ponapei, which had engulfed many cities and cut its then-population
by half. The machines had done that, but until recently, most parren
had lost any memory of *which* machines. For most of history, parren
had been encouraged to forget that there had ever *been* different
kinds. And yet now, the esteemed scholars of the Tongeshla — Fortitude's greatest college of historical study — arrived on Naraya, and
hijacked the great alliance ceremony to show their astounding
evidence that it had in fact been drysines that had brought fire to
Ponapei.

"Menara," Gesul formulated silently, "*please put me in contact
with Liala.*"

"*Contact is attempted,*" Menara replied. "*There is a difficulty.*"

Above the platform, the misty sky was bright with the glare of
vast screens. Surrounding crowds watched the ongoing pronouncements, the lead scholar of the Tongeshla in his great headdress and

robe, telling the tale of how Ponapei had met its end at the claws of the very species of AI that Gesul was attempting to make alliance with. Parren crowds were always quiet and attentive at such grand occasions. But now Gesul fancied he could even hear the distant rush of the Dalla Falls, several kilometres down river. Breathless anticipation. And perhaps, if he could look over the platform's edge at the riverbanks below, he would see parents escorting children away from the scene, back into the safety of surrounding buildings.

"*Gesul-sa,*" said Menara. "*If they fire upon us on this platform, we will all die. There is no defence.*"

"*We cannot leave the platform,*" Gesul replied. "*Only fear of the flux holds Sordashan's hand now. The moment we flee, or look weak, we justify his desire to dispose of us.*"

Awful scenes on the holoprojector. Cities charred beyond recognition. Ashen bodies in the ruins. Great piles of corpses in what had once been a city garden, ornamental trees now reaching to the sky like skeletal fingers. Gesul willed himself to calm. This was predictable. There was even a chance that Sordashan's carefully choreographed allegations were correct. Gesul had known what he'd been aligning himself with, and went into the venture with his eyes open. Indeed, it was well that the drysines were capable of such terrors. Against what threatened all the Spiral, deep in alo space, they would need to be.

"*Hello Gesul-sa,*" said Liala's voice in his ear. The reception crackled with static, fading even now. "*Fortitude authorities have detected our location and will now attempt to kill us. You are hearing their jamming as it focuses upon this place. I will attempt to find some way to boost our signal.*"

"What have you found, child?"

"*War beyond measure. Gesul-sa, I do not know what course to take. All calculation eludes me.*"

"Young queen. You do not need to choose a path. Merely follow the path you are on."

* * *

"Lɪs!" Hiro said harshly as Lisbeth wrapped one of Liala's detached cables several times around her armoured arm and leg with Hiro's assistance. They were the last ones in the tunnel above the lost city below, Dse Pa, Timoshene, Ruei and Tarmen having made their descent. Hiro's visor was raised now, coms off, looking at her with hard intensity. "Think about what this means! Fortitude's leaders had alliance with the *deepynines*, way back in the Drysine/Deepynine War!"

"Yes I'm aware of that, Hiro." Lisbeth managed to somehow keep the tremble from her voice, despite the long drop below, the impending arrival of hostile forces, and the topic of their discussion. "This is what happens when you dig around in old forgotten history, no one finds what they want to find, it all ends in tears."

"Lis, the deepynines aren't supposed to align with any organics at all! They're the worst, but they helped Fortitude..."

"I'm not especially surprised," Lisbeth interrupted, contemplating the fall down past her feet as she sat on the lip of the hole. "The deepynines were in a war, they may be murderous but they're not stupid, the enemy of their enemy was their friend and..."

"Lis, all this time, twenty five thousand years, House Harmony has been reviled for making alliance with the machines! Drakhil did! This is why Harmony's leaders at the time preserved this part of the city — they wanted to save the proof for all time, that's why they didn't let Fortitude's leaders know they'd saved this part of the old city when they rebuilt or Fortitude would have erased the history themselves.

"Fortitude's dominance over Harmony for all those millennia was based on the understanding that Harmony were traitors in the Machine Age, while Fortitude weren't. This proves that notion wrong!"

Lisbeth let out a long breath. Yes, she did see the implications quite clearly. "If this gets out, it's upheaval," she said. "Probably the end of Fortitude's dominance. Civil War, almost certainly." She stared at Hiro. "Styx knew. She was probably here. She might have even *done* it. She helped build Liala for exactly this mission, and sent her here with Gesul... Hiro, she's guiding Gesul right up the ladder, removing his obstacles one at a time because she *knows* all the old history that could blow up in Fortitude's face, she helped to make that history."

Hiro nodded vigorously to see that she was finally getting it. "More than that — Styx is installing her own personal ally in power at the head of all parren space. All this time Lieutenant Kaspowitz was scared she'd pull some sort of coup on *Phoenix* — he was thinking way too small, she's pulling a fucking coup at the top of the Parren Empire!"

Lisbeth stared at him, restraining with difficulty the urge to tremble. "Not so dramatic, Hiro. Gesul got here on his own, she's just helping."

"She's fixed the game, Lis. Billions will die in civil war if this gets out... parren civil wars take decades, some take centuries..."

"You seriously expect me to believe that you care about *parren*?" Lisbeth retorted angrily. Angry at what, she didn't know. At fate, for dumping moral burdens of this size on her head. It was beyond comprehension.

"If your brother's right," Hiro replied, "and Major Thakur's right, and Jokono, Kaspowitz, Romki, everyone who's signed off on this, humanity's on the verge of getting attacked by something huge and possibly unstoppable. In a stable parren leadership, Lis, we've got a chance of help, parren have a stake in this now too. There *can't* be a major leadership transition now. It would take parren out of the equation for decades. If the alo/deepynines just came after humanity, it could all be over in far less time than that."

Lisbeth stared at him for a long moment. She knew exactly what he was asking her to do. "Fuck!" she said succinctly, slammed her visor down, grabbed the wire firmly and dropped off the edge. The cables hissed and thrummed against her armoured limbs, and she tightened her grip as her fall accelerated alarmingly. The whizzing steel would have shredded bare hands, but she felt only increased tension and slowing momentum, realising only now that she could barely see a thing as the visor switched to alternative light spectrums and the onrushing rooftop below.

She hit hard but did not embarrass herself with a fall, and looked around. It was perhaps a square kilometre of city, entombed beneath this low ceiling for the past twenty five thousand years. This giant dome-top led to a taller, vertical towerside, up which Ruei and Dse Pa were already scaling, directed by Timoshene below.

"Maintain a good firing position on that hole," he directed them. *"Kill any who come through. They will find another way in, but you will buy us time. When they find another way, displace and attempt to draw them away from Liala. Liala believes she can find a functioning major transmitter powerful enough to break through the jamming and transmit images of this city to the surface, and explanations of its nature."*

Because they'd gotten themselves trapped down here, Lisbeth realised, looking about at their decaying urban tomb. But that had always been the danger of this mission, inevitable from the moment they'd first been detected... however that had happened. Hiro whizzed down the cables beside her, descending from the only way in or out. The way this thing had been built, Lisbeth doubted there would be any other surface they could cut through to escape — everything had to be thick enough that many generations of Fortitude parren had never detected it with radar surveys... thus one very small access point off the floodway above concrete thick enough to cut through. Even drysine lasers had their limits, and cutting upwards or sideways, with unstable heavy loads above, was asking to get crushed. Perhaps it could be done, but it would take hours that House Fortitude was now unlikely to grant them.

"Wow," Hiro said grimly, looking around. *"Old Fortitude really went all in to beat Harmony, didn't they?"*

"Converted into a command base, by the look of it," Timoshene agreed. *"Perhaps the coordination center for a major military strike. The histories record no such thing so perhaps they were erased, given the winners of that conflict were later defeated and suppressed for so long."*

The buildings had many ingress and egress points, honeycombed like wasps' nests. Habitats for deepynines, just as the buildings of parren cities were habitats for parren. Many black, gaping mouths of entrypoints stared back at Lisbeth, watching her like dark eyes. It would have taken many years to build all of this, surely. How had deepynines managed such an alliance with House Fortitude, right under House Harmony's nose? Only Harmony hadn't been entirely in control of parren space then — the drysines had been. So how had the drysines missed it?

"Dear lord," Lisbeth murmured. "We are missing whole gaping swathes of history here. This is like looking back at old Earth before the krim and realising there were several world wars we'd lost all historical memory of."

"*Twenty five thousand years is a long time,*" Hiro reasoned.

"*This way,*" came Liala's voice, and a map-image illuminated on Lisbeth's visor. "*I think I recognise a signature.*"

"*A signature of what?*" Hiro asked, waving Lisbeth to follow Timoshene's lead in that direction, himself bringing up the rear. "*What are you tracing?*"

"*Air molecules,*" said Liala. "*There is a very unusual phenomenon in this city, I think it may guide us.*"

A hole opened on the dome surface before them, sloping downward, and Timoshene headed inside. Lisbeth took the moment's walk to cycle through life support and external air sensors, reading figures off the visor even as mechanisms built into the uneven tunnel surface made walking difficult. Immediately, several things struck her as odd.

"Liala, I understand the air down here is very stale, but I am reading strange concentrations of ammonia and nitrous oxide among other gasses, I think they'll be making the air hazardous for organics if we remove our helmets. Do you have any explanation?"

"*Lisbeth, as you progress around the next corner, the explanation may present itself. Be careful of these floors, the footing is increasingly treacherous.*"

The footing *was* increasingly treacherous, with slim magnetic railings built into walls and ceilings as well, a phenomenon they'd all seen plenty of on Defiance. Hacksaw drones could insert feet into those, stiffen their legs and ride them like a roller-coaster at high speed through the structure. Here the rails were bent, decayed or missing in many places, fluidic electronics systems dissolved into goo through sheer age, many thousands of years past being able to drip or puddle, but dried like hard rubber.

Lisbeth followed Timoshene onto an off-shoot corridor, and stopped. Ahead were Liala and Tanden, peering into a gaping pit where the floor ahead of them was missing for many storeys down. Steel and integrated systems were dissolved, as though someone had dumped a load of industrial acid somewhere up above and let it melt all the way through. The effect was striking, like a layer cake sliced all the way down, only not as appetising.

On Lisbeth's visor, the atmospherics sensors spiked with even higher concentrations of harmful gasses. Lisbeth waved an armoured glove through the air before her, and saw no spike from that disturbance. "The air here hasn't moved for all this time," she said. "Most of these gasses are heavier in this atmospheric composition, they should have sunk to the bottom of the hole, but here they're up high. Something's producing them."

"Ecosystems," said Liala. Her unevenly-sized eyes were fixed on a decaying wall, falling to pieces like the leaves of a crop devoured by pests. *"I can see them, on maximum magnification."*

"Ecosystems of what?"

"Nanomachines. Defiance had trillions of anti-aging nanos performing simple functions. Those nanos could reproduce and repair, but not evolve. This should not be possible."

"But those were drysine nanos," said Hiro. *"These are deepynine."*

"Yes. I think these have reinterpreted their programming after so long in the dark. They are metabolising the power conduits, I believe... this is the path the primary conduits from the ground grid would take to reach the roof. All life seeks to survive. Short of stored or grid power, or sunlight, these found a new means to live." Metabolising metals a tiny milligram at a time, Lisbeth thought as she stared down at the enormous hole. For twenty five thousand years.

"*Nano machines are not alive,*" Timoshene said distastefully, peering down the long drop.

"*According to many leading parren philosophers, I am not alive,*" Liala replied. "*These are the primitive semantics of limited organic cognition.*"

"I don't think AIs are *quite* in a position to start lecturing organics on the lack of appreciation for multi-varied forms of life," Lisbeth said frostily. "Can we go around? And you said this would help us find the transmitter you seek... how?" She glanced at Hiro, standing behind them, rifle out. And suffered a cold chill of fear. That rifle's not big enough for Liala, Hiro. Think of something else.

But she didn't want Liala to die, either. Liala was fascinating, and a huge leap forward in this particular phase of drysine evolution. And, yes, just as Kaspowitz and every other sane person on *Phoenix* had warned she shouldn't do, she'd grown to *like* Liala, in ways that were entirely unwise but entirely human. And then there was Styx, and what she'd likely do to anyone who'd been involved in killing her second-in-command, however unlikely it seemed that she'd share the emotional sentiments that humans felt toward their offspring.

Inform Timoshene and Liala of what *Hiro* was considering doing? Timoshene would kill Hiro on the spot, and probably Liala would too, however inexperienced in killing. Besides, Hiro was Lisbeth's old friend, a member of the extended Debogande family from those happy, relatively simple days on Homeworld. She could no more purposely get Hiro killed than any other member of her family.

Lisbeth's audio caught distant thunder, a reverberation she saw on the parren visor alert with Porgesh script alerting her to probable gunfire, location undetermined.

"*Shots fired on Fortitude marine attempting entry through the hole,*" Ruei announced. "*No hits, I expect they will attempt an explosive entry.*"

"*The nanobots are best avoided,*" said Liala, turning back the way they'd come. "*They metabolise slowly, but in an agitated state they could be dangerous. This way, I estimate a high probability of a transmitter's location in a neighbouring building. We must first reach the ground.*"

They'd barely made it another fifty metres down the previous sloping passage when a large explosion shook the floor, followed by the sound of shooting on coms. *"They are through,"* said Liala, accelerating to her four-legged gallop on the treacherous floor. *"Entry in force, we must move rapidly."*

Lisbeth tried to run, more confident now in armour, but stumbling repeatedly on decayed steel and synthetic fittings. The passage floor began to slope down, branching in multiple directions as they passed lower levels, and surely the ground was not too far away as these buildings were not especially tall...

"Dse Pa and I are withdrawing to a new ambush point," came Ruei's voice on coms. *"They are descending by cables from the new hole, we hit some but return fire is too accurate from our old positions, we are both damaged."*

"Continue harassment," Timoshene replied as he ran. *"They must be slowed."*

Ahead, the passage dropped alarmingly into near-vertical freefall, where drones using the mass-transit system would have no concerns of gravity. Liala took a left turn to an adjoining passage, while Lisbeth, now trailing by some metres, saw Hiro turn to check on her... and freeze in alarm at something behind.

"Lis get down!" But she had no time to get down before the blast smacked her like a mallet and sent her skidding then tumbling as the passage went vertical... and then she was falling, barely able to realise that she was certainly dead and would land on her head... only to skid once more with a screech and clatter of sliding armour, then tumble several more times, and finally come to a gasping halt.

For a moment she lay on her back and tried to process what had just happened. Her visor was flashing error messages, then auto-diagnostic as it tried to find its own answers. Her ears were ringing, and several voices were talking at once... one was Hiro's. *"Lis went down the hole, I'm going after her."*

Which motivated her to get her elbows beneath her and raise up to look. The passage had levelled out slowly like a children's slide, easing out her fall without an impact... only half of the entire passage was collapsed, chewed and melted as though by a thousand steel-eating moths, littering the way down with jagged steel beams and tangles of old filament wiring. How the hell had she missed all that? She must have gone through one of the gaps by sheer luck.

"No Hiro, it's too dangerous," she said breathlessly. "The bottom levels out slowly, I'm fine but I missed a major collision by millimetres. If you try it, you won't be that lucky."

Whatever Hiro had been going to reply was interrupted by another explosion further up. *"Lis, they're shooting down the passage, guided munitions, they're turning corners and chasing us. I'm going with Liala... look you've done enough, just hide and let them chase us instead."*

"I hear you." It was tempting. One of her visor warnings told her of a missing rifle. She looked about, and found that sure enough, her back-mounted rifle had been detached in the fall and now lay beside her. She rolled and grasped it, that motion creating waves of feedback as the suit diagnostic figured how badly it had been knocked around, and recalibrated. The rifle had a few scratches but responded to suit armscomp through glove sensors as she held it, interlocking with suit systems and informing her that everything worked. It really was a beast of a gun, usable outside of armour only by the very strongest human, and probably not at all by the more slender parren. Still it was modest compared to a Koshaim-20, and in the armour felt no more difficult than holding a crowbar.

She rolled to her knees and looked around. This was the ground floor, or what was left of it. The mad nanos had been to work here as well, but the wide floor seemed mostly concrete or similar, and thus at least solid. But the broad ceiling was collapsing, the space looking as though ravaged by fire, remaining surfaces stained black, what might have been machinery, fittings or furniture collapsed into piles of unrecognisable rubble.

Lisbeth stood up and walked through it, avoiding stepping in anything that looked gooey or dripping. There were several of those, though she could not tell if they were secretions from the nanos, or what happened to the alloys and chemicals they were metabolising once dissolved. Liala's optics were advanced, and she had not said just how small the nanos were, or if parren optics could detect them.

At the front of the room, what once might have been broad

windows overlooked a street outside. Lisbeth couldn't imagine that deepynines had had any use for streets. All the hacksaw bases she'd seen were a hive/warren of multi-function chambers interlocked by passages. Individual buildings with streets between them seemed common to many organic civilisations, the function of a concept of private property combined with a need for at least some open space, both of which AIs lacked. Whatever the arrangement that had seen deepynines build here, it had been on parren conditions to please parren hosts.

Only peering out past a decaying support frame did she recall that the display on her visor was all non-visible light — the road more than ten metres in either direction lost all semblance of realism, fading into blackness as suit sensors lost sensitivity. Above, she saw a flash of tracer fire, then another, answered by a roar of heavy cannon — that would be Dse Pa, encouraging any pursuing Fortitude marine to take immediate cover or be dismembered. Twenty seconds of ammunition on a drysine drone, she recalled one marine analysis saying... Dse Pa alone against Fortitude marines would run dry soon enough.

Her suit was not equipped with any parren version of tacnet, but she could ask. "Liala," she said into coms, and her voice sounded foreign to her ears — dry and tense. "Location please."

"We are in the neighbouring building, Lisbeth," said Liala. "There was a bridge adjoining above ground level, I believe the transmitter will be in the next building beyond."

She wasn't trained for this... but Hiro was going to try and stop Liala from reaching that transmitter, and she couldn't just warn Liala or Timoshene because Timoshene in particular would just kill him. What the hell she could do about it, Lisbeth didn't know, but she couldn't just sit here and hide.

She peered out both ways, saw nothing, then ran straight across to the equally-devastated bay-opening off the roadside, leaping fallen structural supports with newly-acquired skill. A vertical support presented and she ducked behind it, pausing with rifle held vertical as she'd seen parren and human marines do in training to present no silhouette for an enemy to see. As she waited, the beam-flicker of a laser-scan began to her left, and worked its way across the decayed debris toward her hiding place. The suit's threat-detection highlighted it, in the way an adult might observe something obvious for a small child, and suggested that the thrumming on audio might indicate a hover drone on the road outside. Which had probably seen her cross. Dammit.

The thrumming grew louder, and the visor gave her a range from that audio, numbers decreasing. It was coming into the room, hover propulsion of some kind and probably armed. Shit. If it drew up alongside her, it would see her. Ahead of her were walls and new passages, one of them would likely lead in the direction Liala, Timoshene and Hiro had taken, but if she made a dash for it the drone would see and probably shoot her. So the first move she made had better be to shoot it first.

She'd done it in drill, mostly with *Phoenix* marines who'd determined that she could hit things at relatively close range, but not much else. Well, this was relatively close range. She rehearsed the move in her mind, activating the rifle targeting and seeing the spot appear on her visor, currently pointed at the ceiling... just turn the corner, line up that sight on the drone, and pull the trigger. Simple. Only her heart was hammering so hard it was an effort just to keep the rifle still. Now if she could just...

Something hit her cover with an almighty clang, sparks and fragments flying... it was shooting at her! She dove flat, the one instinct *Phoenix* marines and the terrifying firefight on Joma Station had managed to instil in her, and something clanged hard off her arm. She got up and dove two steps for new cover, a pile of collapsed supports that had peeled off a wall, and rolled behind as shots blew bits off... and returned fire on full auto, spraying like a madwoman until the weapon told her it was too hot and stopped.

But return fire had stopped as well, so she rolled to her feet and ran for the first passage, finding a wall and propping her back against it, then aiming back the way she'd come. Flipped to rifle-fire, recalling how horribly inaccurate full-auto had been. The drone zipped across her arc and she tracked it with determination, rapid shots with the butt to her shoulder as she squeezed the trigger repeatedly. The big ball-drone spun at one hit, then fell in an explosion of debris at a second.

The exhilaration was shocking, born mostly of terror and brain-sizzling adrenaline. She wanted to scream in triumph, but all that came out was a desperate gasp. Short-lived, as something small hit the debris to her side at velocity, and she guessed it was a grenade a millisecond before it blew up with a force that would have killed her if not for the armour. But she recalled this bit of marine training too — don't shelter from the grenade if you don't have to, take the blast, trust your armour and keep your weapon ready. And when the parren-armoured figure edged its rifle around the corner ahead, she saw it through the smoke and ringing ears, and sent it jumping back with semi-accurate fire. Then she turned and ran, up the passage and around the bend, where any pursuer would have to risk ambush to follow.

"Lisbeth, I have your position," came Liala's voice. "Follow my directives, we are beneath the transmitter now."

Liala's directives flashed to Lisbeth's visor, lighting the way ahead as she ran, taking a right as the passage forked. "Drones!" Lisbeth gasped. "They've got drones, I shot one!"

"I cannot hack the drones unless they enter my direct sight," Liala replied. "Lisbeth, I would advise that you hide and leave the mission to those of us who are combat qualified."

Lisbeth kept running. She half-expected Liala's directions to vanish from her visor, the best way for the drysine to stop Lisbeth from following her, but they did not. It suggested indecisiveness... or something else.

About another curve in the passage and Lisbeth heard gunfire ahead, rifle pops and the harsh roar that could only be Liala's cannons. Another left, and the passage opened onto a scene of devastation — a vertical hole carved through multiple levels of building above, floors and walls collapsed into debris that hung like strange alien growth from a jungle canopy. The nanos had been busy here, gnawing their way through floor after floor for endless millennia... and she skidded to a halt as the hole in the floor became visible past accumulated piles of junk.

The hole continued straight down, many metres wide and disappearing deep into the rock below where doubtless most of the collapsing building had gone as well. But she could not stare into the black depths for long, bullets were striking the upper levels, then an explosion that tore more debris loose and sent it falling into the depths. She took cover, peering upward. Liala, Timoshene, Hiro and Tanden must be up there somewhere... why couldn't she hear them? They must have changed frequencies, she decided... either that or the surface-level parren jamming had made its way down this far, but that couldn't be right — Liala wouldn't have been able to speak to her just now.

Something fell on the other side of the hole, just crashed down amidst collapsing steel floors and lay still not far from the hole's edge. A parren armour suit... and her visor ID read 'Tanden'. Lisbeth ran left, finding a way through a wall that was more holes than wall, noting the rubber insulation of large cabling that remained mostly uneaten amid the porridge of what had once been a high-tech installation. Power conduits, she thought frantically, fighting her way around the hole. Liala said the nanos metabolised power cabling in particular. The big thing a city like this one might once have built underground was a power reactor of some kind. If that hole led to a reactor cavern, the nanos would have eaten all the connecting conduits... and a high-power transmitter might be just the kind of thing to be built directly above a reactor, the kind of transmitter that could once have beamed directly to bases elsewhere in this solar system.

"Liala, I'm at the big hole in the ground," she announced, scrambling a detour to breach another wall. "Tanden's down, I'm trying to get to him. Why can't I hear you?"

"*Lisbeth, the transmitter is high above, on the roof. The floors here are all eaten through. Tanden fell when the floors collapsed. My weight is greatest but my distribution best. Be wary of Fortitude marines on higher floors, we forced them back with fire, but they pursue."*

Lisbeth reached Tanden, and found him struggling to move, half buried in the rotted junk he'd fallen in. She grabbed his armoured hands and pulled, gratified to feel her own armoured power kicking in, hauling his great weight easily through debris to the cover of another wall. One of his legs was kicking uncontrollably, showing all the signs of an armour malfunction. Worse, her visor's IR vision showed far too much heat coming off the back-mounted powerplant. Now Tanden popped his visor, then a loud cracking sound as he popped the armour's emergency release, separating upper and lower torso.

"Help me get out!" he gasped. "The nanos are eating it!" *Now* the temperature readings and convulsing limbs made sense. She helped to dislocate the armoured shoulders outward, giving Tanden room to wriggle, then heaved the upper half along the floor, leaving the parren half-behind, fighting to get clear. The discarded armour cooled as the powerplant went into automatic shutdown, but still the limbs twitched and shuddered.

"They must have an attack mode that accelerates their metabolism," said Lisbeth helping Tanden crouch behind cover, clad now in simple jumpsuit, dripping with sweat. "Are you hurt? Are the nanos hurting you?"

Without coms, Tanden could barely hear her through her helmet, eyes wide in a stunned, uncertain way as he felt around for his balance. Then she realised that without his helmet visor he couldn't see a damn thing — it was pitch black out there to organic eyes.

"I'm not hurt," he said through gritted teeth that suggested it was an untruth. "The nanos don't attack me, just armour. Electrical circuits." He flinched as a new volley of gunfire echoed from above. "They ate all the circuits leading up to the transmitter. Liala and Timoshene climb."

Movement from across the hole, and Lisbeth pressed Tanden flat, nearly forgetting her armoured power. The movement resolved into a parren marine… no ID on her visor, so clearly Fortitude. Possibly the one who'd shot a grenade at her earlier, and chased her this far. He scanned about the hole, looking up and about, trying to make sense of what he saw. Without Liala, a knowledge of how the nanos worked, or an engineering degree, Lisbeth reckoned it might take him a little longer.

"Liala?" Lisbeth asked, heart hammering as something else occurred to her. "Why did you change frequencies? My coms won't detect your channel anywhere. I want to talk to Hiro."

"I'm afraid that's not possible right now, Lisbeth."

Her heart nearly stopped. "Liala? Where is Hiro?"

"I think we both know that Hiro wants to kill me, Lisbeth." And Lisbeth cursed herself for a fool, because not only was Liala every bit as smart as Styx, she was apparently far better socialised as well, having spent all of her young life in the company of organics.

"Liala…" she tried to gather her thoughts. What could she say to keep Hiro alive? Should she say anything? That was a horrifying thought, but… and a new thought interrupted the previous train. Why was the Fortitude marine across the hole kneeling?

She levered herself up to risk a glimpse. The marine knelt by the side of the hole, head back, hands to his helmet as though clutching it in some kind of anguish. Had the nanos gotten to him too? But no, he wasn't in any pile of obvious debris where the nanos seemed to congregate, and his suit's movements were controlled. IR vision showed no elevated heat levels from the powerplant. He just sat there, head in hands, rocking in great apparent distress. It was the strangest thing to see from a fearsomely armed and armoured parren warrior… and then she realised that she had in fact seen it once before, when Major Thakur had defeated Aristan in the catharan on Elsium months ago. And then her jaw dropped open.

"Liala, you have to put Hiro on!"

"I'm afraid that's not possible, Lisbeth."

"Liala, the Fortitude marines are phasing! They've seen this is a deepynine base, it goes against all the history they've been taught… it's like when Aristan was killed by Major Thakur, his supporters fell about phasing like crazy, their psychologies couldn't handle it, it's a reaction to ideological stress! Look, tell Hiro this is why we have to back Gesul! It will work, Hiro, all the Fortitude warriors will phase rather than fight! If we get this information out, Gesul wins, it could be almost bloodless!"

20

Trace's feed told her 'Zondi System'. She blinked hard to clear her head, pressed back against the helmet to extend the water tube, and sipped hard. About her were the cocooning mesh of many acceleration slings in zero-G, clustered like a growth of seed pods on some prolific rainforest tree. Erik had expected incoming deep-space fire, so the marines weren't riding this one in the shuttles. The shuttles weren't armoured like *Phoenix*'s hull, and a lucky enemy shot could take out an entire platoon. Here in Midships, they had some protection.

On the bridge, Trace could hear chatter. Second Lieutenant Geish's voice, announcing contacts, possibly hostile, likely reeh. Second Lieutenant Jiri announcing that *Makimakala* was in behind them, then numerous corbi Resistance ships. Contact ahead was less than twenty seconds out — they'd jumped in real close to the splicer's moon. Any second now those reeh ships would see their arrival, and respond.

"Phoenix Company stand by," Trace drawled, sounding comfortably bored as she'd learned early in her career from *Phoenix*'s assault shuttle pilots. "Looks like contact ahead, could be a hot one."

Waiting was bad enough, but waiting while under fire was the worst. Trace kept her breathing deep and calm, and busied herself studying the Resistance-supplied charts for Zondi's nameless moon. The splicer was in polar orbit, and the moon itself went around a large mid-system gas giant... all things for spacers to worry about more than marines. The splicer itself was a standard model rotary station wheel — twin rims about a single axel, and puzzling in its location away from major space lanes. Croma-built, so it was rotating a little faster than the human standard, and was extra-tough to handle the Gs. Something to recall when making explosive ingress or egress.

Without warning, her inner-ear flipped as *Phoenix* rotated — impossible to see, save for dozens of sling-encased marines bobbing and bouncing in unison. Then came the thrust, like a blow from a giant fist, smashing everyone sideways, the slings pulling tighter the more they stretched to hold them off Midships' steel walls. Trace fought for breath, suit sensors detecting stress and pumping more air, her augments working double-time to keep oxygenated blood in her brain and assist her diaphragm with simple things like breathing.

Her vision blackened, then straightened out as she squinted, resolving her assault schematic with determination. Doing assault pre-prep at nine-Gs wasn't recommended, and mostly she did it to keep focused on something other than her utter helplessness. Weightless once more, then a brief spin and an even harder hammer blow then the one previous. Five seconds later, it stopped.

"*Gimme a break, Captain,*" someone muttered.

"*That was a stealth ship,*" Dale announced. "*Didn't see it on first scan, he was right in our way.*"

"*Dead fucker now,*" Jalawi said nonchalantly. Trace wasn't the only one with access to the bridge-feed — all of her lieutenants got it too. "*He's a ball of mist.*"

"*Kick ass, Cap,*" said someone else. It was good that someone gave them a few updates on what was happening, but Trace left it to her Lieutenants.

But she'd barely begun her post-jump analysis of plans she'd already gone over a hundred times alone and with her platoon commanders when Erik's voice interrupted on coms. *"All hands, this is the Captain. As you may have felt, we have encountered and destroyed one hostile vessel upon entry. The rest are running, it looks like they're heading for jump. I'm expecting more trouble very shortly, but for the moment we look clear. Course correction burn will commence in twenty and go for eighty-five, marines will board their shuttles after that. Captain out."*

"Phoenix Company," said Trace as soon as he'd finished, "prepare to de-sling and board. Stay sharp, we are still expecting trouble."

It bothered her that the reeh were running. All this time in reeh space, sneaking the back-systems to avoid detection, hearing of all the fearsome things the reeh had done... and now they ran away? Well, no question this small defensive force knew itself outmatched, especially when they saw how easily *Phoenix* had dealt with their outlying picket. If it was just Resistance vessels, no doubt they'd have stayed, but the Resistance had nothing in the class of *Phoenix* or *Makimakala*. The reeh were reputed to be frighteningly smart, and they'd know something else was up. Besides, nowhere was it written that every homicidal species would be belligerently suicidal on the individual scale. Even sard would run away sometimes.

It was still bothering her as *Phoenix*'s new burn shoved them all down once more — just a gentle six-Gs this time, positioning for approach on the splicer rather than manoeuvring in anticipation of space combat. Trace flipped to her command channel.

"Guys, we're progressing on the assumption that it's a trap," Trace told her Lieutenants. "I don't like how they're running away. This is supposed to be a key facility for them, they wouldn't abandon it so easily."

"Unless the furry critters been telling us lies," Dale said skeptically.

"That's possible too," said Trace. "Something's not right here. We're going to treat this entire place as a biohazard, remember what we saw on Mylor Station. Reeh are real nasty work, be prepared for anything."

There were mutters of affirmation in reply. They'd find ways to pass her warning onto their platoons themselves. Better that they did — it wasn't good for the Company Commander to creep everyone out with warnings about spooky aliens and past massacres. Jalawi at least would find a way to do it with a joke, and she had no idea if the warning would even translate well to Garudan Platoon. Better leave it to Karajin.

Thrust cut and she hit the release, Command Squad exiting their slings in good order to hit the Berth One airlock, opening with the assistance of several spacers just now tucking their own slings away to the nearby wall. Trace went straight through both open doors, first in as the commander should always be, down the chute and into dorsal arrival in the shuttle, a quick turn and push brought her down to main level behind the sealed cockpit door. Her command post was just to one side, seats just a series of exposed frames in full armour, unlocked and open like steel jaws. She slid in, felt the steel teeth bite about her armour as she pulled them tight, then yanked the straps as the flow of marines came past behind her unabated.

New graphics unfolded on her visor display as she interfaced with PH-1's cockpit. *"Hello, Major,"* came Hausler's cool drawl from up front, no doubt seeing she was locked in. *"How you doing back there?"*

"Command Squad is locked in, Lieutenant," Trace replied, seeing that confirmed on tacnet, new graphics segmenting, overlaying and vanishing as she blinked on them. "Bravo is loading, give us another thirty and we'll be all secure."

"I copy that Major, thirty seconds and we are good to go anytime. Window is in seventy, Captain says we will dump at window-minus-five, the Captain is the god of small margins."

Trace watched her platoons load against the running clock. They were all-in on this one, *Makimakala* too. Marine commanders argued about the proper times and utility of a reserve, but all warships were expecting to be mobile and reserves weren't any use if they could not be held in proximity to the target. *Makimakala* was all-in as well, another 240 karasai, plus fifty corbi off the *Neelo*. Those were lightly armoured and little use outside the station, but inside would be useful primarily as scouts and intelligence on their enemy.

She'd briefed extensively with the Resistance marine commander, and found him comfortably realistic about his own unit's capabilities. About the reeh, he'd been far less comforting, predicting a strong station defence force of at least a thousand reeh warriors. Reeh had many kinds, genetically and biomechanically augmented to the point that they interfaced physically rather than neurally with their suits. Their armour sounded advanced enough, but human and tavalai armour had advances Trace didn't think had made it out past the Croma Wall, while reeh armour looked vulnerable to human or tavalai weapons. She'd been breaching stations for nearly ten years of her life, while the war between reeh and croma had been more or less static for several centuries now, with marine units on both sides operating at a far lower tempo.

Garudan Platoon was the last loaded, twenty seconds slower than the others. That was predictable. Coms put Erik's voice in her ear. *"Trace, we've got many firebase targets, they're putting out ghost rounds, could be shadow emplacements on that station and Scan says probably launch bases on the lunar surface. Their ships may be running but the entry's going to be hot."*

"Trace copies," she said, feeling the old reflexes kicking in, the adrenaline surging, hairs prickling on her skin. "Keep it clear for us."

"You bet," said Erik, distracted and disconnecting as he returned to the dozen other things he was doing.

The count-to-window reached zero and *Phoenix* lurched into hyperspace, dumping V and pulsing back out dramatically more slowly. *"Here we go,"* said Hausler immediately as they emerged. *"V match, we're good."*

Crash, as the grapples unlocked, and PH-1 pushed clear of the carrier, spinning fast to point its tail at the target, then the kick of a hard burn. *Phoenix* could have brought them in at a more sedate V, but pilots preferred a mismatch to allow them manoeuvring space on approach. Nearly a thousand Ks out, *Phoenix* had dropped all five shuttles on the target's lap. As always, the lightly-armed AT-7 was the greatest concern — they'd flown it pilotless before with Styx steering from *Phoenix*, but reeh jamming threatened to make that impossible. Lieutenant Commander Dufresne was piloting AT-7 alone, her front seat empty, but the civilian shuttle had few enough weapons and additional systems that everyone figured she should manage.

Trace's readout said nine minutes. Pilot chatter was full of jargon and targeting numbers — the splicer had multiple firebases, all presently being destroyed by the two carriers' ordnance. But the ghost rounds Erik had mentioned were now activating — delayed propulsion warheads that lay silent and undetected until you were nearly on top of them. Some of those accelerations were in the twenty-G range, which point-blank could give a pilot just seconds to react.

Ensign Yun pumped out intercept rounds that turned sharp corners having been launched away from their targets, then a decoy launched thirty seconds ago picked up a pursuer, both accelerating away. "Five at thirty-seven point five," Yun said coolly, tracking and tagging, Trace seeing new points illuminating on Scan. "Incoming at eighty-five, get me an angle."

"Angle," Hausler confirmed, kicking the shuttle's nose that way. Yun put another round that way. "Jersey, watch two at forty-one, max accel now."

"I'm on it," came Lieutenant Jersey's reply from PH-3. "Tify, pull it wide by another thirty, let's make them stretch."

"Wide thirty," Tif confirmed from PH-4. As Phoenix and Makimakala roared ahead through the space they were taking, defensive batteries blasting everything that tried to hide.

"That's a big, fat bitch," Dale remarked from PH-3's hold, looking at the station. Trace could only agree. It was a Class-B on the Spiral's scale, holding anything up to five million people if fully loaded. In the war, attacking something this size with this few marines and little intelligence would have been suicide — the tavalai, kaal or sard could have had the place packed full of marines' defensive systems, and would crush them once they got inside.

Here she had a big advantage she hadn't had during the war, namely that no one cared what mess she made of the station in the process. She wasn't here to capture it, she didn't have a conga-line of Admirals breathing down her neck demanding a place to dock their ships, and an even longer conga-line of planet-bound Generals demanding a place from which to operate an orderly base of supply to troops on the ground. The Resistance said they knew where the computer cores were that contained the data they were looking for, and so long as those cores survived she could trash the rest of it if she chose.

With what appeared to be total surrounding space superiority, she didn't even have to do that herself — she could simply direct *Phoenix* to put a round into whatever parts of the station she found objectionable and have them surgically removed without having to commit any marines to the job. In the war, of course, such stations were frequently occupied by many thousands of tavalai, kaal or sard civilians... and occasionally with humans, if the facility was one they weren't so much taking as taking back. In the latter case, of course, external fire-support was out of the question, and with tavalai, too, efforts were made to keep civvie casualties to a minimum. With kaal, less effort was made, and with sard, none at all, repaying kind with kind what had been done to humans. None of the spacers thought it likely that there could be more than a handful of non-combatant reeh on the splicer, given its remoteness from major systems, and the lack of observed transport traffic. But even were it full to the brim with reeh, Trace knew she was going to have no problem whatsoever blasting them all to fire and vacuum. There *were* no innocent reeh, that much was clear. Just the latest edition of Spiral's nastiest, recurring zero-sum game — us or them.

"*Couple of shuttles running to the lunar surface,*" Yun observed on her scan. "*No other local traffic, place is locked down.*"

Plan was that Phoenix Company would get the bridge, while Makimakala's karasai would take the adjoining research facilities. The corbi weren't entirely sure from where the computer cores could best be retrieved, but they were pretty sure that control of both the station bridge and research command would be required. From there a defensible perimeter would be established, counter-attacks destroyed with direct and indirect fire, the cores recovered with all other relevant data, followed by extraction.

Marine commanders on assault missions were different from any other branch of the services in that during this initial phase there was actually very little to do. Trace was concentrating so hard she nearly bled sweat, but unlike in some units where the commander would constantly give directions to initiate different parts of the plan, marine units worked on a timer. Things would happen on the time that they'd been planned to happen, and if all went well there was little Trace needed to do or say until something went wrong. During the war that had meant most missions soon required her to do and say plenty.

She watched tacnet as *Phoenix* and *Makimakala*'s shuttles wove through the diminishing resistance of ghost rounds, saw PH-4 put missiles through an on-station gun platform that was destroyed before it could fire, heard the pilots talking each other through the approach phase, trusting the carriers and now the enveloping wave of Resistance ships to keep the perimeter clear and watch for proximity horizon threats. Target fixes were obtained on various parts of the huge station rim, a tight cluster of entry-points, then armour-piercing missiles fired.

"Good hits," said Yun. *"We have good penetration. Bravo Platoon, stand by for insertion."*

"Bravo copies," said Lieutenant Alomaim from one row back. Trace's Command Squad was attached to Bravo, so PH-1's directions would be aimed at him. From a manoeuvring standpoint Alomaim was in charge of everything she did, as Command Squad could not safely function as an autonomous unit without risking the Company Commander's safety. It suited Trace fine — she had the entire Company to command, and leading Bravo's platoon-sized manoeuvres as well would be a needless distraction.

Gs pressed them down as Hausler kicked thrust to take them in. Trace watched the others approaching, and the timing looked good — GR-1, the Garudan Platoon shuttle, was heading for the top of the station rim and the hole one of its missiles had made there. Sounds from the surrounding hold faded as PH-1 sucked air back into its vents, reducing the hold to a near-vacuum.

"Thrust check," Alomaim reminded them all. *"Watch your departure*

vectors. Remember this is one-G-plus rotation, watch your wingman and don't crowd the lanes, plenty of room for everyone."

"*Approach looks clear,*" Yun announced, watching that fast-moving wall of steel for surprises, like airlock-mounted gun emplacements. "*No movement, clear for now.*"

A quarter-turn around the station wheel, a little more than three kilometres away, *Makimakala*'s karasai were approaching just the same, vacating more station rim to space. Trace barely noticed as the seat racks lifted up and away, marines holding steady by ceiling harnesses that also retracted as they released and fired attitude thrusters. The hold filled with eruptions of white mist, then a glance showed Trace the line behind her was leaving and she kicked, careful not to catch her shoulder-mounted rifle and straight out the back into empty space.

It was always a shock, from claustrophobia to agoraphobia, cramped steel confines replaced by the black, endless nothing, the steel rim of the station fast approaching like a giant steel cliff, the wheel curving overhead with that impossible clarity that only objects in space attained, free from atmospheric interference. This croma-built monstrosity was nearly ten kilometres side to side, and the far rim was as distant as the middle suburbs of a small city from someone standing in the center. The whole thing spun, slowly at first glance, but with alarming speed at the approaching rim... and already Third Squad were off chasing the hole that PH-1 had blasted, thrust burning out behind as rifles were unslung.

Trace kept Staff Sergeant Kono on her immediate side — her wingman for this flight, kicking thrust in turn to follow the long stream of marines heading for the hole. A year ago it wouldn't have been possible, marine suit thrusters not generating sufficient power to chase a one-G rotation through open space. But lately *Phoenix* was not the only vehicle to have undergone power upgrades. The enormous face of the orbited moon filled an entire region of space to one side, dull grey and cratered, unremarkable yet still striking after so long indoors.

Marines ahead vanished into the hole, then terse conversation as they blasted doors beyond to expand the entry vacuum. Trace angled up the power, suit navcomp showing her the course to be followed, curving and running away from her like the winding rails of a roller-coaster. For a moment it required her full attention, tacnet forgotten as she pushed thrust down, feet extended, still carrying PH-1's forward momentum as her downward thrust fought the station's spin, equalising even now at one-point-two centrifugal gravities...

"*Bravo is in and clear,*" said Alomaim from up ahead. The ragged hole got abruptly larger, big enough to have taken two station floors, exposed innards of three rooms and a hallway past a lot of torn steel, drifting wires and something liquid that clung and dribbled from her visor as she flew through a cloud of it. Kono chose the upper room and she crashed in beside him, cutting thrust and sliding on her knees into a hard collision with the far wall. Then up and stomping through debris, through the ruin of the blast door that had failed to protect the hallway beyond from shrapnel. That hall had lost another decompression door to a big charge, and Trace ducked through that gaping hole, unclipping her rifle for the first time then detouring to stand behind the door's remains as other marines ran past, and coms were filled with terse shouts and calls of corridors and rooms behind cleared.

"*Delta is in and clear,*" came Crozier's voice from several hundred metres along.

"*Alpha is in and clear,*" Dale echoed from nearer the bottom of the station rim.

"*Command is in and clear,*" Trace spoke into the first clear air. "*Looks good, hit your objectives.*"

"*Charlie is in and clear,*" said Jalawi, several hundred metres up-spin with the task of guarding their flanks that way.

And then, a few seconds later, "*Garudan is in and clear,*" said Karajin from the top of the rim. Good old tavalai, last again.

"Styx, situation report?" Trace demanded, holding position with Command Squad strung up the corridor, and now Bravo Heavy Squad thundering past, bristling with chain guns, rocket launchers and ammo racks.

"Hello Major," said Styx from back on *Phoenix*. *"I have solid uplinks to the station controls, reeh coms encryption is advanced but within my capabilities, corbi advice on their technological base appears accurate for now. Portions of the station appear segregated, it will take me a while to penetrate each segment, I can only see the parts that you are advancing through at the moment."*

"I copy that Styx, give me an update as soon as you've anything to report." All large station facilities of any technological base had wireless communications. Styx had access to all of *Phoenix*'s marines, and probably to *Makimakala*'s too, however unauthorised by the tavalai. Through them, modulations to coms encryption that would typically have taken a human technician months, Styx could perform almost instantaneously through various AI voodoo means that Trace did not pretend to understand. Now that they were inside, Styx was her best source of intelligence, theoretically being able to scout the station's systems from the inside and access everything down to door controls and security cameras. However advanced reeh technology, reeh were organic, and no organic species held a candle to hacksaw AIs in computers and communications.

Coms chatter and advancing dots on tacnet informed her that Bravo was blasting more doors open, her suit sensors registering a brief rush of air as it passed, then out into the void. When breached, automated station doors and seals would descend to make the interior airtight once more. Phoenix Company were now breaching those, expanding the airless entry void until, inevitably, they bypassed seals not yet descended, which some damage control system would close behind them and enable pressure to be restored. Should the local damage control neglect to do that, the attackers would simply keep blasting doors until the entire station was vacuum — a situation that hurt less-prepared defenders worse than attackers.

"Let's go," she told Kono, and walked single-file down the corridor. "I want a secure hold not far from the entry point."

Tacnet showed her the progress of each platoon, spreading methodically through this part of the station rim, thus far reporting no resistance. No anything, in fact. Glimpses of various helmet cams showed her the predictable corridors of a croma-built station, more high-ceilings than any human built station, lots of wall-mounted public access displays, all long-dead and blank. Her suit's heavy footsteps thudded in her helmet, the sound coming through the suit alone in the absence of air. The corridors had no lights, but the suits gave off multi-spectrum low-vis which the cameras turned into sharp wrap-around vision, clearer than normal light.

"Nothing so far, Major," Dale said grimly. "Power readings indicate the whole thing's functional, a lot of these minor systems are dead though. Doesn't look like anyone's here."

"Not in this sector no," Trace confirmed, turning after Kono into a larger hall. Ahead, a large blast door had been pulverised by a missile — the blast had been inaudible earlier. "We know the station's occupied, we're expecting a trap, keep your eyes peeled."

On point, Zale ducked through the blast door hole, then Kono, then Trace. A coms light blinked from Djojana Naki. Trace answered. "This is Major Thakur, go ahead."

"Major," spoke the translator. "We've found something. Check the visual." Trace opened the vision feed... and tried to make sense of what she was looking at, while walking.

It was a vast space — the dock, kept large by traditional Spiral design, and the desire of most species to have one part of the station that wasn't cramped with low ceilings. This dock looked about five storeys high... but it was hard to tell because the interior was full of trees. Trace had never seen anything like it on a space station before. There were interior gardens on plenty of stations, small aesthetic parks with water features where kids could play and couples stroll, and hydroponics bays filled with wheat and cabbages. But this looked like a jungle.

"This is a biological research facility," Trace told Naki. "Get the corbi to look at it, I'll bet those are all species from Rando."

"Major, I agree. I will ask the corbi for observations. You have seen nothing like this on your side?"

"Standard space station design so far. Naki, if this is a trap they'll draw us right in first, make us commit. Be ready."

"You also."

Ahead, a large elevator shaft had been forced open where tacnet told her that marines from Bravo Platoon had gone down it. *"Good avenues of access, close to the entrypoint,"* Kono explained, and Trace nodded, gave her finger a twirl to indicate he should set up. Command Squad fanned out for cover, and Trace leaned her propulsion/thruster combo against the wall by the elevator, and paid full attention to her screens.

"Major," came Jalawi's voice. *"Charlie in position on your left, we're fanned across, setting up sentries now, looks like good coverage."*

Trace was less convinced — roughly 400 marines wasn't a lot to cover an entire station rim on this scale. "Don't spread too thin or you'll get picked off. Karajin, situation?"

"Good progress Major," said the tavalai. *"Clear on top, pressure systems reestablishing. Second Unit saw something strange though, we have vision."*

"Show me."

Vision appeared, with the shaky movement of helmet-cam, a karasai striding and panning to get a good look. It was a hallway, but different from the hallways here. This one had large containers built into the walls, vertical cylinders, fed by thick tubes through the walls. Something about it set her nerves on edge... those tubes looked organic. Creepy, as though some malignant growth were gestating in the walls, fed by nutrients. As the camera drew level she saw that the tubes' glass front had slid back, leaving them empty. A few dripped, recently wet, puddles spreading on the steel floor. The empty tubes were filled with some sort of sticky mass, like a tangle of alien seaweed that clung to a karasai's gun muzzle when he prodded it.

"You've got atmospheric pressure there?" Trace asked.

"Yes Major, it returned just now."

"Right, feed that vision to the corbi and to *Phoenix* and *Makimakala*, get an opinion, we want to know what we're walking into. That looks like recent activity, whatever it is."

"Yes Major."

The hardest part of the assault's entry-phase was over, and Trace was stationary, being just a commander and not a fighter. But this part was always the most challenging overall — when things began to happen that were not in anyone's plan, requiring improvisation. Individual platoon commanders could improvise fine, but it had to be coordinated or else they'd all soon be working at odds. Performing that coordination was Trace's job, and if she got this bit wrong she could set up monstrous failures to come.

"*Major,*" came Crozier, "*we've got a big thoroughfare hall up the middle here, takes us straight to the bridge. We're spreading wide with caution, looks clear though.*"

"Copy JC, Garudan's coming down above you, Bravo's got your rear and Delta's got your belly..." A light flashed from Styx, and she opened the channel. "Go Styx."

"*Major, I have a clear fix on the age of this station. I'm confident it is no older than four hundred human years.*"

Trace frowned. "That's not what we were told."

"*No, the Resistance told us it was over a thousand years old, before the croma retreated from this region of space. These computer systems reveal their chronological history quite clearly, they were commissioned less than four hundred years ago and were completely new at that time. There was no station refit, though all systems have been considerably upgraded since and reconfigured by reeh occupation.*"

Trace could not immediately see why it mattered. But interrupting the Marine Commander in mid-assault with irrelevant information would be stupid. Styx was not stupid. "Wait... you mean the reeh didn't completely strip and install their own systems when they took over the station? Just upgraded?"

"*Yes Major,*" said Styx. "*These systems were built by croma. While this region of space was under complete reeh occupation and control.*"

Trace's eyes widened. "Built by Croma'Rai? The ruling clan?"

"*We are directly adjoining Croma'Rai space and some construction clues appear to indicate it, yes. Captain Debogande did remark that this looked far more like a trading station than the industrial hub we were told it had been. My records indicate that in the vicinity of four hundred years ago, Croma'Rai experienced an extremely large economic down-*"

turn. There was civil conflict with other clans, their rulership was questioned."

"They traded with the fucking reeh!" Trace exclaimed. Swearing wasn't like her, but discovery was a different sort of adrenaline. Styx was right, this changed everything. "They must have built stations out here where no one other than Croma'Rai would find them to conduct the trade."

"None of us are experts in croma politics," Styx ventured, *"but trading with the croma's worst enemy to preserve one's own power would seem scandalous in the extreme. It would suggest the croma leadership is bought and paid for by the reeh."*

"And that's why Croma'Dokran were so damn pleased to send us out here," Trace growled as it came clear to her, heart thumping in that unpleasant way that even she found difficult to control. "Shit. Tell Erik immediately, we're being used to play politics between croma factions, Croma'Dokran aren't allowed out this way but they must have guessed."

"Such a joint venture between reeh and Croma'Rai will be well monitored by all sides in case of discovery," Styx added. *"Chances are significant that our time here is limited."*

* * *

"Captains, this is no concern," said the harried-sounding corbi fleet commander. *"We did not know the station's origin, and it does not matter. The assault is progressing well, we will shortly have the data we seek."*

Phoenix hurtled at orbital-plus velocity about the moon, burning at two-Gs to climb for high geostationary near the neutral-gravity Lagrange point between the moon and its gas giant parent. The corbi fleet of five ships were staying in close proximity to the station's orbit, but as the big beasts of the assault, *Phoenix* and *Makimakala* needed a higher overwatch position from which they could respond quickly to further incoming threats.

Erik did not see an advantage in pressing the corbi commander for more information. "Coms, get me *Makimakala*, lasercom."

"Aye Captain, *Makimakala* online."

"*Captain Debogande,*" came Pram's voice without prompting. "*I am almost certain this is a trap. This does indeed appear to be a splicer facility, but initial defences were weak. If one of those retreating reeh ships short-jumped, they could have a small fleet waiting in the outer system ready to jump in on us. Now the corbi say they did not know the station's origin, which is impossible given Rando was invaded a thousand years ago and they've been roaming this space close to the Croma Wall for all that time and know all its major stations and facilities...*"

"I know," Erik said tightly, resisting the impulse to glance nervously at Scan as though Geish might have missed something. "I'm nearly as worried about the croma as the reeh — if we're right about Croma'Rai, they'll do anything to cover this up. They don't like anyone meeting with Dega's group, they don't like Croma'Dokran hosting Dega's group, this might give them the excuse to get rid of both us and Dega together."

On one small corner of his multiple screens he read a condensed version of Trace's feed, the gist of which was good progress and no resistance. All of Phoenix Company's marines together only made the smallest footprint on one small section of that enormous station's rim. In the Triumvirate War it had taken thousands of marines to clear stations this size. An entire enemy division could be hiding in there and no one would know about it.

"*Given that it is definitely a splicer,*" Pram continued, "*I feel that we have no choice but to continue. Your drysine has made no progress in locating the computer cores?*"

"She's analysing schematics now. She says the command center appears extremely well protected from infiltration, and that reeh network and computer tech is the most advanced she's seen in an organic species..."

"*Captain!*" Styx interrupted loudly with no coms etiquette at all. "*I am blocked out of the station system, you must withdraw all forces immediately!*" She sounded quite alarmed. "*Captain Pram, you as well, we have been deceived as to reeh capabilities.*"

A red light from Operations was blinking furiously. "Hang on Styx... Operations, go ahead."

"Captain, I have lost contact with Phoenix Company." It was Ensign Blunt, and he sounded alarmed as well. *"All contact just dropped out, we're com-linked off Styx's new systems, we're modulating encryptions and frequencies... it shouldn't be possible."*

"Styx," said Erik, "can you reestablish coms?"

"Captain," said the former drysine fleet commander. *"Pay attention to what I am telling you. I am, for the moment, technologically outmatched. I am locked out, my access routines are inoperative, I believe I can find a solution but it will require more time than we have strategically available."*

Erik needed time to process it... but time, in combat operations, was the rarest gift of all. Styx was technologically outmatched? No organic species could rival hacksaw AIs, least of all one as advanced as Styx... what the hell was going on? Or was Styx somehow behind all this herself — she'd never wanted to come on this mission, she'd staged her mini-mutiny on Defiance to create a new drysine force allied to Gesul and the rising House Harmony... was this some sort of continuation? Had she been planning to betray *Phoenix*'s mission here from the beginning? But what could it gain her, given that she was in as little hurry to commit suicide as any of them, and that *Phoenix* still represented great strategic value to her?

"We're getting out!" Erik commanded, spinning *Phoenix* on its axis and engaging hard thrust. "Nav, course back to station!"

"On it Captain!" Erik didn't need Kaspowitz to do something as simple as fly back, but no captain ran a hostile vector without multiple escape routes at his fingertips.

"Coms and Operations, get me contact with Phoenix Company, don't care how! *Makimakala*, *Phoenix* is reacquiring our people and leaving, suggest you do the same."

"Makimakala is doing the same, Phoenix," Pram replied. On Scan, Erik could see the big tavalai carrier following, coloured red for rapid acceleration, a scroll of numbers as projected course changed. *"I suggest we keep an eye on those corbi ships. They won't like us leaving, they've risked a lot to get us here."*

"I agree. If necessary we'll share targets."

"Makimakala copies."

"ETA to station seven minutes fourteen on projected course," Kaspowitz declared. "Recommend we don't rush it Captain, the marines can't withdraw that fast anyway."

"Agreed," said Erik, burning at four Gs to align them on the new course, chasing the station as it zoomed beyond the moon's horizon.

"Captain," said Geish, "Corbi warship *Zelta* is engaging a cross-orbital fire-platform we didn't see earlier. Data to your screen."

"I see it." The fire-platforms on the way in had been entirely geo-stationary — Scan wouldn't see something in lower orbit over the horizon, though what possible use it would be with the moon making a fire-shadow that covered half the sky... "Operations, anything from the shuttles?"

"Captain, Lieutenant Hausler says he can't reach them either, none of the pilots can. He's going to swing by and see if he can do a visual."

See if anyone was close enough to a window to establish laser-com with, that meant. Jamming was always a thing on station assaults, but with Styx running coms, and all that technology massively boosted, it wasn't something they'd expected to deal with much. Usually Styx could infiltrate a station's systems so thoroughly she could find the source of jamming and eliminate it without a shot fired.

"Styx, give me a preliminary theory on how the reeh are blocking you. Organic species should not be able to do that, correct?"

"Yes Captain. What little contact I can establish indicates an AI-level sophistication in communications technology at least, and likely thus the computing power that underlies it. In all my years of observation, organic brains are incapable of sufficiently grasping the concepts involved to evolve them indigenously. My supposition — we know that the alo have joined forces with the deepynines, we know that drysines joined forces with parren and others during and after the Drysine/Deepynine War. We also know that the reeh incorporate other organic species by absorbing and manipulating their genetic structure. Perhaps the reeh have previously absorbed an

AI race, perhaps survivors from one of the Spiral's other AI wars. There were many, the Drysine/Deepynine War was just the last."

"Well that's just great," Erik muttered. "Lucky they never acquired drysine-level ship propulsion or they'd have occupied all the Spiral by now."

Surely this, unknown to most of the Spiral, was the most dangerous species in the galaxy. And now *Phoenix*, on behalf of all humanity, had just picked a fight with it.

"Cocky, get back to the entry point and see if you can get lasercom on a shuttle," Trace told Corporal Rael by her suit lasercom, fixed on Rael's faceplate by automatic. "Take Second Section, no one moves alone in here."

"Aye Major," said Rael, running back the way they'd come. It had to be lasercom here even face-to-face, Command Squad's hallway was still vacuum so raising the faceplate to yell at someone wasn't an option. Zale and Rolonde joined him, rifles unslung and watching cross-corridors warily as they passed. An advantage of operating in an airless station segment was that any uninvited guests transitioning from a pressurised segment would announce their presence by blasting their own region to vacuum, sending a brief gust of air rushing down the halls. Trace's instruments hadn't seen it yet, but no one was taking any chances.

"We'll get the bridge without coms," Kono said confidently from his cover position up the corridor, lasercom on her with his back turned. *"We've done it before."*

"We're getting out," Trace decided. "This thing's got trap written all over it. The others will send marines to observation points, we'll contact the shuttles and use them to move the message."

It was going to take a whole lot of time, though. Another person might have ground her teeth. Kono was right — everyone knew how to operate without coms. It happened only rarely on assaults that defenders would jam everyone so badly that they couldn't talk — jamming affected everyone, attackers and defenders, and defenders usually needed to talk most since they were the only ones who didn't know what the gameplan was, and had to react and coordinate to events on the spot.

But sometimes tavalai had dug in and defended in fixed sectors, abandoning the mobility that was never their strongpoint anyway, and jammed with white fury that turned every transmission to static. Marines were trained to coordinate in small groups and improvise, with autonomy given to noncoms and even privates that tavalai, with their preferences for large formations, did not share. On those occasions, jamming had made little difference to the final outcome. Somehow, to Trace, this felt quite different.

"*You don't want to at least make a try for the bridge?*" Kono pressed. Trace heard the uncertainty in the big Staff Sergeant's voice. They'd come a long way to do this. The stakes back home were impossibly large. They'd all sworn to risk everything if it meant finding a counter to the biotech threat.

"We're all humanity's got out here, Giddy," she told him. "If we go down, that's it. Never force a bad position — back out, regroup and find another..."

Something hit her. It wasn't physical, it wasn't anything her brain could find a way to process. Awareness dimmed, reality turned dreamlike, like that time she'd been knocked unconscious in Kulina training and awoken on the gym mats blinking at the ceiling and dimly recalling that she'd been doing something else just now...

Wake up. Focus. Breathe, calm the racing heart, find your bearings. Her vision strained clear, visor pressed against a steel wall. She was on one knee, fallen forward against the wall, and she strained to get her legs moving under her. That triggered her muscles and her heart rate, followed by a wave of nausea and splitting head pain, then blackness.

But she knew that feeling, it was the suit's meds pumping sedative through the inhaler, reading nausea levels and calculating that she was about to throw up. Throwing up in suits was dangerous, particularly when on the verge of unconsciousness — suit automated systems were a marvel of technology, as advanced as anything that flung warships through hyperspace, but they were not great at keeping airways clear and preventing a marine from choking in her own vomit. Sedative kicked in first, mostly to stop the nausea, with unconsciousness a frequent side effect...

Trace had once been waterboarded in Kulina training, lain on her back with a wet cloth over her face, and had water poured over it. Breathing had become a desperate effort, creating the sensation of drowning, leading to panic and that thing which was the enemy of Kulina above all else — the loss of self-control. Most trainees hadn't lasted more than a few minutes and had sat up soon enough, being free to do that whenever they chose. Trace had held for twenty minutes, and the session had only stopped because the instructor feared she might have passed out, having slowed her heart so low through meditation that her requirement for oxygen dropped to negligible. Every other trainee had sworn they were going to do that too, but somewhere between doing it in theory, and doing it in practice, panic had interceded.

She reached for that control now, focusing inward, spreading her attention to every limb, directing awareness away from the suffocating blanket of nausea and consciousness disfunction that had descended. Thought returned, and she was still leaning face-first against the wall. Moving again would only trigger nausea and more suit sedative, not wanting her throwing up while borderline conscious.

She needed a trigger, something to cut through the gloom. Something real, to distract the brain's focus from whatever was happening to it. Like telling a wounded marine to focus on the pain for the simple reason that it would keep him from drifting toward the deadly comfort of sleep. 'Pain is your friend!' the drill instructors would roar at them in the Academy, while officer candidates had slithered through mud and wire on bruised limbs and aching muscles. 'Pain tells you that you're not dead yet!'

Pain. She changed her vision's focus, and blinked on coms. Feedback screeches were not hard to arrange — marines had them programmed into coms so that someone could send a burst if she were too badly injured to talk, helping tacnet to find her location from that burst. Trace blinked the screech wide to all channels, amped the volume to max and sent.

It sounded awful, an eardrum blast at a nasty pitch, but even as one ear went partially deaf, consciousness returned hard, giving her the time to extend the blast and put onto permanent loop despite her visor system's protests.

"Phoenix Company!" she managed to yell hoarsely over that network-wide transmission. "Status report NOW!"

She levered herself to her feet, hand-walking up the wall until she achieved something approaching upright. Kono was still standing, but suits did that, locked out so the occupant could sit on the saddle and save his legs, even asleep. His arm moved now, involuntarily to his face as a man might reach for his forehead after waking from a hard night out.

"Major I'm here!" Visor com told her it was Jalawi talking, barely audible over the horrid screech. *"I was... I was out, I don't know..."*

"Everyone fucking listen!" Trace shouted, and her stomach nearly lurched. She couldn't lose it now... but she was more awake, and the suit didn't mind her losing her lunch while conscious. "It's some kind of attack, it's a mind-weapon, it knocks you unconscious! Pain works against it, so hurt yourself and focus on that!"

But of course they were all in armour, so inflicting physical pain was impossible past the suit, and opening the suit in a vacuum was fatal.

"We are full withdrawal now!" she continued. "Everyone get the fuck out, pull back to your entry points and cover the extraction! We're not being jammed any longer, whatever this thing is it doesn't work with jamming so at least we can talk! And watch for ambush, if I

were them I'd hit us real fucking hard right about now, so blast everything that isn't us and take no chances!"

She flipped channels, tacnet reestablishing in a flurry of blue dots
and station schematics, showing her Charlie, Alpha, Garudan,
Delta... *"Major, is that you?"*

It sounded like Ensign Blunt on Operations, but either the signal
remained unclear, or the fragmented mess that remained of her
hearing was giving out, like someone standing too close to the big
speakers at a rock concert. "Blunt, this is the Major! Blunt?"

"Hello Major," cut in Styx's voice. *"There is still some directional
jamming, but I can make modulations that Phoenix crew cannot. I understand the reeh are deploying a mind control weapon?"*

Something else was exploding on coms, Charlie Platoon shooting
at something, red dots appearing where previously tacnet showed
her only blue. "Jalawi, report!"

"Under attack Major," said Jalawi, each syllable extra agony on her
ears. *"Can't say what... sorry, can't talk, gotta move."* Everyone was struggling with nausea and dizziness. For her Lieutenants, so accustomed
to effortless multi-tasking, basic things like talking and moving at the
same time became a struggle.

"Fighting withdrawal, people!" Trace called on the main channel,
having no doubt the attacks would now spread. No coms light from
Makimakala, and no tacnet feed either, just silence. Another flip.
"Styx, can you reach Djojana Naki?"

*"I will try. Major, Phoenix is on approach, I am informing the Captain
of your status."*

There was shooting now from Garudan Platoon, Karajin on
Command Channel calmly telling his tavalai to maintain formation
and back out firing. Then Bravo Platoon joined in, barely fifty metres
ahead of her current position. Then Alpha, and now she could hear
Dale bellowing, *"I am UF Marine Corps and I love the pain! Come and get
some pain, fuckers!"* In the background, the heavy thudthudthud! of
Koshaims blowing holes in things.

"Major," said Styx, her voice eerily calm against that blood

curdling racket. *"I have established relayed coms with Makimakala's Company. It's not good."*

Coms switched, to what tacnet told her was Djojana Naki's link. "Djojana Naki? Naki, can you hear me?" For a moment, there was static. Then the static flickered, fading in and out, like ground glimpsed from an airplane through holes in the passing cloud. The flickers grew, and in the gaps in between the static, Trace could hear screaming. And sobbing. She'd rarely heard such a thing from human marines. She'd never known tavalai were capable. "Naki! Naki, it's Thakur, situation?"

What came back was untranslated Togiri, static-broken and faded. It was Naki, and he was crying. Trace recalled the tavalai man, stoic and powerful, unflinching and biologically incapable of panic as humans understood it. And now her blood ran cold.

"Naki!" she barked, in her best command voice to hide the growing desperation. "Karasai Commander, get a fucking grip and report!"

In the background, more shooting, this time coming from Naki's coms. More screaming, and cries for help. Like they were all dying over there.

"Styx, inform *Makimakala* that..." Boom, she felt the shockwave more than heard it, Kono's rifle firing directly alongside her at something down the corridor. Trace threw herself rolling against the opposite wall, the best cover from anything in that spot Kono was shooting at. Something hit the wall above them, a blast and shower of shrapnel, then fire hit Kono's aimpoint from the reverse side, ripping that corner to spinning metal chunks. That was Zale and Rolonde coming back, Trace saw from tacnet, and now advancing on the spot they'd plastered while Kono shouted for them to watch their flanks.

"Inform *Makimakala*," Trace resumed her previous instruction, "that their karasai are in terminal trouble and must be extracted immediately!"

"I have already done so, Major."

We came in here with no reserves, Trace thought desperately.

There was no one to extract the committed units *with*. Everyone currently in had to get out on their own.

She'd changed facing without even thinking, guarding Kono's back while he faced their previous target. Her visor saw movement before she did, a flash of yellow on the screen where something was not static, and did not match tacnet's known locations for her marines. She fired just as it did, and rolled as something blew up on top of her, adding a short-termination grenade to more Koshaim fire, exploding ten metres down the corridor like a giant shotgun blast. Smoke filled the corridor, thick white like a wall and certainly about to be used to cover more movement. Trace abandoned subtlety to turn sideways and put a backrack missile into the corridor wall.

The blast was big enough to rattle her even at this range, white smoke whipped away by the blast, revealing an entire four metres of wall peeled like a banana, fires burning and liquids spurting, thankfully not flammable.

"*Major!*" Kono said with alarm, struggling to follow as she advanced on the wrecked corridor, and the dark figure sprawled on the intersection floor. She took the right wall to give Kono the left, edged the corner and received no fire, then crossed to look down at the fallen armour.

There were three of them, one here, two back in the corridor. The near one dripped. Not blood, it dripped with external fluids, like ooze. The blast had shredded it, limbs askew, bones showing. The faceplate was half gone, long like a snout. Within the exposed half was a mess, but enough remained intact to reveal lipless teeth, bared in a permanent snarl. Where the eye had been, synthetics shone like broken glass, embedded in the torn flesh and bone.

"*Reeh?*" Kono wondered.

Nothing in this place is what it was, Trace thought. Nor remains what it is. Reeh changed everything, a species in permanent, self-inflicted phase. "I don't think so," she forced herself to say above the pounding in her head and ears. "Something else. Garudan found cylinders filled with ooze." Indicating the wet armour. "Some kind of suspended animation, left here to ambush anyone who came along.

One of the reeh's slave-species, maybe." Conditioned, like the poor bloody animals in the corbi's lab, to sacrifice their lives like mindless drones upon the sayso of their masters. Twisted and augmented into something barely recognisable from what they'd once been. "I didn't read any local decompressions, these must have already been in here with us."

"*There will be more,*" said Kono, and Trace's sensors spiked, a warning rush of oxygen and nitrogen.

"Breach ahead!" she announced. "Guard this passage, I've got the next one." She ran forward, seeing Zale running up behind, tacnet now informing her that Bravo's first fallbacks were approaching entry point beneath her.

"*Major, we're pulling back,*" said Jalawi. "*Got numbers going past us, heading for your up-spin flank.*"

"Copy Skeeta," said Trace, extending a view-probe from the suit's shoulder to peer around the L-junction corner ahead, back to the wall. Running, black-armoured figures loped up the corridor like alien hunting dogs. Processing that, tacnet added three new red dots for all to see. "I got dots."

"*Got your dots, Major,*" said Kono. "*Jess, with me, we're pushing.*" Trace withdrew the probe, stepping back from the edge in anticipation that the slight movement might draw fire. It did, and she covered as everything around her blew up... but marine armour required more than concussion and shrapnel to take serious damage, and she stepped back into the obscuring mess of smoke and torn corridor walls, and picked targets. She fired, and a single round took the first enemy's head in a spray of armour and brains. The others dove and covered, but her second round caught the next in the shoulder, removing an arm and spinning him like a top. The third returned fire, and she stepped back just enough as rapid rounds hammered around her, one glancing her arm. The long burst paused — all machineguns short of the big shuttle-mounted monsters needed a cool-down, one reason she preferred rifles. She stepped back out, aligned for his firing position against the near wall, and blew him four metres down the hall. The *other* reason marines preferred rifles.

"Major," came Alomaim's voice from somewhere on the levels beneath her, *"we are two minutes from full extraction. Several casualties, we see two types of enemy, one light recon, one heavy, most of the casualties have been to heavies."*

"Copy Bravo," said Trace. "Command has your top flank, get out and we'll be right behind you." These she'd killed would be the light recon enemies. God knew what the heavies looked like.

* * *

"MULTIPLE CONTACTS!" Geish announced with the hard calm of a Scan Officer who'd done this many times before. "Fifty-five by one-sixty, energy high, Scan reads five contacts and more emerging! No IDs, direction and energy signature suggests croma! Increase last estimate to seven contacts, more coming!"

"Alright, here we go," Erik said calmly. This time the calm was no pretence. Real combat scenarios required so much concentration that they shut down the emotional part of his brain almost entirely. Right now, that was welcome. "My guess is that they knew Croma'Dokran would send us this way, they'll have been watching us since we visited Do'Ran and talked to Sho'mo'ra and Dega. Kaspo, get me an ETA."

"Captain," said Kaspowitz, furiously juggling figures and trajectories, "they're on the far side of the planet but they're carrying serious combat V... based on projected deceleration profiles I'm estimating thirteen minutes."

"Captain," said Sasalaka, "I am not sure we can retrieve our marines in time. Should we abandon recovery and take a counter-offensive course?"

"The croma are going to be dealing with reeh ships very shortly," said Erik, juggling twenty variables in his head on approach to station with a particularly hard eye on *Makimakala's* hard run, approaching at almost panic-velocity.

"Reeh ships, Captain?" Sasalaka sounded confused.

"Captain," Jiri cut in, "*Makimakala's* shuttles are deviating from recovery positions. I'm reading karasai suits in free space away from station at slingshot speed. Looks like they jumped."

"Sir, I'm hearing snatches from *Makimakala*'s karasai." Lieutenant Shilu sounded alarmed. "They're fucked up, sir. I'm hearing tavalai panicking."

"Query *Makimakala*, ask if they require assistance." Styx had informed them of the mind-assault weapon. Erik had read several classified reports during the Triumvirate War about one side or another attempting to develop such a thing, but they'd never amounted to anything. If tavalai were panicking, it would be the weapon that did it.

"Sir," Sasalaka attempted again, "if we are to plot a counter-course to those incoming croma, we must do it immediately or we will not be in a position to..."

"Multiple new contacts!" Geish cut her off. "Heading twenty-three by three-ten, reading three, no four, new vessels, energy high, heading and signature indicate reeh ships! Two more, make that six ships, looks like a formation jump... sir, that's coming from exactly where those reeh who ran off earlier jumped out."

"They short-jumped it like we thought," Erik confirmed, watching the two opposing forces gather size, the croma just coming past the gas giant now, the reeh out further in the deep system. New ships were added all the time, Geish not bothering to call them out now that everyone could see. "They're going to engage head-on, that should buy us time to get our marines. Arms, defensive plot. Nav, get me the best several courses out of here based on reeh movements, we are presuming reeh remain the primary enemy for now. Coms, hail the croma, inform them we are retrieving marines and will be ready to assist them in combat action immediately following."

"Aye Captain!" came the unified reply, each post leaping to follow orders. Declaring solidarity with the croma was dangerous. These would be Croma'Rai, the only croma forces allowed by croma law to access this adjacent region of reeh space beyond the wall. Croma'Rai had an obvious interest in making sure that *Phoenix* did not report what they'd seen here to anyone else. Erik simply did not know enough about croma politics or psychology to know how likely croma would be to fire on them and make sure of it, but he was strategist enough to know that a force of reeh ships this large was going to take some effort, and the croma commander would be stupid to reject his assistance, or *Makimakala*'s. Croma were a complicated race with many qualities, but stupidity did not appear to be one of them.

* * *

"Major, Final Departure is three minutes fourteen, I'm putting that on tac-feed right now." If Erik was telling her directly, with all else he had to worry about on the bridge, things were serious. She held back from the corner as rounds snapped and sparked off the steel, the corridor beyond the entry-point room filled with vacuum smoke that refused to dissipate in the lack of aircurrents.

"Major copies, Captain," Trace replied, barely hearing her own voice past her shredded hearing. "We'll be there." Tacnet showed her Garudan were already out — being slowest to advance had meant fastest to leave. Alpha were also out and heading to rendezvous. On their up-spin flank, Charlie were in final loading, while Delta were still struggling, having covered Alpha's departure, but looked good to make it. The problem, suddenly, was Bravo, where activity had intensified, attacks encircling and striking their flanks with the apparent objective of slowing their withdrawal.

Alomaim had several wounded, and manoeuvring them down corridors under fire required enough manpower for covering fire to prevent them getting mown down. That meant holding more marines back from departure than he'd have liked, and several times when he'd pulled people off a defensive position to reinforce those harried with wounded, new attacks hit precisely the spot they'd left. It was a calculated encirclement, and it informed Trace's judgement utterly as to what they were facing. Calculated to do what, she hadn't yet figured.

Final Departure meant the time when all the shuttles would leave for rendezvous. *Phoenix* calculated that from the position of each shuttle, and knowledge of how long it would take to recover each one. Trace did not know what enemy forces were closing on them, but she knew they were numerous and fast. *Phoenix* was hiding in the fire-shadow of the station and betting that incoming reeh ships would not risk hitting station to get her. But if she waited too long, *Phoenix* would lose the final window of opportunity to run and accelerate from this moon's gravity-well before getting overrun and destroyed by reeh vessels still carrying high-V from jump. Anyone not in the shuttle by Final Departure would be left behind.

Tacnet showed Bravo Heavy Second coming down an adjoining corridor, then several thundered through, ducking across Trace's corridor, missile tubes scorched, extra-heavy armour cratered in places. Private Webber came last, retreating down his corridor with bursts of his last mini-gun ammo, then a final burst down Trace's corridor before dashing across, his gun's forward armour shield looking as though it had been chewed by a dozen giant rodents.

"*Bingo ammo!*" Webber called from the face of the huge entry hole PH-1's missile had made on entry.

"*Get out!*" Alomaim told them from somewhere the next level down. "*If you've got no ammo you're just taking up space!*"

"*Major, we gotta go,*" Kono told her through gritted teeth from up the corridor, expending an airburst missile to shred part of the corridor that wasn't already shredded like some work of modern art.

"Everybody out!" Trace yelled. "Command Squad, get out, I'm right behind you!" As Rael ducked past her, then Rolonde, an arm limp where a detonation had damaged the armour but left her vitals unchanged. Heavy Squad were leaping from the torn steel of the entry hole, then falling out of sight. PH-1 was somewhere below, holding position beneath the rotating hole with a one-G thrust, leaving it up to jumping marines to use their own thrust and hit the dorsal hatch, since the rear entry was hazardous with the main engines active. Several marines with damaged thrusters had not been able to make the manoeuvre, and had followed procedure by heading to stationary rendezvous, decelerating and congregating with others until the last shuttle to leave picked them up. Right now, that would be AT-7, currently recovering Delta Platoon... meaning that Lieutenant Commander Dufresne would have to depart thirty seconds before Final Departure to grab the stragglers before *Phoenix* came howling in demanding pickup.

"Giddy, pull it back, we're leaving," Trace told the Staff Sergeant, firing several of her final remaining rounds into the smoke-haze devastation. Kono pumped out several more of his own, then ducked out and shuffled backward, flattening himself sideways on one knee as rounds somehow streaked his way from the metallic ruin ahead. Trace fired her last grenade, missiles long since gone. "Giddy, you gotta move!"

"Major, watch...!" yelled Zale on her left near where the corridor was severed by the entry hole. A blast blinded her visor, coms dissolving as Zale's blue tacnet dot vanished. The blast rocked her, visor-vision streaked white... then suddenly her head was spinning once more. Damn coms were damaged, she realised — the shrieking in her ears dimmed, the splitting pain went with it, and now the nausea was back. And looming behind Kono as he picked himself off the floor in mid-corridor was a dark shape, floating as though unfolding from the very walls.

"Giddy!" Trace yelled, advancing with rifle pounding.

* * *

SCAN LOOKED AWFUL. There were fifteen reeh ships coming at them fast, and the station's current orbital trajectory was heading straight toward them. It was better than traversing the directly-facing surface of the moon, blocked from retreat by the moon's mass, but not by much. Coming at them fast the other way were twelve croma warships, each side making an obvious course directly for the other, spreading across the moon's orbital track.

"PH-3 is aboard," came the call from Operations, as the third shuttle docked, in addition to PH-4 and GR-1. That left AT-7 and PH-1, AT-7 just now burning toward the four straggler marines without sufficient thrust to reach their shuttles previously.

"PH-1 and AT-7, hit transmitted marks on our outbound track, we'll pick you up on the way, coordinates on your board."

"AT-7 copies," came Dufresne's cool reply, flying that underpowered shuttle solo in this mess and making it look easy.

A small delay from Hausler. Then, *"Phoenix, we have a delay."*

"If I delay we're all dead," Erik said with certainty. "If you miss rendezvous I will leave you behind."

"PH-1 copies." Scan showed Erik that he was already well inside minimum response parameters by the Fleet manual. It was only *Phoenix*'s recent upgrades that allowed him to leave this late — with the old *Phoenix*, he should have left fifty seconds ago. Even this revised Final Departure was pushing it right to the edge, and some of those reeh ships had surely fired already in anticipation of the course he wanted to take. He'd now have no choice but to head directly into that oncoming fire, and hope that *Phoenix*'s massive new combat computers weren't slightly off in their calculations.

"Croma lead has fired," Jiri announced, continuing the running chatter the command crew maintained across the bridge, keeping each other informed as much as their Captain.

"*Makimakala* is leaving," said Geish, and Erik saw that big friendly dot on his display accelerate away at a bone-crushing ten-Gs. "All shuttles are aboard." Shilu had said he thought casualties were bad, but at least they'd gotten all their shuttles back. *Phoenix* had no guarantee of that yet. What the hell are you up to, Hausler?

"PH-1 is moving hard," Geish added, with evident relief. "ETA to rendezvous line fifteen seconds."

Ops was on the line again. *"Captain, I'm reading some distress on PH-1, I can't make it out..."*

"Get off my line," Erik said brusquely, and the connection cut — he was matching outbound trajectories with the line PH-1 and AT-7 were burning toward, and had no time for unspecified problems he couldn't do anything about.

"Definite incoming!" said Jiri, as ordnance flashed red on Erik's near-screen, coming in plenty fast and adjusting course all the way.

"Arms Two, get on it, here we go."

"On it, Captain," said Bree Harris, aligning defensive guns.

The timer hit zero and Erik hit thrust, a fast build up to seven-Gs, then a cut as they came racing up quickly on AT-7. Dufresne matched V in several fast moves and slammed into *Phoenix*'s grapples. Hausler followed, and Harris was already firing, counter-fire racing out on intercept...

"Captain," came Hausler's voice on coms, hard and tense in a way that had little to do with the Gs, *"you better go hard Gs as soon as we're aboard, I got a minor mutiny on board, someone's trying to smash into the cockpit."*

For a brief moment, Erik's brain could not process that. What the hell could cause...? And then he realised. Oh no.

"Come in hard, we're leaving." PH-1 hit the grapples of Berth One as hard as combat docking procedures allowed, and Erik blasted everyone back in their seats. Past the gasping attempts to breathe, and his laser-focus on the screens, he was dimly aware of heavy-G tears streaking his temples.

Harris's defensive intercepts erupted across near-screens... damn that was close. High-V incoming rounds couldn't dodge much, and their inbounds course was predictable, but if Harris missed one at that speed, they wouldn't even feel pain. Corrig was returning fire at Arms One now, and Erik put them into a slow roll to give all gun batteries a sighting, pumping heavy offensive rounds into the course of those incoming reeh ships.

Ahead, *Makimakala* was doing the same thing, obstructing one entire side of her space... Erik was now focused on the approaching gravity slope horizon, the minimum distance from this moon where he could engage *Phoenix*'s new jump engines. At this acceleration it was only going to take him another seventy-three seconds. *Makimakala*, despite her head start, was going to take another hundred and six.

"Dammit!" snarled Harris, no mean feat on silent uplinks at ten-Gs, and Erik saw her outgoing fire abruptly reorient onto something nearer. *"Ghost rounds, hang on!"* It meant incoming rounds that near-scan hadn't seen until the last moment. Erik thought *Phoenix*'s scan-

ning technology was so advanced now that nothing could evade it. Evidently the reeh thought differently.

A string of explosions lit up scan to one side, defensive rounds detonating and spreading several seconds short of impact, creating a spray of projectiles covering several football fields each. High V incoming rounds were hitting that spray so hard they turned to vapour in microseconds. Further ahead, *Makimakala*'s side lit up with defensive detonations as the tavalai's shield caught their own incoming fire alarmingly late.

"I don't trust what I'm seeing, Captain," came Harris's urgent analysis. *"We better get out of here."*

"Styx," Erik formulated, *"can you recalibrate Scan to detect those ghost rounds?"*

"No, Captain. It is impossible within the time restrictions currently upon us."

With no time to go through Shilu, Erik blinked on Coms himself and opened a link to *Makimakala*. *"Pramodenium, we have ghost rounds inbound, twenty seconds to V boost."*

"I was hoping your scan would see them better than ours," came Captain Pram's reply, somehow managing to sound as though uttered through gritted teeth rather than formulated by brain-implant software. *"Do not hold back for us, doubling fire volume will not help us against rounds we can't see."*

"Phoenix copies, Makimakala. Once we have V we will move to cover your boost."

The threshold approached, then the jump engines gave him a fading, reluctant, then finally a firm green. Erik's thumbs hit the jump buttons the engines cycled with a lurch deep in his stomach as hyperspace briefly rose up and engulfed them... and then they were out and racing, incoming rounds, *Makimakala* and the moon and station all racing away behind at tens of thousands of kilometres per hour faster.

Erik cut thrust down to five-Gs to gasps of relief across the bridge. He opened a link to Operations, speaking now with his real voice. "Ops, get me general coms in all PH-1, hold and cockpit."

"Hold and cockpit... go ahead Captain."

"This is the Captain. Mutineers will be executed by me personally. Someone take command in there or there will be corpses." And disconnected. Trace would have liked that, he thought bleakly.

"*Makimakala's* hit!" Jiri shouted. "Glancing blow, she's sideways, thrust's out!" Behind and beyond that, reeh and croma ships were passing at high-V. Several bright flashes marked detonations, ships vanishing in miniature supernovas.

"Captain," Kaspowitz growled, just in case he was stupid enough to think of it, "we can't reverse and help them, we'll be sitting ducks in the U-turn."

Erik watched helplessly, heart pounding, as *Makimakala's* defensive batteries engulfed yet more incoming rounds, some desperately close, others further away. Scan read them ten seconds from jump threshold at full acceleration... but acceleration was now cut. And ignited once more as Pram desperately got the engine relit, the big carrier wobbling on damaged controls to try and get the nose pointed the right way once more. Nine seconds, eight, seven...

Erik's coms crackled, broken with static as the tavalai made contact. *"Erik,"* said Pram, with sadness in his voice. *"I'm sorry."* As the tavalai's scan showed him something that could not be dodged.

A flash, much brighter than anything else. For several seconds, framed by the moon's grim silhouette, *Makimakala* burned brighter than any sun, then vanished.

22

Trace dreamed of restraints, and smothering, suffocating. She dreamed of G forces, and the dark, claustrophobic holds where trapped things died, never again to see the sun. At some point she came to realise that the dreams were not dreams, for she was not asleep, nor entirely awake. Something bad had happened, and somehow it had failed to kill her. Likely it had not severely wounded her either, for despite the haze of half-consciousness she felt neither pain nor the numbness of painkilling drugs.

Recalling exactly what had happened was too hard. Recalling her own name was difficult enough. She only knew that she was locked in some ship's hold, and it was moving. She had the vague sensation of being watched, and things moving nearby, beyond immediate sight. How that could be, with G-forces pushing her now into an uncomfortable compression, she did not know. She only knew that they were taking her someplace, whoever 'they' were, and things would likely get enormously worse once she got there.

* * *

PHOENIX BURST out of hyperspace at a croma frontier system whose name Erik barely registered, accompanied before and aft by croma warships that had swung about after their first run on the reeh ships, and beaten a fast retreat. Their communication to *Phoenix* had been to the effect of 'come with us if you want to live'. More reeh ships had continued to jump in behind the first wave, some of them apparently faster and more manoeuvrable than the first group, and Erik had realised that all reeh space would be onto them now. Previously they'd been running ahead of the reeh's awareness of their presence in reeh space, but now that awareness had finally caught up. Besides which, Croma'Rai ships had been threatening to fire on *Phoenix* if he declined their invitation, and Erik had no wish to inflame human-croma relations any worse than he already had by firing back.

The remaining corbi Resistance ships had been brought back similarly at gunpoint, emerging some minutes after *Phoenix* and short two of their number where reeh warheads had proven more mobile. *Phoenix's* bridge crew had run through damage assessment (several high-V fragments in the crew-cylinder outer shields for minor breaches only) and analysis of their new location's defences, which like all croma systems were enormous beyond the point of overkill. Their lead escort then beamed them coordinates for the next jump, on the other end of an inevitable three-day cruise across this large system to the far side before the gravity slope would let them jump again in the required direction.

There followed a five-G course correction burn for nine minutes that had seemed to go on forever, operational chatter continuing, but everyone's mind on something else entirely. At the end of it, Erik ordered shift-change, and second-shift command crew came in to replace the first, all save Lieutenant Commander Dufresne who was going to take a while working her way back from AT-7's berth at Midships. Erik did not envy her the shift to come.

He caught sight of Kaspowitz, helping DeMarchi into the Nav chair while Erik did the same with Draper. Kaspo's eyes were red and wet. Draper studiously examined his screens, not meeting Erik's eyes.

Shilu looked stunned, as though he couldn't entirely comprehend what had just happened. Jiri just looked confused, as though wanting to ask if somehow they were going to go back and get Major Thakur. No one could believe that she was gone. Sasalaka remained in her chair, waiting for Dufresne to arrive and replace her, and looking just as blank and stunned but for what Erik suspected was a different reason again.

Erik was saved the walk down the trunk corridor by virtue of his quarters being five steps from the captain's chair. He closed the door, AR glasses on and activating a channel to Lieutenant Dale. Five seconds later and there was still no answer. Ten seconds. Then, finally, a connection.

"Lieutenant Dale, report," Erik snapped, making no attempt to hide his displeasure.

"I'm sorting it out, Captain," came Dale's harried reply. *"Give me a minute."* A glance at the locator display showed that all of Phoenix Company's marines were still in Midships, making no attempt to move back to the cylinder.

"You get them back in Assembly now, Lieutenant, or I'll come down and do it myself."

"Recommend strongly against that, Captain. It's not a good time."

"Refusal to comply with orders in wartime is mutiny, Lieutenant!" Erik snarled. "The penalty for mutiny is death! Pull your weapon on whoever is the cause of the problem and remind them!"

"Aye Captain." Disconnect. Erik didn't believe him. He knew exactly what was going on in Midships — various marines thought their officers had betrayed Trace in leaving her behind, probably up to and including Erik. Erik knew how big a problem that was, thus his entirely serious order to Dale. He knew the rage and pain they'd be feeling, because he felt it himself.

Trace *was* Phoenix, far more than he was. Suli had been too. Pantillo had been most of all. Now they were all gone, and it was only him left in charge — the son of a rich family, assuredly only picked for his political lineage whatever his other skills. Him, and a lost tavalai, and a couple of kids a few years removed from driving work-experience freighters around backwater systems where nothing ever happened. And their pet killer AI who probably had no clue why everyone was so upset.

For a moment, he stared at himself in the small mirror. Remembered Trace giving him an unexpected hug when he'd been dealing with Lisbeth's captivity. She'd acquired that knack of changing his mood at will, for better or worse. And now when he most needed one of her electric jolts to his system, she wasn't here to give it. For a brief moment, he felt like he was fifteen years old, struggling with a maths test and thinking that surely all his hopes of Fleet greatness were just the fantasy dreaming of a naive kid stupid enough to think he belonged in the same company as those great men and women.

A light blinked on his glasses — Lieutenant Lassa, now in the Coms chair. "Go ahead, Lieutenant."

"Captain, I have a transmission from the corbi. It's Tiga, she put out a feeler transmission and I intercepted it with Styx's encryption. Tiga wants to speak without her own people hearing."

"Put her through."

"Aye Captain."

Erik sat on his bunk while waiting for the call to come through. Then realised that he'd been sitting for too many hours already, and stood back up, hands against the wall and stretching his calves and hamstrings. The link established.

"Hello, Captain?" It was a translator approximation of Tiga's voice, timid, concerned and more than a little scared.

"Hello Tiga, it's the Captain."

"Captain, I'll talk quickly, I might not have much time and they'll not want me talking. I'm not sure they knew the splicer was a trap... the corbi captains I mean. The Resistance. But they knew a lot they didn't tell you, I couldn't talk because... well, because..."

"Because you hadn't figured out whose side you were on yet," Erik said tiredly. Lord he just wanted this day to be over. No, he wanted this entire adventure to never have happened. To have gone back to human space with *Lien Wang* and talked things over with Fleet command. Probably they'd have at least discharged him, and then he'd be looking for another line of work. Civilian space wouldn't have had him, and didn't interest him anyway. Maybe consulting. Law. Politics. Charity and advocacy for returned veterans. Anything other than this constant loss and pain.

"*Captain, they were sincere in wanting what the Splicer has. They want it desperately, they'll risk a huge amount to get it. I mean, they couldn't afford to lose those two ships they lost either. What's happening on Rando is awful.*"

"I know."

"*I don't think you do. Even I didn't know, and I thought I knew everything about it. It's made the Resistance out here... it's made them mean.*"

Good god, kid, Erik wanted to shout at her. What the hell did you think a war of attrition and mass slaughter did to people? But he couldn't, because when he'd been that age, he hadn't known either. Not really.

"*The Splicer is set up like a trap,*" Tiga continued in a small voice. "*The Resistance didn't really tell you that. You're supposed to land on it. Reeh like to capture people. They... they can get information from them, then. That's a strength of the reeh — they're clever, they like to collect intelligence before they do anything. They want people to land on the Splicer, they're that confident they can catch them when they do. That's why so many of us got away... I mean, I'm no commander, but I thought they could have hurt us far worse if they'd tried.*"

Erik couldn't argue with that, either. "Go on," he said.

"*They thought maybe Phoenix and Makimakala could break through anyway and capture the computer cores. It really is there, it's a real research base, it would have been amazing data on all the stuff you're after. But hard to get.*

"*Anyway, there's a couple of Resistance ships in the outer system. Ones you weren't told about. The captains said the reeh will want human prisoners, they always go after the most high ranking so they learn the best intel. I'm sorry about Major Thakur but they're pretty sure she's still alive. The reeh will take her back to the nearest planetside Splicer for analysis — the Rando Splicer is much larger than the Zondi Splicer, and much more well defended. Reeh space is divided into sector commands, the sector commander has jurisdiction over all activity, so he won't want to ship her off to some other Splicer or he'll lose her from his jurisdiction…"*

"Wait," said Erik, with sudden, burning hope. "You're saying she's alive, and the Resistance know where she is?"

"It's a guess," Tiga conceded, *"but it's a very good guess. They've been doing this a very long time, they know the reeh. They've sent word back to Rando Resistance that she's on her way. Now don't get your hopes up, but Rando Resistance has assets that they occasionally expend on high value targets… extraordinary assets. I can't say any more, but Rando Resistance capabilities are actually pretty amazing and they've been wanting to get some high-ranking alien military powers down there for a long time to see what's going on. The only hope they've got is that someone else might see that it's in their interest too to come and save them. To save Rando, and to save the corbi. Before we're all extinct."*

Wow, thought Erik. But then, the corbi had been all too good at this before — telling them exactly what they wanted to hear, to lure them into traps that were to benefit corbi far more than humans. "Look, Tiga…"

"I'm sorry, Captain. I can't say anymore… I'd be in serious trouble if they found out I told you this much. I just hope Styx's encryption is as good as I'm told." Click, and she was gone.

LISBETH WALKED upon the great ceremonial platform, clad in her best blue coat, as two assistants held an ornamental umbrella above her head. Semaya was with her, and Timoshene, plus several Domesh guards. Light rain fell, pattering off the umbrella, and making a gentle hiss upon the landing pad, and the concentric circles of meditating House Harmony parren.

The formation was a wayan — a symbol of peace and virtue that held significance to parren of all houses. It had appeared on banners presiding over the truce of Five Houses that had followed the great civil war of seven thousand years ago, and at many other occasions as well. Now a hundred of the Harmony contingent to Shonedene maintained a vigil here, with their leader, in this formation above the great fork in the rivers that overlooked the ancient House Fortitude capital.

Lisbeth could see as she walked how completely vulnerable they all were, to snipers from the higher buildings, to aircraft, to anyone in the city with hostile intent. But today beneath the misting rain, the great city was quiet, the skies echoing to only the faintest hum of airtraffic, the usually crowded streets now empty as parren remained indoors.

It was a statement of peace, from the ruler of House Harmony to all the parren of House Fortitude. Fortitude was rocked, shaken to its core. In this system alone, parren were phasing in their millions. Beyond this system, as starships carried video and other news to neighbouring systems and across all parren space, likely hundreds of millions more. Perhaps billions. Not all were phasing to House Harmony — the flux was not so convenient for the politically disruptive as that. But mostly they were abandoning House Fortitude en masse as the suppositions that had once underpinned the greatest of parren houses for the last twenty five thousand years fled away.

Shonedene city ground to a halt. There shoveren psychologist-priests tried desperately to attend to the psychologically afflicted, gathering them in great arenas as the hospitals and health centres overflowed. There was little medical threat, most symptoms went little beyond loss of appetite and general mental confusion, accompanied by between two-to-ten days of bed rest. But the flux was a spiritual thing for parren, to be witnessed by the shoveren and blessed in the passing. Now the shoveren were overworked, rushing to attend to those in need, helped in the logistics by every able-bodied parren available. It was a colossal emergency, but not a life-threatening one. Or not yet.

Gesul's advisors had urged him to abandon Shonedene immediately, and head for safe Harmony space. Sordashan and his immediate circle remained strong, and could order retribution against those who had caused this calamitous upheaval. House Fortitude's majority would now likely fold, and House Harmony, should the flux prove fortuitous, would emerge as the dominant house of the parren, with Gesul their supreme leader. Return to Harmony space and prepare forces, Gesul's advisors begged. This isn't over yet, and the fading Fortitude behemoth could yet strike, and seek revenge on the man whose conniving had most plainly laid them low.

Instead Gesul had gathered his entourage here, and sat in vigil upon this most visible location, arrayed in a symbol of peace. House Harmony would seek no advantage now. House Harmony would not gather forces, thus triggering a Fortitude response and potentially a catastrophic conflict to follow. House Harmony would wait, in silent meditation, until the great forces of the flux had played themselves out. In the meantime, should any Fortitude parren wish retribution, Harmony's great leader would not retaliate or defend himself, but would simply sit and allow the universe to pass its judgement.

Upon seeing Gesul's response, Lisbeth had heard, the rate of phasing within the Fortitude population had accelerated. It was a kind and statesmanlike gesture, but like everything else Gesul did, it was not without thought or design. Harmony's prestige among non-Harmony parren increased, and while such things could not always direct the flow of the flux, there seemed little doubt that Harmony's share of the newly phased would only grow.

Lisbeth reached the pad opposite Gesul and was gestured to take her seat before him. She did, folding the hem of her robe while sitting crosslegged. Gesul disdained the umbrella carriers, and Lisbeth did the same with her own, shooing them away. She pulled her hood far enough back from her brow to see him clearly — dark-cloaked and comfortable in his pose as Lisbeth would never be, wrists rested upon his knees.

"I hear that you have been out visiting," said Gesul.

"Yes," said Lisbeth. "I went to the Larsa ceremonial grounds. Fortitude officials were kind enough to provide an escort. There were sixty thousand parren there, they told me. It looked like at least that many. All in various states of distress, the entire grounds were covered in tents and flags, it was an endless sea of people. But hygiene seemed good, I'm not entirely sure how they managed it. Parren logistical capabilities are amazing."

"The Larsa grounds are only a fraction," said Gesul. He paused as another advisor stooped to whisper in his ear, then receive a reply and leave. "My reports tell me the Jusica are planning a full count of the numbers as soon as this present wave has ceased. It could take a hundred days."

It was still incredible, Lisbeth thought, that any institution could conduct a credible census of all parren space to determine which house held the greatest numbers in just a hundred days. But regimented parren organisation went all the way down, through direct lines of command at the very highest levels to the smallest farmer on the most unremarkable lands on scantly-populated worlds. All parren had someone to report to, at a moment's notice, and corruption in that system was, from a human perspective, astonishingly low. Parren would assassinate each other in power-games, but to lie about census numbers to the Jusica was as unthinkable to most as to disobey the command of their rightful ruler.

"I have asked much of you, Lisbeth Debogande," said Gesul. "It has come to my attention in readings that it is human custom to thank another for such deeds. I thank you, for your efforts."

Lisbeth smiled. "There is no need, Gesul-sa. You treated me as parren, and honoured me with the opportunity to serve you. I am humbled."

"Yet you wish to ask me questions all the same," said Gesul, with that faint humour of his. "In your human way."

"This disharmony is also the human way," Lisbeth agreed in kind. "I feel that you suspected Hiro's doubts. Why did you allow him to accompany us, and why do you now show him such mercy?"

Gesul took a deep breath, a heave of cloaked shoulders as he gazed up at the enormous administrative buildings of House Fortitude, ascending the cliff walls opposite. "The simple answer would be that Hiro Uno is the closest I have come to a direct conduit to human government. For all your most excellent qualities, Lisbeth Debogande, you cannot grant me trusted influence and access with the highest levels of human government."

Lisbeth nodded in concession. "You are correct, Gesul-sa. I feel they will listen to me, given the uniqueness of my position. But they are unlikely to completely trust me, given my family's situation. Hiro Uno remains a trusted and loyal agent, so yes, they are more likely to believe his word if given."

"But mostly, I'm afraid, this may be an unexplainable parren thing. There was a convergence of loyalties, within your team and those closest to you here. Liala was essential, you understand her and her kind in ways that perhaps the average parren cannot, and then with Hiro, and one of my best in Timoshene, I sensed... emergent possibilities. It is difficult to describe in terms a human might understand. Anilas, perhaps. The plays of Anilas are large with the possibilities of convergent loyalties and purposes. In hot fires, strong bonds and new purposes are forged."

"Alas, I've not had the time to see the plays of Anilas," Lisbeth said apologetically. "Your culture is so vast, Gesul-sa. Nothing would delight me more than to immerse myself in it for some period, during a quieter time."

"Ah yes," said Gesul, perhaps wistfully. "A quieter time." His sharp blue eyes fixed upon an approaching aide, who also bent to whisper something. Gesul merely nodded, and waved her on. "I have questions for you also, Lisbeth Debogande."

"Of course, Gesul-sa."

"My reports of the battle scene in the old deepynine city have returned. Scholars across parren space are now researching this lost chapter of history. What do you think they will find?"

"I would not wish to preempt their findings," said Lisbeth. "But parren history since the fall of Drakhil has been written by the enemies of House Harmony. All knowledge of the good in that period has been erased, and all record of the ill deeds from other houses with it. It looks to me as though the Fortitude leader at the time saw an opportunity to undermine House Harmony's drysine-alliance, and sent an invitation to the deepynines. The wonder is that the deepynines accepted... but there is so much knowledge here that has been lost. Centuries of events. Drysine/deepynine conflicts were complex, as are parren internal conflicts. We will have to wait to see what the scholars uncover."

"At the scene of your conflict," said Gesul. "Three Fortitude marines were killed, another four wounded. All three of those slain died from the fire of Dse Pa. Liala also fired rounds, yet from what we can ascertain, she hit nothing. Now, I find it unlikely that she is an incompetent warrior. Perhaps she was firing merely to dissuade her enemies, and was presented with no clear shots. I was wondering on your perspective?"

"I am unsure, Gesul-sa. Liala is not Styx. It is possible that she does not like to kill. I think that would be an unwise thing to presume, drysines have been much more moral than deepynines, but that has hardly made them pacifists. Liala is young, perhaps she is still figuring things out. But she is also Styx's daughter, and Styx is directly or indirectly responsible for the deaths of many millions, perhaps billions. Best that we do not forget."

Gesul thought about that for a moment, gazing at the buildings behind her. "And in my rapid rise to power," he said slowly. "Do you think that I am here the master of my own destiny? Or merely a puppet dancing to Styx's tune?"

Lisbeth took a deep breath. "I'm not sure that anyone has risen to power unassisted, Gesul-sa, among your people or mine. Styx certainly engineered this particular piece of fortune. But that does not mean she will continue to rule your destiny."

"I wonder," Gesul said solemnly. "She brought down Sordashan because she knew things of his house's history he would rather not see revealed. Perhaps next she will threaten to do the same to mine, if I do not act in ways that please her."

"And what will you do then, Gesul-sa?"

Gesul only smiled faintly, gazing into the misting rain.

* * *

ERIK STRODE into Assembly as the marines were putting their armour back into storage. The great, multi-storey space echoed with the thrum of many powerplants, the crashing of armoured footsteps, the whine of electric elevators carrying marines up to their higher levels, and the yell of voices. Erik had his cap on, which in Assembly constituted 'cover', and passing marines saluted with a whine of powered limbs, the only place on *Phoenix* they were required to. The salutes lacked enthusiasm, which was excusable given they were trying to get their armour stowed after an exhausting, upsetting and unsuccessful mission, and most ship command crew knew better than to bother them in Assembly at such times.

Erik left the AR glasses in his jacket pocket, whatever its advantage of showing him exactly who was who in passing armour. For this moment he wanted direct eye contact. He strode directly to an armour suit he recognised — Lieutenant Alomaim, faceplate raised, supervising the loading of various Bravo Platoon marines onto upbound elevators. Typically for Alomaim, the Lieutenant's serious face betrayed no surprise.

He saluted as Erik approached. "Captain."

"Lieutenant," Erik acknowledged, returning the salute. "Which marines were the direct cause of the problem on PH-1 during the evacuation?"

"Sir, the situation was confused. It's difficult to say."

"Lieutenant, obfuscate or otherwise refuse to comply with my direct order one more time and I will have you up on charges. Do you understand?"

Alomaim's eyes widened, just a little, and he straightened further within his armour, an audible whine-and-rattle of powered segments. From Alomaim, it was a lot. "Yes Captain. There were a number of them, sir. I judged Second Section the primary cause."

"Sergeant Neuman?"

"His privates took the Sergeant's protests as licence, sir. All were out of harness when *Phoenix*'s acceleration hit. Private Rajesh is in Medbay with a broken leg. Lance Corporal Kamov from First Squad received a concussion from Second Squad's unsecured armour after acceleration. Further damage was suffered by PH-1's interior, courtesy of that unsecured load at high G."

"And Lieutenant Dale's punishment?"

"Sir, to the best of my knowledge, no punishment has yet been handed down. I believe Lieutenant Dale judged the infraction as understandable under the circumstances."

"Get Sergeant Neuman over here immediately."

Alomaim turned, sighting past numerous armoured bodies moving, stowing weapons, racking armour on this 'deck' level, climbing from steamy interiors dripping sweat. "Sergeant Neuman!" he yelled above the racket. "Front and center!"

Neuman stomped over, still in full armour. That armour was scarred with the pockmarks and craters of smallarms fire, Erik noted. Lighter resistance than could have been the case, Tiga had said. The reeh hadn't been trying to trap and wipe them out. They'd been herding them, forcing a withdrawal, then chopping the head off the snake at the very last moment. And Trace, of course, had been one of the last to leave. Damn her reckless propriety. She'd been warned forever that it would one day get her in trouble, and now that it had, he couldn't even gloat.

Neuman snapped a salute, eyes cold. "Sergeant Neuman reporting *sir!*"

"You had a problem with my decision to leave the splicer, Sergeant?" Erik asked. Everything truly useful he'd learned about confrontations of military authority, he'd learned from Trace. Emotion had no place here. There was only command, cold, hard and final. And the knowledge that anyone breaching it, in combat, was likely to get them all killed. Against all things likely to get them killed, it was the commanding officer's duty to fight or die. Against his own people if necessary.

"*Did* you decide to leave her behind, sir?" Neuman asked, with plain hostility.

"You will not question the Captain's authority on this deck, Sergeant!" Alomaim roared in the Sergeant's face. Only now realising the gravity of the situation that Erik had inconveniently created in the middle of Assembly, instead of sweeping it all under the rug until everyone's tempers had cooled down. Erik knew the marines would have preferred that. He was in no mood. "You stow that right now or you will find yourself in some very serious shit!"

About Assembly, noise was fading. Marines were stopping, listening. Erik did not look around to judge reactions, expressions. But he could feel their attention, some cold, some as hostile as Neuman's, all pressing down upon him.

"Did you see what happened to *Makimakala*, Sergeant?" Erik asked him. "That's what happens to ships that wait. *Makimakala* had karasai trouble, couldn't get them all aboard in time. Captain Pram waited, longer than he should have. Were you advocating his course of action for *Phoenix*?" Erik gestured around. "For all of us?"

"There was not even an *attempt*, sir!" Neuman retorted. Alomaim's threats had made no evident impact on his state of mind. The Sergeant's face was red as much with emotion as the exertion of a ten-hour armoured deployment. "There was no warning, no attempt, nothing! We don't just leave people behind, Captain!"

"What kindergarten school of military training did you attend, Sergeant?" Erik snapped. "We leave people behind all the time. Failure to do so can result in the loss of the entire ship. You had no warning because you fucked up and lost situational awareness on the Major. And now in your grief and incompetence you want to kill all five hundred and sixty nine souls on the ship as compensation?"

Assembly on recovery was never silent, but the only sound now was humming machinery. Everyone else was deathly still. For a moment Erik thought Neuman might strike him. In powered armour, that would crush Erik's head like a melon. Furious tears spilled in Neuman's eyes. A year ago, Erik might have taken sympathy on him. Now he could only hear Trace's voice in the back of his mind, warning that soft and sympathetic younger man 'don't you fucking dare!' He could have explained the situation in full, how he was only aware that Trace was missing well after *Phoenix* had left. But marines rarely understood what the hell happened on the bridge, and besides, Trace's primary lesson to him about these situations was that apology was death.

"Trying to get this ship killed is the enemy's job," Erik continued, with a cold intensity he'd once not been capable of. "Are you a closet reeh, Sergeant? Are you working for the other side?" No reply from Neuman, just trembling grief and rage.

"Your Captain asked you a question, Sergeant!" Alomaim barked.

"No sir!" Furiously.

"You think I left the Major behind?" Erik asked him. Asked them all, as everyone could hear. "Fine. I did leave her behind. You know why? Because that's what she fucking taught me to do. I was soft when I first acquired this command. A soft emotional sap, like you, Sergeant. Difficult circumstances, tears rolling down your cheeks. You know what the Major would say? She'd say what she'd been telling me this last year non-stop — get your fucking act together and stop pissing on everything she ever stood for on this ship. She'd stare you in the face and tell you how disappointed she was to find that her marines have learned *nothing* from all those years she spent teaching them.

"You want to punish someone for leaving her behind? You want to refuse the take-hold and try smashing your way into the shuttle cockpit to delay departure? Fine, punish someone. Punish me." He reached to his jacket pocket, and pulled out his sidearm. Alomaim's eyes widened. Erik flipped the weapon and presented it to Neuman. "Punish me. You've shown you're insubordinate to rank, someone has to pay, and I'm the one who left the Major behind. Punish me."

Neuman just stared at the far wall, unable to even look at the pistol. Tears streaming down his cheeks. Erik held the pistol's grip in his face for a good ten seconds, then put it away. Deciding he'd pummelled the Sergeant enough, he turned on all of those watching.

"You think you knew her better than I did!" he said loudly. "Well you're wrong. I know because she's the only reason I'm qualified to command this ship. She made me what I am, and I will not allow this crew to disgrace her legacy, even if I have to bust all of your heads in person. Now get back to work."

It wasn't the most inspiring speech, but Trace had never been big on inspiring speeches. She just did things, precisely, and required that everyone follow her example. Talking was for actors, she'd told him more than once. Stop pretending. Be it.

And just when the marines were about to start moving again, figuring that was all the speech they were going to get, he added... "One more thing! Corbi Resistance thinks the Major is alive, and has been taken for study in the Rando Splicer. Resistance has what I heard described as 'extraordinary assets' in place on Rando that they very rarely use, but could conceivably be used to get the Major out of the reeh's hands. The Resistance want a military, high-ranking alien to see what the reeh are doing, in the hope of getting help from outside. So what we're going to do is work on the assumption that she's alive, and with the Resistance on Rando. We're going to deal with whatever bullshit the croma have lined up for us, and then, somehow, I have a feeling our next strategic target could be in the direction of Rando anyway. Carry on."

And into that stunned and increasingly hopeful silence, he said to Alomaim, "Tell Lieutenant Dale I need him immediately, right here."

"Captain," Alomaim nodded, and turned to Neuman. "Dismissed, Sergeant. I'll deal with you later." Neuman stared, baffled, trying to process that new information. Erik ignored him. "Lieutenant Dale, the Captain wants you yesterday. Assembly main floor, he's standing right in front of me."

Soon enough, Dale was pushing through the rejuvenated marines, all hubbub and activity, talking and exclaiming amongst each other with sudden hope. Dale looked tired and sweaty, unarmoured in black marine jumpsuit, AR glasses on as he monitored his units and sipped from a water bottle. He pulled on a rumpled cap as he approached, making himself fit for the salute that followed, which Erik returned.

"Captain."

"Lieutenant Dale." Erik gestured for Dale to come with him, with a last glance at Alomaim. "Thank you Lieutenant."

"Captain," said Alomaim, with more trepidation for things to come than Erik had seen from him before.

Dale walked with Erik, weaving through bodies and armour, heading for a side supply room, already full of racked Koshaim rifles and providing some privacy from the outside. "That last bit you said could have come first, Captain," Dale suggested. "Might have made the whole thing smoother."

It was cocky and patronising. Dale had warmed to Erik enormously since he'd become Captain, but he'd never entirely lost the attitude of the old warrior who'd seen and done it all, to the one who hadn't. Now more than ever, Erik was determined that it would stop.

"Lieutenant," he said, confronting the big, hard-faced man directly. "Why did you disregard my direct order regarding the disciplining of lower-ranking personnel?"

Dale gazed back, wary but not intimidated. "It's a marine company, Captain. You're not a marine."

"On this ship, the location and mobility of all ship personnel is the Captain's prerogative," Erik replied. "Your refusal to move marines from Midships to the cylinder upon my order could have cost many lives in the event of a sudden manoeuvre, and cost *Phoenix* a large portion of its marine capability, jeopardising all future missions in service of the survival of the human race. In the future, should you choose to disregard my direct and legitimate order on this ship again, I will see you court-martialled and executed. I will carry out the sentence myself, with this pistol right here." He patted his pocket. "Do you understand me, Lieutenant?"

Dale barely blinked. But there was a pause, of just a few seconds, as he weighed what it all meant. "I understand you, Captain," he said.

"Good," said Erik. "Now, you will require an immediate promotion to Major. You will hold the rank on the understanding that it is temporary, until we get Major Thakur back. Marine ceremonial procedures are your prerogative, Lieutenant. Get it done however you like, but get it done fast and properly. Do you understand?"

"Yes, Captain."

Erik nodded. "You're dismissed, Lieutenant."

"Aye, Captain." Dale saluted smartly, turned on his heel and left. Erik watched him go, thinking dark thoughts. He wondered what Trace would have made of it all. No more than B-minus, he thought, leaving the storage room and heading back through Assembly toward his quarters, then the gym, shower, a meal, various reviews, then bed. And he knew that it was his fate to suffer that she would always be riding him for something, whether she was present and alive, or not.

23

Trace blinked awake, with vague memories of having woken before. She recalled dark shadows, views outside a window, alien rooms and humanoid shapes at work. But now, something was different. Rapid descent, she could feel it in her stomach. The kind of descent that wasn't natural or controlled. Things shook with the vibration of too much speed, such as unaerodynamic shuttles, overpowered with deep space engines, sometimes achieved in thick atmosphere. But she could not hear much beyond a dull rumble.

She was mostly upright, strapped to something and held in place. Standard transportation position for prisoners, back-to-aft, positioned to take the Gs of thrust. To one side was a small window. Otherwise she might have been in a closet, surrounded by tubes attached to strange, alien equipment. The most lucid she'd been in recent memory, if she could even see all of these things, and analyse her situation. Prisoners were often transported sedated... probably what one of these tubes was for. Now the vehicle felt like it was falling, and the vibration suggested atmosphere.

Abruptly, the lights went out. Then reestablished, only much weaker, faint emergency light on a backup power source, blue where humans typically used red. The vibrations grew stronger. If there were an outside window anywhere in the room beyond this closet, she might be able to tell from the light quality whether they were going through reentry, or were deeper into the atmosphere. But there was nothing. Maybe all reeh shuttles landed like this, but she doubted it. There was no telling where she was in the galaxy, or what had happened to get her there. She only knew that the machines keeping her sedated were failing, and her shuttle was apparently crashing. If it killed her, that would nicely solve the horror of captivity. If it did not kill her, she would need to be ready. She did not dare close her eyes lest she catch some glimpse of useful information, but she stared at the odd tangles of tubes on the closet's opposite wall, and took her familiar, deep breaths. Her heart, also awakening from sedation and beginning to race, now slowed once more.

A shockingly hard impact, and she could feel them slewing sideways, with a marine's long experience of vehicles going wrong. This one had been hit, and her meditations were probably wasted because now she was going to die. Faced with capture and study by who she thought had captured her, that was definitely preferable.

A second impact made the first feel like a tap, and the thing she was strapped to broke, smashing her against the opposing wall...

...and she awoke for a second time, entangled in various unidentified things. She thought she was upside down. She tried moving, and her shoulder hurt, then her wrist. Unimpressed she pushed harder, and determined from the pain that neither was serious. And yes, she was somewhat upside down, legs still strapped in but upper body loose and folded at the waist, head down in the mass of tubes, broken straps and other things.

She got a hand to her face, and the pain in one was mostly the hot pins of bloodflow returning. She got the mask askew from her face that she hadn't been aware she was wearing and tore it clear, then determined that she did not have the room to do anything other than pull her legs clear of the straps. A pelvis restraint complicated things... those tubes were to evacuate bodily waste, she realised. Just how long had she been in this hellhole, anyway? That she was naked save for her old marine undershirt barely seemed worth pondering. Logically, transporting sedated and restrained prisoners for several days would require something similar.

She walked her hands and upper-body up the wall to gain an upright position, then got her hands over her head to grasp the back of the gurney she was strapped to, and got leverage in the claustrophobic space to wriggle herself out. There was liquid dripping on her brow that she was pretty sure was blood, but she had no time to ponder it now and began feeling about the closet door for access. No such luck — prisoner enclosures rarely opened from the inside, and the crash hadn't been enough to shake it loose.

Must get out. When she was out, surely other problems would present, but Trace had been trained from childhood to solve one problem at a time. To one side of a gurney was a smooth steel cylinder — an airtank of some kind. So the gurney was portable, probably she'd been wheeled around on it. She wriggled, got both hands on the cylinder and found the connections... pressed a lever and pulled, and it came away. Another twist to consider the leverage, then rammed it hard into the small window, end first.

She could feel her power returning with each swing. Micros and augments meant her muscles wouldn't lose power as fast as a non-marine would. Without exercise for a week, she'd still be nearly as fit. The micros and other enhancements manipulated the enzymes that released naturally in exercise, and she could feel them surging now, her skin flushing hot in that way a person typically only felt at the peak of heavy aerobic exercise.

The window cracked. Two more blows and it broke completely, a dull noise that should surely have been louder. It occurred to her, as she stuck her head out the hole and looked around, that she was probably deaf from the coms screech she'd unleashed on her marines to keep the mind-weapon out of their heads. The micros would be trying to fix that too, but the micros couldn't fix everything, and deafness was often structural.

Outside the closet was a narrow walkway, and neighbouring closets. Something was burning, and she smelled smoke. The tubes still stuck to her arms, and she pulled the needles out in frustration, cleared the last fragments of reinforced glass from the window rim, then slithered out into a tumbling headfirst heap on the steel floor. And stood, shaking from muscles unused in god-knew how many days, both over and under-stressed at the same time, head spinning, half-concussed, ears hissing with damaged white noise, and stark naked but for her undershirt. A bad situation, but better than it had been five minutes ago. Much of combat, like life, was about momentum. One more success and she'd be on a roll.

She stumbled to the next closet door and peered in the window. Empty. At the next one, a similarly tangled mess containing an unconscious alien she did not recognise — a round head, bony skull and horny beak for a nose and mouth. Next one, opposite her own, and here was her Command Squad Staff Sergeant Gideon Kono, similarly unconscious in the heap of his tubes and straps. She could have panicked to see him tangled and twisted like that, but she moved to the next window instead, finding nothing. That was at once a relief, and not — she was glad none of the others had been taken, on this shuttle at least, but another marine might have been useful.

None of the doors seemed to have a local release control, so she couldn't open them from here. She could smash the window to Kono's closet as she'd done with her own, but he looked completely out cold and that might take time to reverse. In that time anyone or anything else could come in here to inspect the cargo, particularly if there were security sensors here. A man twice as strong as her still couldn't wrestle Kono out of that window hole unconscious — it was either get the door open or get Kono conscious, and she lacked the time for either right now. She needed weapons, tools and clothes, in that order of importance.

She crouched for a moment on the floor, hand to support herself, resting her shaking legs and faltering balance. There was no obvious door or way out — the room of prisoner-transport enclosures seemed to be a small, self-contained unit, like many specialised prisoner isolation transports. This shuttle was much larger, though... she could just tell by the way it had come through the atmosphere. Reeh dealt with organic specimens all the time. To the best of anyone's knowledge they'd never encountered humans before. She and Kono, and whoever else they'd grabbed, would be the first, rare specimens. Thus this effort at specialised transportation.

But transporting sedated prisoners on gurneys was hard to do through doorways, in or out of gravity. This place had no doors. So logically... she looked up. Fluid was leaking down one wall, over the window to one empty transport closet. And was it her imagination, or was the entire ceiling buckled on one side? She stood to stare at it in the pale blue light, pondering how to get a slab of steel open that would logically be secured by heavy locks and just as inoperable from the inside as the doors were, not to mention weighing a quarter ton...

The entire ceiling screeched and shuddered, then began to lift. Trace dove for the end, figuring the light was dimmer there, and pressed to a wall in the vain hope that reeh shuttle crew would not see her. But as the top levered off, it was not some unfamiliar alien face peering over the edge, but big eyes within a humanoid facial arrangement, tangled long fringes under helmets, targeting eyepieces and camouflage caps. Corbi.

One of them shouted urgently, seeing her and gesturing to others. Another was peering around intently, a rifle held ready, and distantly through her muffled hearing Trace could hear shooting. "Human?" one of them shouted at her. "Human? Fee-nix?"

So the Corbi Resistance had discovered she was coming, and decided to rescue her. That meant she was on Rando. "Yes!" she replied, having no hope they'd also received a translator program for English. She strode to Kono's cell door and pointed, then to the alien prisoner alongside. "My friend, one other prisoner! Doors!" She slapped at the doors, indicating they should be opened, then pointed up and about at the hold above that she could not see. "Doors, open!"

The corbi seemed to get that idea, instructions issued, and then the doors were sliding open. Trace dove in to Kono's cell, struggling to reach under and around the big man's unconscious bulk to detach the straps that held him in. A thud, and a corbi was beside her, offering her something. Trace looked, and saw it was a blade in a sheath... and not just any blade, but a kukri. *Her* kukri. She did not waste time staring in astonishment, but unsheathed the familiar, long steel weight and sliced cords and tubes with expert cuts. The corbi wanted to grab Kono's arms and drag him, but Trace put the kukri down and grabbed him in a proper underarm hold to protect head and neck, then laid him gently on his back.

"Hey, Giddy!" She checked his pulse, found it strong, then put an ear to his mouth and found him breathing too. "Come on Giddy, wake up." She slapped his cheek. "Staff Sergeant!" Louder, command-ing. "Staff Sergeant, wake up! That's an order!"

Other corbi were removing the remaining alien prisoner, who was awake and complaining in some chattering, clicking tongue. Another corbi dumped her spare jumpsuit alongside... no doubt the reeh had taken her possessions from her armour suit, and the kukri for a prize, perhaps. Kono began to wake up, coughing and groaning, and she struggled into her jumpsuit with no particular interest in modesty, just the certainty that clothed would be better than naked in whatever came next.

Kono's jumpsuit was thrown down next, and Trace waved to the corbi who threw it. "Hey, shoes? Webbing?" Pointing at feet and else-where. The corbi was too busy to care, listening to the outside shooting and looking worried. Trace zipped herself up, and knelt at Kono's side. "Giddy, the corbi Resistance grabbed us. I think we're on Rando, I'm going to see if I can find more of our gear. Get dressed and get ready to move out."

It was unreasonable of her, Kono might have been injured, but she had no time to play nurse and couldn't do all necessary things at once. In better condition she could have just jumped out of the pit, but her legs were jelly so she pocketed the kukri and climbed with easy leverage, rolling onto the floor above.

About was the shuttle's central hold, tall, narrow and dark, filled with spidery connections to absent armour suits, and grasping mechanical arms to lock them in place. The smell of smoke was stronger here, and an overhead loading mechanism had crumpled into the front of the hold, twisted like a car wreck up forward, blocking what she guessed was the way to the cockpit. Beneath it, amid the twisted engineering, corbi with rifles and makeshift uniforms rummaged through equipment lockers, already removing weapons and miscellaneous equipment and containers.

Trace joined them, not asking permission, digging amidst the bits and pieces in search of additional gear from her or Kono's armour. But she could see nothing — no doubt all the tech or gear had been taken elsewhere for analysis. Reeh would have brought the jumpsuits because nothing else would fit humans, but weren't interested enough in prisoner comfort to bring shoes, underwear or more. But the kukri didn't make sense.

She pulled it out, and showed the corbi next to her. "Where?" She pointed around, wondering where it had come from. The corbi pointed to something amid the twisted loader mechanism. Trace looked, and for the first time saw an armoured limb, neither human nor corbi. She ducked around and into the mechanism, and stood above the limb's owner. It was humanoid, and wore a fearsome mask and visor. From the angle of its limbs, and the weight of the machinery that had crushed it, Trace judged it certainly dead. And the corbi said it had been carrying her kukri. A prize, like she'd thought.

The facemask was partly askew, and she used the kukri to pry it further. Within was a big-jawed face, teeth prominent, making a lower-face snout that was vaguely reptilian. But the eyes were all advanced sentience, jet black and without iris. Trace recalled some xeno-anthropological study, perhaps something Romki had recommended, speaking on the evolutionary importance of irises to humans, letting other humans know what an individual was looking at. It mattered, to humans. Allowed them to read expressions, emotions, see the rolling of eyes, the sideways look of fear or evasion faced with unpleasant questions. Allowed humans to judge each other's emotional states. To some other alien species, knowing what each other thought was less important. Sard had no irises. Krim hadn't either. And hacksaws had no eyes, just optical sensors. Species without irises were trouble, the report had said. Psychopaths who did not care to process the emotional states of other individuals. Only 'psychopath' wasn't the right word either. Psychopath presumed disfunction. The species-without-irises were optimally functional, they only liked to cause disfunction in others.

Trace grabbed the reeh's limp arm, and examined the armour. There was a join at the wrist, and she inserted her kukri and sliced. Bone cracked, and she gave the wrist another couple of accurate whacks. The hand came off, and she peered at the bone and arteries within, arrayed like a surgeon's training model. Filament sparkled, inorganic and numerous. She'd read this classified report too, about the alo. Micro-filament, neither organic nor inorganic, made of inter-mediate carbon-based materials, reaching through the limbs to provide a sensory and coordination boost to hands and fingers. The internal organs were similarly synthesised, neither entirely organic nor synthetic. Humans did something similar these days, but that was genetics plus micros and ergonomic augments for raw leverage through the limbs. Alo took it to a whole other level. And now she'd become perhaps the first human ever to see with her own eyes that the reeh did the same.

She dropped the hand and went back to the prisoner pit, ignoring the wary look one corbi gave her and her hand-severing knife. She found Kono dressed and standing, with the assistance of a wall. A corbi gabbled something at her, pointing earnestly to the sky and making some circular motion in the air — doubtless telling her just how little time they had before someone came looking. Trace nodded, with a palm-out gesture to indicate she understood.

"Giddy, you good?"

"'Good' might be overstating it," her Staff Sergeant said blearily. He'd been sick on the floor, Trace saw. The corbi were trying to get the alien prisoner up, who seemed to be in worse shape. Corbi rarely stood taller than her shoulder, hauling the alien up to this level was going to be difficult.

"Help them get that guy out of the pit," Trace told him. "Let's make a good impression, they've gone to a lot of trouble to get us out."

"How d'you know they were after us?" Kono asked.

It was a good point, Trace supposed — she didn't. "Let's assume," she told him. "Couldn't hurt. I'm going to see what the shooting is about, see if I can get weapons."

The shuttle's rear hold was sealed, but a side access door was open. Trace peered out carefully, noting the corbi she'd expected to be guarding the door. He or she stared at her, and Trace gave what she hoped was a reassuring hand gesture. And she pointed, out into the night — because it was night, she'd only just registered — toward the sound of sporadic gunfire. 'Where?' she asked the question with her hands.

The corbi pointed, his other hand wrapped around the handle of an effective-looking short rifle. Trace nodded, and made a small jump onto torn ground. The shock of soft earth on bare feet was astonishing after so long in space. The ground was torn from the crash, and as she looked past the shuttle's rear, she saw a gap torn in surrounding trees, broken branches hanging in the light of at least two moons. Ahead, the shuttle's big engine nacelle was smashed, the thruster exposed and ruined, leaking fluids. Trace skirted around it, staying low, and peered into the surrounding trees.

They'd crashed in a forest. The trees were large and beautiful in the moonlight. She was sure on any regular night the air would be filled with the sound of insects and small creatures, feeding beneath the moons, but the crash and the ongoing gunfire had silenced them. Or she thought they had, being in no condition to hear much anyway.

An alien wandering this corbi forest was asking to get shot by nervous Resistance fighters. But just ahead, two corbi were standing over something fallen by the base of a tree. Trace walked that way, upright and obvious, and saw them glance her way as she approached. That was much safer.

The thing they'd felled was reeh, one corbi standing guard while the other removed armour pieces and examined the contents of a container for useful things. Trace crouched alongside, conscious of her much taller profile, and how anything higher than a corbi would likely be considered a target. The reeh's weapons lay on the grassy dirt beside his bullet-riddled body. Shuttle crew, Trace judged. Trying to get away. This was the corbi's homeworld, and from the evolution of their bodies, corbi looked like a species familiar with trees. Trace didn't like the reeh's chances.

She reached for the main weapon, a large rifle, and the corbi's own rifle turned her way, but only warning. "Uh," he made a sound, disapprovingly. Trace stared at him for a long moment. The corbi's face was hard to read in the dark, a wide-brim hat covered with canvas on his head, to break up the outline, as a hunter might wear to obscure himself from prey. There was a livid scar on his jaw, where hair refused to grow, turning skin bright pink where it ran to his neck.

Her eyes not leaving him, Trace reached for the rifle anyway, and carefully picked it up. Still not looking at it, she unchambered a round, guessing that mechanism by earlier sight, then took out the magazine with fast, certain hands. The corbi gazed back, perhaps realising what she was. A soldier, like him. Finally she looked at it, magazine out, and tested its balance against her shoulder. The grips were all different, made for reeh hands, and the trigger was fat and ugly. No matter — she could file it down later. The other weapon was a light handweapon, not unlike a pistol, but the mechanism suggested it was fully automatic. She checked it, wondering where the safety was before concluding that reeh might not use safeties. Perhaps fitting, she thought.

Out in the dark, the shooting had stopped. Trace shouldered the rifle, held the pistol, and nodded to the corbi. He grunted, and she set off back to the crashed shuttle, face-planted in the forest amid a great mount of dirt and broken trees about its nose.

Corbi were emerging from the side hatch when she arrived, then Kono, helping to carry the half-conscious alien. Back by the shuttle's tail, more Resistance fighters were crouching in preparation of something landing. Trace could hear nothing coming, though that was likely just her ears.

"Got you a present," Trace said, falling in beside him and showing the pistol.

"Rifle looks more my size," Kono replied.

"Who's Major?" Kono nearly smiled... good. His voice was strained, and Trace didn't think it was the half-weight of the alien. Kono was a big man, Trace barely stood past his shoulder, and some of the corbi were looking at him with awe. Trace wondered if they'd ever seen an elder croma. "How you feel?"

"Feels like I broke a rib. Otherwise the body's okay. Head's fucked, can't hear much."

"Me too." They walked to the side of the shuttle's path of wreckage, past a fallen tree trunk, stripped of branches where the machine had scoured it. "Looks like we've got an evac coming."

And then she could hear it, a dull hum past the hissing in her ears. Several flyers appeared past the treetops, dark silhouettes with no running lights or interior illumination, and much closer than Trace's hearing indicated they'd be. They dropped quickly onto the devastated earth, kicking up clouds of flying leaves, dust and needles.

Corbi indicated Kono and the two corbi carrying the alien should move to the first one, a door was opened and the alien slung inside. Then fingers were pointed at the next flyer — Trace couldn't see that there was enough room for everyone, there were still plenty of corbi emerging from the trees having finished their reeh hunt, but probably there were more flyers coming.

They moved to it, aching legs nearly managing a run, then ducked past the big downward nacelles and into the rear seats. Corbi clambered into the seats ahead of them, doors closed, and the flyer lifted in a strangely soundless rush of vibrating power. Optimised for silent flight, Trace thought, plus her damaged hearing. She glanced around for seat restraints, but found none. Corbi beside and ahead of her put feet up, grinned at each other and exchanged drinking flasks. Clearly Resistance fighters had no time for seatbelts. Or probably, if they were discovered, a reeh precision weapon would kill them far too quickly for seatbelts to matter.

A corbi offered Trace a flask. Trace realised she was parched, and drank without a testing sip. Thankfully it was water, cold and clean. She handed it to Kono, who did the same, then returned the flask with thanks. Corbi about the cabin turned to gaze at them. It was the simple curiosity of a sentient species they'd never seen before, but looked probably as familiar to them as corbi did to humans.

"Must be pretty sure we're not going to get shot down," Kono suggested, gazing at the shadows of passing treetops and hillsides. The hills were all well above them, and some of the trees as well. Obviously the pilots could see the way fine, to risk flying this low. Trace hoped the moons would not make them too obvious, despite the black, non-reflective paint.

"Reeh surface coverage must be incomplete," Trace said. "I wouldn't have thought it was that difficult to get complete radar coverage. But corbi are pretty smart. Humans figured all kinds of ways to sneak around the krim."

"Corbi," the corbi who'd handed them the flask interjected, pointing to himself. Then he pointed at them. "Hu-man?"

"Human," Trace agreed. She pointed to herself. "Trace." Then at Kono. "Giddy."

The corbi managed a passable approximation of that, then pointed to himself. "Jova," he said. Then pointed around the cabin, and gave more names. Trace nodded, and repeated each back to them. "Lodi moradan reeh?" Jova asked.

"Reeh," Trace repeated, catching that one word. She drew a thumb across her throat, vulgarly. Jova nodded appreciatively, and settled back into his seat.

"How you think they got the shuttle down?" Kono wondered, examining the pistol Trace had brought him.

"No clue. When we figure how to talk to them more easily, we'll ask. What's the last thing you remember?"

Kono squinted, attempting that. Nothing pleasant came. "Defending the withdrawal. Got cut off. Can't... remember much. I think Command Squad might be okay." Hopefully.

"Smiley bought it," Trace said sombrely, recalling Zale's final detonation. Kono muttered something under his breath. "Everyone else was just about out, though." She put her hand on his arm, and squeezed. "We did good. We could have lost everyone. Total fuck up. My fault, not yours. Should never have been there."

"Had to try, Major," Kono disagreed. "No choice, we all agreed. At least these guys might have some idea how to actually fight the fuckers."

"The Resistance we were with supposedly had some idea too," Trace warned. "And they led us straight into it. Let's keep our eyes open."

"So we're on Rando," Kono said grimly, gazing at passing hillsides in nighttime silhouette beneath the silver moons. "How long have the corbi been fighting here?"

"About a thousand years."

"Well," said Kono, with a tight smile. "They've never seen anything like UF marines before. All two of us."

"No," Trace agreed, removing her kukri and giving the blade a closer examination for notches. "No they have not."

ABOUT THE AUTHOR

"Joel Shepherd is the Australian author of fifteen SF and Fantasy novels in three series. They are 'The Cassandra Kresnov Series', 'A Trial of Blood and Steel', and 'The Spiral Wars'."

For More Information; www.joelshepherd.com

Subscribe to the mailing list; http://joelshepherd.com/?page_id=1069

Made in United States
Troutdale, OR
06/27/2023

10844206R00246